THE DIABOLICAL SEVEN

There were seven of us and maybe thirty of them. Two beauties roared by on a Harley chopper. The guy in the sidecar had a twenty-foot bullwhip in one hand and some kind of sabre in the other. As they swept by me, the Diablo in the sidecar snapped the whip, shooting out the black snake, slow as a dream. I watched it, entranced, as it wound around my upper arm with a stinging whisper. There was a moment where everything seemed stopped cold, then the whip almost jerked my arm out of the socket as they pulled me along behind the careening bike. But for some reason I didn't seem to be able to feel the dirt and rocks and cactus. At last the guy must have gotten tired of dragging me around, because he let go of the whip.

I got to my feet and began to stagger down the street. I was a mess, evidently, because when my old buddy Shig got to me, his face went white until I made a sound. "I thought you were dead," he said.

What I saw next shocked but no longer surprised me: the twins, still alive and still the same. Last time I had seen them, they w̲ ̲ ̲ ̲ ̲ ̲ ̲ ̲ gore, brought down by flailing Dia̲ ̲ ̲

So there we were, headed up th̲ ̲ ̲ rise. As I passed an open doorwa̲ ̲ ̲ biker jumped out and leveled a saw̲ ̲ at us. I turned without breaking st̲ ̲ ̲ my little Beretta and said "Bang." A b̲ ̲ into his chest. I wasn't fazed. This was̲ ̲

In the end, we killed every one of t̲ ̲ bullet in the last gun killed the last p̲ ̲ last window. The trigger finger was m̲ ̲

WAR IN HELL

Created and edited by Janet Morris

JANET MORRIS WITH MICHAEL ARMSTRONG,
NANCY ASIRE, C.J. CHERRYH,
DAVID DRAKE, BILL KERBY, CHRIS MORRIS,
DIANA PAXSON, ROBERT SILVERBERG

WAR IN HELL

Copyright © 1988 by Janet Morris

A Baen Books Original

Baen Publishing Enterprises
260 Fifth Avenue
New York, N.Y. 10001

First printing, December 1988

ISBN: 0-671-69792-7

Cover art by David Mattingly

Printed in the United States of America

Distributed by
SIMON & SCHUSTER
1230 Avenue of the Americas
New York, N.Y. 10020

CONTENTS

[. . .] IS HELL

Janet Morris

The demon was sitting on a rock in Tartaros when the fiend came up to him with a basket.

Tartaros was hot, as usual, and fiery, as was its wont—a blasted heath across which, in the far distance, Tartarouches, a Fallen Angel, chased damned souls, cracking his fiery lashes at their heels. Among all the unpleasant places in Hell where a soul could languish, Tartaros was one of the unpleasantest, and the demon on the rock wasn't sitting there for his health.

The demon in question was Asmodeus, king of the demons—or had been, until the Devil had decided that Asmodeus needed his comeuppance (or comedownance, this being Hell). Now he was Asmodeus the Resentful, sitting there in a loincloth upon that hot rock, staring out over the blasted heath of Tartaros, regretting the errors that had brought him here.

One of those errors had been falling in love, so far as a demon can, with the once-earthly damned soul of Gertrud Margarete Zelle, better known as Mata Hari. Thus the demon was not surprised when the fiend with

1

the basket raised its head and smiled at him with Mata Hari's smile.

She shifted her basket and her robe fell open, revealing Mata Hari's famous, nippleless breast. She looked at him with a fiendish glitter in Mata Hari's eyes and said, "I've brought you a gift—and a riddle, Asmodeus the once-proud demon lord."

"Terrific," said Asmodeus hesitantly, still sitting with his dark head on his long-nailed fist, naturally wary of a fiend who resembled his beloved and came bearing a gift and a riddle. "What's the catch?"

"It's a riddle, not a catch," said the fiend with a cautious smile and a flirtatious flick of Mata Hari's eyelids. "Don't bother being wary of me. Aren't you Asmodeus, who got caught aiding the traitors in the Pentagram and then turned right around and tried to sell your services to Julius Caesar and that lot?"

"Consulting," said the demon. "I was just doing some consulting for elements of Agency that . . ."

"Ex-Agency types like Mata Hari and Machiavelli—intent on covering up the cover-up of the cover-up of the Pentagram's illicit arming of the Dissident movement—hardly qualify as 'Agency,' " sniffed the fiend whose pert nose was so much like Mata Hari's that seeing it wrinkle made Asmodeus inexpressably sad. "And as for consulting, if what you were doing was 'consulting,' I suppose you're going to try telling me next that you thought what you were doing was perfectly legal when you helped the Dulles Brothers and Bill Casey airdrop lethal aid into Dissident strongholds and—"

"Can we cut the politics?" snapped the demon, and sat upright. Asmodeus was not your storybook demon, all red and warty and snaggle-toothed. He was big, dark—a handsome, charismatic soul that sometimes seemed to be all blue smoke and mirrors, but always seemed to be strong, forceful, indisputably male, and fiery-eyed even when none of the rest of his face could be seen. He'd walked the Earth in its infancy and Hell in all its profundity. He'd been banished to Tartaros for Complicity to Commit Treason, a charge the Devil didn't have to prove—a matter of the company he'd kept.

Looking at the fiend with the basket who'd come to him in the guise of Mata Hari, Asmodeus knew that the Devil wasn't through with him yet—that Tartaros, with its baking and broiling and charcoaling wasteland of Gnostic grief, wasn't sufficient punishment for him. Oh no. The Devil was, judging by the fiend's appearance, still exceedingly p.o'd.

"Okay," preened the fiend, stroking her Mata Hari-hair. "I'll let the politics go, for the nonce. But you *will* let me explain the reason I was sent down here." She fanned herself.

"Explain, already," said Asmodeus, wishing the fiend would get it over with and let him go back to his solitary study of the blasted heath before him. He'd been counting the souls Tartarouches chased across the horizon, and he didn't want to forget his day-total.

"Well," said the fiend, standing up straight so that her hip made the wicker basket jut forward. "Here you've got your basic basket of gifts, and you'll notice that there's more than one gift in here. You only get one. You get to choose."

"I don't like this."

"You're not supposed to like it, demon. It's part of your punishment. You pick the right gift, and your punishment will end—your sentence'll be, well, commuted —and you can go back to New Hell, even get your old desk on Corpse Street back, work for the Insecurity Service, raise all the Hell," and here the fiend grinned, "you want."

"The riddle," Asmodeus reminded the fiend, cautioning himself warily that fiends might be slow-witted, but the Devil was not. This fiend who looked like Mata

Hari certainly hadn't thought this little junket up by her lonesome.

The fiend wiped a pale hand across her brow. "It's hot down here," she said. Asmodeus glared at her. She fingered the items in her basket. "Right," she said at last. "The gifts and the riddle. You ask me 'What's in the basket?' "

She looked at Asmodeus expectantly.

He said, "What's this, a knock-knock joke? I'm not in the mood. I'm tried on a trumped-up charge, eaten alive by a jury of my peers, resurrected from among the dead by an Undertaker with bad breath, then re-arrested as soon as the real Mata Hari tries to ease my suffering. I'm then sent here without so much as a peer review, to languish with only one-trick Tartarouches and a bunch of damned Copts and proto-Christians for company, and you want to tell *jokes?*"

"A riddle, I said. It's a riddle. Now ask me the foolish question," said the fiend, drumming Mata Hari's fingers on the straw of her basket. "Or, Devil take you, you can rot here without so much as one chance in five of ever getting out."

The basket should have burst into flames in the heat of Tartaros long since, Asmodeus told himself by way of comfort. Therefore, the basket and, by implication, the fiend carrying it, weren't real. Or weren't really here. He'd probably fallen asleep in the doomsday heat and was having trouble digesting his long-pig barbecue sandwich.

"Okay, okay," said Asmodeus. " 'What's in the basket?' "

"What Jesus of Nazareth brought to the world," said the fiend. She touched each of five, fist-sized stones in her basket, inclining the basket toward him so that Asmodeus could see that the stones were as alike as peas in the proverbial pod. "You may pick one, but only one."

"Not unless you're willing to be more specific," said the demon, who was now considering getting to his feet, even though the desert of Tartaros was bound to be hotter than the rock on which he'd been sitting so long. He didn't like this fiend who resembled his beloved, and he didn't like the riddle.

"Come on," said the fiend, and her tongue flicked out between Mata Hari's teeth for just a second, its two forks waving. "You know about Jesus—you were on Earth so long. What's to be afraid of?"

"That's two riddles," Asmodeus snapped. Then he looked at the stones again, and he said: "Name the stones before I choose one. It's my right." He was shooting in the dark, but it was worth a try.

"Um . . ." The fiend closed Mata Hari's eyes. Then she opened them and said, "Jesus said, 'Perhaps people think I have come to bring peace' "—she tapped one stone—" 'to the world. They don't know that I've come to bring conflict' "—she tapped another—" 'to the earth: fire,' " and another; " 'sword,' " another; " 'war.' " She touched the last.

"Fine," said Asmodeus, thinking that he had tricked the stupid fiend. "Give me peace."

"Peace it is," said the fiend, smiling, and reached into her basket to hand the stone to Asmodeus.

When he took it in his palm, blazing Tartaros disappeared. The baking sands were gone; the cracked, parched ground was gone. The unremitting glare of the white-hot sky was gone; the fires of the compass points were gone. And the souls and avenging Fallen Angel were gone. There was nothing around him.

Asmodeus floated in a featureless dark void, not black nor gray, not purple nor brown, but devoid of even the absence of color. There was nothing under him. There was nothing over him. There was nothing near him and nothing far from him. All around him, there was nothing.

Worse, he himself seemed reduced to nothing. He had no fingers with their sharp-clawed nails. He had no nose through which to breathe. He had no mouth through which to scream his complaint. He had no terrified bowels through which to void into this non-universe. He had no pulse in his ears, no blood in his veins. And he didn't like it.

Inside the mind that was all Asmodeus could be certain was left of him, he began regretting his choice. He regretted as hard as he could, for a demon stripped of being. He regretted with all his . . . particle of self-awareness. He cursed the fiend and its forbears, trying desperately to hold the thought. But it was hard to hold a thought when you were nothing.

No time whatsoever passed.

And then, with a thumping impact on his rump, Asmodeus was back in Tartaros, back on the same rock he'd been sitting on when the fiend handed him the first stone. And the fiend was there too, but she was much older.

Her nippleless breast was pendulous and scoured with deep stretch marks out of which hairs were growing sideways. Her nose had grown long, and her chin was also sprouting hairs. She smiled at him coquettishly and said, "Peace takes forever." Her voice was reedy. "I almost forgot to come back for you. Well, how did you like your gift?"

"I hated it. You tricked me. I want to exchange it for something else instead."

"You renounce peace?" frowned the fiend. "Isn't that counter to the revolutionary ethic and the altruistic tendencies and the slavish, quasi-religious store you put in the Rule of Law when last we met? Isn't peace lawful, fundamental, inherently good and completely new to your experience? Didn't you like the higher values to which you were so interminably exposed?"

"I was interminably exposed to . . . nothing at all. No choice; no individuality, since I was the only being I encountered; no free will or any other damned thing. That was no gift, I say. I demand a different—"

"Stone. Yes, I see. Well, you're performing according to expectations, anyhow. Here," said the aged crone who looked like Mata Hari but was in truth a fiend, "pick another stone."

The demon Asmodeus hesitated. He wanted to ask how much time had passed, and whether Mata Hari looked like the fiend's simulacrum of her. But he didn't. Asmodeus held out his hand, palm up, and said implacably: "Sword."

Bang. The fiend disappeared, along with her basket, as she held out the second stone to him.

Slap. Down into Asmodeus's hand came the hilt of a sword.

Swoosh. All the fires of Tartaros flared skyward as if a giant was working the bellows of the underworld. And out of that fire came a stumbling, screaming herd of charred and damned souls, headed directly for the demon sitting on his rock, sword in hand.

And behind these souls, bubbling like marshmallows held over a campfire and oozing a sticky white substance and a smell much the same, came the Fallen Angel Tartarouches, cracking his fiery lashes at their heels.

"Kill us," begged the first bubbling marshmallow of a damned soul as it came abreast of the demon's rock. "Put us out of our misery. Kill us, we beg of you!" The soul fell down and grabbed Asmodeus by the knees.

It smelled just like a marshmallow and it oozed white, sticky stuff. Its hands were crusted with black, carbonized skin that flaked off and stuck to Asmodeus's knees. And that sticky white stuff bound itself to him, flakes of skin and flakes of lives and flakes of souls. There were strands of it all over him now, and each strand burned like damnation as the driven souls of Tartaros begged him for death.

Behind the train of them, inexorably mounting around Asmodeus and his rock, still came Tartarouches, whose face was like the flare of a sun gone nova.

Asmodeus lurched to his feet, covered in strings of burning souls, and those strings hung from him like giant cobwebs. He laid about him in the wailing, begging crowd of the black-crusted damned, swinging the great sword in his hand.

He swung and he swung. He struck and struck again. He lopped heads from shoulders and he cleaved breastbones clean to the scrota. And every time he did, some damned soul blessed him, and its essence stuck to his sword.

The sword was twice its weight now, and its edge was getting dull. It was covered with white marshmallow and black crusts, as if it were a tree with some horrid disease.

Unhesitatingly, the line of souls came on. Soon Asmodeus was up to his hips in the sticky stuff of the damned, then up to his waist, then up to his sternum. And still he killed those who begged for death by his sword.

Thus he didn't notice when the corpses began to grow so high that his arms were fouled. When he did, it was too late. The damned were falling on him in desperate profusion, and his sword was stuck in their masses.

When he was up to his neck in them, sick from the sweetness of them, caught in the trap of them like a fly in a spider's web, Tartarouches came up and shook his blazing head at him. "You know what they say, Asmodeus: 'He who lives by the sword. . . .' "

Then Tartarouches flailed the demon with his fiery lashes and strangled the life from Asmodeus' body.

But since 'life' is a relative term when you're a demon stationed in Hell, Asmodeus' soul soon found itself back on the selfsame rock where he had first met the fiend wearing Mata Hari's aspect.

And the fiend was there, smiling a middle-aged Mata-Hari smile.

"You're not old, this time," said Asmodeus, rubbing arms that were just reconstituting around his demon's soul and noticing that those arms were trembling.

"You're not cocky, this time," said the fiend, flashing her breast in their recognition sign.

Asmodeus growled, "Put that away, fiend. I don't like this gift, either. I insist on returning it. Give me another."

"Well, let's see," said the fiend, biting her lip uncertainly, the way Mata Hari used to do. "What have we got left, here? You've got your conflict, you've got your fire, your—"

"Fine. Give me fire," said the demon, not waiting to hear the rest.

The fiend shook her head. One eyebrow went up. She said, "You're sure? Peace negated you. The sword buried you in suffering souls who—"

"Shut up, okay? You're a bitch, you know that? I thought you said one of these gifts would restore my freedom, commute my sentence—"

"That's not exactly what I said, but it's close enough, yes. Now, since you're so nasty, you can have your choice with no word of warning from me." And she threw the stone of fire at Asmodeus.

It hit him in the head. The whole world of Tartaros, which anyone could see was fiery enough, dissolved in a white-hot burst of greater fire, and Asmodeus found himself in the middle of the air. He was a wheel. He was turning in another wheel. He was singing songs of destruction and transformation with his mouth of fiery expanse, and below, souls were cowering.

He was spreading out over a city in a storm of his own destruction. He collapsed walls and seared the bones from every living thing in his path. He rose up into the atmosphere in a blossoming cloud and spread darkness over the land. He was a cleansing fire, and this he knew, but that cleansing was the cleansing of life. He heard another voice in the fire, which told him that the universe was all fire, some igniting, some burning out, but it did not soothe him.

As fire he was mindless. As fire, he was without

purpose but to burn. And he was hungry, ravenously hungry, and straining for oxygen. In the whole universe, there was not enough oxygen for him. He began to gasp. He began to shrink. He began to dim . . .

This time, when he found himself once again on his rock in Tartaros, the whole place seemed cold and dark. The fire of its four compass points barely warmed him. The fire of his soul was all but extinguished.

Now the fiend who was Mata Hari looked like a scorched skeleton, with only the one nippleless breast unscathed. This fish-white, flopping teat she cradled in a blistered hand and she said, "Well, I'm glad that's over. How did you like the cleansing fire?"

"The solution," Asmodeus said in a crackling voice, "to the flaws of man and beast and all of life is not to burn them off like weeds in a field." And he remembered, then, some of the fires he'd been: the fires of the ovens of Europe in which Jews and Slavs roasted; the fires of the Inquisition; the fires of Salem; the fire that ate Joan of Arc alive.

And Asmodeus wept, for among the fires he'd been was also the fire of vulcanism: he had consumed a whole race of dinosaurs; he had struck the earth dumb and blind. He had scoured her clean once. He wanted no part of those fires, or even of the fires of Tartaros, his home in hell.

"Another choice," he said to the fiend hoarsely. "I demand another choice."

"Choose well, Asmodeus," said the fiend, holding out her basket. "There are only two choices left to you—conflict and war."

"And one of these will restore me to New Hell, and to my life as I've grown accustomed to it in Hell?" He waited for the fiend to look him in the eye and answer.

When she said yes, he responded, "Then give me conflict, for we are among the greater evils now."

And conflict she gave unto him, into his hand.

When the demon's fingers closed upon that rock,

within him a great chasm opened. A part of him wanted righteousness, and a part of him wanted mayhem. A part of him wanted love: Mata Hari, the comfort of a soul's esteem, a woman's arms. A part of him wanted revenge upon the very Devil himself, for Satan had unjustly accused and punished Asmodeus, once a faithful servitor.

One part of him wanted to live a life of service, while another part wanted to wreak destruction, if necessary, to make his power felt.

He had visions of Mata Hari down on her knees to him in awe with tears on her face. He had visions of the Devil himself cowering before the might that was Asmodeus. He wanted to forgive all wrongs and begin anew among the hierarchy of his peers; he wanted every one of them prostrated before him in eternal supplication.

He got up from his rock, and there was no fiend there beside him. He walked toward the horizon, which hosted no driven souls now, but only a ring of fire. He walked toward the city he could see in that ring, and wherever he stepped the ground crumbled under his feet.

He was the avenger, and when he reached New Hell, his will would be done.

Then he was not. He was the prophesied Redeemer, who could lift the suffering of all the damned on Judgment day.

And the two parts of him separated there, on the blasted plain of Tartaros, and did battle. The part of him that wanted to bring the world to its knees, to have all the cognizant world beg for his favor, attacked the part that wanted only to alleviate the suffering around him, all the misery of the burning souls that he had seen.

They snarled at one another. They grappled, mincing in, evenly matched, two mirror-perfect demons on a sea of fused sand. And they closed, and wrestled, and fell to a heap on the ground.

The vengeful Asmodeus was screaming in the other's ear: "You want the same as I! You want primacy. You want respect. Awe. Power. Glory. Minions. Dominion over the beasts of the field and the souls of the Elysian fields. You want to get it by trickery, that's all. You want to get it by making them love you. I'm more honest: everyone hates anyone with more power than he himself has, and I want only unsullied power. So let them hate me!"

"No!" cried the other Asmodeus, who got his hands around the vengeful Asmodeus' throat just as his adversary's thumbs closed on his own windpipe. "I want only a rebirth, a better world, though that world be Hell, for all. I want people to honor me because I—"

"Aha!" said the vengeful Asmodeus as he bore down, not only because the twin he fought had fallen into a logic trap, but because he was being choked by his alter-ego as surely as he was choking the adversary that had always been within him.

Neither uttered another word, only the gagging sounds of imminent death. The contest took many by surprise, many onlookers from higher hells who'd assumed there'd be a winner and placed cagy wagers.

There couldn't be: the combatants were too evenly matched, and the death throes of each snapped the neck of his opponent, once breath had truly fled. They died in a flurry of torn betting slips fluttering down from higher hells like snow.

Only one Asmodeus appeared back on the rock, where the fiend stood waiting with its basket. This time, the fiend showed no trace of femininity, of either the human or the fiendish sort. It was all fiend and a mile wide. And it was grinning through jaws the size of a Rolls Royce grille as it said, "Well, want another stone, Asmodeus?"

When he didn't immediately answer, it began to sing

"Roll Away The Stone," very badly, for no fiend ever born can carry a tune.

"Stop! Don't sing, for Satan's sake; don't sing! I'll take the last stone. Give it to me—give me war."

The fiend reached into the basket and pulled out the final stone. As it dropped the stone into the outstretched hand of Asmodeus, once king of the demons, its cackle could be heard to the farthest reaches of blasted Tartaros.

"Have a nice day," the fiend called as the stone met the palm of Asmodeus and all Tartaros faded away.

In its place loomed New Hell, its skyline alight with the rockets' red glare, its bombs bursting in air, and Asmodeus could tell by the light that the Viet Cong were still there, in Decentral Park, lobbing shells at the Roman quarter and anywhere else they could reach.

But there was solid hot mix under his feet, and bright cadmium, poisonous painted dotted lines along the road leading into the Devil's most infamous city.

Here the Dissidents fought the Administration, and elements in the Pentagram and elsewhere funded the Dissidents' struggle. The damned souls fought for a better life in afterlife; a newer New Hell, a more fulfilling wait while they passed the time until the Last Trump.

And Asmodeus, swinging into a ground-eating gait that would get him into New Hell by the time Paradise started to rise, cursed himself for a fool. He should have known which stone to choose to get him home.

It was his fault, not the Devil's, that he'd suffered so. Old Nick was simply trying to get him off the hook without having to admit that His Infernal Temper had gotten the better of Him.

The Devil couldn't admit he was wrong, any more than Asmodeus ever could. The secretive agent of His Infernal Majesty's Secret Service began to whistle as he walked.

Finally, he laughed and said aloud to the dark and restless night, "I really should have known. War was the only sensible choice. War *is* hell, after all."

WISDOM

David Drake

The barroom was hot as Hell. It stank like Hell, too, and whatever the bartender served tasted like a hellish mixture of horse piss and lava. The men crowding the place claimed it was no worse than one venue or another where they'd served in life, but they were lying. Most of them.

When the new man pushed through the swinging doors, a few heads turned—and then all the heads in the bar.

The newcomer was tall. His garments were of the finest quality—a cashmere burnoose and robe over a silk tunic, all of a white so pure that they had no color save the muddy light which they reflected. His headband was red and gold, and the hilt of the dagger hooked through his sash was of silver set with turquoises.

The face framed by the burnoose was English as surely as the clothing was Bedouin.

"Bloody 'ell," said a color sergeant with the red coat and cross-belts of Wolseley's troops at Zagazig—even victors have casualties. "Hit's bloody Lawrence of Arabia!"

They were all men in the bar—making due allowance

for the slight fellow in the corner, naked except for his fur, who notched the rail morosely with a hand axe.

And they were all men of war, of many breeds and every time. Near the furry fellow was an Israeli pilot with a bemused expression. The remains of a flight helmet rested on the bar beside him. The hole in the front was the size a 23 mm cannon shell might have made, and the helmet had no back at all.

Between the two in that corner—perhaps because they were the only ones as short as him in a room full of big men—was a fellow in the oil-stained khaki of an RAF mechanic, shivering despite the heat. He looked at the newcomer, shook his head, and looked away again.

"I scarcely feel the hero *now*," said Lawrence with an engaging, rueful, smile. He stepped into the room, nodding to either side in the easy motion of a prince receiving homage. "My motorcycle stopped a mile from here—"

He snapped his finger in the air. "*Zut*, stopped. No buts or maybes. And put me back on these."

Lawrence's hand gestured airily toward the toes of the military-pattern boots, now scuffed, that poked beneath the embroidered hem of his robes.

They'd all heard of Lawrence here, though few in the bar were of his time and most had died before it. The great came to Hell in their pride . . . and lesser folk with lesser sins, like these whom rumors of war had gathered in a riverside bar, had all eternity to trade stories about their betters.

"New stuff don't work near the river," said a Roman in a cuirass of iron hoops. "Upstream a ways, I hear tell steel swords don't cut. Here, mind, they work just fine."

The British sergeant plucked a note like that of an ill-tuned Jew's-harp from the tip of his rifle's bayonet—just in case the Roman meant something by the look he gave the Redcoat when commenting on 'new stuff'.

"Ah, is that so?" said Lawrence, turning with his back to the bar so that he could survey the room. "I'd heard that the Nile plays its little games in this place. Everything does, of course."

"The Nile, then," said a gaunt man in Afrika Korps khaki. The plastic goggles around his neck had shrunk to beads in a fire that must have scorched the skin from his bones had he been wearing them at the time. His face, like that of the pilot, bore no sign of injury. "It *is* the Nile, you are sure?"

"It's whatever we make it, old boy," said Lawrence in amusement. "That's the way things *are* here, don't you know?"

"Why were you on a motorcycle?" asked the Israeli pilot slowly, his brow furrowed with the effort of remembering. Other memories intruded, causing him to rub his forehead. "Would you not ride a camel, yes?"

Lawrence gave his questioner a smirk of amused disdain. "A skittish motorcycle with a touch of blood in it," he said, "is better than all the riding animals on earth."

He changed down, dragging the heel of his right boot on the inside of the corner. A farm truck was approaching ploddingly, already close enough that the driver's face brightened in surprise at seeing the glittering Brough motorcycle slide through the T-intersection. There was no real danger.

He dropped another gear to keep the big V-twin from lugging for the first twenty feet as the bike came level and straightened onto its new heading. He fed torque to the rear wheel with more eagerness than care. The rear end shimmied, the tire's grip on the pavement doubtful— and when it did hold, the Brough's frame twitched as it tried to control the thrust of the 1000 cc engine.

Rubber held, steel held, and Lawrence held in the gorgeous rush of acceleration like nothing else on earth. Second gear, third—a momentary pause in the vibra-

tion through the seat and handgrips as the harmonics of engine movement cancelled themselves in some of the frame members. . . .

Some. Both boots buzzed outward on the footpegs— and calmed, through that point of peculiar sympathy and back with the rising power curve to the universal quivering of a thousand metal parts directed but not controlled by the human part astride them.

Fourth gear, and the blat from the Brough's fishtail exhausts was lost in wind-rush and the hedgerows.

He leaned over the gas tank, gripping it with his knees and feeling a new source of the hammering vibration that jellied fear and will and thought beyond the present instant. Valves rang against their seats; the push-rods clattered in their long, chromed housings.

His hand opened the throttle in a smooth motion that ended only when the cable reached its stop.

The road was straight and open. It began to compress under him, the slope ahead driven upward into a hill toward which the Brough snarled.

He was still accelerating. Everything but what was directly ahead of him went to brown and a blur.

The crest and a side-road, no traffic but loose gravel and the back end very twitchy, rigid frame allowing the wheel to hop from the pavement and spin unchecked for a fraction of a second before gravity brought it back and made the Brough twist under him as if in an access of lust.

Inertia carried them through. His heart settled, then leaped again with sudden awareness of being alive and the joy of living—in the moment, for the moment.

Faster. The road a yellow line, the hills ahead a blue haze. Alive, man and machine quivering together like sunlight on a pond.

Alive. . . .

"My Arabs called motorcycles devil-horses, you know," Lawrence said to the room with a satisfied smile.

"Thought they were the children of cars—as cars were the children of trains. Not a sophisticated people, rather like children themselves . . . but they could fight."

"You've come here for the war, then?" said a stocky, blond-bearded man whose fingers played idly on the cross-hilt of his sword. His coat of mail was heavy, hot, and stinking with his sweat. He continued to wear the armor because experience of his portion of eternity had taught him that he would be no more comfortable—here—if he took it off.

"Say, yeah," said the Mameluke with baggy pantaloons and a drooping moustache—Turkish by blood, but with only clumsy deference in his voice as he spoke to the man who had freed the Arab world from his race. "*You'd* know. Who is it's fighting, anyhow?"

Lawrence surveyed the room. His expression was as pleased as that of a king scanning his court—or a herdsman leaning over the top rail of his well-filled cattle byre. "Men are, old boy," he said with amusement, letting his body lounge backward against the bar.

"Yeah, but *who*?" grumbled the Roman, who had enough experience of philosophers to know their bullshit paradoxes didn't belong in a discussion of war.

Everyone but the RAF mechanic, hunched over the bar, was staring at Lawrence—waiting for his response, waiting for its *tone*.

Instead of snarling or sneering, Lawrence smiled and said gently, "It doesn't matter, you see, old boy? You know that as well as I do. The only time a man is truly alive is in battle. It's no different here than it was in life."

There was a murmur around the room. A group always mouths agreement with an opinion stated forcefully—at least brief agreement; but the one voice clearly audible was saying, "My wife always claimed the only thing I was good for was killing some other poor fucker, and fuck if I don't think the bitch was right."

"We could have run at Tafileh," Lawrence went on

musingly, quieting the room by pitching his voice so
low that every other voice fell silent. "Considered as
war, that would have been the right decision. . . ."

He grinned tightly at those facing him with bated
breath. "But war, that's a business for politicians. Battle
is what tries men, and we gave the Turks a battle that
day. For no better reason than that they irritated me by
trying to recapture a village they needed as little as I
did—but that *I* decided to keep."

"You defeated them, then?" said the Crusader, his
gaze shifting as he spoke from Lawrence to the Mameluke with baggy trousers and a sabre with a callus-
polished hilt.

"We massacred them," replied Lawrence, his tongue
flicking like a snake's from between his lips. "Or rather,
we chased them like dogs, and the villagers past whom
they ran massacred them. I lost scarcely twenty dead
and only a hundred or so casualties all told. While the
Turks—"

He smiled again, his long-jawed British face momentarily reptilian. "While of the thousand Turks who had
the effrontery to attack me, not fifty of them escaped.
The slopes were littered with them, and the cold that
night finished what our knives spared."

*The sky was as clear a gray as the blade of a kitchen
knife, worn by use and the acids of what it had cut.
Snow lay smooth across the rocks, crusted against the
wind that cut like frozen steel.*

*The bodies were lumps, brown where a stiff limb
raised its uniform into the wind from which flesh no
longer needed protection.*

*His bones ached with the cold. The recent bruise on
his thigh was a particular agony. A fragment of Turkish
shell had struck him there without penetrating during
the battle.*

*That hurt was the only shield he had against the
memory of what he had done.*

He was billeted with twenty-seven of his men in a two-room hut in the village below. They kept down the lice by sprinkling their hair with urine, but nothing could help with the fleas, the stench, or the bitter, smoky fire of green camel dung.

The slopes were as clean and cold as death; but the dead were everywhere, on the ground and in his memory.

Twenty friends in shallow graves, and hundreds of not-friends lumping beneath the snow. All for him, and all for nothing save a chance to pack twenty-eight men into a hut not fit for six. . . .

If he stayed on the slopes, the wind would kill him too . . . but that wouldn't bring the others back.

And it wasn't time; not yet.

"Finished 'em for good, did ye?" said the color sergeant, smiling as his thumb polished one triangular flat of his bayonet. The smile vanished as he recalled the way a similar blade had felt, hot and then a cold that expanded to fill the universe, when a panicked wog thrust him through the chest at Zagazig.

"Oh, the Turks were back in Tafileh the next Spring," said Lawrence off-handedly. "Nothing we could do about *that*, old man; far too many of them. But—"

He fixed the sergeant with his gaze, then swept it regally across the other expectant faces in the room. "But *when* we fought them, we won. And that was all that mattered, then or now."

"I had thought that it was trains you ambushed," said the Afrika Korpsman, speaking stiffly as if still surprised to find that he had lips. "But it was battles you fought, then?"

"Oh, I wouldn't want you to think we skimped on trains, no," Lawrence explained with a smirk. "They were good targets for a mob like mine. Trains can't be defended very well after the locomotive's been blown up by a mine—and they're full of loot."

The smirk broadened. "There's nothing, you know,

that an Arab won't chance for loot. That was one of my problems, you see. It was dashed near impossible to get them to leave an ambush site while there was anything left to steal. I remember once when we blew up a train just south of Mudowwara, and a company of Turks came hot-foot out of the station to drive us away."

"Too many to fight, you mean?" prompted the Roman, stabbing the statement to find the point he was unwilling to assume.

"A squad would have been too many for me to fight by then," Lawrence replied with a laugh. "You see, besides the wounded and a group of Austrian instructors, the train had been packed with the families of Turkish officers and all their household belongings. My men had never dreamed of such loot. They were throwing down their rifles to carry off their new riches in both arms."

. He shook his head in mock amazement at the childishness of the men who had followed him. "If the Turks from Mudowwara had been a little more spirited, why, they'd have bagged us all. And a very bad thing that should have been for us, I assure you. It was a bad war for captives, the war we fought."

He could still hear the cries of the few hospital cases who'd survived the blast. They'd been in the first wagon, just behind the locomotive where the mine had gone off. It was amazing that even these few were alive to scream.

One of the dying had moaned, "Typhus," when Lawrence looked in, so he'd wedged shut the door of the splintered carriage filled with splintered men.

The ground about the wreckage wore a floral beauty of outspread loot: blankets and quilts and carpets, spread for the victors to paw through; jewelry and knick-knacks and cookware. The Arabs made and discarded their selections while women screamed and children wept or stood in dumb amazement, blinking in the desert sun.

A pair of his men were struggling over an eight-day clock. Its weights spun wildly, a golden dazzle between them. One Arab lost his grip; reaction jerked the clock away from the other claimant, and it crashed down in a flutter of gears and mother-of-pearl inlays.

Ignoring it and each other, the men turned to separate piles of Turkish belongings.

The Austrians in blue-gray uniforms were artillery instructors returning from Medina. They stood in a stiff group beside the carriage in which they had been riding. The car's brown sidewalls were flecked with ragged yellow holes where bullets had blasted through and exposed the pine boards beneath the paint. A lieutenant lay on the ground with blood oozing from his mouth and the hole in his chest.

Another Austrian stepped forward. The oilcloth patch on his epaulets bore the single star and braid of an ensign, but he was scarcely a boy.

He had blue eyes and blond hair. It was like looking into a mirror through a decade of time.

"You are English, not so?" the boy murmured in German. "Please, you must fetch a doctor for my friend. He must have a doctor."

Rahail, one of Lawrence's bodyguards, rushed past with his eyes and butter-plaited hair gleaming. He held his rifle high and, in the crook of his right arm, bore a pair of European-style silk dresses from some unimaginable part of the baggage.

He shouted triumphantly to Lawrence and fired in the air. The crash of the shot echoed from the railway embankment and mingled with the other firing—joyful excess and the volleys of the oncoming patrol.

"Your friends will be here soon," Lawrence said. He waved his hand up the line, toward Mudowwara. He knew he couldn't really hear the cries from the front carriage over the sound of guns and steam escaping from the ruined locomotives. "In an hour. They'll take care of your friend."

The wounded Austrian would die despite anything the best physicians in Europe could have done for him. There would be no doctor in the rescue party, and the Turks wouldn't waste the effort of carrying the dying man to Mudowwara.

Lawrence turned away. A pocket pistol snapped, noticeable in the din by its slightness against the muzzle blasts of the Arabs' rifles.

He spun. Rahail had tried to jerk gold buttons from the uniform of an Austrian major. The officer fumbled his little pistol from its patent-leather holster and managed to fire a shot into the ground before Rahail batted the weapon away.

"No!" Lawrence shouted.

Another of his guards laid the muzzle of his rifle against the major's skull and fired. Bone and brains spattered the side of the railway carriage around the splintered yellow of another bullet hole.

There was a wild volley, twenty or more Arabs firing as quickly as they could work the bolts of their rifles. The Austrians spun like ten-pins, caught too suddenly to run or even cry out.

The ensign crumpled at the knees. Both of his hands were clasped to the bloody hole in his chest, but his eyes mirrored those of Lawrence until his face flopped onto the gravel. . . .

He grinned like a sated hawk in the frame of his white burnoose. "One of the Austrians," he said, "objected to the treatment he was getting and fired a pistol at my bodyguards. It got him what anyone but a fool would have expected."

Lawrence glared around the room with tigerish challenge, flicking his eyes over hands resting familiarly on the grips of worn weapons. "We didn't carry around the Geneva Conventions, out where we were playing war. Most of you lot can understand that, can't you?"

Shrugs, smiles on faces scarred by one war or twenty-odd.

There was no need to reply with words, but a Macedonian wearing the gilded bronze armor of a successful mercenary said, "Hold 'em for ransom and make a nice bit a' change, everybody'd say . . . but there was always a few, you know, you didn't want to fight another time."

The furry man in the corner squinted, then tried to stroke the arm of the shivering mechanic beside him. The mechanic clasped the furry hand for a moment, then thrust it away from him in barely-controlled revulsion at human contact.

Lawrence frowned at the pair momentarily, but his face reset itself in a mask of cynical superiority. He said, "I surrounded myself with only the hardest cases, the men who'd been cast from every household in Arabia for murder and insubordination. They fought for me because they knew that I cared for nothing else if they fought—and because they knew that I was harder still than they."

The hands of other men in the bar were often on their weapons, but Lawrence never touched the broad-bladed jambiya in his sash. He leaned back with his elbows on the mahogany rail behind him, surveying the room in a sweep as lazy as that of a vulture's wing.

"The only way to keep order where we were, where I was," he said, the words rolling softly like old brandy over his tongue, "was to be judge, jury, and executioner. I was above their feuds, above injustice."

He smiled tightly around the room. "I knew my duty; and I assure you, I did it when required."

As the sheer-sided gorge narrowed, its atmosphere became filled with the sweat and terror of Hamid the Moor.

The prisoner could walk no farther between the rock walls. Turning to Lawrence and the revolver at the gully's entrance, he blurted, "Aurens Bey, you must believe me. I meant Saleh no harm; only—the sun was hot. And he must always gibe at the way I speak. My rifle—but I did not mean. . . ."

Hamid's fear and his thick Mahgrabi accent made his words almost unintelligible.

"Kneel and pray," Lawrence ordered.

"Aurens—"

"Kneel, damn you!"

He had shouted in English, but the order would have been clear even without the way the Webley's barrel wobbled at the end of Lawrence's out-stretched arm.

Hamid fell on his face with his eyes closed. He was babbling something that could be either prayer or further attempts at justification.

The rain a few days before had pitted the gully's sandy floor and left a damp memory which the weeds overgrowing the top of the crack had protected. Under other circumstances, it would have been pleasant. Now it was too near a reminder of the tomb the place was about to become.

The sun on Lawrence's back had lost all power to warm him.

"Get up."

Hamid's face lifted from the weeds. "Aurens—"

"Get up!"

As Hamid rose, the heavy bullet took him in the chest. He toppled face-down again in the thunderous echoes, screaming, thrashing mindlessly. When his chest lifted in spasms, blood spurted from the wound to soak his robe of brown and maroon stripes.

The gully's floor sloped toward the entrance. Rolling, twitching like a pithed frog, Hamid flopped closer.

He had voided his bowels. That stench filled the air like the blast of the second shot that should have finished him, but the gun-hand was trembling too badly. Sand gouted from the bullet's impact, stinging Law-

rence's bare feet and the knuckles of his hand on the
Webley's grip.

There was a gray-blue entrance hole on the back of
Hamid's flailing wrist. When the limb slashed the ground
convulsively, the exit hole left bloody spatters in the
sand.

Hamid was crying "Allah!" or "Saleh!" . . . or perhaps nothing at all, just crying in a voice that grew
weaker as the blood from the chest wound began to
bubble instead of jetting toward the sky.

Hamid lay on his back. Lawrence leaned over him,
socketing the muzzle of the revolver where the flesh
dipped at the juncture of the Moor's sternum and collar
bones.

The bloody robe fluttered with the roar of the shot,
but Hamid only quivered and lay flaccid, his eyes staring at eternity. . . .

"So you see," Lawrence continued with a dismissive
wave of his hand, "that while as a civilized man myself I
could deplore a mishap with a prisoner . . . well, you
can't make a silk purse of a sow's ear, can you? And—"

He raised a finger for emphasis, a gesture made
indolent by the way his elbow continued to rest on the
bar. "And you must remember that the Turks, were—"
Lawrence smiled tolerantly at the Mameluke whose
grin was too wide and fixed to be unaware "—not to
put too fine a point on it, beasts. As I learned to my
own cost at Deraa."

"Your enemies captured you?" asked a black man
with a cuirass of crocodile hide and a hooked bronze
chopper thrust through his belt.

"Not captured, no," Lawrence replied with a laugh
like a bird trilling. "Dashed if they didn't *conscript* me,
of all things."

He smiled with quiet pride. "I was spying out the
place as I often did, in Arab dress, don't you know?
And the Governor of Hauran himself caught sight of

me. He had me sent for, and I don't suppose I have to
tell you chaps that I thought it was all up with me then.
But deuced if they didn't enroll me as a soldier."

Lawrence shook his head as if in rueful recollection.
"It wasn't just a soldier that the Governor wanted though.
That was clear by the first night when he had me
dragged upstairs to his bedroom. A fat, greasy fellow,
wearing only a robe as he sat on his bed."

"Rank hath its privileges," commented the Roman
with a laugh of coarse remembrance.

"So *he* thought, at least," rejoined Lawrence. "But
he was quite wrong in this case, of course."

He glared in challenge, first at the Roman and then
sweeping the remainder of the room—to rest at last on
the shivering back of the RAF mechanic. No one else
spoke.

"He had the others hold me," Lawrence continued,
his brow clearing of its momentary frown. "He slapped
me with a slipper—so as not to damage my skin, I
suppose. He found me very white, not surprisingly.
When that didn't work, he prodded me with a bayonet
and even bit me—in between his kisses, of course, and
dashed if I didn't prefer his teeth to his lips. And
then—"

In the hush, Lawrence gestured upward with both
palms, his fingers loosely spread. "Then he told the
other soldiers to teach me my business below in the
guardroom—and I don't mind telling you chaps that it
was a deuced unpleasant night I spent there, too."

*Pain was a red-tinged pressure, not sharp at all but
rather buoying him, supporting his mind in its shuddering ambiance.*

*One of the guards came back, buttoning his fly. His
black eyes gleamed like beads of polished cannel coal in
the light of the paraffin lamp. "Is he ready for the
Bey?" the guard called laughingly.*

"Give him a kiss, Tewfik," replied another of the

soldiers as he played with Lawrence's groin. "That'll
bring him around, won't it?"

Tewfik paused, then fumbled his buttons open again.
"No, I'll give him something to kiss, all right," he said.

Each of the whip-strokes criss-crossing Lawrence's
back throbbed against the bench with its own separate
rhythm, like the parts of a motorcycle whirring into a
single serried whole. He could feel his heartbeats in a
hundred blood-suffused ridges. Where the ridges met,
the blood seeping out had a momentary coolness which
brought its own unique character of pain.

Something touched his lips. He vomited.

Tewfik slapped him with a hand as calloused as a
camel's pads. The other guards laughed.

"No, he does me honor," Tewfik snarled. "He makes
sure that I will slide easily. Roll him over."

The only sound for a moment was the thunder of
Lawrence's heart, echoing through the whip-weals.

"The Bey will be angry," a guard said.

"Fuck the Bey," said Tewfik, but he pitched his voice
low. Then he added, "Nasir, go up the stairs a little
way. Anyway, he won't come down here, he'll call us up
to him."

Hands lifted Lawrence by wrists and ankles, as if he
were a sheep about to be flayed. As they turned him,
the air fanned itself against his whip-struck back. The
pain was white and red and universal.

"I'm next," somebody muttered.

Tewfik was heavy. Because the bench was narrow, he
supported his hands on Lawrence's ribs, crushing down
against the weals each time he lifted his hips for another stroke. Pain and pain made a rhythmic counter-
point, a choir of sensation at which Lawrence smiled.

After a time, the soldiers rode him around the room,
two of them dragging Lawrence's legs while a third sat
astride his body. Before they were done with him, he
had surrendered every recess of his body and will to
them. . . .

* * *

"Don't take much of a beating to be worse'n one night's sore asshole," said a Byzantine soldier in trousers and a shirt of iron scales. One of the scales—over his heart—had been punched out by the thrust of a Vandal spear. He glared a challenge at the rest of the room, though he avoided meeting Lawrence's eyes.

"You'd understand if you'd been an officer, my man," said Lawrence distantly. "I couldn't have lost face with the Turks and still been able to lead my men."

He straightened, taking his elbows from the bar for almost the first time since he had entered the room. "The Turks were hard," he said, "so I had to be harder. Hard with them, harder still with my own men. We burned all the dross out of ourselves. The Turks roasted their captives alive, so we—"

Someone in the room was weeping softly, but no one looked away from Lawrence to see who it was.

"—had to give our own wounded a clean death when we weren't able to carry them off," Lawrence continued, oblivious to the vagrant sound. "Which was most generally the case, you chaps understand. We didn't have the luxury of motor ambulances or doctors accompanying our raids. They understood, the poor chaps, but it was hard nonetheless. . . ."

Farraj looked childlike, younger even than his boyish years. The skin from which they had stripped his robes was dead white in contrast to the sluggish bleeding no one could staunch.

The boy's breath whistled thinly through both the entrance and exit holes left by the Turkish bullet.

"Aurens . . . ," old Zagi said doubtfully, looking northward, up the railway line.

The single-cylinder engine of the approaching motorized trolley popped and sputtered harmlessly, like the complaints of an old woman at the boys robbing her orchard. The trolley's Spandau machinegun had a slower,

*implacable note, and the occasional bullet passing over-
head cracked like death itself.*

*Which one would very soon bring, when the range
grew too short for even Turkish gunners to miss.*

*"Aurens . . . ?" Zagi repeated, for there were fifty
Turks accompanying the armed trolley and only sixteen
in the raiding party.*

Fifteen and Farraj.

*"Leave me," the boy whispered. There was a dab of
blood on his lips, lips that Lawrence had been kissing
the night before. "I haven't wanted to live anyway, not
since Daud died."*

*A bullet struck the arch of the bridge. The lead core
ricocheted skyward with the howl of an exorcised demon, but fragments of its steel jacket sprayed the crouch-
ing men.*

*"Aurens Bey," said Zagi, firmly dignified. "He will
die in an hour at best, and we cannot move him since
he screams so when we try. We must leave."*

*"We will leave shortly." Lawrence shifted so that the
nude boy couldn't see that he was drawing the revolver
from beneath his robe.*

*Farraj understood the motion anyway. His eyes were
black with the end of love. "Daud will be angry with
you," he whispered.*

"Greet him from me," Lawrence said.

*His left hand gripped that of the boy. It was tiny by
contrast, and already cold as nothing was cold in the
desert by day.*

*He tried to look at Farraj, but the eyes of both of
them strayed sidewards, toward the revolver.*

*He squeezed the trigger, and the hammer seemed to
take forever to fall.*

"The hard decisions are a part of leadership too, you
know," he said, brushing away the fold of the burnoose
which sweat had glued to his cheek. He let his hand
linger in contact with the smooth cashmere.

" 'ooever leads *this* lot," said the color sergeant, looking balefully around at the men sharing the barroom with him. "Believe you me, 'e'll 'ave 'is bloody work cut out."

"I could lead you," said the man in Arab dress. His voice falsely hinted that he spoke idly.

There was no sound or movement in the room.

"Yes . . . ," he went on, drawling the syllable as his glance glittered across the scarred, hopeful faces turned to his. "Desperate men, all of you, and you need a leader. If you'll trust your souls to me—"

The RAF mechanic moved, slipping through the rank of bigger men like a terrier pouncing in a thicket. His eyes were the colorless shade of blue the sun has burned too long.

"What—" said the man in Arab dress, raising one of his broad, long hands in warning.

The mechanic slipped the silver-mounted dagger from its sheath in the Arab sash. The weapon was a jambiya, sharpened like a razor on both edges of its broad, curved blade.

The mechanic gripped its cold metal by the flares at butt and guard, with the pad of his middle finger barely resting on the hilt's narrow waist. The tip of the blade had hooked beneath the burnoose in a practiced motion, and the steel's inner curve lay against the taller man's neck from ear to Adam's apple.

Weapons and curses crashed all around the room, but it was too late for anyone to affect the situation save the two men touching the knife—with hand and throat.

"How could you kill Farraj?" said the mechanic. He wasn't whispering, but his voice broke repeatedly like radio signals being received through static.

"I—" said the other man.

"He loved you," said the mechanic, the words stronger but trembling with the same emotion that made light quiver eagerly across the flat of the blade. The knife shook like a hound straining to slip its leash.

"I—" The taller man choked. He was straining upward, because his throat moved when he spoke, and each time the steel drew a drop of blood through his skin.

"He loved you," said the mechanic caressingly, "as he loved no one in life but Daud . . . and you'd led Daud to his death already, hadn't you . . . ?"

"Please!" blurted the taller man. He was breathing in short gasps. "Please, you've got to—I've been lying, I swear it now. I never even saw him. My name's Patrick, Major Patrick, and I was on the staff at Alexandria."

Someone in the room cursed. A sword, half-drawn, rang the rest of the way clear of its sheath.

"I *swear* to you!" the imposter screamed. "I didn't kill anyone. I'm not Lawrence!"

The RAF mechanic squeezed his forehead with his left hand. "No," he said in a puzzled voice. "You're *not* Lawrence."

The jambiya cut a glittering arc through the air, slamming down to shudder a hand's breadth deep in the floor of earth and filth.

"You can't be Lawrence," said the little man in the uniform he wore after resigning his commission and re-enlisting under a false name. "I'm Lawrence. May the Lord have mercy on me, I was Lawrence."

He walked out of the bar. The doors clacked back and forth on their sprung hinges.

No one tried to follow.

FALLOUT

Nancy Asire

Napoleon sat at the kitchen table, staring out the window into the predawn darkness, his cup of coffee all but forgotten. Something had jarred him awake, though the house and yard were quiet. He grimaced. Hell being Hell, life was never what one expected; but, even for Hell, lately things had gotten out of hand.

Only two weeks ago, Caesar's Romans had delivered Hadrian to Wellington's house with instructions that the ex-Supreme Commander of Hell's armies be kept out of sight, and hopefully out of mind, for three days. Those three days had turned into six, to ten, then fourteen. A few highly coded messages from Caesar had told Napoleon no more than he already knew: things in Hell appeared to be coming apart at the seams.

ITEM: Rameses, "victor" of Kadesh and present Supreme Commander, was more than slightly upset about altercations that had taken place at Ashurbanipal's palace and Tiberius' villa, in which Caesar and his lads had played more than a simple part.

ITEM: After the aforementioned, Management had called an Administrative Tribunal into session, an event which—to the surprise of everyone listening to the news broadcasts, or reading the *Daily Hell*—had made the news, unaltered by the new Unified Propaganda Information service.

ITEM: Officials of the Government—*highly* placed officials, including one Mithridates (the "Butcher of Asia"), Rameses' second-hand man, stood implicated in collusion, or worse.

ITEM: With things going—ahem—to Hell in a wicker basket, he and Wellington were still in possession of Hadrian, who, as *ex*-Supreme Commander, might be a morsel too juicy to be resisted by anyone with a modicum of ambition in New Hell and environs.

Only one of those items held the slightest ray of hope: he and Wellington had finally convinced Hadrian (by mentioning the Administrative Tribunal) that they were *not* keeping the ex-Supreme Commander prisoner for personal gain, but for his own safety. Hadrian's ultimate understanding, however, had not diminished his autocratic demands *or* tempered his boorish imperial behavior. Keeping Hadrian half-drunk on distilled liquor helped matters some, but it was a triumph of personal self-control that kept Wellington from killing the Roman Emperor for any number of reasons.

"Sit tight, if you can," Caesar had advised at the outset, regarding Hadrian. "I'll help you if I'm able."

"I'll kill the bloody bastard!" Wellington had exclaimed on too many afternoons. "Then we won't need to accept more of Caesar's help and end up further in his debt."

"Patience," Marie always counseled, though her own patience with the current state of affairs had worn quite thin.

At least he and Marie no longer played host to de Vauban. The wounded soldier of the *Grande Armée* had recovered enough to be on his own, though Napoleon had not sent him back to serve as stablemaster and bed-partner to an English lady of Wellington's acquaintance. No. For de Vauban, Napoleon had found a far better position—that of assistant in the bar at the Hellview Golf and Country Club. This put de Vauban within easy reach, gave the soldier a sense of independence, *and* provided Napoleon a window on what was being said in the bar when patrons were deep in their cups and more talkative.

Goebbels had obviously either lost interest in what was going on at Napoleon's and Wellington's houses, *or*, for some reason, had been unable to parlay any of his information into the Management perks he so desperately desired.

And, thank God, the Huns and Mongols had finally gone home, after having participated in the longest back yard barbeque in history.

The telephone rang.

Napoleon instinctively reached for the wall unit, then stopped and let the phone ring two more times before picking it up.

"*Safe line,*" said Caesar's voice, "*but this will have to be quick. We've got problems over here, Napoleon. We think the Assyrians are mobilizing to come at us again.*"

Napoleon straightened in his chair. "Tiberius?"

"Aiding and abetting, or at least uninterested in possible traffic across his grounds."

"What do you need *me* for?" Napoleon asked. "I've got enough trouble as it is with Hadrian—"

"*Just stay on alert. I'll be in touch later. And, Napoleon . . . keep an eye on your own backyard.*"

The line went dead. Napoleon stared at the phone, then slowly placed the receiver back in its cradle.

"Napoleon, who was that?"

He turned: Marie stood at the kitchen door, her eyes bleary with sleep.

"Caesar," he said. "Who else? I think things are going to get interesting again, Marie."

She took the chair at his side. "May you live in interesting times," she murmured, quoting the old Chinese saying.

"Huhn. But they never said you'd have to put up with interesting times after death, did they?"

A few coded phone calls, including one to de Vauban on the grounds of the Country Club, provided Napoleon no helpful information. Everything seemed to be peaceful on *this* side of Decentral Park. "Seemed to be" often turned into the exact opposite, so, after breakfast, Napoleon made an early morning call on Wellington.

Anbec, one of the DGSE men who had taken up residence with Wellington and who, with his three companions, would remain with Wellington until Hadrian was gone, answered the doorbell.

"*Où est Wellington?*" Napoleon asked.

"*Dans la cuisine.*"

Still at breakfast? "*Et Adriene?*"

Anbec snorted. "*Il dort encore. Il est enivré!*"

Drunk and asleep . . . situation normal. "*Bon. Merci.*" Napoleon walked into Wellington's kitchen. "Late breakfast?" he asked.

Wellington set his cup down. "I'm trying," he said with massive dignity, "to arrange things so that I'm awake when His High and Mighty Lordship isn't."

"How's it working out?"

"He's still alive, isn't he?" Wellington took another sip of tea as Napoleon sat down. "What brings you over here?"

"Caesar," Napoleon replied.

"What *now*? As if we aren't doing enough for him already that he—"

"Trouble with the Assyrians, he thinks. Might need some assistance."

Wellington straightened the high collar of his red uniform. "Ours, naturally."

"Not yet. He's put us on alert. Told us to watch our own backyards."

The doorbell rang several times.

"Oh, damn!" Wellington muttered. "Who the devil could *that* be?"

"De Vauban?" Napoleon heard Anbec at the front door, speaking French. "Were you expecting—?"

"I haven't bloody well been expecting *anyone* for the past two weeks and look what I end up with! A house full of surly French and a drunken Roman Emperor!"

It was de Vauban—the Frenchman stood in the door to Wellington's kitchen. *"Mon empereur,"* he said, bowing slightly. *"M'sieur le duc,"* he said to Wellington, and then continued in slow English. "A man came to breakfast at the Club. He had been in the country. He saw many, horsemen . . . knights, *n'est-ce pas?* They come this way."

Napoleon traded a glance with Wellington. "How many?"

"The man said over two hundred."

"Knights?" Wellington echoed. "What the bloody hell is a pack of knights doing in the country?"

"Looting and killing," de Vauban replied.

Napoleon stared. "How far off are they?"

"The man guessed five or six hours by horseback."

"Damn, Wellington. With Caesar possibly needing help, and these knights headed *our* way. . . ."

"Where are *you* going, Napoleon?"

Napoleon was halfway to the back door. "Caesar had better know about this." He turned to de Vauban. "Stay here, *mon ami*. Wellington still has no phones, so if he needs you to run a message to me, do it." He looked at Wellington. "Tell the DGSE men what's going on. I'll be back as soon as I can."

"Caesar's tried to call you two times," Marie said, as Napoleon let himself into the kitchen. "He wants you to call him immediately."

"Wonderful." Napoleon shut the door behind him. "We've got trouble, Marie. De Vauban—"

"I know . . . he told me. He came here first."

"Do you know where our guns are?"

"Will it come to that?"

"More than likely." He snatched up the phone and punched in a number. "I don't want to be caught with—Hello, Caesar?"

"*Wellington needs some kind of communications,*" Caesar said, all Roman efficiency. "*We can't have either of you out of touch. Here's the situation. The Assyrians are mobilizing. I'll need you down at Louis XIV's to cover my rear. A division of mounted warriors is heading eastward, right toward Louis' and Maria-Theresa's. Maria-Theresa I can trust to defend herself, but Louis . . .*" Caesar snorted derisively. "*He'll sit on his butt in that opulent palace of his and never stir a hair. Probably invite the bastards to a* soirée *or something.*"

"Uhn . . . Julius. Hate to rain on you, but I've got trouble on *my* side of the Park, too. We've got a force of about two hundred knights headed our way. I don't want to leave when—"

"*You've got Wellington there, don't you? Use him, man! I need you over here. Hell's degenerated into total chaos . . . here and everywhere. Things downtown have deteriorated into street fighting and worse.*"

"*Merde!* If Wellington finds out, he'll be off to Queen Victoria before I finish telling him the rest of the story."

"*He won't get far. No one can make it through that mess to the English quarter. Can I depend on you?*"

Napoleon rubbed the bridge of his nose. "Do you need Attila?"

"*No. You can have him.*"

"All right. I'll set up some kind of defensive line here and leave as soon as I can. Give me a few hours."

"*Good. and, Napoleon . . . while you're down at Louis', kick the idiot out, will you? I'd much rather have you as the French power base than him.*"

Napoleon stood looking at the phone long after Caesar had hung up, then placed the phone back in its cradle and turned to face Marie.

"I've got to defend Louis XIV's palace—there's a division of horsemen headed toward that area. The Assyrians are coming at Caesar from the other side of the villa."

"What about us?" Marie asked.

"I'll leave Wellington in charge." Napoleon snatched up the phone again, punched in Attila's number and waited. "Attila! Yes . . . it's me. Get yourself down here . . . on the double! Full alert!"

He hung up the phone. "Gather up every weapon we have in the house, Marie, and all the ammunition you can find. I'm going back to Wellington's."

"Now what?" Wellington asked, standing in the opened doorway.

"For God's sake, Wellington . . . let me in, will you?"

"Oh . . . sorry." Wellington stepped back. Two of the DGSE men sat watching TV; Anbec had detached himself from the group and stood at Wellington's shoulder.

"Anbec," Napoleon said in rapid-fire French, "we need some field phones and medium-sized weapons. How soon can your connections move on it?"

Anbec's eyes narrowed. "Inside an hour."

"*Bon! Allez!*"

Anbec rapped out an order; he and his two companions headed for the garage.

"Napoleon." Wellington's voice had an edge to it. "What the bloody hell's going on?"

"I'm getting you weapons. You'll be in charge of things over here. I've got to help Caesar."

"What?" Wellington grabbed Napoleon's arm. "One more time . . . *what's happening?*"

"Nobody knows! Hell's turned upside down. Things have degenerated into a whatever-you-can-grab-it's-yours party!"

"Just around the Park?"

"No." Napoleon turned to go. "Everywhere, as far as Caesar can tell."

"*Everywhere?* That means the English quarter could be having a tough go of it. I can't stay here, Napoleon . . . I've got to help my countrymen."

Napoleon sighed and gently removed Wellington's hand from his arm. "You can't get through, *mon ami.* They'll have to make do without you."

"But . . . Queen Victoria *needs* me! I'm her Iron Duke! I—"

"Shit, Wellington! She's *got* Montgomery! She's *got* Marlborough! Shall I list all her other famous British generals in alphabetical order? *You're* all the way down with the W's."

"But . . ."

"You can't get through. Do you hear me? *You can't get through!* Settle down, man. I can't think of anyone I'd rather leave here behind me."

Wellington drew a deep breath. "You *mean* that? After Waterloo? After—"

"I mean it. Besides, you'll fight nastier than anyone else I could pick right now. *You've* got the brandy in your basement to protect, to say nothing of your Steuben glass."

Attila stood waiting in Napoleon's living room, clad in his war-gear: leathers, sturdy boots, and metal helm. His shield and his weapons—sword, bow and arrows, and two spears—he had leaned up against the wall. The gold-butted pommel of the long dagger stuffed into his belt winked in the light as he turned around.

"What's going on?" Attila asked.

Napoleon told him about the knights, giving all the details. "That's where we stand," he said, shutting the front door. "Can you mobilize your Huns quickly?"

Attila's narrow eyes glittered. "How long have we got?"

"Around four hours . . . maybe more, maybe less."

"They'll be here."

"Good. What about the Mongols? Can you get your hands on any of them?"

"Hey! Subodai owes me. No problem." Attila stood straighter. "From what Marie tells me, Hell's going to Hell, heh?" He grinned at his own joke. "Are you leading us?"

"No. I've got to help Caesar. Wellington's in command."

"*Wellington?* He'll be too worried about getting his uniform dirty to—" He sighed. "Who's going to sit on Hadrian?"

"The DGSE men. They're also going to get us some communications devices and some light armaments."

Attila's face lit up. "Hooohah! *Now* we're talking!"

"Move, Attila! Get your horsemen here inside two hours. I want those knights stopped *before* they reach the neighborhood."

"Right!" Attila walked to his weapons, snatched them up, and headed toward the door. A wide grin split his face. "This *could* be more fun than a barbeque!"

Napoleon leaned back against the door after Attila had gone, his eyes closed, his mind filled with possible strategies and maneuvers. He wished he had been at Louis' more often; not being familiar with the lay of the land put him at a disadvantage, but left him no more ignorant than the division of horsemen approaching from the west.

Louis. Useless Louis. Interested in nothing more than the perpetuation of his glorious legend. His opulent life-style, the multitudinous parties and balls . . . the entire outward show of power and prestige. . . .

Louis was a fraud.

In life, he had led armies, fought wars, and made France one of Europe's greatest nations.

But after death, finding Hell his reward, Louis had lost his nerve.

Few of the French had understood why Napoleon

had not taken over the French power base when he had come to Hell. Especially the old *grognons*—the old grumblers of the *Grande Armée*. None of *them* had been able to see it.

But Napoleon's reasons sprang from the past. In life, he had lifted his people to the pinnacle of worldly power, given them and everyone in his Empire better laws, roads, schools, and a chance for anyone with ability to succeed. And what was his reward? A one-way trip to Hell.

Had it all been for nothing? The dreams, the chance for glory and immortality . . . the hushed promises of a star?

Napoleon bowed his head and hooked his thumbs in his jeans pockets. He was not, like Louis, one who rested on his laurels. After not all that long in Hell, he saw that he could best help his people if he stayed in the background, out of the limelight, periodically serving in Hell's army under commanders he could have whipped any five of on a bad day. The Devil must have thought the entire situation amusing—the last thing *l'empereur* Napoleon would have wished.

Remember the briar patch, B'rer Rabbit.

And so, he had done the exact opposite of what anyone expected. Let Louis live in his palatial spread across the Park, he had told himself. Let Louis have all the glory. Meanwhile, establish underground connections with people who *truly* make things move in Hell. A string pulled here . . . a string pulled there . . . and, *voilà!* suddenly someone's life in Hell might grow marginally better.

And, above all, be ready to jump when the shit hit the fan.

The fan was running; the shit was on the way.

Did he now move in on Louis, kick the useless idiot out, and assume command of the French in Hell? Augustus would be pleased, as would Caesar. Napoleon had known this long before Caesar admitted as much on the phone. And other power bases in Hell would take heart if a strong hand guided the French instead of one only fit to wave to dancers on a ballroom floor.

Ambition. In Hell, where did it lead?

To a balancing act . . . a walk across the edge-thin blade of a sword stretched over deeper Hells than the one he inhabited. One misstep, one minute miscalculation. . . .

He heard Marie in the rear of the house, gathering what weapons they had, and started off down the hallway to help her. What would happen, would happen. He had thought it through thousands of times before. He would act only as he *could* act, and *only* when the proper set of circumstances had arrived.

With another quick look at his watch, Napoleon paced up and down the living room. The few quick phone calls he had made had set up a rendezvous with some of his old comrades from the *Grande Armée*. They were to contact as many cavalrymen as they could, and assemble in the woods by the armory.

So much for that. But where the devil was Anbec with the communications devices and the light armaments? Anbec's absence had troubled Napoleon more than the fact Attila had not arrived. Attila would turn up . . . he always did. Hell itself would freeze over before Attila was late to a fight.

He caught Marie watching him pace. Clad in a pair of jeans, wearing a jeans jacket over her blouse, she had been sitting silent so long he had forgotten her.

"Napoleon." She rose from the chair by the window. "We'll have to be going soon."

"I wish you'd think twice about coming with me," he said. "I'd feel better if—"

"Do you think I can't help you? That I don't know my weapons? After all the hours you spent with me, I think I know one end of a gun from the other."

"You do," he admitted. "You're a damned fine shot. But—"

"But, nothing!" She drew a deep breath and walked to his side. "You're not going off without me again. I chose to spend my eternity with you, not waiting for you to come back from somewhere else! I either go *with* your permission, or follow you without it."

The front door banged open and Wellington charged in, his face beet-red with anger.

"Now he's done it!" he yelled, slamming the door behind him. "The bloody fool's done it for sure!"

Napoleon dragged his mind away from Marie. "Who's done what?"

"*Who?* Hadrian, *that's* who! He's up now and sporting a monumental hangover. Swore up and down a fly walking across the ceiling woke him. And His Imperial Majesty's imperial mood is—" Wellington scowled. "—Lord! It's worse than ever!"

Napoleon lifted an eyebrow. "He's had hangovers before, and—"

"You don't understand! He overheard me telling de Vauban about my plans for defending the Country Club! *I* thought he was still asleep, or I wouldn't have—" Wellington sputtered for a moment. "And *then*, he—oh, so magnanimously—offered to serve as our commander!"

"Shit."

"That's what I said." Wellington spread his hands in appeal. "What am I to do? The condition *he's* in, he won't—"

"Oh, keep him fuzzed out," Napoleon suggested. "A bit of brandy here and there should do the trick."

"But . . . That royal ass will make *mincemeat* out of anything I plan!"

"Then don't let him close to the meat, *mon ami*. Keep him occupied with the mince."

Wellington muttered something under his breath about how he would much rather be fighting with his English and began prowling nervously up and down the living room. Napoleon exchanged a quick look with Marie and let Wellington go, knowing the Iron Duke's mettle: he would swing around when the time came.

The telephone rang.

Napoleon got to the study before Wellington, snatched up the receiver, and fended off the Iron Duke with a glare.

"*Les armes . . . nous les avons!*" Anbec said briefly. "*À côté! Mais, nous n'avons pas des communications.*"

"*Zut! Que faire?*"

Anbec quickly explained. "*Nous les trouverons.*"

"*Merveilleux!*" Napoleon replied. "*Merci, Anbec, merci. À tout à l'heure!*"

"They've got the weapons?" Marie asked as Napoleon hung up the phone.

"Yes, but no communications." Napoleon looked up at Wellington. "He's tried everywhere . . . the French, Americans, Italians . . . God! Everyone! But he swears he'll find us something, even if he has to *rent* it!"

As Napoleon, Marie, and de Vauban drove off down the street headed toward the armory, Wellington's heart sank. Napoleon trusted him . . . had left *him* in command, despite what Hadrian might maintain; had put Attila at his beck and call . . . Attila and the Huns and Mongols who followed him.

Waterloo, be damned.

He could *not* think of his countrymen. Queen Victoria had other British generals to help her. But none of them were her beloved Iron Duke, who had served as her Prime Minister, and who had saved the British Empire from—

—the very man who trusted Wellington enough to leave the defense of the neighborhood in his hands.

Wellington cursed under his breath. "Attila, you've been out and about. What's the condition of the rest of the neighborhood?"

"Hah!" Attila sat in one of Wellington's less expensive chairs, one booted leg thrown across its arm. "The DGSE men are in the garage, working with their weapons. Anbec's *still* trying to get our field phones. As for the rest of the neighborhood—" Attila made a rude gesture. "Crazy Louis is out in his back yard digging a bomb shelter."

"A bomb shelter?" Wellington stared, trying to envision Louis XVI with a shovel in his back yard digging madly away. "These are *knights*, dammit . . . not the 1st Airborne!"

Attila shrugged. "Little idiot said he wanted to be prepared for anything. And I couldn't find anyone else. They're probably barricaded in their houses." A nasty little smile touched Attila's face. "The only one who's interested in helping is our new neighbor—"

"—the Tulsan. Damn! Where is he?"

"Out with Yanush, looking over the horses. Says he used to have a quarter horse would put all of them to shame. Where's Hadrian?"

Wellington drew a deep breath. "In the bathroom, getting dressed in whatever we could find for him to wear. He doesn't want to direct a battle in a toga."

"Your sheets, he means. Har!" Attila made the sign against the evil-eye in the direction of the bathroom. "Now what?"

"We divide our forces. We'll leave some of your horsemen here in case the knights get around us at the Club. You have someone you can trust to lead them?"

"Yanush."

"Good. We can set up our command post at the Country Club. From there—"

An explosion rocked the house, rattled the windows, and sent Attila running to the front window.

"Gods! Someone's bombing the Park!"

Wellington had arrived at the window only seconds after Attila. A black cloud of smoke rose from deep in Decentral Park. Lord! If the Viet Cong thought the fire was coming from the Country Club—

The front door burst open and Tommy Hendron, late of Tulsa, Oklahoma, dove into Wellington's entry hall.

"Jeez-us!" he swore, slamming the door. "Hey, y'all! Saw a plane fly over. Who the hail's bombin' who?"

Wellington stared at the Tulsan who, from all appearances, seemed ready to protect his waterbed, his wet bar, and all his assorted other treasures. The ex-businessman carried a .22 rifle in one hand, a western-replica .45 was holstered at his hip (riding lower than normal because of Hendron's beer belly), and a machete was stuffed into the other side of the gun belt.

"Who's bombing whom?" Wellington echoed. "Damned if *we* know."

"Purty dumb way t'fight a war," the Tulsan growled. His face brightened. "Way-el . . . I'm here, yer Dukeship, if ya need me."

Another explosion shook the house.

"Damn, Attila! If the Cong think *we're* behind this—"

"Cong?" Hendron walked over to the front window. "Vee-yet Cong? From Vee-yet Nam? We've got them little slant-eyed devils 'round here?"

Attila turned from the window. "You were at a party with them."

"Y'all joshin' me? The bobby-que?" Hendron's eyes widened. "Ya mean all them little fellers dressed up in black pee-jamas? Them?"

"Them," Attila said.

"Shee-it."

"I wish Napoleon was here," Wellington said. "He'd—"

"Ya mean Napol-yun ain't gonna fight with us? Where'd *he* go?"

"To help Caesar." Wellington looked at Attila. "We've got to keep the Cong from shelling us. If—" He stopped, stared at the Tulsan, feeling the slightest tug of an idea. "I've got it!" he exclaimed, and started off toward his kitchen.

"You've got what?" Attila called after him.

"An idea!" Wellington snatched open his refrigerator

door and rummaged a bit, cursing Hadrian who had depleted most of what had been there. "Ribs!" he muttered. "Where are the damnable ribs?"

"What do you want ribs for?" Attila asked, coming to stand behind Wellington's shoulder.

"Bargaining power!" Wellington grabbed out a ziplock pack, slammed the refrigerator door. "Got them!"

"Now what in hail . . . ?" The Tulsan eyed the ribs. "Hey, yer Dukeship . . . whatcha lookin' at *me* for?"

Five minutes later, Tommy Hendron, armed with a yardstick on the end of which was tied a white rag, and carrying a handful of ribs, set out across Wellington's front yard toward the Park.

"We've got you covered!" Attila shouted from the front door, two of the DGSE men on either side of him, their automatic rifles aimed at the Park. "Talk loud now!"

"Talk loud now!" Hendron shouted back. "I'll *scream!*" He halted at the edge of the street, looked nervously up at the sky, and began waving his yardstick. "Truce!" he bellowed toward the Park. "Thet ain't us who's bombin' ya! 'Member thet bobby-que?" He waved the ribs over his head. "Ya'll kin git more of these here ribs, if ya blow them bastards outta the sky!"

An explosion answered him from farther back in the Park. Hendron turned and bolted for Wellington's front door.

"Outta my way!" he shouted, but Attila and the two DGSE men had already jumped back from the doorway. Hendron leaned up against the wall, panting. "Ya'll sure that was worth it?" he asked. "D'ya even think them little gooks heard?"

"They're always watching us," Attila said. "They heard you."

Wellington took the ribs back from Hendron. "Thank you, sir. We need all the help we can get." He glanced at Attila. "Let's move. We're running late. With Yanush here, we can turn our attention to the Club."

"Wellington. Are you ready to assist me?"

Wellington cringed and turned toward the hallway leading back to the bedrooms. Hadrian stood there, his eyes not all that focused, weaving slightly on his feet. Dressed in tunic and cloak, he looked decidedly Roman.

"My table cloth," Wellington murmured in a strangled voice. He felt Attila's restraining hand on his arm. Another explosion rumbled out of the Park.

It was not going to be a fun day at the Club.

Louis' palace lay atop a low hill at the end of a very long driveway. Napoleon stood for a moment at the end of that drive, looking at the woods, the rise and fall of the land, trying to get some sense of the ground he would be defending. If he planned to erect any perimeter defense, he would have to move quickly. Maria-Theresa had already set up her own defenses: Napoleon had seen men, cannon, and horses moving in the trees that surrounded the Austrian Empress's palace. As for Louis—

Anyone could have ridden up his drive: as far as Napoleon could tell, the entire grounds stood unprotected.

"Louis, you're a fool," he muttered under his breath, and turned back to his jeep where Marie and de Vauban waited.

The Romans had gifted him with the jeep when he had stopped and parked his car on the north side of the armory. "Caesar says he's sorry he can't give you more," the legionary who delivered the jeep had said. Napoleon had not complained: a jeep with a machine gun mounted in back was a damned sight better than nothing.

The assembled French soldiers seemed capable and ready to fight anything Napoleon pointed them at. Since Napoleon had asked for cavalry, few of the one hundred men had modern weapons; but each man carried the arms he had used in life: pistols, sabres, and lances.

Napoleon sighed softly, climbed into the jeep's driver's seat, beside Marie, and started up the driveway to

Louis' palace, followed by his cavalry. The secure feeling of command wrapped him—a pattern all too familiar in life, and one he had avoided after death. It would be so easy to take leadership of the French from Louis . . . so damned easy. Yet, was it worth it in the long run?

As he brought his jeep to a stop in front of the grand staircase leading up to Louis' palace door, Napoleon counted at least another hundred French soldiers waiting for him. Infantry, these fellows, come to give him their help even if they had no horses. To a man, they leapt to their feet as he climbed out of the jeep and helped Marie down.

"*Vive l'empereur!*" they shouted, lifting their rifles above their heads. "Long live the Emperor!"

Well, Louis, Napoleon thought, as he waved to the assembled men and ascended the steps with Marie at his side. *What will you make of* that *cheer, I wonder?*

When Wellington, the Tulsan, Attila, and Hadrian arrived at Hellview Golf and Country Club, they walked into a scene of total chaos. Denizens of the Club clamored for news; management had none, and stood wringing its collective hands at the very thought of knights trampling across the meticulously maintained grounds. Those few Club members who had been standing in the parking lot when Attila and his Huns and Mongols had arrived, had sent up a ragged cheer, unsure at first if *these* were the horsemen they were to fear.

There was no room, Wellington could see at a glance, for a command post. Hadrian stalked back and forth, still bleary from his hangover, asking questions and making suggestions. Wellington controlled himself with difficulty, longing to stuff a corner of Hadrian's cloak into the ex-Supreme Commander's mouth.

Hadrian was now trying to explain his battle plans to the Hunnish and Mongol captains; they stared at the Roman Emperor as if he were speaking Swahili. Wellington looked around the lobby, crammed with curious Club members, and smiled slightly.

"I say, commander," he said, touching Hadrian's shoulder. "It's beastly crowded in here . . . doesn't give a man like yourself proper room to think. Shall we adjourn to the bar?"

Hadrian shrugged his cloak back on his shoulders. "Not a bad idea, Wellington. Lead on."

Wellington exchanged a quick look with Attila and tipped his head back. The Hunnish King's narrow black eyes glittered with amusement as he caught Wellington's unspoken plan. It took Attila and several particularly surly looking Huns only a minute or two to empty the bar of its patrons.

"Not you!" Wellington caught at the bartender's arm before the man could leave. He slipped the fellow a bill of largish denomination, and smiled. "Seven and seven for His Majesty there. Doubles. Yes, he's the one in the tablecloth." His voice lowered. "And whatever you do, don't tell him what's going on. Give the rest of us sparkling water."

Hadrian, meanwhile, had taken up residence at a table by the window, his chair turned so he could look out across the polo field in the very direction from which the knights should ride.

"Are your scouts back yet?" he asked Attila, as the Hun sat down beside him.

"Soon. Any moment now."

"Good. When we know where these vagabonds are, we'll be able to greet them with the deaths they deserve."

Hyperbole and Hadrian were old, old friends.

Wellington waited until the bartender had the drinks ready and led the way to the table.

"A drink, commander?" he said. "I'm a bit dry, myself."

Hadrian nodded and gestured to the table before him. "Another good idea, Wellington. I'm pleased that you haven't forgotten how to serve me." He lifted the glass as Wellington took a chair, and downed it in several quick gulps. "Gods! Sweet stuff, isn't it? But not bad. I'll have another," he said to the bartender, who stood attentively nearby.

Attila coughed into his drink and Wellington strove mightly to keep a grin off his face. A few more glasses of Seven and Seven, and the defense of suburbia would be in good hands.

Any hands but Hadrian's.

"No! I won't have it!" Louis yelled. "Get your soldiers off my property!"

Napóleon stared at the Sun King: Louis would have a fit if he did not calm down. "*M'sieur,*" he said, "you have a mounted company of madmen headed at your palace, and—"

"Maria-Theresa can handle any invaders!" Louis shouted. "I don't need you and your rabble here!"

Rabble, eh? "This rabble you speak of, *m'sieur,* is made up of Frenchmen like yourself. Like me."

"You're not French!" Louis snarled. "You're a damned Corsican! Now get out of my palace!"

Napoleon turned his back on Louis and walked across the marble entry hall, his hands clasped behind his back. Louis' temper had already broken; his own would soon follow.

When he and Marie had entered the palace, leaving de Vauban outside with the jeep, Napoleon had counted all of Louis' retainers he could see: his own men outnumbered them considerably. And more than half those retainers and guards of honor had given him bows and salutes that told where *their* allegience lay.

Now, close to twenty of Louis' guard stood backing the Sun King, their muskets held at attention.

Napoleon looked at Marie who stood by the door, her face white and her expression difficult to read. *What should I do, Marie? What do you want me to do?*

"Who do you think you *are,* barging in here with

your troops, and telling *me* what to do?" Louis demanded, stalking across the entry hall. "I'm the King here, and I don't need any *parvenu* Emperor trying to take over *my* kingdom!"

"You aren't going to *have* a kingdom if you don't get off your fat butt and *do* something!" Napoleon snapped, turning around to face the flamboyant, velvet-clad figure of the Sun King. "Maria-Theresa is busy defending *her* territory. You're expected to at least *try* to defend yours!"

Napoleon could have sworn Louis' long, curled wig lifted an inch off the monarch's head.

"Guards!" Louis bellowed. "Throw this . . . this . . . *Corsican* out on the street!"

Not a one of them moved.

Napoleon looked Louis directly in the eyes. "*Ah, va te faire foutre!*" he said.

The gutter language, telling Louis precisely what he could do with himself, had its desired effect.

The Sun King stepped back, as if slapped in the face. Perhaps no one had ever spoken to him like this . . . during life or after death.

"Guards!" Louis screamed.

"I suggest not," said a soft voice from the door.

Napoleon turned his head: Marie held her Uzi in steady hands, the long black gun aimed at Louis' heart.

"And don't tempt me," Marie said, her voice still quiet, as she walked to Napoleon's side. "I'm a *very* good shot."

De Vauban and several of Napoleon's men burst through the opened door, weapons cocked and ready. At the sight of Louis being held at gunpoint by Marie, a deafening silence fell on the entry hall.

Napoleon shrugged. "As you will, *majesté*," he said, nodding to Louis. "You have left me no choice. *I* will assume command."

* * *

Hadrian snored. When he was drunk, he snored louder than when sober. At the moment, his snores threatened the windows.

Wellington paced up and down by the bar, glancing every now and again at the figure of the ex-Supreme Commander stretched out on the table top, near to falling from the chair.

Attila's scouts had returned with good news and bad news: the knights rode only a half hour away, exactly where expected, but there were *four* hundred of them, twice the number reported.

Damn, damn! Where was Anbec with the field phone?

Attila stomped into the bar, a flask of *kumiss* in his hands. "You were right," he said without preamble. "The knights *have* split up. Two hundred of them look like they're going west of here—"

"Oh, bloody hell! Right at our houses!"

"—and the other two hundred are headed straight for the Club. What's your plan?"

Wellington stopped pacing and leaned back against the bar. "We've got more room to fight *here*," he said at last. "Put more men at the edge of the stream that runs behind the houses. Yanush has sixty warriors with him now, doesn't he?"

"Yes."

"Send him forty more."

"That only leaves *us* with seventy-five."

"If what I have in mind works," Wellington said, "that will be just about right."

Louis languished in his upstairs bedroom, screaming and cursing himself hoarse. Fortunately, the bedroom sat far to the rear of the palace, and no one but those unfortunates assigned to guard duty had to put up with the noise.

With no more than a nod of his head, Napoleon had taken over Louis' palace. Jubilation swept through the

French who waited outside: their Emperor had taken command at last.

Marie watched silently, her Uzi held loosely at her side.

Napoleon had tried to get in touch with Caesar, using Louis' baroque-style telephone, but had found no one at home but Augustus. The news from that quarter was ominous; Augustus, however, had cheered up a bit at finding out who now held power to his west. He said he would tell Caesar what had happened, and lend—the stress was on *lend*—Napoleon a field phone to use until things had settled down.

Now, came time for the real fight.

Still clad in his jeans and workshirt, Napoleon had spoken to his soldiers, standing a bit above them on the long stairway leading to the front doors of Louis' palace. He told them he had learned the lay of the land from Louis' retainers (who had also given him detailed maps), information he sought to put to immediate use.

Louis had plenty of cannon, but they were old and kept mainly for show. Napoleon distrusted them: any weapon not kept constantly cleaned and in use could turn on its wielder. So, he was left with his cavalry, the few infantry that had showed up, and the jeep with its machine gun.

To say nothing of Marie and the Uzis.

The scouts he had sent to the west had just returned: the company of mounted warriors had swelled to nearly four hundred. Odds such as these Napoleon had faced undaunted in the past, but he would rather the opposing sides be a bit more equal.

Mais, c'est la vie . . . ou bien, c'est la querre!

He divided his cavalry into two troops, sending both ahead to wait on either side of a wooded valley just to the northwest of Louis' palace. Half the infantry would follow him toward the end of that valley, to serve as a lure to the horsemen.

Now, as he drove the jeep across the finely manicured lawns toward the forest that hid the valley, carrying the borrowed field phone with him, Napoleon hoped the bait would keep the horsemen from going down toward the road. The fifty men he had left guarding the front of Louis' property would be of little help if the horsemen managed to by-pass the cavalry trap, but the idea of reinforcements was hardly out of the question. More French soldiers would be en route to Louis' now that word had gotten out who was running the place.

If not. . . .

In all his years in Hell, Napoleon had never once—save for his initial visit—seen the inside of the Undertaker's rooms. He had no desire to break the record now.

He would think of something.

He always did.

Though Wellington could not see the knights, he knew where they rode: smoke lay on the horizon, possibly from a few farms that lay to the south of the Country Club.

Attila's scouts reported that the first two hundred knights had swept around the east end of Golgotha Park and now rode straight north, a direction which would take them right across the golf course toward suburbia. The other two hundred knights headed directly for the club house.

Wellington paced up and down the bar, past the snoring Hadrian, to the window, then back to the bar again. It was hard to tell what would—

The telephone sitting on the bar rang, and Wellington snatched up the receiver. "Hello?"

"*Anbec.*" The DGSE man's voice sounded utterly weary. "*Communications! Seulement un. Je l'avais!*"

"Where?" Wellington asked.

"*À votre maison! Vite!*" Anbec said, and hung up.

"O Lord!" Wellington set the receiver back in its cradle. He glanced up at the Tulsan who stood by the door. "Mr. Hendron . . . if you would be so kind as to run back to my house, Anbec, one of the Frenchmen there, has the communications—the field phone we've been waiting for. Hurry! Please!"

Hendron slapped the stock of his .22 rifle and grinned. "I'm on my way!" he said, turning and rushing out of the bar. "YAH-HOOOOOO!"

The Tulsan scrambled across the stream that ran between the golf course and the back yards, clambered up the steep bank behind Wellington's house, and gained the back yard soaked to his knees and sporting a long scratch down the side of his face where a bush had scraped him.

Catching his breath, he dashed across the yard toward Wellington's back door.

"Hey, y'all!" he bellowed, pounding on the door. "I've cum fer thet field phone y'all have fer his Dukeship!"

The door opened and a hand dragged Hendron inside.

"What'cha think yer—?" He stopped in mid-sentence as the man who faced him lay a finger across his lips.

"*Silence!*" the fellow hissed, and eased the back door shut. "*Je suis Anbec. Suivez-moi!*"

The name rang a bell; Hendron followed readily enough, comforted he still had his weapons.

"Where's thet field phone?" he whispered loudly.

"*C'est ici,*" Anbec said quietly. "Here."

"What's goin' on?"

Anbec made another shushing noise, guided Hendron into the living room and pointed out the front window.

Ten black-clad Viet Cong, armed to the teeth and beyond, squatted waiting on Wellington's front lawn.

"Oh, shee-it!" the Tulsan moaned. "Now where the hail did his Dukeship put them ribs?"

From what the scouts told Napoleon, the mounted division headed toward them was comprised mostly of medieval types, armed with crossbows, longswords, and pikes. Marauders—these horsemen still had some sort of discipline, operating more than likely beneath the clenched fists of a few captains.

Cannon fire rumbled from Maria-Theresa's palace now. If all four hundred horsemen had attacked the palace, the Austrians would be hard put to keep them off. Sheer numbers would propel the invaders past the cannon to face Maria-Theresa's infantry.

Napoleon guessed not all the invaders had turned aside to attack the Austrians. If they had sent out scouts of their own, they would think Louis' seemingly unprotected palace a far more alluring target than Maria-Theresa's.

Marie sat at Napoleon's side, her face very still in the sunlight. He was not quite sure what to do with this new Marie. She was undeniably brave, but he had never seen her so grimly determined, so ready to face actual fighting. He sensed Hatshepsut's influence here . . . Hatshepsut *and* Kleopatra.

Hoofbeats—the sound of approaching horses. De Vauban stiffened in the rear of the jeep, his hands resting on the machine gun. Napoleon glanced at Marie, and she smiled at him.

The first of the horsemen galloped over the rise that led down into the valley, then jerked his horse to a sliding halt. His comrades rode up behind him and stared down into the valley.

Napoleon knew what they saw: a thin line of foot soldiers stretched across the end of the valley, Louis' unprotected palace glittering seductively in the background. He pulled his jeep to a stop sitting sideways to the milling horsemen on the rise, took a slow breath and lifted his hand, feeling the eyes of his men fastened on him. In the momentary silence, he waited.

"EEEEEEYAHHHH!"

The scream came from a hundred or more throats, as

the distant horsemen began their charge into the valley, swordblades glinting in the light.

The damned knights were singing something as they cantered toward the Club. Attila shook his head and trotted his horse back to the trees where his men waited, concealed by leaf and bough. Singing. Huhn. Just before he rode into hiding, he glanced over his shoulder and caught a good glimpse of the device borne on the shields the knights carried.

A black cross on white, duplicate on their surcoats.

Teutonic knights.

He swore under his breath. A meaner, nastier bunch of knights had never terrorized Europe. Attila put the stress on "knights," for he thought his own armies had not done all *that* bad a job in terrorizing Europe themselves.

Oh, well. The meaner they were, the harder— No, that was not the way the saying went. Attila shrugged and held his horse steady, waiting in the shade of the trees.

The Tulsan had not returned with the field phone and that boded ill, but Wellington could spare no more than a brief good thought aimed at suburbia. He had more pressing problems of his own.

He stood at the end of the polo field, along with twenty-five of Attila's Huns, all men who had seen some service with the National Guard and were therefore familiar to varying degrees with modern technology. Each of these men had not only brought weapons befitting Hunnish warriors, but carried a .45 pistol shoved into his belt.

A last look down the polo field to where Attila and his men waited hidden behind the trees. The knights had caught sight of the Club, and had broken into a gallop toward it. Now, if Attila and his men were ready. . . .

A loud screech drifted over the polo field. Attila and

fifteen men rode out from behind the trees toward the knights. Suicidal, that ride, had it gone to completion. But at the last moment, the Huns and Mongols spun their horses around and darted off to the side, releasing arrows from their small, recursive bows.

For each arrow shot, one of the oncoming knights tumbled from his saddle, but it would take more than arrows to slow them down. *Come on, Attila!* Wellington whispered silently. *Get your lads together!*

But then the other Huns and Mongols swept out from behind the trees, their horses at a dead run, aimed at both flanks of the charging knights. Harsh Hunnish and Mongol cries filled the air, rising above the roars of anger that came from the knights.

Wellington turned to his twenty-five comrades and gestured briefly. Each man knew exactly what was expected of him. Behind them, armed with whatever guns they could find, stood the staff of the Country Club. At Wellington's signal, they trotted off toward one of the sand traps that skirted the eighteenth green.

The Huns and Mongols were like hawks attacking a herd of elephants. The knights rode larger and more powerful horses, but the very size of those animals put them at a disadvantage. Each knight wore heavy chain mail and plate armor, and once horse and man were aimed in a particular direction, it would be difficult to stop. The more lightly-clad horsemen of the steppes, mounted on horses trained to dart and swerve, galloped in and out of the company of knights.

Swordblades flashed, dulled now with blood, as the Huns and Mongols fought in what seemed to be undirected madness. The polo field lay littered with bodies now: most of the dead were knights, but Hunnish and Mongol warriors had fallen as well.

The knights drew closer. Wellington straightened his shoulders and hefted the .45 in his right hand. He and his comrades must move now, or be trapped with their backs to the Club.

* * *

When the charging horsemen had gained half the valley, well within range of his infantry, Napoleon brought his hand down. A fusillade rang out and the first ranks of charging horsemen fell beneath it. At the same moment, the two squads of cavalry galloped out from the woods on either side of the valley, thundering down on the startled enemy.

Mayhem reigned. Again, Napoleon's infantry fired, perhaps the last clear shots they could make, for the invaders and the French cavalry were now caught up in an equine dance of death on the valley floor.

It was difficult to tell, but Napoleon estimated he had faced two hundred or more horsemen. His own hundred cavalry had the advantage of surprise on their side, but this battle would be a close thing.

He glanced over his shoulder: de Vauban had the machine gun trained on the melee but, like the infantry, was held from shooting for fear of hitting his own troops.

"Damn!" The more heavily-armored invaders were beginning to take their toll on the light cavalry who dared not disengage. Napoleon looked up and down the line of his infantry. "Advance fifty paces!" he called. "Fire when clear!"

The infantry started forward and Napoleon looked at the battle again. He saw the distant figure of an enemy soldier waving a gun. *Dieu en ciel!* The enemy had firearms of their own.

A squealing horse bolted out of the fighting, dragging a French cavalryman whose foot had caught in the stirrup, and galloped off toward the woods. Napoleon cursed again, and grabbed up his Uzi.

The battle intensified. Napoleon's infantry had advanced their fifty paces and now took aim at any of the enemy they could get a clean shot at. Screams of men and horses rang out over the valley.

Another round of shots from the French. Enemy

horsemen tumbled to the ground, horses reared, blood spattered everywhere. Napoleon squinted into the dust: the invading horsemen rode reduced by over half their number. French losses were not as great as he had feared at first.

An opening appeared in the battle. "Now, de Vauban!" Napoleon yelled. "Fire!"

De Vauban opened up against a group of twenty horsemen who charged toward the French foot soldiers. Damn! It was a sight to see them fall!

Slowly, the tide of battle turned to the French—the opposing sides were now equal, and the infantry had yet to see hand-to-hand combat. Though the enemy seemed determined to fight to the last man, they had lost their initial ferocity. For the first time since the battle had begun, Napoleon felt the knots in his stomach loosen.

"Napoleon!"

He turned as Marie touched his shoulder, and looked up toward the top of the rise.

Another two hundred horsemen had gathered there—enemy, all of them—small distant figures on the horizon. Swordblades and pikes glittered as the invaders prepared to charge.

Attila ducked a slashing swordstroke, stabbed out with his own blade, and felt its tip slide into the knight's throat. Kneeing his horse aside, he darted back out of the fighting, and glanced over his shoulder: he and his men had slowed the knights to near a stop. The eighteenth green lay just over the low rise before them.

"Yip! Yip! Yip!"

That was Mongol, a cry for help. Attila reined his horse around for another charge at the knights.

Suddenly, over the top of the rise rolled thirteen golf carts, each carrying two men—one holding a shield and the other brandishing a .45 pistol. And there, riding in the center cart, waving his men forward, his red British general's uniform conspicuous among the leathers of the Huns and Mongols, came Wellington.

The knights' horses panicked at the sight of the carts. Shrilling, bucking and kicking, they spun in terror and tried to escape the horrible rolling objects headed at them.

On the other hand, the Mongol and Hunnish mounts, used to motorized traffic around the polo field, might have been galloping across an empty meadow.

"YIIIII-HAH!" Attila yelled, waving his sword at the Huns and Mongols. "Ride, you bow-legged wonders! Ride! Let's kick some ass!"

Tommy Hendron stood on the Duke of Wellington's front doorstep, a plateful of barbequed ribs in his hands, and ten Viet Cong staring impassively at him.

"Y'all want more of these here ribs," he said, hoping like hell the little gooks could not hear his voice tremble, "y'all be on *our* side. Hear? *We* ain't shootin' at ya. *We* didn't chase ya off from the bobby-que." He took a deep breath. "Any of you fellers talk English?"

Silence.

"Lookie, here," Hendron said. "We ain't gonna bother ya. The Park's yours, rot proper. You can keep thet ol' Park for all eternity, unnerstand? Jes' don't shell *us*, OK?"

More silence.

The Tulsan felt his courage slipping down to the toes of his muddy boots. "Lemme offer ya this. Y'all leave us alone, an' we'll have *another* bobby-que real soon now."

Ten very satisfied grins greeted him and ten black-capped heads nodded.

Hendron's knees threatened to collapse from relief.

Wellington took aim and shot at another knight whose panicked horse had gone beyond handling. The kick of the gun lifted his hand, but his aim was true, and the knight tumbled backward from the saddle.

"Enough, Toka!" Wellington yelled at his Hunnish companion. "Stop the cart!"

Toka grinned widely, and brought the golf cart to a slow halt. Wellington looked over the battlefield: between Attila's mounted warriors, the golf carts, and the .45 pistols, the knights had not stood a chance. What few of them survived, had raced off toward the south, a few of Attila's pistol-armed men in hot pursuit.

"My green! O, Lord! Look what's happened to my green!"

Wellington turned around in the golf cart: the Club's grounds keeper, well known for his fussy maintenance of the golf course, was wandering around the eighteenth green, his shoulders slumped.

"God!" the man wailed. "Look! Hoof-marks in the turf! And blood! There's blood *everywhere!*"

Attila rode up to the side of Wellington's golf cart, his sword red to the hilt. The King of the Huns sported a blackening eye, two swordcuts to his right leg, but sat his horse grinning widely.

"Got the bastards, heh?" he said. "Damned fine idea, Wellington! Haven't had so much fun since—"

"Let's get some help to Yanush," Wellington interrupted. He glanced around at the gathering Huns and Mongols who were still mounted. "To the houses! We'll come up on the bloody bastards' rear!"

Attila barked a command, and set out toward suburbia, following by his screeching men. With a small sigh, Wellington waved a hand after the Hun, and led his golf cart brigade forward.

"Aaaaghh!" he heard from behind him. "My green! My precious green! Ruined! All my work! Shot to hell!"

Hendron sat on Wellington's door step, doling out what few ribs he had yanked from the refrigerator and microwaved into warmth. The Cong seemed content to squat on the front lawn, each politely waiting his turn to stand and take the offered food.

Damn! If my friends back in Tulsa could see me now!

He could hear the sound of fighting back by the stream, on the opposite side. Attila's horsemen had obviously tangled with the invading knights. Hendron shifted uneasily on the doorstep, unsure what the outcome of that fight would be.

The door opened behind him and he glanced up over his shoulder: Anbec stood there, the field phone in his hands.

"Take," he said, extending the phone to Hendron and eyeing the Viet Cong with some trepidation. *"C'est l'empereur Napoléon."*

Napoleon? Hendron passed out the last rib, wiped his greasy hands on his jeans, and took the field phone from Anbec.

"What's wrong with Napol-yun?" the Tulsan asked.

"Trouble," Anbec said in his broken English. "Big trouble!"

Napoleon glanced up as what remained of his cavalry fought with desperate fierceness against the few horsemen left from the original force that had ridden at Louis' palace. The infantry had fallen back to form a small square around Napoleon's jeep.

The other two hundred invading horsemen gathered for their charge down the rise into the valley.

He had two choices; he could retreat back to Louis' palace, or he could call for help . . . *any* kind of help.

"Eagle to Lion!" he shouted into the field phone, using the code words he and Wellington had chosen. "Mayday! Mayday!"

The phone crackled with static: he heard a torrent of Latin, and knew he was close enough to Caesar's battle to be picking up Roman communications. He cursed and changed the frequency.

"Eagle to Lion!" he yelled again. "Dammit, Wellington! Where the shit *are* you?"

This time he got an answer. In French.

Anbec!

"Can you get us any help over here?" Napoleon asked. A quick glance up: the enemy had started to move.

"Where are you?" came Anbec's voice. *"Coordinates?"*

Coordinates? Napoleon lifted an eyebrow. Artillery? He snatched up one of the maps from the floor of the jeep. "Anbec?"

Nothing. Napoleon's heart sank, but he quickly located his position on the map.

"Hey, yer Emperorship, what's yer coordinates over there? Where's yer enemy?"

The Tulsan? With the field phone? What the hell was going on in suburbia. Napoleon gave his coordinates, those of the enemy, then repeated them once more.

"Gotcha!" came Hendron's voice over the field phone. *"Y'all hang tight, now . . . hear?"*

Hang tight? Napoleon set the phone on the floor beside him and snatched up his Uzi. Marie glanced at him, her face gone white. De Vauban swivelled the machine gun around so that he had a better aim on the approaching enemy and cut loose with a short round fired directly into a group of horsemen who had broken through the French cavalry and charged toward the jeep. Men and horses screamed and tumbled to the ground. Marie took sight with her Uzi and downed another horseman.

Napoleon lifted his own gun, chose his target at random, and fired: horse and rider spun around and fell heavily.

"Infantry!" Napoleon yelled. "Staggered fire! Wait for my command!"

Only around ten men were left alive of the first wave of invaders, but the additional two hundred horsemen galloped closer to the entrance of the valley.

Dieu! If we're going to get help here, it had better come—

The scream of incoming shells. Napoleon crouched low in the jeep, pulling Marie down beside him.

"Turn!" he bellowed to the cavalry. "Infantry! Hit the dirt!"

A series of explosions shook the ground. Clouds of dust rose over the valley. Another rain of shells . . . more explosions.

"Damn!" de Vauban yelled. "Who's shelling the enemy?"

"Who cares?" Napoleon yelled back. "They're decimating them!"

The French infantry cheered at the sight of invading horsemen being blown apart. The cavalry drew back, regrouped, and waited the word to charge.

Napoleon watched the sky, listening after the last explosion for any more incoming shells.

What was left of the enemy milled in total confusion, some of them opting for flight.

The shelling was over.

Napoleon waved a hand toward the other end of the valley.

"*Allez!*" he called out. "Let's clean up!"

The battle over, Napoleon brought his jeep to a halt, threw on the brake, and stopped the engine. De Vauban leaned up against the side of the jeep, staring at the still-hot machine gun, and Marie sat slouched back in her seat, the Uzi held loosely in her hand.

The valley was full of bodies—invading horsemen, fallen French, and their horses. Napoleon briefly wondered if Reassignments was still in commission: none of the bodies had disappeared.

On the other hand, with Hell turned upside down as it was, perhaps Reassignments was backed up.

Out of his hundred cavalry and fifty infantry, Napoleon possessed sixty-two men. He reached forward and rubbed a fingertip over the bullet holes in the jeep's windshield, only now remembering the shots that had come close to sending him to the Undertaker's. *If* he could have gotten in.

The vision of newly dead taking a number and waiting in the hallway came close to making him smile.

The surviving French were helping their wounded comrades now, and Napoleon could hear no more artillery from Maria-Theresa's. It was possible *all* the invading horsemen had fought in the valley: Maria-Theresa's palace had been too well-defended. Now, everything was silent, save for the moans of the wounded.

"A close one, *mon empereur*," de Vauban said.

Napoleon nodded. He considered himself fortunate to have lost just over half his men. It could have been far worse.

"Marie?" he asked, turning to her. Her blond hair was tangled by the wind, and a smudge of dirt ran across one cheek.

"I'm fine, Napoleon," she said, setting the Uzi down at her feet. She reached out and took his hand. "We make a pretty good team, don't we?"

He grinned, leaned over and kissed her, not caring if de Vauban watched or not.

A burst of static and angry voices came from the field phone, lying all but forgotten in the confusion under the front seat. Napoleon snatched it up: had Wellington and Attila successfully defended suburbia? And who had shelled the enemy?

Latin was all Napoleon heard from the field phone—Romans yelling at Romans. He tried another frequency.

"*Hey, yer Emperorship! D'ya read me? Come in! Come in!*"

The Tulsan!

"I read you," Napoleon said. "Where's Wellington?"

"*Rot here . . . he jes' arrived.*"

A rustle of static.

"*Napoleon?*" It was Wellington's voice. "*What the devil's going on over there? Hendron tells me—*"

"Did you get rid of the knights?" Napoleon interrupted.

"We certainly did. They didn't even make it across the stream to the houses!"

"Where's Hadrian?"

"Sleeping off another drunk at the Country Club. We only lost around forty men. How did your battle go?"

"Not as well. Who the hell did you get to shell the enemy for us?"

"You're not going to believe this—"

"Try me."

"Viet Cong."

Napoleon stared at the field phone in his hand. "Cong? How the shit did the Cong get messed up in this?"

"They were hungry, I guess. Hendron talked them into shelling the coordinates you gave for the enemy in exchange for a future barbeque."

"Damn. Just what we need. Where did Anbec come up with the field phone?"

Wellington laughed. "He pulled a raid on Goebbels' house. Sneaky little bastard had one hidden in his basement. He left the bugger locked up in the fruit cellar."

"That's appropriate. Listen, Wellington, I'll talk to you later. I've got to secure Louis' palace and make sure the grounds are fully defended. I'll bet you dinner at the Club this idiocy isn't over yet."

"How's Caesar doing?"

Napoleon shook his head. "Can't tell. I'll check in with Augustus and find out."

"Good show. Try to make it home in one piece."

Wellington's transmission went dead.

Napoleon sighed, leaned back in his seat, and closed his eyes: things would never be the same for him again. He now stood in control of the French power base in Hell. What he would do about that, and what he would do with Louis, were situations he did not want to think about yet.

Right now, for his own neighborhood security, and

because an Emperor *always* paid his debts, one problem loomed over all the others.

Just how many Viet Cong lived in the Park, and how the *hell* was he going to afford the ribs?

GILGAMESH IN URUK

Robert Silverberg

Oh dream of joy, is this indeed
The lighthouse top I see
Is this the hill? is this the kirk?
Is this mine own countree?
—Coleridge: *The Ancient Mariner*

"Surely you would agree, Gilgamesh, that it's better to reign in Hell than be a slave in it!"

"I think you have that phrase a little wrong," said Gilgamesh quietly. "But never mind. We have lost the thread of our discourse, if ever there was one. Did I mock you? Why, then, I ask your forgiveness, Sulla. It was not my intention."

"Spoken like a king. There is no grievance between us. Will you have more wine?"

"Why not?" Gilgamesh said.

The gritty smear of browns and yellows that was the western desert of Hell appeared to stretch on before Gilgamesh and his companions for a million leagues: past the horizon, and up the side of the sky. Perhaps it actually did. The narrow shoddy highway that they

were following was vanishing behind them as soon as
they passed over it, as though demons were gobbling
up its cracked and pitted paving-stones, and ahead of
them the road gave the impression of traveling in several directions at once.

Day and night the caravan rolled steadily onward
across this dismal barren land. They were journeying
up the coast above the island-city of Pompeii, hoping to
find a city whose very existence was at this moment
nothing more than a matter of conjecture and speculation.

Gilgamesh drank in silence. The wine was all right.
He had had worse. But he could remember, after thousands of years, the joy that had come from the sweet
strong wine and rich foaming beer of Sumer the Land.
How many flagons he and Enkidu had quaffed together
of that dark purple stuff, in the old days of their life!
Indeed it made the soul soar upward. But in Hell there
was no soaring, and the wine gave small joy. It was only
a momentary tickle upon the tongue, and then it was
gone. You expected no more, in Hell. Once, at the
beginning, he had thought otherwise. Once he had
thought this to be a second life in which true accom-
plishments might be achieved and true purposes won,
and true pleasures could be had, and great kingdoms
founded. Well, it was a second life, a life beyond life,
no question of that. But the wine had no savor here.
Nor did a woman's body, nor did a steaming haunch of
meat. This was not a place where joy was to be had.
One simply went on, and on and on. Hell was by
definition meaningless, and so all striving within it was
meaningless also. He had come to that bleak awareness
long ago. And it had puzzled him then that so few of
these great heroes, these Sullas and Caesars and Pha-
raohs and all, had learned the truth of that in all their
long residence here.

He shook his head. Such thoughts as these were not
appropriate for him any more. No longer could he look
with contempt on other men's ambitions, ever since he

had had the Knowing of his soul at the hands of Imbe Calandola in Pompeii.

He reminded himself that he too had dabbled in kingship in Hell: even he, aloof austere Gilgamesh. Had quested for power in this chaotic place and gained it, and founded a great city, and ruled in high majesty. And then had forgotten it all and gone about Hell piously insisting that he was above such worldly yearnings.

Diabolical Calandola, the black cannibal chieftain and seer, had forced the troublesome reality upon Gilgamesh during his sojourn in Pompeii. The giant sorcerer Calandola, his body glistening with unguents made of human fat, awakening revelations in the Sumerian with a devil's brew of wine mixed with blood, and a monstrous sacrament of forbidden flesh.

Through his witchcraft Calandola had shown Gilgamesh New Uruk, the Uruk of Hell, and had stripped away the years to let him see what he had forgotten: that he too once had desired as others did to reign in Hell, that he had founded that great Uruk, that he had been its king. So it ill behooved him to scorn others for their ambitions and their pride in their achievements. He had forgotten his own, that was all. You could forget anything in Hell. Memory was random here. Whole segments of experience dropped away, thousands of years of hurly-burly event. And then would return unexpectedly, leading you into the deepest contradictions of spirit.

Gilgamesh wondered now whether the fever of powerlust that he had claimed so to despise might not seize him again before long. Hell was a great kindler of opposites in one's breast, he knew: whatever you were most certain you would never do, that in time you would most assuredly find yourself doing.

"*Look* at this place!" Sulla muttered. "Uglier and uglier. Worse and worse!"

"Yes," said Gilgamesh. "We have reached the edge of nowhere."

Originally there had been seven Land Rovers in the expedition—the gilded bullet-proof palanquin of Sulla of Pompeii, who was not a king but who conducted himself as if he were; two lesser vehicles for Gilgamesh of Uruk and Herod of Judaea, who had been kings in their former lives but felt no need to burden themselves with crowns in Hell; and four more that carried baggage and slaves. But on the third day the roadbed had gaped suddenly beneath the rear vehicles of the baggage train and the lastmost Land Rover had disappeared amid tongues of purple flame and the discordant wailing of unseen spirits. Then two days later Sulla's magnificent motor-chariot had developed a leprosy of its shining armor, turning all pockmarked and hideous, and its undercarriage had begun to melt and flow as if eaten by acid. So now five Land Rovers remained. Sulla, disgruntled and fidgety, rode with Gilgamesh, consoling himself with prodigious quantities of dark sweet wine.

Their goal was Uruk: not Gilgamesh's ancient Uruk in the land of Sumer on Earth, but the great and fabled New Uruk of Hell, which for all any of them knew might be only a figment of some liar's overheated imagination.

This supposed Uruk, Gilgamesh thought, could be anywhere: to the north, the south, the east, the west. Or some other direction entirely. Or nowhere at all. Uruk might indeed be only a rumor, a vision, a wishful fantasy: mere vaporous hearsay, perhaps. They might spend a hundred years in search of it, or a thousand, and never find it.

There was no denying the folly of this endeavor, then. But not to search for Uruk would be folly also.

Sulla had heard that it was a city overflowing with jewels, and there was nothing he coveted more. And by good report Gilgamesh had learned that in Uruk he was likely to find his long-lost friend Enkidu, whose company he desired above all else. How could they not attempt the quest, then? Even if Uruk did not exist, they must at least attempt it. If there are no beginnings, there are no fulfillments.

Sulla of Pompeii, squirming beside Gilgamesh in the lead Land Rover, said uneasily, "I thought we would be traveling through a region of marshes and lakes, not a desert. This place looks like nothing that was shown on the map the Carthaginian sold me."

Gilgamesh shrugged. "Why should it? The map was a dream, Sulla. This desert is a dream. The city we seek is possibly only a dream too."

"Then why were you in such a hurry to set out from Pompeii to find it?"

"Even if it may not exist, that in itself is no reason not to search for it," Gilgamesh replied. "And once we are resolved on the quest, searching sooner is better than searching later."

"No Roman would talk such nonsense, Gilgamesh."

"Perhaps not, but I am no Roman."

"There are times when I doubt that you're even human."

"I am a poor damned soul, the same as you."

Sulla snorted and handed a fresh flask of wine to a slave to have its cork drawn. "Listen to him! A poor damned soul, he says! Since when do you believe in damnation, or any such New Dead idiocy? And that note of sniveling self-pity! A poor damned soul! You couldn't snivel sincerely if your life depended on it." The dictator of Pompeii accepted the opened flask of wine, took a deep thoughtful pull, nodded, belched. Sulla was a heavy-bodied balding man, blotchy-faced and red-eyed, a bold warrior gone soft outside from too great a fondness for drink. He offered the bottle to Gilgamesh, who drank indifferently, scarcely tasting the stuff.

"I spoke sincerely," Gilgamesh said after a time. "We are all damned in this place, though that seems to mean different things to different folk. And we are all poor, no matter now many caskets of treasure we amass, for everything is demon-stuff here, without substance to it, and only a fool would think otherwise."

Sulla went crimson, and his blotches and blemishes stood out angrily. "Don't mock me, Gilgamesh. I'm willing to accept a great deal of your arrogance, because I know you were something special in your own day, and because you have many qualities I admire. But don't mock me. Don't patronize me."

"Do I, Sulla?"

"You do it all the time, you condescending oversized Sumerian bastard!"

"Is it mockery to tell you that I accept the fact that the gods have sent me to this place with a flick of a finger—even as they have sent you here, and Herod, and so many others who once drew breath on Earth? Do I mock you when I admit that I am and always have been nothing but a plaything in their hands—even as you?"

"You, Gilgamesh? A plaything in the gods' hands?"

"Do you believe we have free will here?"

"There are some who rule and some who are slaves," said Sulla. "Even in Hell, I live in a palace bedecked with rubies and emeralds, and I have hundreds of servants to draw my baths and drive my chariots and prepare my meals. Here as once in Rome I am a leader of men. Is that by accident? Or is it by free will, Gilgamesh? By my choice, by my diligent effort, by my hard striving?"

"Those meals you eat: do they have any savor?"

"It is said I set the finest table in this entire region of Hell."

"The finest, yes. But do you get any pleasure from what you eat? Or is the finest not but a short span from the meanest, Sulla?"

"Jupiter and Isis, man! This is *Hell!* Nobody expects the food to have much taste!"

"But yet you have free will."

"The inconveniences of this place don't have a demon's turd to do with the question of free will, which in any case is a foolish issue, a lot of gasbag vapor dreamed up by New Dead idlers. Why are some men kings here and some slaves, if not that we shape our own destinies?"

"We have debated this point before, I think,' said Gilgamesh with a shrug. He turned away and stared out at the landscape of Hell.

Mean jagged cliffs that looked like chipped teeth rose on both sides of them. The air had turned the color of dung. The earth was palpitating like a blanket stretched above a windy abyss. Black gaseous bubbles erupted from it here and there. Everything seemed suspended in a trembling flux. A blood-hued rain had begun to fall, but not a drop reached the parched ground. Lean dog-like beasts that were all mouth and fangs and eyes ran beside the highway, leaping and screeching and howling. Far away Gilgamesh saw a dark lake that appeared to be standing on its side. The road ahead still veered crazily, drifting both to the right and left at the same time without forking, and seeming now also to curve upward into the sky. A demon-road, Gilgamesh thought, designed to torment those who dared travel it. A demon-land.

"The Carthaginian's map—" Sulla said.

"Was all lies and fraud," said Gilgamesh. "It turned blank in your hands, did it not? Its purpose was to swindle you. Forget the Carthaginian's map. We are where we are, Sulla."

"And where is that?"

Gilgamesh gestured with his hands outspread, and leaned forward, narrowing his eyes, seeking to make sense out of what he saw before him.

All was confusion and foulness out there. And, he realized, it was folly to try to comprehend it.

In Hell there was never any hope of understanding distances, or spatial relationships, or the passing of time, or the size of things, or anything else. If you were wise, you took what came to you as it came, and asked no questions. That, Gilgamesh thought, was the fundamental thing about Hell, the particular quality above all others that made it Hell. *You took what came to you.* Nobody was the shaper of his own destiny here. If you believed you were, you were only deceiving yourself.

Suddenly all the madness outside disappeared as if it had been blotted out. Thick gray mist began to spout from fissures in the ground and clung close as a cotton shroud, enfolding everything in dense murk. The Land Rover came to a jolting halt. The one just behind it, in which Herod of Judea was riding, did not stop quite as quickly, and bashed into Sulla's with a resounding clang.

Then invisible hands seized the sides of Sulla's Land Rover and began to rock it up and down.

"What now?" Sulla grunted. "Demons?"

Gilgamesh had already swung about to seize his bow, his quiver of arrows, his bronze dagger.

"Bandits, I think. This has the feel of an ambush."

Faces appeared out of the mist, peering through the foggy windows of the Land Rover. Gilgamesh stared back at them in amazement. Straight dark hair, dark eyes, swarthy skins—an unmistakably familiar cast of features—

Sumerians! Men of his own blood! He'd know those faces anywhere!

A mob of excited Sumerians, that was who was out there—clustering about the caravan, jumping about, pounding on fenders, shouting.

Sulla, aflame with rage and drunken courage, drew his short Roman sword and fumbled with the latch of the door.

"Wait," Gilgamesh said, catching his elbow and pulling him back. "Before you get us embroiled in a battle, let me speak with these men. I think I know who they are. I think we've just been stopped by the border police of the city of Uruk."

*　　*　　*

In a huge dank basement room on the Street of the Tanners and Dyers the man who called himself Ruiz sat before his easel under sputtering, crackling floodlights, working steadily in silence in the depths of the night. He sat stripped to the waist, a stocky, powerful man past his middle years, with deep-set piercing eyes and a round head that had only a fringe of white hair about it.

The work was almost going well. Almost. But it was hard, very hard. He could not get used to that, how hard the work was. It had always been easy for him up above, as natural as breathing. But in this place there were maddening complications that he had not had to face in the life before this life.

He squinted at the woman who stood before him, then at the half-finished canvas, then at the woman again. He let her features enter his mind and expand and expand until they filled his soul.

What a splendid creature she was! Look at her, standing there like a priestess, like a queen, like a goddess!

He didn't even know her name. She was one of those ancient women that the city was full of, one of those Babylonian or Assyrian or Sumerian sorts that could easily have stepped right off the limestone reliefs that they had in the Louvre. Shining dark eyes, great noble nose, gleaming black hair gathered in back under an elaborate silver coronet set with carnelian and lapis. She wore a magnficent robe, crimson cloth interwoven with silver strands and fastened at her shoulder by a long curving golden pin. It was not hard for the man who called himself Ruiz to imagine what lay beneath the robe, and he suspected that if he asked, she would undo the garment readily enough and let it slip. Maybe he would, later. But now he wanted the robe in the painting. Its powerfully sculpted lines were essential. They helped to give her that wondrously primordial look. She was Aphrodite, Eve, Ishtar, mother and whore all in one, a goddess, a queen.

She was splendid. But the painting—the painting—

Mierda! It was coming out wrong, like all the others.

Anger and frustration roiled his soul. He could not stop—he would keep on going until he finally got one of them right—but it was a constant torture to him, these unaccustomed failures, this bewildering inability to make himself the master of his own vision, as he had so triumphantly been for all the ninety-odd years of his former life.

There were paintings stacked everywhere in the room, amid the ferocious clutter, the crumpled shirts, unwashed dishes, torn trousers, old socks, wax-encrusted candlesticks, empty wine-bottles, discarded sandals, fragments of rusted machinery, bits of driftwood, broken pottery, faded blankets, overflowing ashtrays, tools, brushes, guitars that had no strings, jars of paint, bleached bones, stuffed animals, newspapers, books, magazines. He painted all night long, every night, and by now, even though he destroyed most of what he did by painting over the canvases, he had accumulated enough to fill half a museum. But they were wrong, all wrong, worthless, trash. They were stale, useless paintings, self-imitations, self-parodies, even. What was the use of painting the harlequins and saltimbanques again, or the night-fishing, or the three musicians? He had done those once already. To repeat yourself was a death worse than death. The girl before the mirror? The cubist stuff? The demoiselles? Even if this new life of his was truly going to be eternal, what a waste it was to spend it solving problems whose answers he already knew. But he could not seem to help it. It was almost as though there were a curse on him.

This new one, now—this Mesopotamian goddess with the dark sparkling eyes—maybe this time, at last, she would inspire him to make it come out right—

He had made a bold start. Trust the eye, trust the hand, trust the *cojones*, just paint what you see. Fine. She posed like a professional model, tall and proud, nothing self-conscious about her. A beauty, maybe forty years old, prime of life. He worked with all his old assurance, thinking that perhaps this time he'd keep control, this time he'd actually achieve something new instead of merely reworking. Capture the mythic grandeur of her, the primordial goddess-nature of her, this woman of Sumer or Babylonia or wherever she came from.

But the painting began to shift beneath his hand, as they always did. As though a demon had seized the brush. He tried to paint what he saw, and it turned cubist on him, all planes and angles, that nonsensical stuff that he had abandoned fifty years before he died. *Mierda! Carajo! Me cago en la mar!* He clenched his teeth and turned the painting back where he wanted it, but no, no, it grew all pink and gentle, rose-period stuff, and when in anger he painted over it the new outline had the harsh and jagged barbarism of the Demoiselles d'Avignon.

Stale and old, old and stale, old, old, old, old.

"Me cago en Dios!" he said out loud.

"What is that?" she said. Her voice was deep, mysterious, exotic. "What are those words?"

"Spanish," he said. "When I curse, I curse in Spanish, always." He spoke now in English. Everyone spoke English here, even he, who in his other life had hated that language with a strange passionate hatred. But it was either that or speak ancient Greek, which he found an even worse notion. He marveled at the idea that he was actually speaking English. You made many concessions in this place. Among his friends he spoke French, still, and among his oldest friends Spanish, or sometimes Catalan. With strangers, English. But to curse, Spanish, always Spanish.

"You are angry?" she said. "With me?"

"Not with you, no. With myself. With these brushes. With the Devil. How hellish Hell is!"

"You are very funny," she said.

"Droll, yes, that is what I am. Droll." He put his finger to his lips. "Let me work. I think I see the way."

And for a moment or two he actually did. Bending low over the canvas, he gave himself up fully to the work. Frowning, chewing his cigarette, scratching his head, painting quickly, confidently. The wondrous goddess-woman rose up from the canvas at him. Her eyes gleamed with strange ancient wisdom. And the painting turned, it turned again, it showed bones and teeth where he wanted robes and flesh, and when he fought with it it took a neoclassical turn, with gaudy late-period slashes of color also and a hint of cubism again trying to break through down in the lower left. An impossible hodgepodge it was, all his old styles at once. The painting had no life at all. An art student could have painted it, if he had had enough to drink. Maybe what he needed was a new studio. Or a holiday somewhere. But this had been going on, he reflected, since he had first come here, since the day of—he hesitated, not even wanting to think the filthy words—

—the day of his death—

"All right," he said. "Enough for tonight. You can relax. What is your name?"

"Ninsun."

"Ah. A lovely name. A lovely woman, lovely name. You are Babylonian?"

"Sumerian," she said.

He nodded. There was a difference, though he had forgotten it. He would ask someone tomorrow to explain it to him. This whole city was full of Mesopotamians of various kinds, and yet in the five years he had lived here he had not managed to learn much about them. Five years? Or was it fifty? Or five weeks? Somehow you never could tell. Well, no matter. No matter at all. Perhaps this was the moment to suggest that she slip out of that lovely robe.

There was a knock at the door, a familiar triple knock, repeated: the signal of Sabartés. This would not be the moment, then, to suggest anything to the priestess, the goddess.

Well, there would be other moments.

He grunted permission for Sabartés to enter.

The door creaked open. Sabartés stood there blinking: his friend of many years, his confidante, his more-or-less secretary, his bulwark against annoyance and intrusion—now, maddeningly, himself an intruder. These days he had the appearance of a young man, with plump healthy cheeks and vast quantities of wild black hair, the Sabartés of the giddy old Barcelona days, 1902 or so, when they had first met. But for the eyes, the chin, the long thin nose, it would be impossible to recognize him, so familiar had the Sabartés of later years become. One of the minor perversities of Hell was that people seemed to come back at any age at all. It was not easy to get accustomed to. The man who called himself Ruiz looked perhaps sixty, Sabartés no more than twenty, yet they had known each other for nearly seventy years in life and some years more—ten? Twenty? A thousand?—in the life after life.

Sabartés took everything in at a glance: the woman, the easel, the scowl on his friend's face. Diffidently he said, "Pablo, do I interrupt?"

"Only another worthless painting."

"Ah, Picasso, you are too hard on yourself!"

He looked up, glaring fiercely. "*Ruiz*. You must always remember to call me Ruiz."

Sabartés smiled. "I will never get used to that." He turned and looked with admiration and only faintly disguised envy at the silent, stately Sumerian woman. Then he stole a quick glance at the canvas on the easel, and a sequence of complex, delicate emotions flitted across his face, which after the many decades of their friendship the man who called himself Ruiz was able to decipher as easily as though each were inscribed in stone: admiration mixed with envy once again, for the craftsmanship, and awe and subservience, for the ge-

nius, and then something darker, which Sabartés tried
in vain to suppress, a look of sadness, of pity, of almost
condescending sorrow not unmingled with perverse glee,
because the painting was a failure. In all the years they
had known each other in life, Picasso had never once
seen that expression on Sabartés' face; but here in Hell
it came flashing out almost automatically whenever
Sabartés looked at one of his old friend's new works. If
this kept up, Picasso thought, he would have to deprive
Sabartés of the right to enter the studio. It was intolerable to be patronized like this, especially by *him*.

"Well?" Picasso demanded. "*Am* I too hard on myself?"

"The painting is full of wonderful things, Pablo."

"Yes. Wonderful things which I put behind me a
million years ago. And here they come again. The brush
twists in my hand, Sabartés! I paint *this* and it comes
out *that*." He scowled and spat. "*A la chingada!* But
why should we be surprised? This is Hell, no? Hell is
not supposed to be easy. Once I had only the dealers to
wrestle with, and the critics, and now it is the Devil.
But I beat them, eh? And I will beat him too."

"You will, indeed," said Sabartés. "What is the name
of your new model?"

"Ishtar," said Picasso casually. "No. No, that's not
right." He had forgotten it. He glanced at the woman.
"*Como se llama, amiga?*"

"I do not understand."

English, he reminded himself. We speak English
here.

"Your name," he said. "Tell me your name again,
guapa."

"Ninsun, who was the Sky-father An's priestess."

"A priestess, Sabartés," Picasso said triumphantly.
"You see? I knew that at once. We met in the market-
place, and I said, Come let me paint you and you will
live forever. She said to me, I already live forever, but
I will let you paint me anyway. What a woman, eh,

Sabartés? Ninsun the priestess." He turned to her again. "Where are you from, Ninsun?"

"Uruk," she said.

"Uruk, yes, of course. We're all from Uruk now. But before this place. In the old life. Eh? *Comprende?*"

"The Uruk that I meant was the old one, in Sumer the Land. The one that was on Earth, when we were all alive. I was the wife of Lugalbanda the king then. My son also was—"

"You see?" Picasso crowed. "A priestess and a queen!"

"And a goddess," Ninsun said. "Or so I thought. When I was old, my son the king told me he would send me to live among the gods. There was a temple in my honor in Uruk, beside the river. But instead when I awoke I was in this place called Hell—so long ago, so many years, everything still so strange—"

"You are a goddess also," Picasso assured her. "A goddess, a priestess, a queen."

"May I see the painting you have made of me?"

"Later," he said, covering it and turning it aside. To Sabartés he said, "What news is there?"

"Good news. We have found the matador."

"*Es verdad?*"

"Absolutely," said Sabartés, grinning broadly. "We have the very man."

"*Esplendido!*" Instantly Picasso felt an electric surge of pleasure that utterly wiped out the hours of miserable struggle over the painting. "Who is he?"

"Joaquin Blasco y Velez," said Sabartés. "Formerly of Barcelona."

Picasso stared. He had never heard of him.

"Not Belmonte? Joselito? Manolete? You couldn't find Domingo Ortega?"

"None of them, Pablo. Hell is very large."

"Who is this Blasco y Velez?"

"An extremely great matador, so I am told. He lived in the time of Charles IV. This was before we were born," Sabartés added.

"*Gracias.* I would not have known that, Sabartés. And your matador, he knows what he is doing?"

"So they say."

"Who is *they?*"

"Sportsmen of the city. A Greek, one Polykrates, who says he saw the bull-dancing at Knossos, and a Portuguese, Duarte Lopes, and an Englishmen named—"

"A Greek, a Portuguese, an *Ingles,*" Picasso said gloomily. "What does a Portuguese know of bullfighting? What does an *Ingles* know of anything? And this Greek, he knows bull-dancing, but the *corrida,* what is that to him? This troubles me, Sabartés."

"Shall I wait, and see if anyone can find Manolete?"

"As you have just observed, Sabartés, Hell is a very large place."

"Indeed."

"And you have been organizing this bullfight for a very long time."

"Indeed I have, Pablo."

"Then let us try your Blasco y Velez," Picasso said.

He closed his eyes and saw once again the bull-ring, blazing with color, noise, vitality. The banderilleros darting back and forth, the picadors deftly wielding their pikes, the matador standing quietly by himself under the searing sun. And the bull, the bull, the bull, black and snorting, blood streaming along his high back, horns looming like twin spears! How he had missed all that since coming to Hell! Sabartés had found an old Roman stadium in the desert outside Uruk that could be converted into a *plaza de toros,* he had lined up three or four bulls—they were hell-bulls, not quite the real thing, peculiar green-and-purple creatures with double rows of spines along their backs and ears like an elephant's, but *por dios* they had horns in the right place, anyway—and he had found some Spaniards and Mexicans in the city who had at least a glancing familiarity with the art of the *corrida,* and could deal with the various supporting roles. But there were no mata-

dors to be had. There were plenty of swaggering warriors in the city, Assyrians and Byzantines and Romans
and Mongols and Turks, who were willing to jump into
the ring and hack away at whatever beast was sent their
way. But if Picasso simply wanted to see butchers at
work, he could go to the slaughterhouse. Bullfighting
was a spectacle, a ritual, an act of grace. It was a dance.
It was art, and the matador was the artist. Without a
true matador it was nothing. What could some crude
gladiator know about the Hour of Truth, the holding of
the sword, the uses of the cape, movements, the passes,
the technique of the kill? Better to wait and do the
thing properly. But the months had passed, or more
than months, for who could reckon time in a sane way
in this crazy house? The bulls were growing fat and
sleepy on the ranch where they were housed. Picasso
found it maddening that no qualified performer could
be found, when everyone who had ever lived was somewhere in Hell. You could find El Greco, here, you
could find Julius Caesar, you could find Agamemnon,
Beethoven, Toulouse-Lautrec, Alexander the Great,
Velasquez, Goya, Michelangelo, Picasso. You could even
find Jaime Sabartés. But where were all the great matadors? Not in Uruk, so it seemed, or in any of the
adjacent territories. Maybe they had some special corner of Hell all to themselves, where all those who had
ever carried the *muleta* and the *estoque* had gathered
for a *corrida* that went on day and night, night and day,
world without end.

Well, at last someone who claimed to understand the
art had turned up in Uruk. So be it. A *corrida* with just
one matador would make for a short afternoon, but it
was better than no *corrida* at all, and perhaps the word
would spread and Belmonte or Manolete would come
to town in time to make a decent show of it. The man
who called himself Ruiz could wait no longer. He had
been absent from *la fiesta brava* much too long. Per-

haps a good bullfight was the magic he needed to make the paintings begin to come out right again.

"Yes," he said to Sabartés. "Let us try your Blasco y Velez. Next week, eh? Next Sunday? Is that too soon?"

"Next Sunday, yes, Pablo. If there is a Sunday next week."

"Good. Well done, Sabartés. And now—"

Sabartés knew when he was being dismissed. He smiled, he made a cavalier's pleasant bow to Ninsun, he flicked a swift but meaningful glance toward the covered canvas on the easel, and he slipped out the door.

"Shall I take the pose again?" the Sumerian woman asked.

"Perhaps a little later," said Picasso.

The city was just as Gilgamesh had seen it in his vision, that time in Pompeii when Calandola had opened the way for him and given him the Knowing. It was a shimmering place of white cubical buildings that sprawled for a vast distance across a dark plain rimmed by towering hills. A high wall of sun-dried brick, embellished by glazed reliefs of dragons and gods in brilliant colors, surrounded it. Looking down into Uruk from the brick-paved road that wound downward through the mountains, Gilgamesh could see straight to the heart of the city, where all manner of structures in the familiar Sumerian style were clustered: temples, palaces, ceremonial platforms.

It was for him as though the endless years of his life in Hell had fallen away in a moment, and he had come home to Sumer the Land, that dear place of his birth where he had learned the ways of gods and men, and had risen through adversity to kingship, and had come to understand the secret things, the truths of life and death.

But of course this was not that Uruk. This was the Uruk of Hell, a different place entirely, a hundred times larger than the Uruk of his lost Sumer and a

thousand times more strange. Yet this place was familiar to him too; and this place seemed to him also like
home, for his home was what it was, his second home,
the home of his second life.

He had founded this city. He had been king here.

He had no memory of that—it was all lost, swallowed
up in the muddle and murk that was what passed for
the past here in hell. But the Knowing that Calandola
had bestowed on him had left him with a clear sense of
his forgotten achievements in this second Uruk; and,
seeing the city before him in the plain exactly as it had
looked in his vision, Gilgamesh knew that all the rest of
that vision must have been true, that he had once
been king in this Uruk before he had been swept away
down the turbulent river of time to other places and
other adventures.

Herod said, "It's the right place, isn't it?"

"No question of it. The very one."

They were all three riding together in the first Land
Rover now, Sulla and Gilgamesh and Sulla's prime minister, Herod of Judaea, with their baggage train close
behind them and half a dozen of the low, snub-nosed
Uruk border-guard vehicles leading the way. Herod
was growing lively again, more his usual self, quick-
tongued, inquisitive, an edgy, nervy little man. It had
given him a good scare when the caravan had been
halted by that sudden fog and surrounded by those
wild-looking shouting figures. He had been certain that
a pack of demons was about to fall upon them and tear
them apart. But seeing Gilgamesh step calmly out of his
Land Rover and all the wild ones instantly drop down
on their faces as though he were the Messiah coming to
town had reassured him. Herod seemed relaxed now,
sitting back jauntily with his arms folded and his legs
crossed.

"It's very impressive, your Uruk," Herod said. "Don't
you think so, Sulla? Why don't you tell Gilgamesh what
you think of his city?"

Sulla gave the Judaean prince a cold, sour look. He was immensely proud of his grotesque and fanciful Pompeii, that sorcerer-infested metropolis of baroque towers and clotted, claustrophobic alleys.

"I haven't seen his city yet, Herod."

"You're seeing it now."

"It's walls. It's rooftops."

"But aren't they the most majestic walls? And look how far the city stretches! It's much bigger than Pompeii, wouldn't you say?"

"Pompeii sits on an island," replied Sulla frostily. "Its size is limited by that, as you are well aware. But yes, yes, this is a very fine city, this Uruk. I look forward to experiencing its many wonders."

"And to getting your hands on its treasure," Herod said. "Which surely is copious. Is that the treasure-house down there, Gilgamesh, that big building on the platform?"

"The temple of Enlil, I think," said Gilgamesh.

"But certainly it's full of rubies and emeralds. My master Sulla is very fond, you know, of rubies and emeralds. He's here to fill his purse to overflowing with them. Do you think they'll mind in this town if he helps himself to a little of their treasure, Gilgamesh?"

Sulla said, scowling, "Why are you baiting me like this, Jew? You make me regret I brought you with me on this journey."

"I simply try to amuse you, Sulla."

"If you keep this up, it may amuse me to have you circumcised a second time," the Roman said. "Or something worse." To Gilgamesh he said, "Does any of it start to come back to you yet? Your past life in Uruk?"

"Nothing. Not a thing."

"But yet you're sure you lived here once."

"I built this city, Sulla. So I truly believe. I brought people of my own kind together in this place and gave them laws and ruled over them, just as I did in the other Uruk on Earth. But all knowledge of that has fled from my mind." Gilgamesh laughed. "Can *you* remember everything that has befallen you in Hell since first you came here?"

"If I had been king of some city before Pompeii, I think I would remember that."

"How long have you been here, Sulla?"

"Who can say? You know what time is like here. But I understand some two thousand years have gone by on Earth since my time there. Perhaps a little more."

"In two thousand years," said Gilgamesh, "you might have been a king five times over in Hell, and forgotten it all. You could have embraced a hundred queens and forgotten them."

Herod chuckled. "Helen of Troy—Kleopatra—Nefertiti —all forgotten, Sulla, the shape of their breasts, the taste of their lips, the sounds of their pleasure—"

Sulla reached for his wine. "You think?" he asked Gilgamesh. "Can this be so?"

"The years float by and run one into another. The demons play with our memories. There are no straight lines here, and no unbroken ones. How could we keep our sanity, Sulla, if we remembered everything that has happened to us in Hell? Two thousand years, you say? For me it is *five* thousand. Or more. A hundred lifetimes. Ah, no Sulla, we are born again and again here, with minds wiped clean, and the torment of it is that we don't even know that that is the case. We imagine that we are as we have always been. We think we understand ourselves, and in fact we know only the merest surface of the truth. The irreducible essence of our souls remains the same, yes—I am always Gilgamesh, he is Herod, you are Sulla, we make the choices over and over that someone of our nature must make—but the conditions of our lives fluctuate, we are tossed about on the hot winds of Hell, and most of what happens to us is swallowed eventually into oblivion. This is the wisdom that came to me from the Knowing I had of Calandola."

"That barbarian! That devil!"

"Nevertheless. He sees behind the shallow reality of Hell. I accept the truth of his revelation."

"You may have forgotten Uruk, Gilgamesh," said Herod, "but Uruk seems not to have forgotten you."

"So it would appear," said Gilgamesh.

Indeed it had startled him profoundly when the Sumerian border guards had hailed him at once as Gilgamesh the king. Hardly was he out of the Land Rover but they were kneeling to him and making holy signs, and crying out to him in the ancient language of the Land, which he had not heard spoken in so long a time that it sounded strange and harsh to his ears. It was as if he had left this city only a short while before—whereas he knew that even by the mysterious time-reckoning of Hell it was a long eternity since last he could have dwelled here. His memory was clear on that point, for he knew that he had spent his most recent phase of his time in Hell roving the hinterlands with Enkidu, hunting the strange beasts of the Outback, shunning the intrigues and malevolences of the cities—and surely that period in the wilderness had lasted decades, even centuries. Yet in Uruk his face and form seemed familiar to all.

Well, he would know more about that soon enough. Perhaps they held him in legendary esteem here and prayed constantly for his return. Or, more likely, it was merely some further manifestation of Hell's witchery that spawned these confusions.

They were practically in Uruk now. The road out of the hills had leveled out. A great brazen gate inscribed with the images of serpents and monsters rose up before them. It swung open as they neared it, and the entire procession rolled on within.

Sulla, far gone in wine, clapped the Sumerian lustily on the shoulder. "Uruk, Gilgamesh! We're actually here! Did you think we'd ever find it?"

"It found us," said Gilgamesh coolly. "We were lost

in a land between nowhere and nowhere, and suddenly Uruk lay before us. So we are here, Sulla: but where is it that we are?"

"Ah, Gilgamesh, Gilgamesh, what a sober thing you are! We are in Uruk, wherever that may be! Rejoice, man! Smile! Lift up your heart! This city is your home! Your friend will be here—what's his name, Inkibu, Tinkibu—?"

"Enkidu."

"Enkidu, yes. And your cousins, your brothers, perhaps your father—"

"This is Hell, Sulla. Delights turn to ashes on our tongues. I expect nothing here."

"You'll be a king again. Is that nothing?"

"Have I said I feel any wish to rule this place?" Gilgamesh asked, glowering at the Roman.

Sulla blinked in surprise. "Why, Herod says you do."

"He does?" Gilgamesh skewered the little man with a fierce glare. "Who are you to pretend to speak what is in my mind? How do you imagine you dare know my heart?"

In a small voice Herod said, shrinking back as though he expected to be hit, "It is because I was with you when you had the Knowing, Gilgamesh. And had the Knowing with you. Have you forgotten that so soon?"

Gilgamesh considered that. He could not deny the truth of it.

Quietly he said, "This city must already have some king of its own. I have no thought to displace him. But if the gods have that destiny in mind for me—"

"Not the gods, Gilgamesh. The demons. This place is Hell," Herod reminded him.

"The demons, yes," said Gilgamesh. "Yes."

They were well within Uruk now and the caravan had come to rest in the midst of a huge plaza. At close range Gilgamesh saw that Uruk was only superficially a Sumerian city: many of the buildings were in the ancient style, yes, but there was everything else here too, all periods and styles, the hideous things that they called office buildings, and the sullen bulk of a power-plant spewing foulness into the air, and an ominous-looking barracks of dirty red brick without windows, and something that looked like a Roman lawcourt or palace off to one corner. A crowd was gathered outside the Land Rover, many in Sumerian dress but by no means all; there was the usual Hellish mix, Old Dead and New, garbed in all the costumes of the ages. Everyone was staring. Everyone was silent.

"You get out first," Sulla said to Gilgamesh.

He nodded. A gaggle of what were obviously municipal officials, plainly Sumerian by race, had assembled alongside the Land Rover. They were looking in at him expectantly. They seemed worried, or at least puzzled, by his presence here.

He stepped out, looming like a giant above them all.

A man with a thick curling black beard and a shaven skull, who wore the woolen tunic of Sumer the Land, came forward and said—in English—"We welcome Gilgamesh the son of Lugalbanda to the city of Uruk, and his friends. I am the arch-vizier Ur-ninmarka, servant to Dumuzi the king, whose guests you are."

"Dumuzi?" said Gilgamesh, astonished.

"He is king in Uruk, yes."

"He who ruled before me, when we lived on Earth?"

Ur-ninmarka shrugged. "I know nothing of that. I was a man of Lagash in the Land that was, and Uruk was far away. But Dumuzi is king here, and he has sent me to give you greeting and escort you to your lodgings. Tonight you will dine with him and with the great ones of the city."

Dumuzi, Gilgamesh thought in wonder. That pathetic weakling! That murderous swine! Surely it is the same one; for in Hell everything that has befallen befalls over and over, and so Dumuzi is king in Uruk once again, the same Dumuzi who in the old life, fearing Gilgamesh the son of Lugalbanda as a rival, had sent

assassins to slay him, though he was then only a boy.
Those assassins had failed, and in the end it was Dumuzi
who went from the world and Gilgamesh who had the
throne. No doubt he fears me yet, Gilgamesh suspected. And will try his treacheries on me a second
time. Some things never change, thought Gilgamesh: it
is the way of Hell. As Dumuzi will learn to his sorrow,
if he has new villainy in mind.

Aloud he said, "It will please me greatly to enjoy the
hospitality of your king. Will you tell him that?"

"That I will."

"And tell him too that he will be host to Sulla, ruler
of the great city of Pompeii, and to his prime minister,
Herod of Judaea, who are my traveling companions."

Ur-ninmarka bowed.

"One further thing," said Gilgamesh. "I take it there
are many citizens of Sumer the Land dwelling in this
city."

"A great many, my lord."

"Can you say, is there a certain Enkidu here, a man
of stature as great as my own, and very strong of body,
and hairy all over, like a beast of the fields? He who is
well known everywhere to be my friend, and whom I
have come here to seek?"

The arch-vizier's bare brow furrowed. "I cannot say,
my lord. I will make inquiries, and you will have a
report this evening when you dine at the palace."

"I am grateful to you," said Gilgamesh.

But his heart sank. Enkidu must not be here after all;
for how could Ur-ninmarka fail to know of it, if a great
roistering shaggy giant such as Enkidu had come to
Uruk? There is no city in Hell so big that Enkidu would
not be conspicuous in it, and more than conspicuous,
thought Gilgamesh.

He kept these matters to himself. Beckoning Sulla
and Herod from the Land Rover, he said only, "All is
well. Tonight we will be entertained by Uruk's king."

*   *   *

Dumuzi, at any rate, seemed to do things with style. For his visitors he provided sumptuous lodgings in a grand hostelry back of the main temple, a massive block of a building that seemed to have been carved of a single slab of black granite. Within were fountains, arcades, so much statuary that it was hard to move about without bumping into something, and towering purple-leaved palm trees growing in huge ruby-red planters that glistened like genuine rubies. Perhaps they were. Gilgamesh saw Sulla fondling one covetously as though contemplating how many hundreds of egg-sized stones it could be broken into.

Each of the travelers had a palatial room to himself, a broad bed covered in silk, a sunken alabaster tub, a mirror that shimmered like a window into Paradise. Of course, there were little things wrong amid all this perfection: no hot water was running, and a line of disagreeable-looking fat-bellied furry insects with emerald eyes went trooping constantly across the ceiling of Gilgamesh's room, and when he sprawled on the bed it set up a steady complaining moan, as though he were lying on the protesting forms of living creatures. But this was Hell, after all. One expected flaws in everything, and one always got them. All things considered, these accommodations could hardly be excelled.

Half a dozen sycophants appeared as if from a closet to help Gilgamesh with his bath, and anoint him with fragrant oils, and garb him in a white flounced woolen robe that left him bare to the waist in the Sumerian manner. After a time Herod came knocking at the door, and he too was garbed after the fashion of Sumer, though he still wore his gleaming Italian leather shoes instead of sandals, and he had his little Jewish skullcap on his head. His dark curling hair had been pomaded to a high gloss.

"Well?" he said, preening. "Do I look like a prince of Sumer the Land, Gilgamesh?"

"You look like a fop, as always. And a weakling,

besides. At least your toga would have covered those flabby arms of yours and that spindly chest."

"Ah, Gilgamesh! What need do I have of muscles, when I have *this?*" He touched his hand to his head. "And when I have the brave Gilgamesh the king to protect me against malefactors."

"But will I, though?"

"Of course you will." Herod smiled. "You feel sorry for me, because I have to live by my wits all the time and don't have any other way of defending myself. You'll look after me. It's not in your nature to let someone like me be endangered. Besides, you need me."

"I do?"

"You've lived in the Outback too long. You've got bits of straw in your hair."

Automatically Gilgamesh reached up to search.

"No, no, you foolish ape, not literally!" said Herod, laughing. "I mean only that you've been out of things. You don't understand the modern world. You need me to explain reality to you. You stalk around being heroic and austere and noble, which is fine in its way, but you've been paying no attention to what's really been going on in Hell lately. The fashions, the music, the art, the new technology."

"These things are of no importance to me. Fashion? And music? Music is mere tinkling in my ear. Art is decoration, a trivial thing. As for this new technology you speak of, it is an abomination. I despise all the inventions of the New Dead."

"Despise them all you like, but they're here to stay. The New Dead outnumber us a thousand to one, and more of them arrive every day. You can't just ignore them. Or their technology."

"I can."

"So you may think. A bow and a couple of arrows, that's good enough for you, right? But you keep running afoul of things you don't comprehend. You blun-

der on and on and you get yourself out of trouble most
of the time pretty well, but you fundamentally don't
know what's what, and sooner or later you'll come up
against something that's too much even for you. Whereas
I have kept up with modern developments, and I can
guide you through all the pitfalls. I'm aware, Gilgamesh.
I know what's happening. I stay in touch. Politics, for
example. Do you have the foggiest notion of the current
situation? The really spectacular upheavals that are going
on right now?"

"I take great care not to think of them."

"You think it's safe, keeping your head in the sand
that way? What happens on the far side of Hell can
have a tremendous impact on how we operate here.
This isn't your ancient world, where it took forever and
a half just to carry the news from Rome to Syria. Do
you know what a radio is? A telephone? A microwave
relay? Like it or not, we're all New Dead now. You may
still be living like a Sumerian, but the rest of the people
here are neck-deep in modern life."

"They have my compassion," said Gilgamesh.

"You don't know the slightest thing about the revolutionary movements swirling in half a dozen cities back
East, do you? The whole Dissidence? The Rebellion
against the Administration? What Achilles is doing, and
Che Guevara, and Frederick Barbarossa? The latest
deeds of Rameses? The present status of Hadrian? No,
no, Gilgamesh, you're out of things. And proud of your
ignorance. Whereas I have kept up with the news,
and—"

"I have spent time in New Hell, Herod. I have seen
Julius Caesar and Machiavelli and Augustus and Kleopatra
and the rest of that crowd putting together their petty
schemes. Why do you think I went to the Outback? I
wept with boredom after half an hour among them.
Their intrigues were like the squeakings of so many
mice to me. Whatever they may be planning to do, it
will all wash away like a castle of sand by the edge of

the sea, and Hell will go on and on as it always has.
And so will I. The demons who are the masters here
laugh at the pretentions of the rebellious ones. And so
do I. No, Herod, I haven't any need of your guidance.
If I choose to protect you against harm, it'll be out of
mercy, not out of self-interest." He glanced at his watch.
"It grows late. We should be on our way to the feast."

"The wristwatch you wear is a despised invention of
the New Dead."

"I take what I choose from among their things," said
Gilgamesh. "I choose very little. You are not the first to
try to mock me for inconsistency. But I know who I am,
Herod, and I know what I believe."

"Yes," Herod said, in a tone that was its own nega-
tion. "How could anyone have doubt of that?"

Gilgamesh might have pitched him from the window
just then; but the sycophants returned to lead them to
the feasting-hall. Sulla, waiting for them amid the splen-
dors of the lobby, greeted them with wine-flushed face.
He had spurned Sumerian robes altogether and was
decked out in a purple toga and high gilded buskins in
the Greek style.

As they moved toward the door Sulla caught Gilgamesh
by the wrist and said quietly, "One moment. Tell me
about this king we are about to meet, this Dumuzi."

"If it is the same one, he succeeded my father
Lugalbanda on the throne of Uruk—the first Uruk—
when I was a boy, and drove me into exile. He was a
coward and a fool, who neglected the rites and squan-
dered public funds on ridiculous adventures, and the
gods withdrew the kingship from him and he died.
Which made the way clear for me to become king."

Sulla nodded. "You had him murdered, then?"

Gilgamesh's eyes widened. Then he laughed, seeing
how quickly Sulla had drawn the correct conclusion of
murder from the innocent phrase, *the gods withdrew
the kingship from him.* This man might be a drunkard
but his mind was still shrewd.

"Not I, Sulla. I had nothing to do with it. I was in exile then; it was the great men of the city who saw that Dumuzi must go, and the priestess Inanna who actually gave him the poison, telling him it was a healing medicine for an illness he had."

"Mmm," said Sulla. "You and he take turns succeeding one another in the kingship of Uruk, here and in the former life. Now it's his turn to rule. And yours may be due to come again soon. Everything revolves in an endless circle."

"It is the way of this place. I am used to it."

"He was afraid of you once. He'll be afraid of you still. There'll be old grudges at work tonight. Perhaps an attempt at some settling of scores."

"Dumuzi has never frightened me," said Gilgamesh, making the gesture one might make to flick away a troublesome fly.

Sabartés said, "Which is it, Pablo, that has you so excited these days? That you have a new mistress, or that we are finally to have a bullfight for you to attend?"

"Do you think I am excited, brother?"

With a sweeping gesture Sabartés indicated the litter of sketches all about the studio, the dozen new half-finished canvases turned to the wall, the bright splotches everywhere where Picasso, in his haste, had overturned paints and not bothered to wipe them up. "You are like a man on fire. You work without stopping, Pablo."

"Ah, and is that something new?" Rummaging absentmindedly in a pile of legal documents, Picasso found one with a blank side and began quickly to draw a caricature of his friend, the high forehead, the thick glasses, the soft fleshy throat. A little to his surprise he saw that what he was drawing was the old pedantic Sabartés of the last years on Earth, not the incongruously young Bohemian Sabartés who in fact stood before him now. And then the sketch changed with half a dozen swift inadvertent strokes and became not Sabartés but a demon with fangs and a flaming snout. Picasso crumpled it and tossed it aside. To Sabartés he said, "She will be here soon. Do you have anything you must tell me?"

"Then it *is* the woman, Pablo."

"She is splendid, is she not?"

"They were all splendid. La Belle Chelita was splendid, the one from the strip-tease place. Fernande was splendid. Eva was splendid. Marie-Therese was splendid. Dora Maar was—"

"*Basta,* Sabartés!"

"I mean no offense, Pablo. It is only that I see now that Picasso has chosen once more a new woman, a woman who is as fine as the ones who went before her, and—"

"You will call me Ruiz, brother."

"It is hard," said Sabartés. "It is so very hard."

"Ruiz was my father's name. It is an honest name for calling me."

"The world knows you as Picasso. All of Hell will know you as Picasso too as time goes along."

Picasso scowled and began a new sketch of Sabartés, which began almost at once to turn into a portrait of El Greco, elongated face and deep-set sorrowful eyes, and then, maddeningly, into the face of a goat. Again he threw the sheet aside. He would not mind these metamorphoses if they were of his own choosing. But this was intolerable, that he could not control them. *Painting,* he had liked to tell people in his life before this life, *is stronger than I am. It makes me do what it wants.* But now he realized that he must have been lying when he said that; for it was finally happening to him, just that very thing, and he did not like it at all.

He said, "I prefer now to be known as Ruiz. That way none of my heirs will find me here. They are very angry with me, brother, for not having left a will, for having forced them to fight in the courts for year after year. I would rather not see them. Or any of the

women who are looking for me. We move on, Sabartés.
We must not let the past pursue us. I am Ruiz now."

"And you think that by calling yourself a name that is
not Picasso you can hide from your past, though you
look the same and you act the same and you paint day
and night? Pablo, Pablo, you deceive only yourself! You
could call yourself Mozart and you would still be Picasso."

The telephone rang.

"Answer it," said Picasso brusquely.

Sabartés obeyed. After a moment he put his hand
over the receiver and looked up.

"It is your Sumerian priestess," said Sabartés.

Picasso leaned forward, tense, apprehensive, already
furious. "She is canceling the sitting?"

"No, no, nothing like that. She will be here in a little
while. But she says King Dumuzi has asked her to
attend a feast at the royal hall tonight, and that you are
invited to accompany her."

"What do I have to do with King Dumuzi?"

"She asks you to be her escort."

"I have work to do. You know I am not one to go to
royal feasts."

"Shall I tell her that, Pablo?"

"Tell her—wait. Wait. Let me think. Speak with her,
Sabartés. Tell her—ask her—yes, tell her that the king's
feast is of no importance to me, that I want her to come
here right away, that—that—"

Sabartés held up one hand for silence. He spoke into
the telephone, and listened a moment, and looked up
again.

"She says the feast is in honor of her son, who has
arrived in Uruk this day."

"Her *son?* What son?" Picasso's eyes were blazing.
"She said nothing about a son! How old is he? What is
this son's name? Who is his father? Ask her, Sabartés!
Ask her!"

Sabartés spoke with her once again. "His name is
Gilgamesh," he reported after a little while. "She has

not seen him since her days on Earth, which were so long ago. I think you ought not to ask her to refuse the king's invitation, Pablo. I think you ought not to refuse it yourself."

"Gilgamesh?" Picasso said, wonderstruck. "*Gilgamesh?*"

Motorized chariots painted in many gaudy colors conveyed them the short distance from the lodging-hall to the feasting-place of the king, on the far side of the temple plaza. The building startled Gilgamesh, for it was not remotely Sumerian in form: a great soaring thing of ash-gray stone, it was, with a pair of narrow spires rising higher than any of Pompeii, and pointed arches over the heavy bronze doors, and enormous windows of stained glass in every color of the rainbow and a few other hues besides. Ghastly monsters of stone were mounted all along its facade. Some of them seemed slowly to be moving. It was very grand and immense and massive, but somehow also it seemed flimsy, and Gilgamesh wondered how it kept from falling down, until he saw the huge stone buttresses flying outward on the sides. Trust Dumuzi to build a palace for himself that needed to be propped up by such desperate improvisations, Gilgamesh thought. He loathed the look of it. It clashed miserably with the classic Uruk style of the buildings that surrounded it. If I am ever king of this city again, Gilgamesh vowed, I will rip down this dismal pile of stone as my first official act.

Herod, though, seemed to admire it. "It's a perfect replica of a Gothic cathedral," he told Gilgamesh as they went inside. "Perhaps Notre Dame, perhaps Chartres. I'm not sure which. I'm starting to forget some of what I once learned about architecture. I had some instruction in it, you know, from a man named Speer, a German, who passed through Pompeii a while back and did a little work for Sulla—peculiar chap, kept asking me if I wanted him to build a synagogue for me—what use would we have for a synagogue in

Hell?—but he knew his stuff, he taught me all sorts of things about New Dead architectural design—you'd be astounded, Gilgamesh, what kinds of buildings they—"

"Can you try being quiet for a little while?" Gilgamesh asked.

The interior of the building actually had a sort of beauty, he thought. Paradise was still glowing ruddily in the sky at this hour, and its subtle light, entering through the stained-glass windows, gave the cavernous open spaces of the palace a solemn, mysterious look. And the upper reaches of the building, gallery upon gallery rising toward a dimly visible pointed-arch ceiling, were breathtaking in their loftiness. Still, there was something oppressive and sinister about it all. Gilgamesh much preferred the temple in honor of Enlil that he had built, and still well remembered, atop the White Platform in the center of the original Uruk. *That* had had grandeur. *That* had had dignity. These New Dead understood nothing about beauty.

Dumuzi's sycophants escorted them to the other end of the palace, where the building terminated in a great rounded chamber, open on one side and walled with stained glass on the other. A feasting-table had been set up there and dozens of guests had already gathered.

Gilgamesh saw Dumuzi at once, sumptuously robed, standing at the head of an enormous stone table.

He had not changed at all. He carried himself well, with true kingly bearing: a vigorous-looking man, heavy-bearded, with thick flowing hair so dark it seemed almost blue. But his lips were too full, his cheeks were too soft; and his eyes were small, and seemed both crafty and dull at the same time. He looked weak, unpleasant, untrustworthy, mean-souled.

Yet as he spied Gilgamesh he came down from his high place as though it were Gilgamesh and not he who was the king, and went to his side, and looked up at him, craning his neck in an awkward way—it was impossible for him to hide the discomfort that Gilgamesh's

great height caused him—and hailed him in ringing
tones, as he might a brother newly returned after a long
sojourn abroad:

"Gilgamesh at last! Here in our Uruk! Hail, Gilgamesh,
hail!"

"Dumuzi, hail," said Gilgamesh with all the enthusi-
asm he could find, and made a sign to him that one
would have made to a king in Sumer the Land. "Great
king, king of kings." He detected a quick flash of surprise in Dumuzi at that: plainly Dumuzi was not expecting much in the way of subservience out of him.
Nor would he get much, Gilgamesh thought; but Dumuzi
was king in this city, and proper courtesy was due a
king, any king. Even Dumuzi.

"Come," Dumuzi said, "introduce me to your friends,
and then you must sit beside me in the place of honor,
and tell me of everything that has befallen you in Hell,
the cities you've visited, the kings you've known, the
things you've done. I want to hear all the news—we are
so isolated, out here between the desert and the sea—
but wait, wait, there are people here you must meet—"

Forgetting all about Sulla and Herod, who were left
behind gaping indignantly, Dumuzi thrust his arm
through Gilgamesh's and led him with almost hysterical
eagerness toward the feasting-table. It was all Gilgamesh
could do to keep from knocking him sprawling for the
impertinence of this offensive overfamiliarity. He is a
king, Gilgamesh reminded himself. He is a king.

And the desperate bluster behind Dumuzi's effusive
cordiality was easy enough for Gilgamesh to see. The
man was frightened. The man was scrambling frantically to gain control of a situation that must be immensely threatening to him.

For thousands of years Dumuzi had had the leisure
in Hell to reflect on the shameful truth that he had
been, in his earlier life, the feckless irresolute interpo-
lation between the two great royal heroes Lugalbanda
and Gilgamesh, a mere hyphen of history. Now he was

king again, having risen by some mysterious law of incompetence to his former summit. And now here was that same hulking Gilgamesh for whose sake he had been thrust aside once before, materializing like an unwelcome spectre in New Uruk to claim his hospitality.

Of course Dumuzi would be cordial, and effusively so. But all the same it was likely to be a good idea, Gilgamesh thought, to guard his back at all times while in Dumuzi's city. Cowards are more dangerous than heroes, for they strike without fair warning; Dumuzi, tremulous and resentful, might work more harm than Achilles in all his wrath could ever manage.

A moment later these gloomy ruminations went completely from his mind; for a voice he had not heard in more centuries than he could count, but which was so different from any other man's that not even in Hell could it ever be forgotten, came pealing across the room, calling his name.

"Gilgamesh! Gilgamesh! By the Mother, it is truly you! By the Tusk! By the Horns of God! Gilgamesh, here!"

Gilgamesh stared. A man seated near the head of the banquet table had risen and held his arms wide outspread in a gesture of greeting.

Gilgamesh's first thought was that he must be New Dead, for alone in this great hall this man wore the strange formal costume of the most recent arrivals in Hell, what they called a business suit: tight gray pantaloons that hugged his legs, and a stiff-looking wide-shouldered half-length coat, not exactly a tunic, of the same close-woven gray woolen material, with a white vestment under it, and a narrow strip of blue cloth knotted about his throat and dangling down his chest. He was tall, too, as New Dead often were—taller by far than any of the Sumerians in the room but for Gilgamesh himself.

Yet there could be no mistaking that voice. It was a voice that came from the dawn of time, from the lost world that had been before the Flood, and it rang through the great room like a brazen trumpet, hard and clear. No New Dead had ever had a voice like that.

Nor was his lean face that of a New Dead, clean-shaven though it was. His skin had the burnished gleam of one who has faced the winds and snows of a world without warmth. His cheekbones were broad and strong, his lips were full, his nose was straight and very prominent, his mouth was extraordinarily wide. His eyes were wide-set too, far apart in his forehead, and one of them was missing from its socket: an ancient scar slashed crosswise over the left side of his face.

This man had been king of the cave-dwelling Ice-Hunter people, in that time before time when even the gods were young; and there had been a time in Hell when Gilgamesh had known him well.

Gilgamesh felt a chill of astonishment. How long had it been, he wondered, since they had enjoyed high merriment together in the great windy hall of the Ice-Hunter folk on the northern reaches of Hell—that vast cavern hung with woolly beast-skins where the huge curving tusks of the hairy elephants were scattered like straws on the floor, and the thick mead flowed in rivers, and the smoky fires burned high? A thousand Hellish years? Three thousand? It had been in his earliest days in Hell, that simpler, easier time that now seemed forever lost.

"Vy-otin!" Gilgamesh cried. With a whoop he rushed forward, mounting the dais on which the stone feasting-table sat, holding out his arms in a lusty embrace.

"So you have not forgotten," the Ice-Hunter said. "I thought for a moment you had."

"No, by the breasts of Inanna, how could I ever forget you! The old memories are brighter than anything after. Last year is hazy for me, but those old times, Vy-otin, you and I and Enkidu, and Minos, and Agamemnon—"

"Ah, but you looked doubtful a moment, Gilgamesh."

"You confused me with these New Dead clothes of yours," said Gilgamesh reproachfully. "You, who lived when the world was new, when the great shaggy beasts roamed, when Sumer itself was nothing but a muddy marsh—you, decking yourself out like some tawdry twentieth-century creature, someone out of—what do they call it, *A.D.*?" He made it sound like an obscenity. "I remember a man in fur robes, Vy-otin, and a necklace of boar's teeth around his throat, and armlets of shining bone, not this—this *businessman* costume!"

Vy-otin said, laughing, "It's a long story, Gilgamesh. And I go by the name of Smith now, not Vy-otin. In this hall you can call me by my true name. But in the streets of Uruk my name is Smith."

"Smith?"

"Henry Smith, yes."

"Is that a New Dead name? How ugly it is!"

"It is a name that no one can remember as long as five minutes, not even me. Henry Smith. Sit with me, and we'll share a flask or two of this wine of Dumuzi's, and I'll tell you why I dress this way, and why my name is Smith now."

"I pray you, Vy-otin, let your story wait a while," said Dumuzi, who had been standing to one side. "There is someone else to whom Gilgamesh owes greetings, first—"

He touched Gilgamesh by the elbow, and nodded toward the other side of the table. A woman had risen there, a magnificent dark-haired woman of splendid stature and regal bearing, who stood calmly smiling at him.

She was a wondrous creature, radiant, beautiful, with shining eyes and the poise of a goddess. It was as if light emanated from her. Plainly, by the look of her and by her dress, she was Sumerian. She wore the robe of a priestess of An the Sky-father. She was within a year or two of Gilgamesh's age, so it seemed, or perhaps a little younger than that. Her face was familiar, though he

could not place it. From her size and majesty she
seemed surely to be of royal stock, and her features led
him to think she might even be his own kinswoman.
Some daughter of his, perhaps? He had had so many,
though. Or the daughter of his daughter's daughter to
the tenth generation, for here in Uruk as everywhere
else in Hell there were folk of every era living jumbled
all together, and one might meet one's own remote kin
at every turning, distant ancestors who seemed to be
mere boys, and one's children's children who looked to
be in their dotage—

Dumuzi said, "Will you not go to her and show your
respect, Gilgamesh?"

"Of course I will. But—"

"You hesitate?"

"I almost know her, Dumuzi. But the name slips
from my tongue, and it shames me not to recall it."

"Well it should shame you, Gilgamesh, to forget your
own mother!"

"My *mother*?" said Gilgamesh, with a gasp.

"The great queen Ninsun, and none other. Are you
addled, man? Go to her! Go to her!"

Gilgamesh looked toward her in wonder and awe. Of
course it was plain now. Of course. The years fell away
as though they had never been, and he saw his mother's face, the unmistakable features of the goddesslike
wife of Lugalbanda, king of Uruk, that great woman
who had brought the hero Gilgamesh into the world.

But yet—yet—

What tricks Hell plays on us, he thought. Never once
had her path crossed his in the hundred lifetimes of his
second life. He had not seen his mother since the days
of that other world long gone; and he remembered her
as she had been in her latter years, still majestic, still
regal, but her hair white as the sands, her face lined
and seamed; and now here she was in full robust beauty
again, not youthful but far from old, a woman in glori-

ous prime. He had been only a child when last she had looked like that. No wonder he had not recognized her.

He hastened to her now, and dropped down on his knees before her, taking the hem of her robe and putting it to his lips. The thousands of years of his wanderings in this vile harsh land became as nothing; he was a boy again, in his first life, and the goddess his mother was restored to him and stood before him, agleam with warmth and love.

Softly she said his secret name, his birth-name, that no one but she was permitted to utter. Then she told him to rise, and he came to his full height, folding her against his bosom: for, tall as she was, she was like a child beside him. After a time he released her and she stepped back to look at him.

"I despaired of ever seeing you again," she said. "In all the places I have lived in Hell I have heard tales of great Gilgamesh, and never once, never ever, have I been where you have been. I saw Enkidu once, from a distance, in a great noisy mob: that was in New Albion, I think, or the Realm of Logres, or perhaps the place they call Phlegethon. I forget, now. But we were swept apart before I could call to him. And when I asked of Gilgamesh in that place, no one there knew anything of him."

"Mother—"

"And then I came to this new Uruk, knowing you had been king here, and thinking you might still hold your throne—but no, no, they said you had taken your leave of this city long ago, that you had gone hunting with Enkidu and never returned, more years ago than anyone could remember. And I thought, very well, the gods have no wish to let me see my son again, for this is Hell and few wishes are granted here. But then the word came that you were approaching the city. Oh, Gilgamesh! What joy it is to behold you again!"

"And my father?" Gilgamesh asked. "What of the divine Lugalbanda? Surely he must not be here, for he is a god, and how can there be gods in Hell? But do you know anything of him?"

Ninsun's eyes clouded a moment. "He is here too, of that I am certain. For those who were made gods after their lives in Sumer are gods no longer, and dwell in Hell. You elevated me to godhood, Gilgamesh, do you remember?"

"Yes," he said, only a murmur.

"And you yourself—they ranked you with the gods also. It makes no difference. Those who lived as mortals die as mortals, and come to this place."

"You know with certainty that Lugalbanda is here, then?"

"I think he is. Of him I have heard not one word in all the time I have been here. But some day he and I will find one another again, that I know."

"Yes," Gilgamesh said once more, nodding. It had never occurred to him that his father might indeed be somewhere in Hell, and the possibility aroused excitement and amazement in his breast. "In Hell all things happen, sooner or later. You will be reunited with the king your husband and live by his side as the Sky-father ordained, for you and he were mated for all time and this span in Hell has been but a brief separation; and I—"

An odd look came then into Ninsun's face. For an instant she lowered her eyes, as though abashed. The queenly splendor, the goddess-glow, went from her, and for that instant she seemed to be only a mere mortal woman.

"Have I spoken amiss?" Gilgamesh asked.

She said, "You have said nothing that should not have been said. But I would have you meet my friend, Gilgamesh."

"Your—friend—?"

Color rose to her cheeks in a curiously girlish way that he was altogether unable to associate with his memories of the regal presence of his mother. She nodded toward an elderly man sitting beside her, who got now to his feet.

Standing, he was less than breast-high to Gilgamesh, a short balding man, *very* short, not so tall by half a head as Ninsun herself; and yet as Gilgamesh looked more closely he saw that there was a strange elemental force about this man, a look of enormous power and commanding strength, that made him seem not nearly as short as he actually was, made him look, indeed, kingly in size and stance. It was the depth and breadth of his shoulders and torso that gave him that potent look, Gilgamesh thought: that and his eyes, which were the most intense that the Sumerian had ever seen, more penetrating, even, than those of Imbe Calandola the mage. Astonishing eyes, they were, dark and glittering, the eyes of a hawk, the eyes of an eagle—no, the eyes of a god, merciless eyes, all-seeing eyes. They blazed like black jewels in his face.

Gilgamesh realized abruptly that this strange and powerful little man must be his mother's lover; and it was a disturbing thought indeed.

Hard enough to find her transformed into a young woman again, beautiful and for all he knew lusty; but harder still to think of her with a woman's earthy nature, seeking a man's bed, this man's bed, this old man, this man who had no hair, his arms about her, his fingers probing the secret places of her body that only Lugalbanda the king had known—

Fool, he thought. She is your mother, but she is also a woman, and was a woman before she was your mother. She has not seen Lugalbanda for five thousand years, and all vows are canceled in this place. Did you think she would remain chaste for the whole five thousand years of her life in Hell? Do you think she should?

Still, why this man?—this old man, so short, not even any hair on his head, his leathery skin deeply folded, lined—

"I am called Ruiz," the little man said. "She is your

mother? Good. You are a fitting son. She should be the mother of giants, this woman. The mother of gods, eh? And you are the famous Gilgamesh. *Mucho gusto en conocerlo*, Senor Gilgamesh." Ruiz grinned and put out his hand, casually, confidently, as though they were equals, standing eye to eye, one giant to another. He was the biggest little man Gilgamesh had ever known.

Gilgamesh began to understand why his mother had chosen this man; or rather, why she had allowed herself to be chosen by him. He was like an irresistible force, a river running unstoppably toward the sea.

"Pablo is an artist," Ninsun said. "A painter, a man of pictures. He is making a picture of me." With a little laugh she said, "He will not let me look at it. But I know it will be a very great picture."

"There are difficulties," Ruiz said. "But I will conquer them. Your mother is extraordinary—her face, her presence—I will make such a painting of her as the Devil himself will want to buy. Only I will not sell it to him. And then, after her, you, eh, Gilgamesh?"

"Me?"

"To pose. I will put a mask on you, the head of a bull, and you will be my Minotaur. The finest Minotaur ever, the true man-monster, the creature of the Labyrinth. Eh? Eh? What do you say, Gilgamesh? I like you. You know, this Sunday, *el domingo que viene*, there will be a bullfight in Uruk. You know the bullfight, eh? *La corrida*? You know what it is, to fight with bulls?"

"I know what that is, yes," said Gilgamesh.

"Good. Of course. You will sit with me that day. We will observe the fine points, you and I. You like that? The seat of honor, beside me." The little man's amazing eyes gleamed. "And tomorrow you come to me and we begin to plan the posing, eh? We must begin at once. I will make you great with my painting."

"He is great already," said Ninsun quietly.

"*Por supuesto!* Of course. He is a king, he is a

legend, we all know that. But there is greatness and
greatness, eh, Gilgamesh? You will be my Minotaur.
You know? The son of Minos, but not really Minos's
son, but *en realidad* the son of the bull, who I think
was Poseidon. Eh? You will pose for me?"

It was only barely a question. This man, Gilgamesh
saw, did not regard his questions as questions, but as
commands. The curious urgency of his desire to paint
him was amusing, and, in its way, compelling. A mere
painter, an artisan, a dauber on walls, was all he was,
and yet he seemed to think that making a painting of
Gilgamesh wearing a bull-mask was a matter of the
most supreme importance. Maybe it was. It mattered at
least as much as anything else here. To his surprise
Gilgamesh found himself liking this little man, and
even respecting him. And not even resenting him for
having taken possession of Ninsun as apparently he
had. He felt an affinity with him that he had felt for
very few of the New Dead. This Ruiz was like someone
out of a much older time, when the distinctions between gods and men were not as great as they later
became. He had about him a demigod's nature. It took
only a single glance to see that.

"Yes," Gilgamesh said. "I will pose for you, Ruiz. I
will come to you tomorrow, yes."

Dumuzi said then, "To your seats, everyone! It is
time for the wine! It is time for the meat!"

They had drunk the night away. Sulla was asleep in
his seat, snoring. He had been bored and restless
throughout the feast, feeling neglected and out of place.
Herod sat slouched over a flask of golden wine, the
same one he had nursed half the evening; he looked to
be frayed and weary, at the last edge of his endurance,
but he seemed determined to hang on. He was talking
earnestly with a lean, dark, heavily-bearded man in a
flowing white robe. Dumuzi, puffy-eyed and pale, was
also clearly making an effort at staying awake, though

his head was nodding. Across the way, Ninsun looked tired but game, and little Ruiz beside her showed no sign of fatigue whatever; his eyes were keen and gleaming still, and he was scrawling drawings by the dozen on the table napery, on dirty plates, on any flat surface that came to hand.

Vy-otin, still impeccable in his crisp and no doubt miserably uncomfortable New Dead clothes, came to Gilgamesh's side and said quietly, "Come, let us go for a little walk. The air is fresher outside, and I have things to tell you. Some advice for you, perhaps."

"Yes," Gilgamesh said. "Of course."

Rising, he bowed to Dumuzi—how costly that was to his spirit, bowing to Dumuzi!—and asked to be excused. The king feebly waved his hand. Gilgamesh and the Ice-Hunter chieftain went down the long high-vaulted aisle of the feasting-hall toward the distant doorway.

By early morning light everything had a red glow. Paradise hung low in the sky, as though it meant to touch the tips of Hell's mountains before noon.

Gilgamesh said, "How peaceful it is at this hour. Even in Hell, one finds peace now and then."

Vy-otin's wind-tanned face turned stern. His single eye was bright and fierce. "Peace? The only peace you'll find in Uruk is the peace of death. Get yourself out of this city, old friend, as quickly as you can."

"I have only just arrived, Vy-otin. It would be discourteous to leave so soon."

"Stay, then. But only if you're weary of your present life."

"Am I in danger, do you think?"

"Tell me this, and what you tell me will be secret, by our ancient oaths of loyalty: Have you come to Uruk to regain its throne, Gilgamesh?"

The Sumerian halted abruptly. "Do you think that's why I'm here?"

"Dumuzi does."

"Ah, does he? He was ever full of fear."

"And he will have you killed if you remain here," said Vy-otin.

"He will try to, yes. I would expect that of him. He won't find killing me that easy."

"He is king in this city, Gilgamesh."

"And I am Gilgamesh. I will stay as long as I please. No one of Sumerian blood will dare raise a hand against me."

"Not everyone in Uruk is Sumerian," Vy-otin said. "No more than one out of ten, perhaps. There are plenty here who'd like the glory of slaying the famous Gilgamesh. Dumuzi won't lack for assassins."

"Let them come. I can defend myself."

"Indeed. But it's true, then, that you are here to take his throne from him?"

"No!" cried Gilgamesh angrily. "Why does everyone assume that? I don't want his throne or any other. Believe me. I lost my appetite for power a long time ago, Vy-otin. That is the absolute truth. Believe me. Trust me in this. Trust me."

"That is three or four times in one breath that you ask me to believe you," Vy-otin said. "It has always seemed to me that only a man who doubts his own words would ask so passionately to be believed."

Gilgamesh, stung, gave the Ice-Hunter a furious glare. "You believe I'm lying to you, then?"

"I think you may be lying to yourself."

"Ah," Gilgamesh said. His hands trembled. He felt rage surging up and down his body—and subsiding. For a long moment he was silent. "Anyone else, Vy-otin, and I would have struck him down for those words. But not you. Not you." He grew quiet again; and then in a very low voice he said, "I will tell you the truth: I no longer know my own soul. I say to myself that I shun power, that I loathe ambition, that I have only scorn for those who scramble for preferment in the land of Hell. And yet—and yet—lately, Vy-otin, there

are times when I feel the old fires rising, when I see
that I am not as different from other men as I like to
think, that I too am driven by that vain urge to clamber
to the top of the mountain—" He shook his head. "The
truth is I am not at all sure of my own purposes any
longer. Perhaps Dumuzi does have something to fear
from me after all. But I tell you this, Vy-otin, that I had
another reason beside seizing the throne for coming to
Uruk."

"Which was?"

"I learned from a sorcerer in the city of Pompeii that
Enkidu might be here, my dearest friend, the brother
of my soul, from whom I have been apart far too long."

"I remember Enkidu, yes. The great hairy roistering
man, like a wild bull."

"I came here to find him. Nothing more than that.
That is the truth. I swear to you, that is the truth as I
believe it."

"Do you have any certain knowledge that he is in
Uruk?"

"Only a vision, inspired in me by the wizardry of a
black mage. But I think it is a sure vision."

"I wish you joy of the search, then, and all good
fortune," said Vy-otin, seizing both of Gilgamesh's hands
in his. "By the Horns of God, I will help you in any way
I can! But be careful in this city, Gilgamesh. Dumuzi is
sly and slippery, and he hates you more than you can
imagine. He would send you to Hell a thousand times
over if you were not already here."

"I will be wary of him," Gilgamesh said. "I know
Dumuzi's ways from the other world."

They walked on for a long while, neither of them
speaking. The glow of Paradise deepened and climbed
and the morning air grew warm. The houses and shops
of Uruk began to come to life.

After a time Gilgamesh said, "You have not told me,
friend, why you wear this absurd garb of yours."

"I have come to like it," said Vy-otin.

"Perhaps so. But it is an odd costume for one who was born at the beginning of time."

"Do I seem that old to you, Gilgamesh? Think of the Hairy Men, who look so near to apes. *They* are truly ancient. Who knows when they lived? It must have been long ago, for they are nothing like us, though they tell us they are our cousins. My time was only ten thousand years before yours. Or perhaps fifteen. I am a man like you."

"Ten thousand years is not a sneeze, Vy-otin. Your time was much before mine. About the Hairy Men I cannot tell you. But you come from a world I never knew, and it was very long before mine. Why, you lived before the Flood!"

"So you like to say." Vy-otin shrugged. "Perhaps so. I know nothing of your Flood. In my time the world was deep in ice. The sun was bright, the air was cool, the wind cut like a knife. The huge shaggy beasts roamed the land. It was the grandest of times, Gilgamesh. There were just a few of us, you know, but we were magnificent! You should have seen us, running to the hunt, moving between the dark leafless trees like ghosts! By the Horns, I wish you had been there with us! I wish I were still there now."

"You had made it all live again in your palace in the north," said Gilgamesh. "With the great tusks on the floor, and the furry skins on the walls, and your people gathered around you. Why did you leave that place?"

"You were king in this very city. Why did *you* leave?"

"How can I say? We move about in Hell without understanding anything. Perhaps I was slain, and awoke somewhere else, New Hell, perhaps, or some other city far away. I have no memory of that. The memory has been stolen from me."

"Not from me," said Vy-otin. "I was killed. A stupid brawl, some drunken Egyptians—I made the mistake of getting between them. I went to Reassignment and was gone a thousand years, or maybe two, and when I came back I was somewhere else far from any place I knew. Do you know the city of Dis, Gilgamesh?"

"Dis? No."

"On the far side of the Western Sea."

"I thought there was nothing on the far side."

"Hell is infinite, friend. I lived in Dis a long while, and then I crossed the sea, and now I live in Uruk. My people are scattered and no one remembers the palace in the north. Everything changes, Gilgamesh, and not for the better."

"And you decided to dress as New Dead in the city Dis, is that it? Why?"

"So they wouldn't know I was prehistoric. For that is what they call me, *prehistoric*, as though I were some kind of animal."

"They? Who?"

"The scholars," Vy-otin said. "The philosophers. The archaeologists. The dull prying boring New Dead folk. Let me tell you what happened, Gilgamesh. In Dis I fell in with a man of the New Dead, short and ugly, but strong, very strong, a musician: Wagner was his name. And his friend, who was called Nietzsche, if you can think of that as a name, and another one, a Jew like your Herod, but older, with a white beard. He was named Freud. We sat up drinking all night, the four of us, just as you and I have done here tonight, and when dawn came they asked me my name and I told them that it was Vy-otin, and that I was of the old Ice-Hunter folk, that I had lived in a cavern during the cold times and lost my eye in a battle with a tiger of the snows. And I told them a thing or two more of how my life had been. Suddenly this Wagner cried out, 'Wotan! You are Wotan!' And Nietzsche said, 'Yes, the very man.' And old Freud began to laugh, and said that it was quite possible, that there would be no question that myth had roots in reality and that I might well be the myth in the flesh."

"I have trouble understanding all this," said Gilgamesh.

"This Wotan, who also is called Odin, was a god, long after your time and mine, a one-eyed god of the cold northern lands. Those three, they were convinced that I was the original of this Odin, this Wotan, do you see? That I had become a legend, the wise one-eyed king of the snow-country, and over thousands of years the people of the north had come to worship me as the father of the gods."

"And if that is so? What is that to you?"

"Only that those three foolish men were dancing with joy, to know that they had the archetype of a great myth right there at the table with them. I said I am who I am, and they brushed me aside. Who I was was of no importance to them. They thought I was quaint, a primitive, a savage. A beast. I think they were amazed that I was capable of speech at all. It was what they wanted me to be that excited them: the archetype. That was what they called me, the archetype. I asked them what an archetype was and they spent hours explaining it to me, when one word would have done. It means the original. I am the original Wotan, if you would believe those three. All the great myths, they said, come down out of the prehistoric dawn of mankind, and here was a man out of that dawn sitting right there with them in the tavern, and it made them delirious with a fever of the mind. *Wotan!* Wagner cried, and he wanted to know if I had had any daughters. Freud, though, asked if I had sons. And Nietzsche wanted to know if I believed in God. Ah, those three, Gilgamesh! One had written operas about Wotan—you know what an opera is? Singing and noise, and costumes—and one had written philosophy, and the third one claimed to know more about the way of life in my times that I knew myself. They each saw their own reflections in me. And they asked me ten thousand thousand questions, and called others to see me, scientists and thinkers, and made such a fuss and a bother that I would have given them my other eye to let me alone. By the Mother, they drove me crazy! I fled from them finally. I am no god, Gilgamesh, and I am no archetype. I am only a simple man of the Pleistocene, and—"

"The what?"

"It is what the scholars call the epoch when I lived. When ice covered everything and the shaggy animals lived." Vy-otin laughed. "*Pleistocene*. You see? Their silly words infect me. *Prehistoric*. Do you think we thought of ourselves as prehistoric men? Mere grunting beast-men? That was not what we were. We had poetry. We had music. We had gods. *Aurignacians*, that is their name for us. It means nothing to me, that name. *Archetype*." Vy-otin shook his head. "I fled, and I hid from them. And now I call myself Henry Smith, and I pretend I am New Dead, so that the scholars can't annoy me any longer—the deep thinkers, the philosophers who would tell me what I am. Let them study someone else. Let someone else be prehistoric for them. Let someone else be an Aurignacian archetype."

"You don't *look* New Dead, Vy-otin."

"No?"

Gilgamesh smiled. "Not to me. To me you look like a one-eyed Ice-Hunter chieftain dressed up in New Dead clothing. A barbarian just like me. You look Pleistocene. You look—what is it?—Aurignacian. Definitely an Aurignacian. You look like an archetype, Vy-otin."

Vy-otin smiled also, but without much warmth. "Be that as it may," said the Ice-Hunter, sounding a little testy. "I will not play their game. And woe betide you, my friend, if you find yourself some day among a pack of philosophers. They'll give you no peace; and by the time they're done with you you won't be sure of your own name."

"Perhaps so," said Gilgamesh. "In the Outback once I met a poor crazy man of the New Dead who mistook me for a Cimmerian, one Conan by name, and wanted to worship me, or worse. What a sad fool he was! It was more of that archetype business, I think."

"They are all such fools, these modern men," Vy-otin said.

"But foolishness was not invented yesterday," said Gilgamesh. "We had our share of it in my time. Possibly so did you."

"Indeed," said Vy-otin.

Gilgamesh stared thoughtfully at his old friend, and suddenly found himself wondering about his own gods, Sky-father An and Enlil of the storms and Enki the compassionate and all the rest. Had they once been men themselves, and been turned by time and human gullibility into archetypes? If he wandered Hell long enough, would he find the originals of the gods of Sumer the Land gathered in some tavern in the City of Dis, telling each other tales of the good times before the Flood?

It was not something that he cared to think about.

In silence once more they walked back toward the feasting-hall.

Gilgamesh said, "So that was the advice you had for me? That I should keep away from philosophers?"

"That, and being on your guard against Dumuzi."

"Yes. Yes, that too. But I should fear the philosophers more, if your experience is to be any guide. Swords and daggers I can handle. But buzzing men of words? Pah! They madden me!" He saw Herod now, coming out of the feasting-hall looking much the worse for his night's carouse. The little Judaean leaned woozily against the intricate reliefs of the hall's dark facade and drew breath again and again, and rubbed his eyes, and ran the back of his hand across his lips. His white Sumerian robe was stained with wine, his skullcap was askew. "Do you see that one?" Gilgamesh asked. "He traveled with me from Pompeii. Words, all words! Give him an ear and he'll buzz at you for hours. No more courage than a flea. And yet he claims he was a king once too."

"Gilgamesh?" Herod called, shading his eyes in the

glare. "There you are, Gilgamesh!" Walking in an uncertain way, as if he expected his ankles to give way at any moment, he came toward the Sumerian and said, "Been looking for you. Can I talk with you?"

"Go on."

Herod glanced uneasily at Vy-otin. He said nothing.

"What is it?" Gilgamesh said.

Herod said, still uneasy, "I've managed to pick up some information this night. A few things that ought to interest you."

"Speak, then."

"Your mother's friend? The man who wants to paint you?"

With mounting impatience Gilgamesh said, "What about him?"

He goes by the name of Ruiz here. But do you know who he really is, Gilgamesh? He's *Picasso!*"

"Who?"

"Picasso. Pablo Picasso!" Herod, bloodshot and stubble-faced as he was, seemed almost apopletically animated. "He's hiding from some ex-wife or ex-girlfriend, that's why he's going under another name. But one of Dumuzi's courtiers told me who he actually is. Isn't that fantastic? Of course you'll let him paint you, won't you? He'll turn you into a masterpiece the likes of which Hell has never—" Herod paused. "You aren't impressed. No, you aren't, not at all. You don't even know who Picasso is, do you? Only the greatest New Dead artist who ever lived! I've studied these things, you know. New Dead art, music, architecture—"

"Is it not as I told you?" Gilgamesh said to Vy-otin. "An endless buzzing. A torrent of words."

"All right, you don't care," said Herod sulkily. "Let him paint you anyway. I thought you'd be glad to know who he was. But that wasn't the most important thing I wanted to tell you."

"Of course not. You save what is important for last. How considerate. Well, speak, now!"

But again Herod was still, and looked uncertainly toward Vy-otin.

"This man is my dear friend and brother Henry Smith," said Gilgamesh. "I have no secrets from him. Speak, Herod, or by Enlil I'll hurl you as far as—"

"Enkidu is in Uruk," Herod blurted hastily.

"*What?*"

"The big rough-looking man, the one you seek. Your friend, the one you call your brother. Isn't that Enkidu?"

"Yes, yes!"

"The courtier told me—an Assyrian, he is, name of Tukulti-Sharrukin, very drunk. Enkidu appeared here last week, straight from Reassignment—perhaps the week before, who can tell? Anyway, he showed up in Uruk and went right to the palace, because he had heard a rumor you were here, or had had a dream, or—well, whatever. He thought you might be at the palace. But of course you weren't. He kept asking, 'Where is Gilgamesh, where is Gilgamesh? He should be here.' Dumuzi became very upset. He didn't like the idea that you might be anywhere in the vicinity."

Gilgamesh felt a thundering of excitement within his breast. "And where is Enkidu now?"

"The Assyrian wasn't sure. Still here somewhere. A prisoner somewhere in Uruk, that's what he thinks. He promised to find out for me and let me know tomorrow."

"A prisoner?" Gilgamesh said.

"By the Tusk!" Vy-otin bellowed. "We'll find him! We'll free him! By the Mother! By the Horns of God! A prisoner? Enkidu? We'll tear down the walls of the place where he's kept!"

"Gently," Gilgamesh said, putting a hand to Vy-otin's shoulder. "Stay calm. There are ways and ways to go about this, Vy-otin, my friend."

"You said his name was Henry Smith," said Herod softly.

"Never mind that," Gilgamesh snapped. To the Ice-Hunter he said, "Haste would be wrong. First we must find out if Enkidu is truly here, and where he is, and who guards him. Then we approach Dumuzi, carefully, carefully. He is a weak man. You know how one must deal with weak men, Vy-otin. Firmly, directly, taking care not to send them into panic, for then they might do anything. If he slays Enkidu out of fear of me I could be another thousand years finding him again. So we must move slowly. Eh, Vy-otin? What do you say?"

"I think you are right," the Ice-Hunter said.

Gilgamesh turned to Herod. A pitiful little man, he thought. But a clever and a useful one.

"A good night's work," he said, smiling warmly. "Well done, King Herod! Well done!"

"This will be your mask," Picasso said. "Here. Here, put it on."

He moved about the big, ugly underground room like some chugging little machine, rearranging the heaps of clutter, kicking things out of his way, pushing them aside. Gilgamesh looked at the mask that had been thrust into his hands, puzzled. It was as ugly as everything else in this room: a massive bull-snout of papier-mache, with huge black nostrils and great jutting square teeth. There was one staring red eye along the left side and another on top, and short sharp curved horns made of wax protruded at peculiar angles. Clumps of thick crinkly black fur were glued to it everywhere. A sour smell rose from the thing. He was supposed to fasten it, apparently, by tying the cord that dangled from it around his throat.

"You want me to wear *this*?" Gilgamesh asked.

"Of course. Put it on, put it on! You will be my Minotaur!" Picasso waved his hands impatiently. "I made it today, especially for you."

Only a day had gone by since Dumuzi's feast. The mask, hideous though it was, was highly elaborate, surely the product of many days of work. "How is that possible?" Gilgamesh said. "That you could have made this so quickly?"

"Quickly?" Picasso spat. "*Cagarruta!* What do you mean, quickly? That mask took me more than an hour!"

"You are a sorcerer, then."

Picasso laughed, and went on clearing space in the studio.

Gilgamesh put the mask aside and wandered around the room, peering at the paintings stacked against every wall. They were horrifying. Here was a woman with two faces on one head, and it was impossible to tell whether she was looking straight at you or showing you the side of her head. Here was a picture that was all little boxes, that made your eyes jump around until you wanted to weep. Here were three monsters with mocking faces. Here, a woman with three breasts and teeth between her legs.

The shapes! The colors! No one had ever seen such scenes, not even in Hell. Surely there was some witchcraft being practiced here. In old Uruk, Gilgamesh thought, he would have ordered these paintings to be burned, and the painter to be driven from the city with whips. And yet he found himself beguiled despite himself by these works. He could sense the little man's powerful and playful mind behind them, and his formidable strength of will.

"Are you a sorcerer?" Gilgamesh asked.

"*Por favor.* The mask. Put it on."

"A demon of some sort?"

"Yes," said Picasso. "I am a demon. The mask, will you?"

"Show me the picture you have made of my mother."

"It is not finished. It keeps changing. Everything keeps changing. I will put the mask on you myself." Picasso crossed the room and snatched it up. But he was too short; Gilgamesh rose above him like a wall. "*Dios!* What a *cojonudo* monster you are! Is there any need for you to be so big?" He shoved the mask upward toward Gilgamesh's chin. "Put it on," he said. "*Ahora a trabajar*. It is time for us to work, now."

He said it quietly, but with great force. Gilgamesh slipped the mask over his face, nearly gagging at first at the stink of glue and other things. He tied it behind his neck. There were slits through which he could see, though not well. Picasso beckoned him to a place under the bright, intense electrical lights and showed him how he wanted him to stand, arms upraised as if ready to seize an onrushing enemy.

"All these other pictures, you have painted using models?" Gilgamesh said, his voice muffled and rumbling inside the mask. "They are things you have actually seen?"

"I see them in here," said Picasso, tapping his forehead. He lit a cigarette and stepped back, staring at Gilgamesh so unwaveringly that the power of that keen gaze felt like the pressure of knives against the Sumerian's skin. "Sometimes I use models, sometimes not. Lately more often than not, because of the difficulties. I tell myself that the models will help, though they do not, not very much. This place, this Hell, it is shit, you know? It is *mierda*, it is *cagada*, this whole place is *un gran cagadero*. But we do what we can, eh, King Gilgamesh? This is our life now. And it is better than the great darkness, the big *nada*, eh? Eh, king? Hold your arms up. The legs apart, a little. Thrust forward from the hips, as though you are going to stick it into her, eh, just as you stand there." He was painting already, swift broad strokes. Gilgamesh felt a quiver of uneasiness. What if this really was some kind of sorcery? What if Picasso could capture his soul and put it on that canvas, and meant to leave him locked up in it forever?

No, he told himself. Nonsense. The little man was just what he said he was, a painter. A very great painter, if Herod could be believed. There might be a demon inside him, but it was the same kind of demon that

once had been in Gilgamesh, that had driven him onward to go everywhere, see everything, learn everything, devour everything. I understand this man,
Gilgamesh thought. The difference is that in Hell I
have grown quiet and easy, and this one still burns with
the restlessness and the hunger.

"You were always a painter?" Gilgamesh asked.

"Always. From the cradle. Don't talk now, eh?"

How casually he orders a king around, Gilgamesh
thought. Just a little bald-headed man wearing only a
pair of ragged baggy shorts, sweat running down the
white hair of his chest, a cloud of cigarette smoke
surrounding him, and he has no fear of anyone, of
anything. It was not hard now to see how he had captured Ninsun. This man, Gilgamesh thought, could probably have any woman he wanted. Even a queen. Even
a goddess.

"Do you know?" Picasso said, after a long while. "I
think this time it will work. The painting holds. The
others, they turned in my hand. This one holds. It is
the charm of the Minotaur, I think. The bull rules in
Hell! I am a bull. You are a bull. We are in the arena all
the time. I could not become a matador, so I became a
bull. The same with you, I think. It makes no difference: the power of the bull is in both. In your city, did
they fight the bull?"

"I fought one once," Gilgamesh said. "Enkidu and I.
It was the Bull of Heaven, with the power of Father
Enlil in him. He was let loose in the city by the
priestess Inanna, and ran wild and slew a child; but
Enkidu and I, we caught him, we danced with him, we
played him, we fought him down. Enkidu wearied him
and I put the sword in him."

"Bravo!"

"But it angered the gods. They took Enkidu's life, by
way of revenge. He wasted away and died. That was
the first time I lost him; but I have lost him again and
again here in Hell. I must search for him forever. It is

our fate never to be together too long. That man is my brother; he is my other self. But I will find him again, and soon. They tell me he is in Uruk, a prisoner. You may have seen him, perhaps—he is as tall as I am, and—"

But Picasso did not seem to be listening any longer.

"The bullfight on Sunday," said Picasso. "How you will love it! We will sit together in the seat of honor, you and I. Sabartés has found a matador of whom I know nothing, but perhaps he will be good, eh? It is very important that the matador be good. Mere butchery, that is shameful. The *corrida* is art. Lift the arms, yes?"

He has not heard a word of what I said to him about Enkidu, thought Gilgamesh. His mind went elsewhere when I spoke of killing the Bull of Heaven. He hears only what he wants to hear. When he wants to hear, he listens, and when he wants to talk, he talks. But in his soul he is the only king. No matter, Gilgamesh thought. He is a great man. And Herod is probably right: he is a great painter. Even if all that he paints are monstrosities.

"It goes well," Picasso said. "The image holds true, you know? The power of the bull. No cubism today, no blue, no rose." His arm was moving so quickly now that it seemed to be not a single arm but three. His eyes were ablaze. Yet he gave no appearance of haste. His face was fixed, still, expressionless. His body, but for that unceasing arm, seemed totally relaxed. Gilgamesh ached to see what was on that canvas.

The mask was hot and stifling now. The Sumerian felt that if he kept it on much longer he would choke. But he dared not move. He was caught in the little man's spell. Sorcery, yes, definitely sorcery, Gilgamesh thought.

"Do you know why I paint?" Picasso asked. "I say each time, What can I learn of myself today that I don't know? The paintings teach me. When it isn't me any more who is talking, but the pictures I make, and when they escape and mock me, then I know I've achieved

my goal. Do you know? Do you understand? No? Ah, it
makes no difference. Here. Here, we can stop now.
Enough for today. It goes well. *Por dios*, it goes well!"

Gilgamesh lost no time working himself free of the
mask. He gasped for fresh air, but there was none. The
room was heavy with the scent of sweat.

"Is it finished?" he asked. He had no idea how long
he had posed, whether it was ten minutes or half a day.

"For now," said Picasso. "Here: look."

He swung the easel around. Gilgamesh stared.

What had he expected to see? The picture of a tall
muscular man with a bull's hideous face, gaping mouth,
swollen tongue, wild red eyes looking in different directions, the face that was on the mask. But there were
two naked men in the picture, crouched face to face
like wrestlers poised to spring. One was huge, black-
bearded, with powerful commanding features. Gilgamesh
recognized himself in that portrait immediately: it was a
remarkable likeness. The other man was much shorter,
stocky, wide-shouldered, deep-chested. Picasso himself, plainly. But his face could not be seen. It was the
short man who was wearing the mask of the bull.

Three assassins were waiting for him when he stepped
out into the Street of the Tanners and Dyers. Gilgamesh
was neither surprised nor alarmed. They were so obviously lying in wait for him that he hardly needed them
to draw their weapons to know what they were up to.

They were disguised, more or less, as Uruk police, in
ill-fitting khaki uniforms badly stained below the arms
with sweat. One, with a big blunt nose and a general
reek of garlic about him, might have been a Hittite, and
the other two were New Dead, with that strange yellow
hair that some of them had, and pathetic straggly beards
and mustaches. They had guns.

Gilgamesh wasted no time. He struck one of the New
Dead across the throat with the edge of his hand and
sent him reeling into a narrow alleyway, where he fell
face forward and lay twitching and croaking and puking.

On the backswing Gilgamesh rammed his elbow hard into the Hittite's conspicuous nose, and at the same time he caught the other New Dead by the wrist and twisted the pistol free of his grasp, kicking it across the street.

The New Dead yelped and took off at full speed, arms flailing wildly in the air. Gilgamesh drew his dagger and turned to the Hittite, who had both hands clapped to his face. Blood was pouring out between his fingers.

He touched the tip of his dagger to the Hittite's belly and said, "Who sent you?"

"You broke my nose!"

"Very likely. Next time don't push it into my elbow that way." The Sumerian said, with a little prod of the dagger, "Do you have a name?"

"Tudhaliyas."

"That's not a name, it's a belch. What are you, a Hittite?"

Tudhaliyas, looking miserable, nodded. The blood was flowing a little less copiously now.

"Who do you work for, Hittite?"

"The municipality of Uruk," said the man sullenly. "Department of Weights and Measures."

"Were you here to weigh me, or to measure me?"

"I was on my way to the tavern with my friends when you attacked us."

"Yes. I often attack strangers in the street, especially in groups of three. Who sent you after me?"

"It would be worth my life to say."

"It will be worth your life to keep silent," said Gilgamesh, prodding a little harder. "One shove of this and I'll send you on your way to Reassignment. But you won't get there quickly. It takes a long time to die of a slash in the guts."

"Ur-ninmarka sent me," the Hittite murmured.

"Who?"

"The royal arch-vizier."

"Ah. I remember. Dumuzi's right hand. And who were you supposed to kill?"

"G-G—G-Gil—"

"Say it."

"Gilgamesh."

"And who is he?"

"The former k-king."

"Am I Gilgamesh?"

"Yes."

"I am the man you were told to kill?"

"Yes. Yes. Make it quick, Gilgamesh! In the heart, not the belly!"

"It wouldn't be worth the trouble of having to clean my blade of you afterward," said Gilgamesh. "I will be merciful. You'll live to belch some more."

"A thousand blessings! A million blessings!"

Gilgamesh scowled. "Enough. Get away from me. Show me how well you can run. Take your puking friend over there with you. I will forget this entire encounter. I remember nothing of you and I know nothing of who it was who sent you upon me. You didn't tell me a thing. You understand? Yes, I think you do. Go, now. Go!"

They ran very capably indeed. Gilgamesh leaned against the wall of Picasso's house and watched until they were out of sight. A nuisance, he thought, being waylaid in the street like that. Dumuzi should show more imagination. Persuade some demons to have the pavement swallow me up, or drop a cauldron of burning oil on me from the rooftops, or some such.

He looked around warily to see if anyone else lay in ambush for him. There was a faint ectoplasmic shimmer on the building across the way, as though some diabolic entity were passing through the walls, but there was nothing unusual about that. Otherwise all seemed well. Briskly Gilgamesh walked to the end of the street, turned left into a street calling itself the Street of Camels, and went onward via the Corridor of Sighs and the

Place of Whispers to the great plaza where he was lodged.

Herod was there, bubbling with news.

"Your friend is indeed a prisoner in Uruk," he said at once. "We've found out where he's being kept."

Gilgamesh's eyes widened. "Where is he?" he demanded. "What have they done to him? Who told you?"

"Tukulti-Sharrukin's our source, the Assyrian courtier who likes to drink too much. Your friend is fine. The Assyrian says Enkidu hasn't been harmed in any way. He's being held at a place called the House of Dust and Darkness on the north side of the city. The House of Dust and Darkness! Isn't that a fine cherry name?"

"You idiot," Gilgamesh said, barely containing his anger.

Herod backed away in alarm. "What's wrong?"

"Your Assyrian is playing jokes with you, fool. Any man of the Two Rivers would know what the House of Dust and Darkness is. It's simply the name we used in the old days of Sumer for the place where dead people go. Don't you see, we're *all* in the House of Dust and Darkness!"

"No," Herod said, edging still farther back as Gilgamesh made menacing gestures. "I don't know anything about Sumer, but that's what the building is actually called. I've seen it. The name's written right over the front porch in plain English. It's just a jail, Gilgamesh. It's Dumuzi's special upscale jail for his political prisoners, very nice, very comfortable. It looks like a hotel."

"You've seen it, you say?"

"Tukulti-Sharrukin took me there."

"And Enkidu? You saw him?"

"No. I didn't go inside. It's not *that* much like a hotel. But Tukulti-Sharrukin says—"

"Who is this Assyrian? Why do you have such faith in what he tells you?"

"Trust me. He hates Dumuzi—something about a

business deal that went sour, a real screwing, he and
the king going partners on a land-development scheme
and the king goniffing up the profits. He'll do anything
to stick it to Dumuzi now. He told me all about it the
night of the feast. He and I hit it off like *this*, Gilgamesh,
just like *this*. He's a member of the tribe, you know."

"He's what?"

"A Jew. Like me."

Gilgamesh frowned. "I thought he was an Assyrian."

"An Assyrian Jew. His grandfather was Assyrian am-
bassador to Israel in King David's time and fell in love
with one of David's nieces, and so he had to convert in
order to marry her. It must have been one devil of a
scandal, a royal niece not only marrying a *goy* but an
Assyrian, yet. David wanted to murder him, but he had
diplomatic immunity, so the king had him declared
persona non grata and he was sent home to Nineveh,
but somehow he took her with him and then the family
stayed kosher after he got back to Assyria. You could
have knocked me over with a straw when he said he
was a Yid, because he's got that mean Assyrian face
with the nose coming right out of the forehead, you
know, and the peculiar curly beard they all wear, but
when you listen for a little while to the way he speaks
you won't have any doubt that he's—"

"When I listen for a little while to the way *you*
speak," said Gilgamesh, "I feel like strangling you.
Can't any of you Jews ever keep to the point? I don't
care who this ridiculous tribesman of yours did or did
not marry. What I want to know is, will he help us to
free Enkidu or won't he?"

"Don't be an anti-Semite, Gilgamesh. It doesn't look
good on you. Tukulti-Sharrukin promises to do what he
can for us. He knows the guy who runs the main
computer at the House of Dust and Darkness. He'll try
to bugger up the software so that Enkidu's name gets
dropped from the prisoner roster, and maybe then we
can slip him out the back way. But no guarantees. It

isn't going to be easy. We'll know in a day or two whether it's going to work out. I'm doing my best for you, you know."

Gilgamesh closed his eyes and breathed deeply. Herod was a colossal pain in the fundament, but he did get things done.

"All right. Forgive me my impatience, Herod."

"I love it when you apologize. A minute ago you had that I-suffer-no-fools-gladly gleam in your eye and I thought you were going to knock me from here to New Hell."

"Why *should* I suffer fools gladly?"

"Right. But I'm not all that much of a fool." Herod grinned. "Let's get on to other things. You know that Dumuzi has a contract out on you, don't you?"

"A contract?" said Gilgamesh, baffled again.

"Zeus! Where did you learn your English? Dumuzi wants to have you killed, is what I'm saying. Tukulti-Sharrukin told me that too. Dumuzi's frightened shitless that you're going to make a grab for power here, and so—"

"Yes, I know. Three buffoons tried to jump me as I was leaving Picasso's. One of them admitted that he was working for Dumuzi."

"You kill them?"

"I just damaged them a little. They're probably halfway to Pompeii by now, but I suppose there'll be others. I'll lose no sleep over it. Where's Sulla?"

"At the baths, trying to sober himself up. He and I have an audience with the king in a little while. Sulla wants to set up a trade deal, swap Dumuzi a couple dozen of his spare necromancers and thaumaturges and shamans for a few barrels of the diamonds and rubies and emeralds that he thinks Dumuzi possesses by the ton."

"Even a fool could see there is no great abundance of diamonds and rubies in this city."

"You tell Sulla that. I'm just an employee. The Devil

has put it into him that this city is overflowing with precious gems, and you know how he salivates for precious gems. He'd sell his sister for six pounds of sapphires. *Meshuggenah. Goyishe kup.* Well, he'll find out. How did things go with you and Picasso?"

"He made me wear a strange mask, a bull's face. But when he painted me, he was in the painting too, and the mask was on him. I could not understand that, Herod."

"It's art. Don't try to understand it."

"But—"

"Trust me. The man's a genius. Have faith in him. He'll paint a masterpiece, and who gives a crap which one of you has the mask? But you don't understand these things, do you, Gilgamesh? You were great stuff in your time, they all tell me, a terrific warrior and a splendid civil engineer, even, but you do have your limits. After all, you have a *goyishe kup* too. Although I have to admit you manage all right, considering your handicap."

"You use too many strange words. *Goyishe kup?*"

"It means you have Gentile brains."

"Gentile?"

"It means not Jewish. Don't be offended. You know how much I admire you. Do you and Picasso get along all right?"

"We find each other amusing. He has invited me to sit with him at the bullfight on Sunday."

"Yes, the bullfight. His grand passion, watching skinny Spaniards stick swords into big angry animals. Another *meshuggenah*, Picasso. Him and his bullfights. A genius, but a *meshuggenah*."

"And a *goyishe kup?*" Gilgamesh asked.

Herod looked startled. "Him? Well, I suppose so. I suppose. But a genius, all the same. At least he makes great paintings out of his bullfights. And everyone's entitled to a hobby of some sort, I guess. An obsession, even."

"And what is yours?" said the Sumerian.

Herod winked. "Surviving."

It was one of those nights that went by in a moment, in the blink of an eye. That often happened in Hell; they were balanced by the days that seemed to last a week or two, or a month. Gilgamesh had been here so long that he scarcely minded Hell's little irregularities. He could remember clearly enough how it had been on Earth, the days in succession coming around at predictable intervals, but that seemed unreal to him now and woefully oppressive. Sleep meant little here, meals were unimportant; why should all the days be the same length? What did it matter?

Now, by common consent, it was Sunday. The day of the bullfight. The calendar too fluttered and slid about, no rhyme, no reason. But the bullfight was to be held on Sunday, and the bullfight was today, and therefore today was Sunday. Tomorrow might be Thursday. What did it matter? What did it matter? Today was the day he would be reunited with Enkidu, if all went well. That was what mattered.

The night, brief as it was, had been enlivened by a second attempt on Gilgamesh's life. Nothing so crude as a team of thugs, this time, but it was simpleminded all the same, the old snake-in-the-ventilating-shaft routine. Gilgamesh heard slitherings in the wall. The grille, he discovered, had been loosened, probably by the maids who had come in to turn down the bed. He pushed it open and stood to one side, sword at the ready. The snake was a fine one, glossy black with brilliant red markings and eyes like yellow fire. Its fangs had the sheen of chrome steel. He regretted having to chop it in two; but what alternative, he wondered, did he have? Trap it in a bedsheet and call room service to take it away?

The same motor-chariots that had transported Gilgamesh and his companions to the royal feasting-hall a few

nights before were waiting out front to bring them to
the stadium that morning. The bullfight, evidently, was
the event of the season in Uruk. Half the city was
going, judging by the number of cars traveling in the
direction of the arena.

Herod rode with Gilgamesh. The driver was a
Sumerian, who genuflected before Gilgamesh with ob-
vious awe: no assassin, not this one, unless he was one
of the best actors in Hell.

The bullfight was being held well outside the city, in
the sandy hill country to the east. The day was hot and
overcast. Some long-fanged bat-winged demon-creatures,
purple and red and green, soared lazily in the hazy sky.

"It's all arranged," said Herod in a low voice, leaning
toward Gilgamesh. They were near the stadium now.
Gilgamesh could see it, tier upon stone tier rising from
the flat desert. "Tukulti-Sharrukin will try to spring
Enkidu from the House of Dust and Darkness just as
the bullfight's getting started. We'll have half a dozen of
Sulla's men posted nearby, with three of the Land
Rovers. Everybody knows what to do. When Enkidu
comes out of the jail building, he'll get into one of the
Rovers and all three will take off in different directions,
but they'll all head out this way."

"And Vy-otin?"

"Smith, you mean?"

"Smith, yes!"

"He'll be waiting just outside the stadium, the way
you wanted. When the Land Rovers show up, Smith
will meet the one with Enkidu and bring him in, and
lead him to the box where you and Picasso will be
sitting, which is right next to the royal box. Dumuzi
will have a stroke when he sees him."

"If not when he sees him, then when I embrace him
before the entire town," Gilgamesh said. "The hero
Gilgamesh reunited with his beloved Enkidu! What can
Dumuzi say? What can he do? Everyone will be cheer-
ing. And after the bullfight—"

"Yes?" Herod said. "After the bullfight, what?"

"I will pay a call on King Dumuzi," said Gilgamesh. "I will speak to him about the unfortunate error of judgment that led his officials to imprison my friend. I will do it very politely. Perhaps I will speak to him also about the state of law and order in the streets of his city, and about proper maintenance of the ventilating systems of his hostelry here. But that will be afterward. First we will enjoy the pleasure of the bullfight, eh?"

"Yes," said Herod glumly. "First the bullfight."

"You don't look pleased."

"I never even liked to go to the gladiators," the Judaean said. "And they deserved what they did to each other. But a poor dumb innocent bull? All that bleeding, all that pain?"

"Fighting bulls is an art," Gilgamesh replied. "Your great genius Picasso the painter told me so himself. And you are a man of culture, Herod. Think of it as a cultural experience."

"I'm a Jewish liberal, Gilgamesh. I'm not supposed to enjoy cruelty to animals."

"A Jewish what?"

"Never mind," said Herod.

The chariot pulled up in a holding area in front of the stadium. At close range the circular structure was enormous, a true Roman coliseum on the grand scale, five or perhaps six levels high. The topmost tier was partly in ruins, many of its great stone arches shattered; but the rest of the building seemed intact and splendid. There were throngs of people in colorful holiday garb walking around on every level.

As he got out of the car Gilgamesh caught sight of Vy-otin, in slacks and a loose short-sleeved shirt, waving to him from a point near one of the ticket booths. The long-legged Ice-Hunter chieftain stood out clearly above the short, square-hewn, largely Sumerian crowd all about him.

He came over at once. "There's trouble," he said.

"Enkidu?"

"You," Vy-otin said. "One of my people overheard something in a washroom. Dumuzi's putting snipers on the top tier. When things start getting exciting and everybody's yelling, they're going to open fire on Picasso's box. The prime target is you, but they're likely to hit Picasso too, and your mother, and anyone else who's close by. You've got to get out of here."

"No. Impossible."

"Are you crazy? How are you going to guard yourself against shots from the sky? Someone your size will be the easiest target in the world."

"How many men do you have here?" Gilgamesh asked.

"Nine."

"That should be plenty. Send them up on top to take out the snipers."

"There'll still be a risk that—"

"Yes. Maybe there will. Where's your warlike spirit, Vy-otin? Have you truly become Henry Smith? Dumuzi can't have put a hundred sharpshooters up there. There'll be two or three, is my guess. Five at most. You'll have plenty of time to find them. They'll be easy enough to spot. They won't be Sumerian, and they'll be looking nervous, and they'll have rifles or some other cowardly New Dead armament. Your men will locate them one by one and push them off the edge. No problem."

Vy-otin nodded. "Right," he said. "See you later."

Picasso closed his eyes and let memory come seeping back: the old life, the thyme-scented tang of dry Mediterranean air in the summer, the heat, the crowds, the noise. If he didn't look, he could almost make himself believe he was eight or nine years old, sitting beside his tall sandy-bearded father in the arena at Malaga again where the bullfights were the finest and most elegantly conducted in the world. Sketching, always sketching, even then, the picador on his little bony blindfolded old horse, the haughty matador, the major of the city in his

grand box. Or he could think this was the bull-ring of
La Coruña, or the one at Barcelona, or even the one at
Arles in southern France, an old Roman stadium just
like this one, where he would go every year when he
was old, with his wife Jacqueline, with his son Paul,
with Sabartés.

Well, all that was long ago in another world. This was
Hell, and the sky was murky and the air was thick and
acrid, and the crowd around him was chattering in
English, in Greek, in some Mesopotamian babble, in
just about everything but good honest Spanish. In the
midst of the hubbub he sat motionless, waiting, hands
at his sides, silent, solitary. There might well have been
no one else around him. He was aware that the priestess-
woman Ninsun was beside him, more splendid than
ever in a robe of deep purple shot through with threads
of gold, and that her giant son the warrior Gilgamesh
sat beside him also, and the faithful Sabartés, and the
little Jewish Roman man, Herod, and the other Roman,
the fat old dictator, Sulla. But all those people had
become mere wraiths to him now. As he waited for the
corrida to begin he saw only the ring, and the gate
behind which the bulls were kept, and the shadows cast
by the contest that was to come.

"It will not be long now, Don Pablo," Sabartés murmured. "We have been waiting for the king. But you
see, he is in his box now, *el rey*." Sabartés gestured
toward his left, to the royal box just alongside theirs.
With a flicker of his eye Picasso saw the foolish-looking
king waving and smiling to the crowd, while his courtiers made gestures instructing everyone to cheer. He
nodded. One must wait for the king to arrive, yes,
he supposed. But he did not want to wait any longer.
He was formally dressed, a dark blue business suit, a
white shirt, even a necktie: the *corrida* was a serious
matter, it demanded respect. But in this humidity he
was far from comfortable. Once the fight started he
would no longer notice the weather or the pinching at

his throat or the sweaty stickiness along his back. Just
let it start soon, he thought. Let it start soon.

What was this? Some new commotion close at hand?

The huge Sumerian was up and prancing about and
shouting. "Enkidu! Enkidu!"

"Gilgamesh!" bellowed a newcomer, just as enormous but twice as frightful, shouldering his way into
the box. "My own true brother! My friend!"

This one was a Sumerian too, by the look of him. But
he was strange and shaggy, almost like a beast, with a
fiery, smouldering look about him and black hair tumbling into his eyes and a beard so dense it hid most of
his face. Another Minotaur, Picasso thought: an even
truer one than the first. They were embracing like two
mountains now, Gilgamesh and this other, this Enkidu.
Gilgamesh was like a child in his excitement. Now he
clapped Enkidu on the back with a blow that would
have felled a dragon, and now he dragged him over to
meet Ninsun, before whom Enkidu fell in a pose of
utter devotion, kneeling and kissing her hem, and now
Gilgamesh was nodding toward Dumuzi's box and both
men began to laugh. "And this," said Gilgamesh, "this
is the painter Picasso, who is a great genius. He paints
like a demon. Maybe he *is* a demon. But he is very
great. This is his bullfight, today."

"This little man? He will fight bulls?"

"He will watch," Gilgamesh said. "He loves that
more than anything, except, I think, to paint: to watch
the bulls being fought. As was done in his homeland."

"And tomorrow," said Picasso, "I will paint you, wild
one. But that will be tomorrow. Now the bulls." Out of
the corner of his mouth he said to Sabartés, "Well? Do
we ever commence?"

"Indeed, Don Pablo. Now. Now."

There came a great flourish of trumpets. And then
the grand entry procession began, the *cuadrillas* coming forth led by a pair of mounted *alguaciles* in eye-
dazzling costumes. Everyone crossing the great arena,

the banderilleros, the picadors riding hell-horses, and then finally the matador, this Blanco y Velez, this Spaniard of the time of Charles IV.

Sabartés had organized everything very well, Picasso thought. It all looked as it was supposed to look. The men, the subordinates, moved with dignity and grace. They understood the grandeur of the moment. And the matador showed promise. He held himself well. He was a little thicker through the middle than Picasso was expecting—perhaps he was out of shape, or maybe in the time of Charles IV the style had been different, matadors had not been so slender—but his costume was right, the skintight silken trousers, the richly embroidered jacket and waistcoat of satin embroidered in gold and silver, the hat, the cape, the linen lace shirtwaist.

The procession halted before the two boxes of honor. The matador saluted the king, and then Picasso, who was the president of the bullfight today. The king, who had been staring at the newly arrived Enkidu as though he were some sort of demon that had materialized in Picasso's box, and whose face now was as dour and foul as bile, acknowledged the salute with an offhand flick of his hand that Picasso found infuriating in its discourtesy. *"Puerco,"* he muttered. *"Hijo de puta."*

Then Picasso rose. As president he carried the keys to the bull-pens. With a grand swing of his arm he tossed them out to one of the *alguaciles*, who caught them nicely and rode over to release the first bull.

"And so we commence," said Picasso quietly to Sabartés. *"Al fin,* we commence."

He felt himself settling into the inviolable sphere of concentration that always enveloped him at the bullfight. In a moment he would feel as though he were the only one in the stadium.

The bull came galloping forth.

Madre de dios! What a horror! That was no bull! That was an evil monster!

Sabartés had told him what to expect, but he had

never quite grasped it, apparently. This could have been something out of one of his own paintings. The creature had six many-jointed legs, like some giant insect, and two rows of terrible spines on its back that dripped a nasty fluid, and great flopping ears. Its skin was green with purple blotches, and like a lizard's. There were horns, short and curved and sharp and very much like a bull's, but otherwise this was pure hell-creature.

Picasso shot a venomous look at Sabartés. "What have you done? You call that a bull?"

"We are in Hell, Pablo," said Sabartés wearily. "They do not send bulls to Hell, only human beings. But this will do. It is much like a bull, in its way."

"*Chingada!*" Picasso said, and spat.

But they were making a brave attempt down in the arena. The banderilleros were dancing around the bull, striving to plant their little lances in the beast's neck, and sometimes succeeding. The hell-bull, maddened, charged this way and that, going for the horses of the picadors, who warded it off with thrusts of their pikes. Picasso could see that these were experienced men out there, who knew what they were doing and were doing their best, though plainly the hell-bull puzzled them. They were trying to wear it down to make it ready for the Hour of Truth, and by and large they were achieving that. Picasso felt the bullfight slip around him like a cloak. He was wholly engulfed in it now. He saw nothing else but the bull and the men in the ring.

Then he looked toward the matador, waiting his moment to one side, and everything turned sour.

The matador was frightened. You could see it in his nostrils, you could see it in the angle of his chin. Perhaps he had been a master of his art back there in the time of Charles IV, but he had never fought anything like this thing, and he was not going to do it well. That was plain. He was not going to do it well.

The trumpets sounded. It was the moment.

Blanco y Velez came forward, holding out the *muleta*, the little red silk cape, and the *capote*, the big work cape. But he moved stiffly, and it was the wrong stiffness, the stiffness of fear rather than the stiffness of courage. The picadors and the banderilleros saw it, and instead of leaving the ring they withdrew to one side, exchanging uneasy glances. Picasso saw it. The hell-bull saw it. The matador's moves were awkward and hesitant. He didn't seem to know how to use his capes— had the art not progressed that far, in the time of Charles IV?—and he had no grace and he took quick, mincing steps. He led the bull around and around, working closer and closer to him, but that should have been beautiful and it was merely depressing.

"No," Picasso said under his breath. "Get him out of there!"

"He is our only matador, Pablo," Sabartés said.

"He will die. And he will die stupidly."

"He looked better when I saw him yesterday. But that was with a heifer."

Picasso groaned. "He will die now. Look."

There had been a shift of equilibrium in the ring. Blasco y Velez was no longer working the bull; the bull was working Blasco y Velez. Round and round, round and round—the bull picking up speed—the picadors trying now to intervene, Blasco y Velez backing away but now finally putting a brave face on things, trying a desperate *veronica*, a *farol*, a *mariposa*, a *serpentina*, a *media-veronica*—yes, yes, he knew his work, he understood the art, except that he was trying to do everything at once, and where was his control, where was his stillness, where was his art? The bull, passing him, snarled and nipped him in the shoulder. Blood flowed. Blasco y Velez jumped back and went for his sword— forbidden, to use the sword in mere self-defense—but the bull knocked it from his grasp with a contemptuous whirl, and swung on past, throwing down a picador's horse and goring it, and coming back again toward the matador—

"No!" came a tremendous roar from Gilgamesh's shaggy friend, the huge Enkidu.

And then the new Sumerian giant leaped from the stone bench and vaulted down into the arena.

"*Enkidu!*" Gilgamesh cried.

Picasso gasped. This was becoming crazy, now. This was turning into a nightmare. The big Sumerian picked the hapless matador up and tossed him aside to safety as though he were a doll. Then he came toward the bull, caught it by the double rows of spines, swung himself up easily onto the beast's back, and began to throttle it.

"No, no, no!" Picasso muttered. "Clown! Butcher! Sabartés, stop this idiocy! What is he doing? *Riding* the bull? *Strangling* the bull?" Tears of rage crowded into his eyes. His first *corrida* in who knew how long, and a dreadful one, and now it was dissolving into absurd chaos. He stood on his seat, bellowing. "Butchery! Madness! For shame! For shame!"

Enkidu was in trouble. He was on the bull, but in another moment the bull was going to roll over and kill him, or hurl him loose and fall upon him with its hooves. That was the one thing Gilgamesh saw, and nothing else mattered to him. To have won him back once more, and then to lose him again in this craziness of a bullfight—no, no, it could not be.

It was like that time when the Bull of Heaven was loose in old Uruk, and Enkidu had mounted it and seized it by its horns and tried to force it to the ground. It had taken both of them to slay the bull that time. It would again.

He snatched up his sword. Herod saw him and grabbed at his arm, crying, "Gilgamesh! No! Don't go our there!" The Sumerian swatted him aside and clambered down over the edge of the box. Enkidu, holding on with difficulty atop the plunging, bucking monster, grinned to him.

The whole stadium seemed to be going insane.

People were up, milling about, screaming. Fist-fights were breaking out everywhere. Dumuzi was on his feet, eyes wild, face purple, making frantic gestures. Glancing upward, Gilgamesh had a quick glimpse of struggling figures outlined against the rim of the arena. Dumuzi's snipers, fighting with Vy-otin's men? And farther up, a flock of demon-birds circled in the sky, ghastly things with gaping beaks and long shimmering wings.

The bull, lurching from side to side, was trying to shake Enkidu free. Gilgamesh rushed forward and took a spew of the bull's sweat in his face. It burned like acid. He drew his sword, but the bull backed out of range, and twisted itself so violently that Enkidu nearly was flung from its back.

Yet he showed no fear at all. He held tight, thighs gripping the bull's back just in front of the spines, and took a firm hold on the thing's diabolical horns. With all his great strength he fought to force the bull's head downward.

"Strike, brother, strike!" Enkidu called.

But it was too soon. The bull had plenty of fight left in him. It whirled wildly around, and the scaly skin of its flank caught Gilgamesh across the ribs and drew blood. It leaped and bucked, leaped and bucked, slamming its hooves against the ground. Enkidu flailed about like a pennant flapping in the breeze. He seemed about to lose his grip; then he called out in his most confident tone and rose again, rearing high above the creature's razor-sharp back. He regained his grip on the horns and twisted, and the bull yielded and weakened, lowering its head, turning so that the nape of its neck was toward Gilgamesh.

"Strike!" Enkidu called again.

And this time Gilgamesh drove the blade home.

He felt a quivering, a shudder, a powerful movement within the creature. It seemed to resist its death a long moment; but the blow had been true, and suddenly its legs collapsed. Gilgamesh extended a hand toward Enkidu as he sprang free of it and came down beside him.

"Ah, brother," Enkidu said. "Like the old days, yes?"

Gilgamesh nodded. He looked outward. On every level of the stadium there was frenzy, now. Gilgamesh was amazed to see that Dumuzi had left the royal box and had leaped into Picasso's. As though fearing for his own safety, the king had one arm tight around Ninsun's waist and held Picasso with the other arm around his throat, and was dragging them from the box, struggling with his two hostages toward the exit.

"Your mother," Enkidu said. "And your little painter."

"Yes. Come on."

They rushed back toward the stands. But suddenly Ninsun twisted about and reached toward one of the guards in the box adjoining. When she swung around again a dagger was in her hand. Dumuzi attempted to shove Picasso against it, but as Gilgamesh stared in amazement his mother pivoted away with the agility of a warrior, reached around, drove the dagger into Dumuzi's side. In the same instant Sulla, coming from the rear, put his sword through the king's middle. Dumuzi fell and was swept under foot. Picasso stood unmoving, as if lost in a dream. Ninsun looked at the hand that still held the dagger as though she had never seen her hand before.

"Up here!" Vy-otin called to Gilgamesh, not from Picasso's box but from the royal one. "Quickly!"

The Ice-Hunter extended a hand. Gilgamesh jumped upward beside him.

"On the royal bench. Fast!"

"What—"

"Dumuzi's dead. He panicked when the snipers didn't

open fire, and tried to escape with Picasso and your mother as hostages, and—"

"Yes. I saw it."

"You're the king here now. Get up there and act like one."

"King?" Gilgamesh said, struggling to comprehend.

Vy-otin shoved him. He caught hold of the edge of the royal bench and pulled himself up on it, and turned and looked upward toward the many tiers of the arena. The sky had darkened and was full of screeching demons. Surging mobs were boiling back and forth. Everyone seemed to have gone berserk.

He extended his arms. "People of Uruk!" he cried, in a voice like an erupting volcano. "Hear me! I am Gilgamesh! Hear me!"

"Gilgamesh!" came the sudden answering roar. "Gilgamesh the King! Gilgamesh! Gilgamesh!"

"You're doing fine," Vy-otin said.

He felt figures close around him. Herod, Sulla, Vy-otin—Enkidu—Ninsun—Picasso—

He turned to them.

"By Enlil, I swear to you I did not come here to make myself king," he said angrily.

"We understand that," said Herod.

"Of course," said Sulla.

"Keep waving your arms," said Vy-otin. "They're starting to settle down. Just tell them to take their seats and stay calm."

"Gilgamesh!" came the great roar again. "Gilgamesh the King!"

"You see?" Vy-otin said. "You're doing just fine, your majesty. Just fine."

Yes. Yes. He felt the rush of oncoming power now, that sense of strength and righteous force that the word *majesty* summed up. Perhaps he had not come here to make himself king, but now he was king all the same, king of Uruk in Hell as once he had been king of Uruk in Sumer the Land. He gestured and felt the crowd in his hand. "People of Uruk! I am your king! Take your seats! All of you, take your seats!"

They were obeying now. The stadium grew quiet.

Enkidu said, "Have them send out another of those bulls. You and I will fight it, Gilgamesh. We'll fight all the bulls they can throw at us. Yes? Yes?"

Gilgamesh glanced at Picasso. "What do you say? Shall we continue the bullfight?"

"Ah, *companero*, that is no way to fight a bull, the way you two do it. It is not what I came here to see, this jumping on the bull's back." Then the little man laughed. "But that is no bull, eh, King Gilgamesh? So why must it be fought according to the Spanish way? Go. Go. Commence your reign with a *corrida* in the Uruk style. Show us what you can do, my friend. I will sketch you as you work."

Gilgamesh nodded. To Herod he said quietly, "Get the late king out of here, will you? And have the arch-vizier and the rest of the court officials rounded up." With a gesture to Enkidu to accompany him he leaped down again into the bull-ring. He shouted to the *aguaciles* across the way and the gate opened and a second hell-bull came charging forth. Calmly the new king of Uruk waited for it with Enkidu at his side.

AN APPROPRIATE HELL*

Diana L. Paxson

Tim Scanlan was trying to decide whether to twist the harper's neck first, or to snap the harp's strings. Overtones whined as the harper struggled to retune; he muttered to himself as a peg slipped. This was the sixth time the harp had gone sour since that sorry fellow, Lightborn, had told Scanlan to wait here. It was like listening to a beautiful woman with the voice of a shrew.

To damage a clarsach would be nearly a sacrilegious thing, but this harper had boasted how he played for the great Elizabeth while her officers hanged his fellows and burned their harps. The harper was in Hell for serving an English queen, and that man Lightborn was here because he had killed an English king. But Tim Scanlan had got his death fighting for Ireland, so why the bloody Jesus was *he* here?

Perhaps the woman he had come to see could answer him.

They had said she was looking for men. He had heard it in the pub in New Hell to which his need for some human contact had drawn him. But he'd not the funds to drink himself into forgetfulness, and the few drinks

*Irish legal phrase. Copyright © 1988 by Diana L. Paxson

he'd been able to cadge had not even begun to dull his
bewilderment. Only one thing made any sense. Queen
Maeve of Connaught was fighting, and she wanted men.

"You there—how long must I be waiting?" Anxiety
sharpened his tone.

As if in response, a harpstring snapped, drawing blood
as the bronze wire flicked across the harper's hand.
The harper glared and Scanlan glowered back at him.
He had traded blacker looks across the Belfast barri-
cades when he was still a man.

"It's Herself will decide that, you Ulster cockerel,
and it's not for the likes of you to judge Her." The
harper grimaced again, rested the curve of the harp on
the wooden floor and began to fish about in the soundbox
for the end of the broken wire.

Scanlan sighed and leaned back against the wall,
wondering if harps went out of tune in heaven. At least
he would not have to listen to this one anymore. Coals
glowed dully in the grate, but Scanlan felt no warmth
from them. The flames that had billowed around him
after the gelignite went off had been hot enough—in
the moment or two before consciousness had winked
out Scanlan had thought for sure it was a first taste of
what was coming to him. But Hell was cold and wet
and full of Irish—at least this corner of it seemed to be.
The priest and the ministers were both wrong.

The door across from him swung open, the wind of it
stirring the worn tapestry so that the brown bull in its
center quivered as if about to charge. For a moment
Scanlan saw only darkness in the doorway, and then
suddenly there was a woman there and Scanlan was
getting to his feet instinctively as she came into the
room.

"I am sorry to have kept you waiting, Mr. Scanlan.
There was a small disturbance on the road."

Scanlan blinked, momentarily stunned by the rich
music of her voice and the clashing colors of her clothes.
Red and russet and blue chequerings swirled as she

shrugged off her heavy cloak and handed it to Lightborn, who had followed her, deft-footed and obsequious, into the room. Beneath the cloak she was wearing a purple jumpsuit that clung to a figure as richly curved as the Mountains of Mourne.

She sank into the shabby armchair, stretched out one leg so that Lightborn could tug off her muddy boot and leaned back, smiling. The movement led the eye along the white column of her throat to the cleft between her breasts and Scanlan swallowed.

"Every moment was an eternity—" he said huskily, "and it had been longer still if I had known who I was waiting for!" Legs that seemed suddenly strengthless lowered him back into his chair. "If you are the Queen of Connaught, then legend did not lie!"

She straightened a little to look at him and the band of gold that held her auburn hair flashed back the light of the fire. There was gold at her neck and on her wrists as well, and little tongues of flame danced in her violet eyes. Her movement sent Lightborn sprawling; she frowned while he rearranged his angular frame, apologising, then put out her other foot. The mud on her boot was splashed with red.

"I am Maeve," her full lips curved as she smiled. "You speak well for a warrior. Are you a scholar too?"

Scanlan shrugged. "I read literature for two years at the University in Reading. It was a good cover." It had seemed a good joke at the time to use the British scholarship to cover his IRA work in Britain. "I did letter bombs, car explosives—once I nearly got the Home Secretary—" He looked at her, suddenly self-conscious. Would she think he was boasting?

He *was* good with explosives! It was not his fault that the last bomb had had a defective fuse. Abruptly the face of the woman who had been beside him in the Post Office came vividly to memory. She had not had the stunning beauty of the great lady he faced now, but he'd noticed her sweet face, and the shining copper of her hair. And once more, in memory, he saw her expression change, saw her leaping toward the pram with her kid in it, into the flames.

"You are a warrior then—" Maeve said smoothly, "but you are one who knows the great tales." Her violet gaze dispelled his visioning. "You know about me . . ." It was not a question.

Scanlan felt himself growing hot as he remembered what he had read about her—Maeve of Cruachan, Queen of Connaught, as noted for her prowess in the bed-chamber as on the battlefield. She smiled as if she could read his thoughts as the Brothers used to at school.

Lightborn slipped brocade slippers onto her feet and unfolded himself into a formal stance. "Will my lady require something to drink? Perhaps some tea?"

Maeve shook her head. "Later, perhaps. I will call. Leave me now, and take him with you—" she gestured toward the harper, who was still struggling with his recalcitrant strings. Sniffling with frustration, the musi-cian gathered up his pliers and his coils of wire, lifted his instrument by its curved pillar, and followed Lightborn out of the room.

Scanlan looked at Maeve, still hearing the echoes of the confessional. But he was damned already, surely. He straightened and grinned back at her.

Slowly Maeve crossed her long legs. The movement drew his eyes to the smooth swell of her thighs. Beside her left hip rested a sheathed commando knife whose hilt had been wound with gold wire. A .38 pistol was strapped to her right thigh and her hand rested on the butt, fondling it.

"And how long have you been a warrior, then, Tim Scanlan?" she asked.

"I joined the Provos when I was sixteen."

She nodded, understanding that he meant the Provi-sional wing of the IRA that had carried the fight to the enemy when the old soldiers, the "Officials," seemed to have lost their nerve.

"You know explosives, then, and you are also good with a gun?"

"I've used the Armalite—" he assured her, remembering the little combat rifle that had become almost an extension of his hand, "and the M-60—the machine gun—a bit. We didn't have many of those." He cleared his throat. "What weapons do you use here?"

The violet eyes held his. "Whatever we can get. This war has gone on for a very long time."

Scanlan leaned forward. "Lady, I have to know—in New Hell they told me that you needed men . . . but why are you fighting? What for?"

Maeve frowned, and for a moment she almost looked old. Then she looked up at him. "You answer me first, Tim Scanlan. Didn't they tell you I'm at war with Con'or of Ulster? And you are from Belfast. So why did you come to me?"

Scanlan swallowed. "They told me that Brookeborough is with Con'or, along with every fucking B-Special any true-born Irishman ever killed, and General Monroe and that traitor Sam Turner of Newry and the rest of the bloody Orangemen. When they tried to clear us out of Armagh in 1795 they used 'To Hell or Connaught' for a warcry . . ."

"And you're already in Hell so you thought you would try Connaught?" Maeve's head came up, and Scanlan thought of a thoroughbred scenting wind.

"I've been thinking—" he said slowly. "They always told us that if we died for Ireland we would win a martyr's crown in heaven. Well, somebody was lying, for, saving your presence, ma'am, there's little enough to remind me of heaven here. But there's a stronghold full of fucking Orangemen in Emain Macha calling themselves Irish—and that is the reason I came to you."

Maeve sat very still. The thick fringe of her lashes

kept him from seeing the expression in her eyes. Scanlan
licked his lips and began again.

"They've made an earthly Hell of Belfast, and surely
if I and the other brave lads are here instead of in
heaven it's because Ireland still is not free. Where
should a soldier be but face to face with his enemy? It's
my thought that we've been given a second chance to
serve Ireland. When Ulster is free of the damned
Orangemen, then maybe the Good Lord will give us
our reward! Isn't that why you've been fighting for so
long?"

"Don't speak that name!" Maeve glanced quickly
around her. "Don't say it even when you think you're
alone, or you may find there's worse than the Orangemen
here. Don't speak the holy names, and don't talk about
getting Out. The Angels have ears everywhere . . ."

"Worse than the bloody English!" Scanlan nodded.
He had seen Satan's soldiers in New Hell; they looked
mean, but his quarrel was not with them.

"I could give you a dozen reasons why I'm at war
with Con'or," Maeve went on slowly. "To put Fergus
back on his throne that Con'or stole from him, to avenge
Ferdiad that would have married my girl Finnabair, or
maybe for reasons of my own . . . You're new, and
you're a fair lad. This time I'll not hold the asking
against you. But remember—" she had risen and a long
step brought her before him so that he had to look up
the length of that beautiful body to see her eyes.

"Remember, if you follow me, it must be without
question."

She was standing so close that Scanlan could smell
the scent of horses, and the sharp tang of sweat, and
the woman-scent, like a musky perfume. He felt the
hot blood flushing his fair skin and engorging his cock,
hard and painfully throbbing against the constraint of
his corduroys.

Without thinking he pulled her against him, rolling
his heated face against the sweet joining of her thighs.

She ruffled his brown hair and he began to tremble. Then her grip tightened, forcing his head up and back, and he looked up at her.

"Maeve—" he whispered desperately, "Maeve . . ."

"Not even that question," she said. She was not smiling now. Still holding him in that fierce gaze, she began to pull the tab of her zipper down. She was wearing nothing underneath the jumpsuit.

Her breasts fulfilled the promise of the tight-fitting garment. He reached up and cupped first one, then the other. They were white, blue-veined, with nipples that offered themselves to his hungry lips like dark rose-buds. Maeve leaned over him and let him feed.

Maeve's hair was like dark fire in the shadowed room, and Scanlan thought of the old lovesong that was a song of love for Ireland too.

"Róisín Dubh!" he whispered as his lips tasted her silken skin, "My dark Rosaleen!"

This could not be Hell! he thought dimly, not when a queen from the songs of glory was in his arms. His whole body ached now, wanting her. A childhood of priestly warnings against impurity had combined with a lack of money and a war that took all his energy to leave him little time for women. There had been one or two encounters, awkward and guilt-ridden, but mostly sex had been something to look forward to when he married, some time in a nebulous future when the fighting was over and a man could support a family.

Only for him there had been no future, only the dreams. And this was a dream in his arms now, surely, this sweet woman-flesh pressed against him and the soft voice murmuring love-words in a Gaelic older than anything he had learned in school.

With a groan Scanlan slipped his hand across the smooth fabric and silky skin of her belly to find the tag of the zipper. But her belt kept him from opening it any further. He reached for the golden buckle and Maeve's strong hand closed over his.

"No . . ."

Startled, he looked up at her.

"No, my hero—" Maeve said huskily. "Not this way, and not here. You want to fight for me, don't you?"

Unable to speak, Scanlan nodded. His body was shaking with a sweet torment and his hands tightened on her buttocks. She did not mean it, he thought. Her eyes were dilated too, and her breath came fast. They could not stop now. He caught his breath raggedly.

"When we have fought Con'or I will give myself to you." Maeve's voice was harsh—with passion or with sorrow? Even in his anguish, Scanlan understood that she was not playing, but it did not make it easier to bear. He shifted position, trying to hold her, and the change of pressure sent a wave of sensation through his imprisoned cock so intense he scarcely knew if it were pleasure or pain.

He gasped, and she gripped his hands and detached them and stepped away.

"You will fight Con'or—" her glowing eyes held his desperate gaze.

"Yes . . ."

"You will obey me better than you ever did your commander—"

"Yes . . ." It was more of a gasp than a word.

"And when we have fought him I will be your reward!"

"Yes!" His eyes fed on her flesh, glowing dimly in the light from the coals. She nodded, and then, very slowly, closed the jumpsuit up again.

"Wait here. Someone will show you where to sleep. You came just in time—we attack Con'or tomorrow." Maeve moved past him, and for a moment her hand rested upon his bent head.

Then she was gone, and there was only the heatless fire in the grate, and the far fiercer fire within him. Scanlan sat trembling, trying to let the tension that locked his muscles drain away.

Tomorrow—he thought—*tomorrow* . . . He tried to

imagine Maeve's naked body, but the images kept shifting to bodies sprawled obscenely in death upon a Belfast road. His hands tried to recapture the curve of her breast, but all they could remember was the smooth stock of a rifle. When the fighting was over then he would have the reality, but the night seemed very long.

"Emain Macha—"

Tim Scanlan lifted himself on his forearms to follow Sean Russell's pointing finger down the hill and across the dull pewter of the river. There was a building down there—stone and timber walls partly hidden by leafless trees. He had been raised on tales of the Ulster Heroes—the knights of the Red Branch—but he had never been to the place where Con'or's hall was supposed to have been. He wondered whether this one looked like the original.

At least it had stopped raining. Heavy clouds hung on the horizon, dyed red as blood by a hidden sun. The bare branches stood out against it, black and sharp and tangled as barbed wire. Good weather for fighting, thought Scanlan.

The scene reminded him oddly of something he had seen before—some one of the many fights whose details were already becoming obscure. The curve of the hill seemed familiar, but somehow distorted, as if he were looking at it through old glass. He looked again, and found it already less strange.

And how long will it be, he wondered then, *before I forget what the true Ireland is like and accept this as the only reality?*

"The place looks strong," he said aloud. "Are we going to assault it?"

"Come back down the hill, lad, and maybe you'll find out!" Russell squirmed backward until he was below the line of sight from the summit, then half-rose and made his way back to the hollow where the others were gathering.

Scanlan took another look at Con'or's stronghold. There was some movement down there, and dark shapes rose like blown cinders from the bare trees. The sound of cawing came clearly through the still air. Crows, he thought, or ravens—they were too far away to tell. The carrion-eaters were well-represented in the ecology of Hell.

When he got back down the hill, Cet MacMatach was arguing with Patrick Pearse about strategy. Cet, muscular and ruddy with the anachronistic mix of clothing and weaponry that characterized most of the fighters from Maeve's own time, looked as if he could blow the tall, stooping Pearse away.

"I say we must go in straight and strike them with all our power!" Cet gestured broadly and Pearse flinched. "We've superior numbers, man, and the new guns, and if they think they got the queen in that last ambush they'll not be expecting us."

"And if you are wrong?" said Pearse in his slow, careful way. He cradled his Lee Enfield rifle more securely in the crook of his arm. "What back-up will there be? We've learned the value of that, surely!"

"We bloody well should've," muttered Russell. "If Pearse had paid attention to planning in 1916, all Ireland would be free."

Scanlan nodded. The Germans had been forced to scuttle the shipload of guns they had offered the rebels when the promised guide never arrived to pick them up, and for that reason and several others, involving poor communications and split leadership, the Easter Rebellion had failed. It had been a shock to Scanlan to find Pearse here, but suddenly Scanlan saw it as an odd kind of a reward—a chance to continue fighting for Ireland.

"Well, it's Herself will have the deciding of it," said Cet. "Herself and the Lord Fergus, so calm yourself, my lad."

Something changed in Pearse's face at the reference

to Maeve. It was the look one saw on a man in church sometimes when he bowed to the Holy Mother. Had Pearse been Maeve's lover? Scanlan's body still ached when he thought of her, even with the prospect of battle to distract him. He had seen death before; he had known fighting, but never a woman like Maeve.

Then he heard a pony neigh. The hazel branches rustled and Maeve was there, wearing black fatigues and a cloak striped in red and yellow and green. A man followed her, stocky, grizzled, with the heavy, proud walk of a champion bull, and Cet saluted him, laughing.

Scanlan straightened to attention, realizing that this must be Fergus MacRoech, Ulster's rightful king. But Con'or had tricked him out of the lordship, and he was fighting to get it back again. He *had* been Maeve's lover—all the legends said it—but Scanlan did not think the man would have such haunted eyes if the affair were still going on.

She is mine, he told himself, feeling the throb in his crotch again as he looked at her. *She promised me. When we're together the others won't matter any more.*

"Is he in there?" asked Pearse eagerly. The other men crowded around to hear the answer. Scanlan recognized one or two of them from pictures of IRA martyrs he had seen in the news when he was growing up.

Fergus nodded. "Con'or himself, with Bricriu and Conn O'Neill. Most of his lads have gone for a shipment of arms from Capetown. If we take the place before they return we can claim sovereignty."

"Will the Fallen Angels allow it?" asked Pearse dubiously.

"Be damned to the bloody Angels!" muttered Russell. "And to think I used to complain about the Brits!" His quick look behind him belied the cocky words, and Scanlan shivered.

"Once we are in possession, I believe they will," said Maeve, setting her hand on the hilt of her sword.

"Well then, what are we waiting for?" Cet grinned.

"You'll take the gate with the new men, and the Lady and I will come in upon them from the back and sides," said Fergus. "There is a woman in that house who has given me copies of the keys."

Scanlan thought he could guess how Fergus had paid for that information. It was more proof that the King was no longer Maeve's man. He picked up his rifle and made his way over to her.

"He said the new men were to follow Cet—" Scanlan nodded toward Fergus. "But I'm requesting permission to come with you."

Maeve looked at him enigmatically and he remembered that he had promised not to question. But this was the order of Fergus, not hers. After a moment she smiled, and he thought, *Sweet Mother, I could take her on the bare ground before them all!* Maeve touched his cheek and nodded. Scanlan caught sour looks from some of the other men and from one of them a cynical grin, but that did not disturb him now.

Fergus gave a low-voiced order and they began to move, soft-footed as cottagers poaching a landlord's deer. A tune was echoing in Scanlan's memory—he tried to remember the words:

" *'Twas in the town of Belfast, all the month of May
Three youthful Irish soldiers set out upon their way
A mission to accomplish, Ireland's freedom which we need,
And the leader of that gallant band was Lieutenant
  Billy Reid."*

Still humming, Scanlan shouldered his Armalite and followed Maeve around the hill.

The place was quiet. Too quiet, thought Scanlan, holding his position at Maeve's shoulder as they moved out from the shelter of the stables across the courtyard to the side door. There should have been someone mucking out stalls or repairing tack at that hour, but even the horses were gone. But if everyone was away getting the new guns as Fergus had said, of course both stables and garages would be deserted now. Scanlan cursed himself for an old woman and kept going.

The other—six men and three women—flattened themselves against the wall as Maeve crouched over the door trying to work the key. Through the dirty window Scanlan saw brooms leaning against a wall and a staircase leading upward. Then Maeve had the door open and they slipped through.

The stairs creaked as they went up them; then they heard the muffled crack of a rifle from somewhere else in the house and Scanlan forgot about trying to move silently. He heard yelling from the front of the house and more rifle fire and knew the attack on the gate had begun, then a pistol fired with a roar that seemed to echo endlessly in the enclosed stairwell, and Scanlan, turning, saw buff jackets and knew abruptly that there had been a good reason for his misgivings.

"Shannon, McGill—guard our rear!" snapped Maeve. "And you others, after me!" Bullets ricocheted past them as they scrambled the rest of the way up stairs. Maeve sent three men ahead to hold the hallway, then held the door as the rest of her force came through. Shannon was the last of them, for McGill had taken a bullet in the thigh and two others who had been hit in the first exchange lay still sprawled on the stairway.

Scanlan fired down the stairs, then jumped out of the way of two men who were dragging over a chest to block the doorway. A bullet sang past and dropped one of them; they shoved it into place and retreated down the hall. More fire greeted them as they turned the corner, and they lost two more men.

Absurdly, the song was still running through Scanlan's head. He bent to check one of the girls, found no pulse, and laid her down again.

"But the bullet caught our Billy, his life it took away.
And there on a street in Belfast an Irish martyr lay."

Maeve moved ahead and motioned to Scanlan to follow her. As the others started after them another door opened and three men with orange armbands stepped out, covering them. Slowly they raised their hands. Scanlan fired twice, at an angle to avoid hitting his own men, then the Armalite jammed. For a moment he hesitated, but Maeve was already turning the corner, leaving the captured men behind.

Scanlan reversed his useless rifle and used it to club the man nearest him, then dashed after the queen. When he caught up with her he saw that her knife was out and there was blood on it. Her eyes were very bright and she began to speak, then stopped, listening.

Scanlan held his breath and heard faint shouting. Then the wooden floor vibrated with the pounding of many feet. He exchanged a look with Maeve and they slipped through the door behind them, searching for cover. It already held a body, still twitching and pooling red upon the floor. Maeve dragged it out of sight from the corridor.

Scanlan pointed to the table. "We could barricade the door—"

She shook her head. "If it is our own lads we'll need to be able to get out to them." They could hear the clatter of footsteps now. Maeve grabbed Scanlan's arm and pulled him behind the door, leaving it half-open so that they could peer through the space between the door and the frame.

Scanlan held his breath as a blur of sleeves, legs, heads and weapons flickered past the narrow field of vision. Did they belong to Ulster or Connaught? Maeve had not moved. Then he glimpsed an Ulster Defence Association badge on a khaki sleeve.

He stiffened and took a step sideways. Maeve's hand vised his arm and fractionally she shook her head. He drew breath to protest, remembered the danger, and his promise, and shut his lips. The men they had left in the corridor were prisoners by now. He and Maeve should go back, try to rescue them, but Maeve shook her head.

"Our only chance is to join up with the others—" she whispered when the slot showed only the opposite wall and the sound of feet was fading down the hall.

Scanlan's eyes fixed on her face. *For you*, he thought, *for you alone I will give up my own will and honor*.

Maeve smiled slightly and her full lips formed a kiss. For another moment she stood still, listening, then slipped around the door. Lightly she ran forward and Scanlan came after her. They came to a landing where the corridor split. There was a carved table against the wall beneath a portrait of a man in lace and periwig that looked like the cheap prints of King Billy they sold at the Orange parades. Staring eyes seemed to follow him as he rounded the corner to the stair.

A shot whined past his ear and he ducked back. King Billy's blank eyes mocked him. Then there was another shot and Maeve rolled around the corner and pulled herself up beside him, swearing softly.

"There's near a dozen of them down there," she whispered. "I don't know what's become of our own lads. There was heavy firing from the main gate, and it may be that Cet never got through at all."

Scanlan nodded. They had never expected the place to be so heavily defended. Had someone betrayed them, or had the reconaissance been inadequate? One would think that with so much at stake they would have been extra careful, but there was always the bad example of the Easter Rebellion. He grimaced.

It's holy terrors in a fight we are, but a little weak on staffwork. But if I had taken more care with the gelignite I would not be here, he reminded himself, *so I'm not the one to go throwing stones*.

"My rifle's jammed—" he said aloud. Maeve looked at him and handed over the M-60 she had been carrying.

"Take this—it's never been my weapon anyway, and give me your cap—"

Scanlan handed it to her and she hung it on the end of the useless Armalite, then poked it out over the stair. Instantly more bullets spat by, and she nodded in satisfaction.

"Get over to the other side—" she told Scanlan. "When I draw their fire again give them a good round with the machine gun."

Scanlan slithered across the top of the stairs and flicked off the safety of the M60 just as Maeve held up his cap again. Sound exploded from below; Scanlan heaved the machine gun into position and pressed the trigger, bracing himself as it leaped to life in his arms, stitching bullet holes through bannister and parquetry. Someone yelled and the firing from below stopped; he wrestled the M60 back and sent another burst across the entryway.

Maeve was getting to her feet. Scanlan stopped firing, and in the throbbing silence heard someone in the corridor down which they had come. Maeve gestured and darted down the stairs; Scanlan hefted the machine gun and scrambled after her. A bullet seared the top of his hand and he leaped the rest of the way down, looking for cover.

But men were coming through the big front door now, and Maeve was between him and them. He yelled at her to get down, then something struck his arm and the M-60 slipped from suddenly nerveless fingers, bouncing and spraying bullets at every impact indiscriminately until it came to rest.

Scanlan stood cradling his arm, staring around him. Maeve drew her sword and shouted—in exasperation and fury, not in fear. Someone laughed and came at her, his own blade casting a confusion of shattered color across the floor as it caught the light of the stained-glass window of the Red Hand of Ulster glowing balefully in the dim light of Hell.

Maeve's blade sheared the air and clanged against her opponent's, twisted and slid along it with a screech of anguished metal and tore into the soft flesh of the man's arm. Blood splattered around them, doubly crimson in that lurid light, and the man yelled.

He fell back and another came at her, a big, fair man with close-set green eyes, taunting Maeve as if they'd both done this too many times before.

"The Devil damn you Conall!" she shrieked. "May the demons that live beneath the black lake drag you down into their slime, may the fire burst your bones—" her cursing continued, and Scanlan's lips twisted in a kind of grin. How could she damn Conall when they were both already in Hell? But he noticed that the big man was not laughing, and sobered with an abrupt, appalled suspicion that maybe the torments she was wishing on Conall were real.

"If I'd a spear I would thread your guts through your backbone!" she raged. "I would destroy you as Cuchulain was destroyed by Lugaid!" Maeve slashed furiously, and Scanlan wondered if in her madness she was seeing Conall at all. She was like the Morrigan in her battle fury, he thought, and he heard ravens shriek outside.

Then Conall leaped forward. Scanlan saw the red flare as his blade came down; Maeve's sword lifted to parry, but she was off-balance, and the smooth arc of Conall's sword was only momentarily disturbed as it struck hers and tore it away.

For a moment everyone stood still. The silence rang in Scanlan's ears. Then from behind the crowd of Ulstermen came a laugh.

"My game, I think, this time!"

Maeve's head came up, and defiance replaced the despair that had darkened her eyes. Conall Cernach the Victorious grinned and raised his sword in salute as the others parted to let the speaker through.

Scanlan blinked, remembering how the drab folk of Belfast had stared when the Italian film crew came through. And yet, before the British beat it out of them, the Celts had had an eye for color too. Scanlan

had not minded Maeve's somber splendor—perhaps he
was only startled to see a man in such colors—a man, a
king, King Con'or.

The king moved slowly out to face Maeve, drawing
off driving gloves of supple cordovan leather and stuff-
ing them into the pocket of the long cashmere coat he
wore. The coat was royal blue, with some kind of cham-
pagne colored fur on the turned up collar that matched
his ash-fair hair. Still watching the queen, Con'or un-
buttoned the coat, revealing slacks of white slubbed silk
and a saffron silk shirt, open nearly to the waist, though
the profusion of chains and the golden torque at his
neck thus displayed were nearly lost in his curling chest
hair.

"You've lost none of your skill, my dear, but it's a
discourteous way to come calling. Surely there should
be more ceremony between sovereigns?" Con'or smiled
and stroked his forked beard.

"Fuck your ceremony!" said Maeve. Her fingers
twitched toward the hilt of her dagger. Scanlan stepped
sideways, wondering if he could get between her and
Conall when she made her move.

"No, Maeve—" Con'or had seen the movement too.
"Don't even try." He gestured, and a lean, dark man
with a basilisk's eyes came forward, leering, to pluck
the knife from her side.

"Thank you, Bricriu," said Con'or. His gaze was still
on Maeve. "As for fucking, well that's the problem
now, isn't it—" His pale eyes shifted to Scanlan's face
for a moment, the first time the king had noticed him,
with what might have been a smile.

"It was with you, certainly!" Maeve spat at him. "I
had reason enough to leave you, and it's no good luck
with women you had after. Ethne my sister had a sorry
life with you, and then there was poor Deirdre, running off with the first young man she saw rather than be
your queen. Do you remember how she looked with

her brains splattered across the stone? Did you desire her then, Con'or?"

"I've got what I desire . . ." the King said dangerously. "I have Maeve of Connaught in my power."

"Are you going to kill me, then?" Maeve laughed.

"Now what good would that do?" asked Con'or. "But my men are skilled in the Five Techniques, Maeve. I can get anything I want from you."

Scanlan shuddered. One of his brother's friends had been among those detained under the Special Powers Act in 1971, and he had told them a bit about what had been done to him. Hooding, wall-standing, deprivation of food and sleep and constant "white noise" combined with beatings to produce a system of torture the Inquisition would have envied—a gift from the civilized British to the citizens of Northern Ireland. The Five Techniques had been hellish enough on earth—Scanlan did not want to know what they were like in Hell . . .

"Oh, Con'or, Con'or—" Maeve shook her head wearily. "Why not do the one thing that would help us all? Let us make alliance. If we fight together, who can stand against us?"

"The Angels . . ." The words fell cold and heavy as hailstones, dousing Maeve's fire. "They will never allow it."

"There was only one man of us ever got himself out of here," rumbled Conall, "and that was Cuchulain, and he had a Christian saint to help him."

"There is only one way for you to buy safety, Maeve, and that is to swear allegiance to me. Half your men are dead or my prisoners. Bring the rest into my service and I'll show you how to deal with the Angels. Cooperating with them is by far the safer way—" said Con'or smoothly. "Those in favor can get arms, supplies—"

"And silk shirts!" Maeve added bitingly. She looked around her, fixing each of Con'or's men with her eagle gaze. "But what else should I be expecting? Diarmuid MacMurrough, there behind you, is the man who first invited the English into Ireland. Conn O'Neill sold his country to Elizabeth, and Leonard McNally there betrayed the United Irishmen in 1795. And then there are all these new lads with their orange armbands. With the practice in selling your nation to the English you have among you it's no wonder you're so quick to sell out to the Angels of Hell!"

Con'or took a swift step forward and backhanded Maeve across the face. There were rings on his fingers, and when he pulled his hand away her lip was bleeding. A deep growl began in Scanlan's throat and he started to move; someone grabbed him and he looked into the grinning face of one of Paisley's Volunteers. He started to struggle, felt his good arm jerked painfully upward, and quieted.

"Woman, will you be still?" hissed Con'or. "They'll carve dice out of your bones!" He stepped back and motioned to McNally. "Take them away!"

"Maeve, Maeve, my dark rose, do not despair. Surely Fergus or Cet will manage a rescue—come now, my love, let me hold you and believe that all will be well . . ." Scanlan eased down beside the queen and put his aching arm around her. The manhandling he had received had not quite disjointed it, and it was more serviceable than the other. She had bound it up for him with a strip from his shirt, but it throbbed dully where the bullet had passed through.

Now she sat with her knees up and her head bowed upon them, and he could feel her shoulders shaking through her cloak's thick wool.

"Ochone! Ochone! Why do I still try?" she whispered. "I can call curses on Con'or and all the men of Ulster, but they're none the worse for all my ill-wishing, and there are all my brave lads laid out cold in the courtyard waiting for the Undertaker to torture them some more."

"It's only another battle—" he tried to reassure her.

"You'll get free from here and have your revenge. Isn't that the story of the Irish, now—to be defeated over and over and never destroyed?"

"Oh indeed . . ." Maeve sighed. "But where has it gotten us? There has to be another way. If it were me and Con'or only then force of arms might decide it, but he is getting weapons and supplies from New Hell, and I have not the resources to oppose him. Oh, it has gone on so long—so long! And no matter who wins, the end is always the same!"

Scanlan stirred uncomfortably, remembering Ian Paisley's contorted face flickering on a TV screen, and the mirror of it on Rory O'Grady orating at an IRA funeral. *And what did they say at my own funeral?* he wondered then. But he knew—"*Let us continue this holy battle so that the sacrifice of this brave young man may be justified . . .*"

He shook his head in confusion; it hurt to think about it, and what use was thinking anyhow—fighting was all he knew how to do. And here was the fairest woman in all Ireland weeping against his shoulder, and somehow he had to comfort her. At least Con'or had locked them up together, and that was more mercy than he had expected. In the dim reddish light that came through the high window he made out the dim shapes of piled crates. There were bare boards beneath them, and dust in the air. It was some kind of storeroom, then, and the two of them had been shoved in with the rest of the rubbish to await Con'or's disposal.

His arm tightened, and Maeve turned and pressed her face against his chest. He could smell the spicy scent of her hair, and the need that had never quite left him since the moment he had first seen her stirred once more.

"Ah, Maeve, Maeve, my dark queen," he murmured into her hair, "how I love you, *'Tá grá agam 'm lár duit lé bliain anois, Grá cráite grá casmhar, grá ciapaithe . . .'* There is a terrible love in my heart for you for a year

now, An aching, tortured, anguished love—" It was a
verse from Róisín Dubh, nearly the only Gaelic song he
knew, but he had never understood the truth of it until
now.

Scanlan felt her grow still in his arms and knew that
she was listening. Ignoring its aching, he lifted his
wounded arm so that he could stroke her hair.

"My darling, your hair is like the shadows of the
sunset, and your skin is as white as the foam that curls
off the sea-wave. Let me comfort you, Maeve—let me
love you. At least we have that much left to us . . ."

Maeve straightened and turned to face him. Her eyes
were like pools of shadow.

"Do we?" she asked softly.

He took her hand and carried it to his lips, turning it
to kiss the soft center of her palm. "I have fought for
you, my queen," he said huskily. "Remember your
promise to me . . ."

"I remember," she said slowly, "and you are a fair
young man with the light of life still in your eyes and
the warmth of life still clinging to your limbs. All the
girls in Belfast must have sighed with love for you.
When you came here, did that one they call the Welcome Woman take you to her bed?"

Scanlan grimaced. "She tried," he admitted, "but
there was nothing in her to tempt me from purity . . ."

Maeve smiled at the churchly turn of phrase. "And
there is in me?"

Scanlan felt himself flushing. Though he had died
fighting for his religion, he'd had little to do with the
Church since he was a boy. But childhood training died
hard. If the Brothers had preached as strongly against
fighting as they did against fornication he might not
have been here now. But then he would not have had
the queen of all women in his arms.

"For you I would brave Hell's flames!" he said wryly,
mocking himself. And what did he have to lose? He was
in Hell already, and it was cold—cold, and only Maeve's

lips were warm. He tipped up her chin and kissed her,
and her mouth opened beneath his. His hand moved
across her thick hair and down the smooth skin of her
neck, seeking the fastenings of her shirt. Her cloak
slipped from her shoulders and he heard her breath
come faster as he cupped the softness of her breast.

"I will not say no to you, Tim Scanlan," she said
brokenly. "And maybe it will be different—maybe you
are the one . . ."

He scarcely heard. His pulse was pounding, and a
sweet fire burned beneath his skin. He dragged off his
leather jacket and folded it into a pillow on top of
Maeve's cloak, and she sank back beneath him, still
kissing him even as he fumbled with the closing of her
trousers and she deftly released him from his. His arm
still hurt, but that didn't matter now; in a curious way it
even spiced his urgency.

Maeve's breathing quickened as he began to do to
her all the things he had imagined in the long hours the
night before when he could not find sleep. Her breasts
must be kissed until the nipples stood up hard and
throbbing as his own cock was now. He gasped as her
hand closed around it, gripping, stroking until he thought
he would explode.

"Not yet—" he tried to whisper, "not this way." But
somehow he contained his excitement as he struggled
to slide her pants over the swell of her thighs and the
softness between them opened itself to his probing
hand.

She was already wet and ready. Both of them groaned
as Scanlan pushed into her, and her arms and legs vised
around him, her mouth fastened on his as if she would
suck out his soul. He gripped her shoulders and thrust
with all the strength in him, again, and again.

Ecstasy carried him from one plateau to another until
it was almost pain. He had never before had such
endurance, and the woman bucked beneath him as if it

were a contest between them, grunting as if she struggled toward some distant goal.

The sweat rolled off Scanlan's body, and the air chilled
his bare skin. He lost all sense of the identity of the
woman beneath him. She was the means to the completion he was so desperately seeking—if he could only
find it he would have his victory.

Think fire! Think of fire! he told himself as the cold
air touched him. And the vision of fire came to him—
orange fire billowing as the gelignite exploded and the
red hair of the girl who had died with him swirling into
flame. All her clothing had been burning, but still she
had struggled forward to clasp what was left of her
child.

Scanlan groaned, but it was in anguish, not in ecstacy.
Mechanically he pounded Maeve's eager body, but
though need still impelled him, he realized in horror
that his cock was softening, shrinking. Maeve felt it too
and stopped moving, but it was too late—Scanlan slipped
out of her, fumbled to push his member back in but it
was no good, it was no good and then she was cursing
him and pushing him away.

Scanlan woke cold. His muscles had stiffened; when
he tried to move it was agony. He was alone.

It took him a few moments for him to realize that,
still longer to understand it. He had been dreaming
that he was in Ireland, waiting in a leaky garage with
the other lads for a British patrol to pass. It had been a
long wait, and a damp one, but a couple of bottles of
Guinness had helped them to pass the time, and at the
end of it they had killed three of the soldiers and only
lost one of their own.

At the time they had called it a fair exchange, even a
victory. But now he was remembering the woman who
had been caught in the cross-fire. In his dream he was
bending over her, trying to give her artificial respira-

tion, but no matter how he pumped and labored, there was no life in her at all.

"Maeve—" he murmured brokenly, "Maeve . . ." and the sound of his own voice brought him to full consciousness at last. Groaning, he turned over and the corner of a crate jabbed his side. Crates—the store room—memory flooded back, a reality worse than any nightmare because this night would not end.

And the queen was gone. Scanlan curled back into fetal position, remembering his failure. But they had both been beaten, exhausted. It was not his fault, he just needed to rest, to recover, to try again. Next time it would be different—if there was a next time. Had they taken her away thinking of him as less than a man? Scanlan pushed himself upright, anger and anguish warring within him.

"Hey!" the shout echoed dully. "Hey, you bloody fucking Orangemen—somebody! Come here, you bastards—" the shout scraped his throat. His harsh breathing sounded loud in his own ears.

Scanlan hauled himself to his feet, jammed his shirt back into his trousers and fastened them. Then he forced aching muscles to carry him to the shut door.

It was locked—he had expected that. He gripped the knob and threw his weight against it. Something about chest level was holding it—a bolt, probably. He pressed himself against the hard wood and it groaned as Maeve had groaned in his arms. Images exploded in his imagination—Maeve lying beneath him, Maeve pinned beneath Con'or or one of his bullies; Maeve being racked, beaten, raped in a parody of the act he'd been unable to accomplish.

What were they doing to her now?

After that Scanlan lost track of time, caught in a mindless cycle of guilt and fury and fear. His hands were bruised and his wound had started bleeding again, but he hardly felt the pain. At some point, though, he understood that he could not claw his way to freedom, and he picked up a piece of lumber and began to batter at the door.

He was still striking out a haphazard percussion to his stream of hoarse obscenities when they finally came for him.

"What is your name?" The voice was cool and at the same time oddly oily. Scanlan blinked, trying to focus, knowing he had heard it before. A blow rocked him and he shook his head, muttering the words. What did it matter if they knew who he was?

"Where were you from?" asked the voice, and when he did not answer immediately, snapped an order. This time the beating was more inventive. Scanlan glimpsed UDA armbands. Finally they gave him a moment to catch his breath again.

"I'm from the Falls, damn you!"

"Ah—a Belfast man." There was a blur of motion and someone brought Scanlan water. He drank eagerly, though it did not satisfy his real thirst—it was like scratching an amputated limb. Still, even the illusion of drinking eased him. He lifted his head with a sigh and for the first time focused on his interrogator.

It was Bricriu Poisontongue—lank-haired and lantern-jawed, sitting behind a table in a leather coat and a silk cravat and pigskin gloves on his long hands. Well, he should have expected that.

"What were you doing fighting for Connaught, lad?" Bricriu's tone reminded Scanlan of the priest at home, but there was an edge to it. "You're an Ulsterman— Con'or is your king."

"Con'or is the Protestants' king. He would be a fine lord for Ian Paisley, but he's none to me!"

"Catholic? Protestant? Pagan?" said Bricriu. "Whatever makes you think that matters here?"

"What matters is that I'm an *Irish*man!" answered Scanlan. "And the sin of every one of us is to have left Ireland divided and in slavery!"

"My dear boy—" Bricriu raised one eyebrow. "If the Irish were able to unite, this would not be Hell!"

"Then why are you fighting?" Scanlan felt himself losing his fragile control.

"To unite the Irish under Con'or as High King . . ." Bricriu's tone was enigmatic.

"I'd rather serve Maeve . . ." said Scanlan sullenly.

Bricriu looked at him and laughed. "I'm sure that you tried, lad—I have no doubt you did try."

A pulse began to pound in Scanlan's throat. "What have you done to her?"

"What have I done?" Bricriu's tongue dripped with venom. "D'you think I'd dip into a pot that's been stirred by every spoon in Ireland?"

Scanlan's muscles tensed and immediately his guard pressed on the wound in his arm, gripping until he went limp and the sweat stood out on his brow.

"You took her away—where is she?" he gasped.

"Such passion—" Bricriu shook his head. "And still he does not understand. The queen requested an interview with King Con'or, Mr. Scanlan. It was she who decided to abandon you."

Scanlan swallowed and stared at Bricriu, seeing the other man's malicious comprehension of the question he did not trust himself to ask.

"Yes, you did understand me," Bricriu added almost gently. "She's gone, Scanlan—she has made treaty with the king. There were six of you alive after this sorry attempt at an attack upon us, and here you will stay. Maeve has agreed to disband her army, to give up this futile attempt to dispute my Lord Con'or's power. You might say that we have won the war. Con'or will rule all the Irish here now—does that meet your requirements? He will graciously accept your allegiance if you choose to offer it, or you may remain imprisoned. The choice is up to you . . ."

Scanlan scarcely heard what he was saying. He was remembering the things that Maeve had said.

"It's not possible—" words came despite his will. "She said that she loved me." He was babbling now. Bricriu's laughter echoed in the hollows of his skull.

"And don't you think she has said the same things to every other man? She admitted it herself once, that she was 'never without one man in the shadow of another.'"

Scanlan turned on him. "If she's left me it's my own fault!" he exclaimed, desperate to defend her, to preserve at least his belief in what had been between them. "I tried—I couldn't be a man to her—a woman like that needs a man's love . . ."

His words were lost in the noise that came from the other men in the room, from Bricriu, from the guards— something that should have been laughter but was instead the essence of pain.

"Yes, Maeve needs a man's seed inside her, and she opens her thighs to every new lad that comes to her, hoping for just that thing. But she won't get it, not ever, not here . . ." Bricriu's words seared all the tender surfaces Scanlan had exposed. "She didn't tell you, did she, lad—she let you think that the fault was yours . . . Ah, now you begin to understand!" Bricriu's poison tongue dripped the words into Scanlan's soul.

She knew—she knew! That's why she made me wait, and now she has betrayed me—oh, Róisín Dubh, oh my Dark Rosaleen!

"What, did you think you were in Ireland?" Bricriu went on. "This is Hell, lad, and once you've failed with Maeve—you'd best face it now—you will never be a man again!"

But there was one thing Scanlan could still do. He was moving before Bricriu's words were done, and this time his captors could not stop him. If he was no man then men's frailties could not hold him. He felt blows and welcomed all the pain, for at least he could feel it, and make others feel it too.

His first kick sent the table crashing, knocking Bricriu backward. Scanlan did not wait to see what happened to him. He was already whirling, fists sledge-hammering the first UDA man with blows to the solar plexus and over the heart and then a smash into the throat that sent the man the rest of the way down.

The other guard's pistol barked and Scanlan felt a hot poker sear his side. As he turned, the pistol spoke again, knocking Scanlan backward. He could not feel his left leg, but amazingly, he was still upright. Cursing, he lurched forward and the third bullet went wild.

The door slammed open. More men crowded into the room, too many to fire without hitting each other. A pistol butt struck numbingly on Scanlan's right shoulder. He whirled on his good leg and his left hand chopped. He heard the crack of the man's neck, staggered and flailed to keep his balance, to control his failing limbs.

Still extended, he saw the blade flare in Bricriu's hand. Fire ripped his belly, he tried to hold his guts in as he fell. Then nailed boots thudded into his ribs and the side of his head, driving sight away.

"Enjoy it—this is the only climax you will ever have!" Bricriu's voice was almost gentle.

Scanlan felt the sharp point touch his chest, and the great muscle spasmed as the sword pierced his heart. In the red darkness into which he was falling he thought that Maeve was holding him, and even when the rest of his body had ceased to twitch and shudder his lips were still trying to form her name.

Róisín Dubh . . .

Maeve . . .

For a time that was no time Scanlan drank darkness. Then came another eternity in which he floated on waves of pain. But each wave moved him a little closer to the shores of consciousness, though he fought to stay under, to drown.

And then finally he knew who he was, though he could not guess where. He knew only the tickling agony as torn muscles were forced back together and organs replaced and made to function once more. Through blurred eyes he saw a gaunt, gray-skinned face. When his tortured lungs drew breath he smelled the essence of Hell.

Scanlan closed his eyes, but oblivion eluded him. The voice of the Undertaker rasped his ears, and all he could remember was his hatred of Con'or. Once there had been another war and Ireland, but he could not remember what they had been fighting for.

Scanlan lay and suffered as the Undertaker painstakingly rebuilt his body into something that could support a semblance of life again, and tried to remember what it had been like to be a man.

THE MAN IN THE BLACK CAPE TURNS

Michael Armstrong

The man in the black cape turned and glanced over at the pale Norwegian sitting next to him in the back seat of the jeep. The tall Norwegian stared ahead at the road, his ice blue eyes intent on the private's driving, his cropped white hair rustling slightly in the open 4 × 4. The private, a short fourteenth-century Venetian, wrestled with the steering wheel as the jeep bounced over the shell pocked road running south out of New Hell.

At the top of a dike separating the city from the Phlegethon Swamp, the jeep passed through a short tunnel. The driver flicked on the headlights; the walls of the tunnel throbbed and beat, and red blood trickled down the sides of the artery out of New Hell. The man in the black cape winced as the portal read his Mark, heard the men next to him groan in their own pain, the tunnel confirming that all were New Dead and allowed to enter. He rubbed his left hand where the invisible code burned into his skin, sighed when he saw the end of the tunnel dilate open and let them out. A cloud of red steam whirled around the men in the jeep as they came into the Phlegethon Swamp, down onto the causeway to the New Hell Universal Airport.

Steam rose from the bloody swamp on either side of the South Road. More a series of creeks and ponds, the swamp was a vast delta bordered on the north by New Hell, on the east by the Sea of Sin, and on the west by the Great Range, a wall of mountains that was all mountains, a range whose shape could change with the weather and become one week the Himalayas, another the Pyrenees, sometimes just the low, beaten Smokies.

Hummocks dotted the Phlegethon Swamp, small mounds of mud rising from misty ooze. On the mounds could be heard the crack of whips as demons patrolled the swamp, forcing the damned back down into the blood their lives had spawned. A thin stream of clear water fed the swamp, a stream that cut back into the mountains in a long, winding valley, circling back and joining other streams, other rivers in Hell. As the jeep drove down the causeway, beasts with runny sores rose from the boiling swamp, slinging gobs of crusty red mud at the spinning wheels. The man in the black cape pulled his cape tight around him, and ignored the mud as it spattered against his cape and hissed into pink fog.

A low thrumming sound came from the south, and the man in the black cape glanced up. A black painted C-130 Hercules flew straight over the road toward them, about five hundred feet up, one of its right engines smoking. The cargo plane wobbled its wings, lost altitude, wobbled its wings again.

"What . . . ?" the man in the black cape asked.

"He's not going to make it," the Norwegian said. "He's trying to bring it down on the road. Pull over, driver!"

The driver swung the wheel hard to the right, drove toward the narrow shoulder. A damned soul crawled up on the road, swung an arm out at the jeep as it passed by, then screamed as the jeep crushed its fingers.

"Keep straight, *autista*," the man in the black cape said.

"Signor?" The private glanced back at the two men.

"*Avanti*," the man in the black cape said. "No way in Hell a Herky Bird can land on this road." He reached to his side, pulled out a chromed submachine gun that looked somewhat like an Uzi. The man in the black cape stood up and leaned against the back of the driver's seat, his left arm raised horizontal before him, his right arm braced on the left arm.

"Signor," the driver said, "the plane may be flying for the Resistance."

The man in the black cape paused, lowered his gun, then raised it again. "If so," he said, "they have completed their mission—or failed. In either case, they will not fly again."

The Herc's wings wobbled again. Its left engine screamed as the pilot fought for lift. The co-pilot waved frantically at the men in the jeep—*away, away*, he seemed to be shouting. The cargo plane's flaps came down, the pilot trying to raise the nose at the same time, to let the tail take the impact. Flames shot out of the outside engine and licked down the wing.

Slamming his foot to the accelerator, the private tried to shoot under and beyond the Herc. The men in the jeep could see the blank patches where the plane's insignia had been scraped off, the scratches on its belly from previous rough landings, the spinning wheels of the landing gear. The man in the black cape sighted along the barrel, raised it slightly, and fired three quick bursts down the length of the belly.

The first burst hit just aft of the nose gear, the second burst hit dead center, and the last burst hit behind the cargo doors at the tail. Each burst seared through the thin aluminum skin of the Herc and crawled over the surface and into the frame, a spreading blue shimmer, three swarms of manic fireflies suddenly adhering to the plane.

Almost instantly the blue shimmer spread completely over the Herc, enveloping it, devouring it. The skin crisped away, revealing the struts of the wings and fuselage, then those, too, flashed away. The man in black lowered his gun, swung his cape around him as the jeep drove through a cloud of swirling black ash. He glanced back down the road, saw two hunks of charred meat tumble to the earth. Several rectangles of clear Lexan scraped along the road, oozing into little brown globs. The driver took his foot off the accelerator and let the jeep coast to a stop.

"My Lord," the Norwegian said.

"*They wouldn't have made it*," the man in the black cape said. He sat down, resting the gun on his lap, watching it until he heard the hum of its recharging batteries die down. "We wouldn't have, either. They are returned to Satan." He motioned at the driver. "Drive on. Take the next left."

"That gun," the driver said, glancing back. "It's a Teller, a plasma gun—I know."

"You know nothing, *autista*," the man in the black cape said. "Drive on."

"Si, signor."

The driver set the jeep into gear, continued down the road. The causeway curved slightly to the west, then straightened out again, rising up on a drier area of the swamp. A herd of damned ran through the ankle-deep boiling red blood and across a narrow road on the left, chased into the swamp on the other side by a galloping centaur. The driver downshifted, turned the jeep down the road past a sign that said AERONAUTI-CAL CONSTRUCTION FACTORY. The road snaked along a filled-in area of the swamp, on the north side of the airport.

Turning south, the access road ended at a complex of huge hangars between the intersection of the north and east runways and the sea. Extending from the complex to the sea was a long canal, with a tanker docked at the end. A short apron connected the complex to the main runways. Across the runway from the Aeronautical Construction Factory were the main terminals of the airport, northwest of the cross made by the two intersecting runways. Torched buildings dotted the complex, their blackened frames thin fingers thrusting into the morning light of Paradise. A black star airport cursed with wind shears, fog, faulty radar, and a short runway that ended ten yards from the edge of a cliff, countless wrecks littered the edges of the airport. Ragged men and women stripped the wrecks, crawling over a virtual museum of flight: Fokkers, B-29s, MiGs, F-4 Phantoms, Stealths, and dozens of other planes. Craters gouged the tarmac, the runway. Some holes were patched with gravel, other holes were left gaping. New Hell Universal Airport—Beirut International, the New Dead liked to call it.

A gate blocked the entrance to the ACF. The driver stopped the jeep and stuck out his left hand to the guard, a Somocista National Guardsman. The Somocista ran a laser scanner over the driver's Mark. The man in black sniffed, extended his hand to the guard, looked away as the guard scanned the hidden tattoo. The guard read the dot matrix readout flickering across the scanner's screen, nodded as a light blipped green.

"Signor Pound?" the guard said to the man in black. "General Nobile is expecting you. He did not say anything about your companion."

The Norwegian glared at Pound, stuck out his hand to the guard. The guard confirmed the Norwegian's identification, raised his eyebrows at the name. He grunted, and stepped back from the jeep. "I see. Go to the main hangar straight ahead." He pointed to the largest of six hangars at the complex, a rusted building with a grimacing skull logo peeling on the side.

As they pulled up to the main hangar, a man in a crisp wool uniform, one star on his lapel and epaulets, flyer's wings on his chest pocket, stepped out of a small door on the side. Tall and narrow, the general had deep brown eyes, a long, aquiline nose, and a cleft chin below a thick lower lip. The driver hopped out, saluted, then helped the two men in the back get out. Pound waved him away, and the driver got in the jeep and drove off.

"*Ezra Pound,*" the general said. "It is an honor to have you here." He stood rebar straight, bowed, extended a hand to Pound, and shook hands with the poet. He turned to the Norwegian, smiled, his face briefly frowning, then smiled again. "Roald," he whispered.

"Umberto," the Norwegian said. "I see we both pay for our past sins."

"Such men as we do not pay for past sins, but only create new ones."

"Excuse me, general," Pound said. "I had not realized you knew Commander Amundsen."

"Back in the World, I had the honor of serving under the Commander on the *Norge,*" Nobile said. He bowed at Amundsen. "Even in his death he honored me, for the White Eagle died searching for me and my lost men when my third airship, the *Italia,* crashed in the Arctic."

Amundsen waved a hand at Nobile. "It was nothing, Umberto. I would have done the same for my worst enemy. The bond of the polar explorer is strong."

"I see," said Pound.

"But you, Signor Pound . . . You honor me with your presence here, *now,*" Nobile said. "You are an inspiration to us at the Aeronautical Construction Factory. My men listen to your every broadcast. I want to assure you that you have boosted our morale considerably."

Pound waved a hand at Nobile, shaking his head. "*Grazie,* general, *grazie.* It is the least I can do for you who are engaged directly in the glorious fight against those who would subvert the true order of Hell."

"Directly?" Nobile shook his head. "You misjudge me, signor. I build blimps." He glanced at the hangar.

"I *attempt* to build blimps, but with the shortages, the bureaucracy . . ." He sighed. "In any case, my aircraft are not weapons of war, but vessels for scientific inquiry, as Commander Amundsen well knows " Nobile fluttered his right hand at the hangar. "Come, gentlemen, come. Let me show you my latest project."

The poet and the explorer followed Nobile into the vast hangar. Gas torches flickered as a man welded plates of the gutted shell of what looked like a B-25C fuselage. The plane had been flipped, and its bottom had been attached to a triangular shaped frame extending fifty feet in front of the plane, two hundred feet behind. Large silver spheres hung from the ceiling, and folds of gray rubber, dusty with talcum, were piled on the floor.

"The *Italia II*," Nobile said. "The N-5." He pointed at the fuselage. "My crew works hard, but at this rate . . ." He shook his head. "Well, perhaps we will have it complete in a year."

"It will be completed in a month," Pound said. "Please, your office. I have good news for you."

They stepped into a glassed office off the main bay. Nobile motioned Pound and Amundsen to two cracked leather chairs in front of a peeling and shellacked desk, then sat down in an equally dismal wooden chair behind the desk. Pound spread his cape behind him, reached around, swung his gun from behind his hip, and unsnapped the sling. Nobile looked at the gun, stared at the smooth silver gleam of the barrel.

"Not *another* Uzi?" Nobile asked.

Pound shook his head, smiled, ran a hand along the gleaming barrel. "No. Just an Uzi body, to fool the citizens. It's a Teller semi-automatic, with ten plasma rounds."

"An uncommon weapon." Nobile pursed his lips. "Pardon my asking, signor, but exactly whom do you represent? Your message this morning said you would be coming from the Ministry of Propaganda to do a

piece on our efforts, so I assumed . . . but this?" He
shook his head. "It is not my experience that propagandists
—let alone poets—are issued such exotic weapons, if
they dare go armed at all."

Pound looked up at the red sign along the glass wall
of the office, with letters six inches high that read
HYDROGEN IN USE: EXTREMELY FLAMMABLE.
NO FUMARE. "May I smoke, general?" he asked,
pulling a white tin out from a vest under his cape.

Nobile nodded. "The hydrogen has not yet been
pumped from the tanker into our storage tanks—a labor
dispute, I understand. It is safe."

"Care for one?" Pound stuck a cigarette in his mouth,
lit it, extended the tin to Nobile.

"No, I cannot abide Hell tobacco." Nobile sniffed the
tin. "Is that *real* tobacco?"

"Balkan Sobrannies, si," Pound said.

Nobile shook his head. "No . . . no, it is tempting,
but I cannot."

"Commander?" He waved the tin at Amundsen, who
shook his head. "No?" Pound clicked the tin shut,
slipped it back in a chest pocket of his vest. "General, I
am more than I represent. The details are complicated,
but let us just say that Lord Satan himself has taken an
interest in your project."

"Lord . . . Satan himself?" Nobile winced at the name.
"You are an emissary of His?"

"Of sorts." Pound sucked on the cigarette, let the
smoke tickle his lungs, then blew it into Nobile's face.
"Of sorts. The performance of the N-4 blimp in the
Mountain Campaign did not go unnoticed in high
circles—very high circles. His Infernal Majesty has seen
the utility of your airships in certain kinds of campaigns."

"*Performance?*" Amundsen asked. "The word I got
was that the N-4 *blew up.* Excuse me, Umberto, but as
I told you on the *Norge,* you must isolate the hydrogen
bags well from the exhaust of the engine nacelles. One
spark . . ."

"She was brought down by a Red Eye missile right up the pipes, Roald." He shuddered. "I grieve for the agony those aviators must have suffered. My ship . . . when I sell my ships, I cannot be responsible for their misuse." Nobile shook his head. "But, no, she did not perform to my specifications. The N-4 should have been able to go higher."

Pound fluttered a hand. "*Pfah*. She performed admirably. Your blimp took out Che's Forty-Second Camp with little more than a GE Minigun in the bow. Lord Satan is convinced such aircraft have their uses." Pound set the cigarette down on the edge of Nobile's desk, pulled out a small velvet bag from his vest, and opened it on the desk top. A minor mound of one-hundred-gram platinum diablos spilled out. "I understand that you are having problems with finances."

Amundsen snorted. Nobile ignored him, stared at the pile of dusky-silver coins. "To say the least, Signor Pound."

"This is the first appropriation." Pound pushed the coins toward Nobile. "More will come. If you are having trouble getting help, materials, anything, let me know." He smiled. "I have ways of tweaking the bureaucracy."

Nobile picked up a diablo, held it to the light. "*Grazie*, Signor Pound. *Grazie*." He set the coin down. "What I really need most is helium. Helium, not hydrogen. Hydrogen is so dangerous. Can you get us helium?"

"You do not want helium, Umberto," Amundsen said. "The lift is so much better with hydrogen."

"So you say, but the safety factor . . ." He turned to Pound. "Can you get helium?"

Pound shook his head. "That is the one thing I cannot do," he said. "There is not enough helium in Hell to . . . to make up a rat's fart. You must make do with hydrogen."

"This is what I have been told," he said. "Well, one

cannot be too choosy." Noble looked back at the pile of platinum.

"Good, then," Pound said. "Lord Satan would like the *Italia II* built in a month. Can you arrange quarters for me here? I will be assisting you in the construction —no, no, general, I will stay out of your way. I am only here to run liason with New Hell. It will be my ship, you see. Crew, ship . . . everything. There is a mission I must embark on. Lord Satan has given me a mission, and I have chosen your blimp for that duty. I *need* that blimp, do you understand?"

"Yes, yes. A month? I will see what I can do, signor." Nobile glanced at Amundsen.

"*Buono,* Umberto. *Buono.*" Pound grinned, stood. Nobile and Amundsen rose. "There is one other thing," he said. "This expedition—it will require Arctic experience, do you see? We must have the most experienced polar leaders working on this expedition."

"Si, si," Nobile said. "I already have some of the original *Italia* crew working with me: Biagi, Arduino, Behounek . . ."

"Yes, yes," Pound said. "But you need an experienced leader, a daring man of vision, a skilled commander . . ." He held out a hand to the Norwegian.

"Roald?" Nobile shook his head. "*No.* No, I *cannot* . . . I mean, I am sure the commander has other duties."

"My duty . . . My assignment is to do as Lord Satan and His agents wish," Amundsen said. "If he wishes me to work with you . . ."

"I . . . ." Nobile shook his head. "Well, of course. Of course." He held out his hand to Amundsen. "It will be an honor to work with you again, Roald."

Amundsen took his hand. "And with you, Umberto."

"Well," Pound said. "Good. I trust that the two of you will make great progress. A month, then? We can leave in a month?" Nobile nodded. "*Benissimo.*" He slung the Teller back over his shoulder, and walked to the doorway.

He paused, looked back at Nobile and Amundsen. "Of course, need I tell you the price of your failure, Umberto?" Pound smiled. "The Red Tent? Surely you remember the Red Tent, general? Ah, yes. Satan can arrange it, an eternal torment, custom designed: the rotting ice, your men starving before you, the summer sun beating down, the bears stalking you, the pain, the misery, the humiliation . . . You will not fail me, Umberto. You will not fail." He glared at Roald Amundsen. "And you, commendatore? You know the price, too. Need I say it?" Nobile and Amundsen said nothing.

"Do not fail," the poet said.

With a flourish, Ezra Pound gathered his black cape around him and marched out of the blimp hangar.

Crouched down behind a pile of crates, Pound stared at the man in the hangar doorway. In the dim lighting of the hangar, the inflating blimp seemed like a flaccid gray condom, a dark drape of dashed desire suspended from the ceiling. Outside the hangar Pound could hear the dull thump of a mortar attack on the New Hell airport, but inside the hangar was quiet, save for a faint hiss coming from the bank of hydrogen tanks on the south wall. Pound watched the man enter, smiled when he saw the man turn, his silhouette distinct against the ruby light glowing down from the EXIT sign overhead. Nobile: Pound recognized the cleft chin and the long nose easily. Nobile sniffed, and Pound sniffed with him, smelling the subtle hint of mustard that marked Hell hydrogen.

"Damn fools," Nobile muttered, walking over to the tanks.

They'd started inflating the hydrogen bags that morning. Pound remembered how nervous Nobile had been, the argument Nobile and Amundsen had had. Only the shell of the gondola, the main nacelle, and the spine had been finished. The engine nacelles had been mounted, but the motors had not yet been installed. Nobile and Amundsen agreed that the blimp skin and the ballonets had to be inflated, so the rudders and elevators could be fitted, the wiring, the cables, and the electronics installed. But Nobile had argued that they wait to pump in the hydrogen, while Amundsen had said pumping in the hydrogen now would save time later. They'd compromised on a mixture strong enough to suspend the weight of the ballonets and the blimp bag alone, but Pound could tell that it still made Nobile uncomfortable. He smiled to himself, pleased at the discord he'd created in Nobile's enterprise.

And now Nobile, paranoid Nobile, had come in to make a final check. *Buono,* Pound thought, *buono.* Nobile stepped to a bank of switches to the left of the door, and turned on the ceiling exhaust fans, venting any built up hydrogen out. Nobile walked to a row of tanks beyond where Pound hid.

Just as Nobile got to the tanks a foot scraped to the left. Nobile whirled. A lighter flickered in the velvet gloom just before the inflating blimp. Nobile dashed to a post next to the tanks, and Pound saw him grope for something—a fire extinguisher. The lighter flickered again, revealing a figure in black hunched before the flame. The general ran toward the flame, shouting, screaming as the dark figure held the lighter up to a bottle, and a wick in the bottle burst afire.

"No!" Nobile yelled. "The hydrogen! You cannot!"

Pound raised the Teller from his cape, sighted down it, rubbed the barrel. He clicked the safety off, checked to see that the red charging light glowed. His finger rested on the trigger, but he did not press down.

The dark figure pulled his arm back, paused, the flaming wick illuminating his face: a classical face, long nosed, full lipped, with deep black eyes. A red flower bloomed in the man's left orbit. His legs buckled beneath him. Another red flower bloomed in the man's chest, and the bottle shattered, a cloud of flaming gasoline enveloping the man's arm and then his body. The cracks of two rifle shots reverberated around the steel walls of the hangar. The humming fans sucked the fumes up to the ceiling. Nobile stepped forward, washed the exhaust of the CO_2 extinguisher over the burning corpse of the saboteur.

Pound watched as Nobile sniffed the air again, imagined Nobile's thoughts: *No tell tale smell of ozone . . . Good. The hydrogen had not ignited. The precious reserves of gas had not blown. The* Italia II *had not been destroyed.* Nobile put the fire out, and Pound stared fascinated at the frost collecting on the charred body, on the face. Something clicked in the darkness, metal on metal. A tall, pale man with ice blue eyes and short cropped white hair stepped into the light, slid the bolt back on a Krag 6.5 mm rifle.

"Roald," Nobile said.

Ah, thought Pound. He had wondered. He debated standing, revealing himself, but decided to stay put.

Amundsen ejected a cartridge, slung the carbine over his shoulder. "The blimp is safe?"

"I turned the exhaust on as soon as I smelled the hydrogen. It vented in time."

"Good, Umberto. Good." Amundsen kicked at the dead man. "Did you recognize him?"

"Dark, perhaps Spanish, perhaps Latin American. Probably one of Che's men? Who else? It's a good thing you had your rifle, Roald."

"Did I tell you about the polar bear in Greenland, Umberto? Yes? Ever since . . . In Hell, there are always polar bears. Be armed, Umberto."

Nobile shook his head. "No, Roald, not anymore. I am sick of war, sick of killing. If someone kills me . . . Well, here we do not die, eh?"

"Umberto, Umberto . . ." Amundsen shrugged. "The inflating? It is going well?"

Nobile nodded. "With the night shift, we should have the bag inflated by next week. And then . . ."

"And then we can begin the campaign."

"The expedition, Roald. The expedition. You will have your part of the crew ready?"

"Ready when you are." Amundsen looked around at the dark hangar. "Shall I close up?"

Nobile ran a hand though his hair. "Would you? I had a few calculations to run in my quarters. This mess . . . ?"

"I will take care of it, Umberto."

"Thank you, Roald. Good night then, commander."

"Good night, general."

Pound watched as Nobile set the fire extinguisher down and left the hanger. Amundsen kneeled, poked at the charred body. Flakes of black skin had begun to fall away from the corpse, revealing his identity, as the Undertaker's wraiths pulled him back to Reassignments. The Norwegian looked around, reached down, grabbed something around the corpse's neck, then pulled his hand back.

"Drop it, commendatore," Pound said, rising from the crates. "He will go back to Satan soon enough."

Amundsen dropped the ripcord, the tag that some souls—particularly soldiers and saboteurs—wore that supposedly took their bodies back instantly to the Undertaker. He whirled, the Krag sweeping before him. Pound swept his cape back, let Amundsen see the gleaming silver barrel of his plasma gun. The Norwegian relaxed, lowered his rifle. "Ez," he said. "Your man?"

Pound glanced at the healing corpse, falling into the floor, down into Hell, back to his Remaker. "My man? No." He stepped up to the body, glanced at the renewed face fading into the earth, shook his head. "I do not recognize him. Why did you want to send him back so quickly?"

"Are you implying that I knew him? That *I* hired this saboteur?" Amundsen raised the rifle. "Me? He was a mess; I wanted to clear the hangar of the body; isn't

that what the ripcord does—clean up messy bodies?"
Amundsen waved his rifle at the patch of charred concrete where the saboteur's body had been. "If this had
been my man, if I wanted him to succeed, why would I
kill him?"

Pound shrugged. "Who said he did not succeed? You
rattled Nobile. The poor man. He will go back to kick
Biagi, rail at me tomorrow to increase the guard on the
hangar, accuse you of incompetence for insisting that
the hydrogen be pumped now. You are sand in Nobile's
gears, Roald. Who said that the saboteur did not
succeed?"

Amundsen looked away. "I do not need this, fascisti."

"Ah, but you do . . . How goes your work? Will the
blimp be ready? Will it be built to your specifications?"

He snorted. "Do not cross me. I know what I am
doing. The *Italia II* will fly as planned."

"I know that," Pound said. "As *we* planned. Does all
work the way you want it? Will the engines sputter in
the cold? Will the bag of the blimp shred from the
prop's ice? Will the nacelle be rent from its supports?
Are your men building the quality aircraft that you
desire?"

Amundsen stared at the silver folds slowly filling, like
pus draining into a blister. "The blimp will be built as I
desire."

"Then all is well." Pound slung the Teller back over
his shoulder, behind his hip. "Come then, White Eagle, and I will tell you what I want done *next*."

Paradise hovered almost directly over the Aeronautical Construction Factory, its horrible light obscured by
high red clouds that soared over even the mountain
tops of the far off Himalayas. The great doors of the
main hangar creaked open, and the ruddy light oozed
into the cavern and over the nose of the *Italia II*, the
N-5. An I-beam track had been spiked into the tarmac,
and a dolly attached to the track, four wheels on the

underside of the I-beam, four on top, with plates connecting the wheels. A pylon rose up from the dolly and was attached to the nose of the blimp, so that the blimp rode the track like a monorail. The main nacelle—the fuselage of a Mitchell B-25C bomber—hung from the spine of the *Italia II*, a nose wheel mounted on the fuselage's back just touching the I-beam. Two ground crews pulled the blimp out of the hangar with ropes attached to the bow of the keel.

Pound, Nobile, and Amundsen stood outside the hangar, watching the blimp emerge. A low breeze blew in off the sea, gently pushing the *Italia* back and forth, the pylon swiveling. The ground crews stopped, straining at the ropes, keeping her steady. Giuseppe, Nobile's second in command, walked up to the nacelle door, pulled down a folded stairway, and turned to Nobile.

"Ready for inspection, Dr. Nobile," he said.

Nobile nodded at the small man, motioned to Pound and Amundsen. "Signor Pound? Commander?"

The four men entered the main nacelle, the salvaged fuselage. The fuselage had been mounted upside down, so the cockpit and forward turret faced down, and the dorsal turret was now a ball turret on the nacelle's belly. GE Miniguns replaced the old M2 machine guns. Nobile walked forward, to the main wheel mounted in the center, just aft of the forward turret. The main wheel controlled the rudders, and a wheel mounted to the left controlled the elevators. Behind the controls was a radio console, the engine console, and a navigator's station. Jump seats lined the starboard bulkheads aft of the main wheel, and through a small hatchway was a cargo hold. A ladder went down to the ball turret, and another ladder went up to a catwalk running the length of the blimp's spine. Nobile walked up to the rudder control, rubbed his hands over the smooth oak of the wheel.

"Well?" asked Pound. "Is she ready?"

Nobile turned. "What do you think, Roald? Shall we take her out?"

Amundsen shrugged. "A short trip? Why not? Do you have your crew?"

Nobile turned to his second. "Giuseppe, get Francis, Ettore, and Vincenzo." He nodded to Amundsen. "My men. Radio, technician, engineer, and motorman. Who do you take?"

Amundsen smiled. "Just one: Malmgren, the navigator."

Nobile frowned. "*Malmgren?* He is here, too? Where? How?"

"My doing, Umberto," Pound said. " I pulled a few strings in Reassignments—lucky for Malmgren. He was running a weather station at a Reeducation Camp near Thebes."

Nobile spat. "I'll not fly with him. I had thought Vigleri, not Malmgren. Do you know what he did?" Nobile turned his back on them, walked to the doorway. He turned back to Pound, Amundsen. "Bungler. Fool. I will not fly this blimp with Malmgren."

"*Basta*," Pound said. "Malmgren is *my* choice, not Roald's. This is my expedition. You will fly on my terms, or the blimp will not fly at all. I do not need this, general." He pulled the Teller forward, raised it straight up. "One shot, Signor, and it is finished, all of us, fried to a crisp and back to Reassignments. Is this what you want?" He clicked the safety off.

"Why not?" Nobile asked. "Malmgren will get us there soon enough anyway." Pound stared at Nobile; he looked down. "No, I do not want this." Nobile sighed. "*Malmgren*, then. But I do not like it."

"Since when have we liked anything in Hell, general?" Pound walked up to Nobile, put an arm on his shoulder. "Malmgren will be fine. He knows the weather. We will need such a man."

Nobile looked at Giuseppe, held his hand up. "My friend? Get Malmgren."

Giuseppe had paused at the bottom of the stairway; he nodded, went down.

"A shake-down cruise, then," Nobile said. "Let us get one thing clear now, signors. For this flight, I command, *capiche?*"

Pound nodded. "It is your trip. But on the expedition, it will be *my trip*. Amundsen will make any command decisions, at my direction—like with the *Norge*—*capiche?*"

"Understood. Signor Pound, do you wish to test the guns?" Nobile waved toward the forward turret.

Pound smiled. "In my old age I denied the Bloody Sestina, but here in Hell, there *is* no wine like the blood's crimson. Gladly, general. Let us send some damned in the Phlegethon Swamp back to their Re-Maker." Pound slipped into the bow gunner's station, just forward of the main wheel.

Nobile's crew came on board, clambered to their stations. A blond man of medium height came on last, looked down at Nobile's gaze. He turned to Amundsen. "Commander? What station?"

"Aft, Finn. Navigation." He waved at a table. "A short course, over the swamp."

"Aye, sir." Malmgren glanced at Nobile. "General, the Himalayas are up today. There may be mountain waves. Stay clear of them, sir."

"Thank you, Malmgren. I will." Nobile turned to the men. "Stations, please."

The ground crew pulled the *Italia II* five hundred yards out from the hangar, on an apron heading southwest to the main runway. Nobile motioned through an open port to the ground crew, and they let go the ropes. Francis touched a switch, winding them in. The *Italia II* swiveled into the wind, its bow pointed west toward the sea.

"Vincenzo," Nobile said to the motorman, "Start engines, reverse, quarter props."

"Engines reverse, quarter-props."

"Francis, elevators level."

"Level, doctor."

"Giuseppe, request clearance from the tower."

Giuseppe turned the radio on, spoke in Greek to the tower. "Cleared for take-off, Doctor," he said.

"Release pylon."

A click came from the bow, and the blimp fell back from the pylon and the track. "Pylon released," said Francis.

Nobile glanced at Amundsen, at Pound forward in the ball turret. "Ready, gentlemen?" Amundsen nodded; Pound waved. "Vincenzo, full props, forward. Francis, elevators forty-five degrees. Gentlemen . . ." Umberto Nobile smiled, looked out the forward port of the *Italia II* at the gray tarmac a dozen feet below them. "Up ship!"

The *Italia II* rose lazily into the wind, its four props thrumming quietly, the blades of each engine four triangles flickering in the low light. Nobile gently eased the rudder to port, let the wind catch the blimp's tail and turn the airship around, with the westerly wind at her back. Steering clear of the air space over the New Hell airport, the *Italia II* followed the dike that curved southeast on the border of New Hell. Rockets rose from the deep forest bordering Decentral Park—Cong at it again, Pound thought—and then popped harmlessly over the Roman Quarter. The blimp rose higher, to about a thousand feet, then leveled off.

Nobile took her down over the Phlegethon Swamp, along a meandering creek that twisted south and below the airport. Pound clicked on his headset, spoke back to Nobile.

"Take her down on a strafing run," he said, "on that herd right there—" he pointed down to a marshy plain in the midst of the swamp. "I want to see how this Minigun works."

"I have no wish to slaughter innocents," Nobile said.

"*Innocents?*" Pound turned, glared back at Nobile.

"You think those fuckers are *innocent*? You're talking about some of the most savage souls ever to walk the earth. Why do you think they're in the Plain of Blood—because they jerked off one too many times?"

"They are innocent now, signor," Nobile said.

"*Christ.*" Pound slammed his hand against the front of Nobile's console. "Look, we'll kill souls far more innocent by the time this expedition is through. I need to know how these guns work."

"It's *my* mission now . . ." Nobile said.

"Ah: true—I'd forgotten," said Pound. "Okay then: May I pretty please do a strafing run? I'll shoot out . . . those hummocks, okay? No innocents."

Nobile flicked a switch. "The forward gun controls the rudders and elevators now. As you turn the gun, so will the ship turn."

"That's more like it," Pound said. "Okay. Give me full throttles."

Nobile glanced back at his motorman. "Vincenzo, full throttle, all props." He armed the gun, rotating one of six barrels to the top so that it was loaded and ready.

"A-hah!" Pound yelled. He threw the arming switch. The drive whirred and the barrel clicked forward 60 degrees. Tilting the GE Minigun forward, the blimp followed a brief second afterwards, the nose tipping at a 45-degree angle. The *Italia II* cast a long shadow on the swamp below, and the ship went down to meet its shadow.

Pound clutched the twin handles of the Minigun and pushed back against the hard plastic of the gunner's seat, his eyes intent on the darkling plain below, his teeth crimping his lower lip. A herd of damned ran up a stream bed, into the mountains, two chasing centaurs cracking whips over their heads. The damned glanced up at the blimp coming down on them, darted to the left and right, and were pushed back together by the centaurs. Pound smiled. He tilted the Minigun to the right, dipped it slightly, and squeezed the trigger.

The six barrels of the gun whirred as they rotated, puffs of white smoke whisping in front of the Lexan bubble of the turret. A thousand rounds—one brief burst—spiraled down to Hell, a hot ribbon of lead ripping into the back of a centaur on the right, sundering man-body from horse-body. The detorsoed horse galloped on, tumbling into a ravine. The centaur's torso rolled over, staring up at the blimp, at Pound, with burning eyes. *Enough, Ez*, a voice said inside Pound's head, but he ignored it, and swung the Minigun to the left. When the second centaur had fallen to the ground, a gash of red down its spine, Pound swept the gun across the herd, finger twitching over the trigger, ready to wipe them all out. But the *Italia II* wriggled back and forth, engines howling, the skin of the blimp snapping in the torsion of Pound's indecision. He sighted the Minigun level on a man running straight and proud at the head of the herd, his red braid whipping across his back, then squeezed the trigger.

Basta, the voice said inside his head, and the gun jammed. Pound felt an electric, stabbing pain lance up his crotch, and jerked back against the gunner's set. He let go of the minigun. "Take it back, Nobile," he said through clenched teeth. "Take control back."

"No wine like the blood's red crimson, Pound?" Nobile asked. He flicked a switch on his command console, and swung the main wheel around, so the plain, and the mountains, were at the blimp's stern.

Pound got up from his seat, took a deep breath. He turned to Nobile. "Your ship performs well, general. I think it is ready for the expedition."

Nobile smiled. "Ready when you are, signor." He flew the *Italia II* down, back to the airport. When he had the airship flying level and true, he nestled it up to its pylon like a babe seeking its mother's teat.

Exactly one month from when he had first walked into the main hangar of the Aeronautical Construction

Factory, Ezra Pound strode out of the hangar, his black
cape flowing behind, his steps matching the progress of
the *Italia II* as it was wheeled out on its track. The
blimp's ballonets had been pumped to bursting with
almost pure hydrogen. Her fuel tanks were heavy with
diesel. Her holds had been loaded to capacity with
supplies for the Democratic Resistance, and her guns
ready with round after round of ammunition, each bullet blessed by the Black Pope, each assigned to some
Dissident. Pound looked at the flat black veneer of the
blimp, inspecting every rivet, every stitch of her skin,
pleased that she had been built to his exacting specifications. His heart glowed with pride at the American flag
he had insisted be painted on the ship, the 48 stars
gleaming in Paradise's early light. Below the flag, to
accommodate Nobile, was the tricolor flag of Italy, with
a bundle of fasces separating the two insignia, and the
letters ITALIA II painted on her sides. The Resistance
would know who came to them, Pound thought. They
would not doubt it.

Nobile saluted Pound as he walked up to the aviator
and his crew: Giuseppe, Francis, Ettore, and Vincenzo.
Nobile's eyes glared at Pound, fierce and proud. Pound
stopped, waved his hand at Nobile and at the blimp.
He raised his right hand, glanced at his watch.

"We must depart. Is your crew ready?" asked Pound.

"Ready, except for Malmgren," said Nobile. "And
the commendatore."

"They are on their way, I suppose? Ah—Finn comes."
Pound glanced at Malmgren, hurrying up the tarmac.

Malmgren stopped, panting. "General," he said. "Signor Pound. The commander . . ." He gasped for breath.

"*Yes?*" Pound asked.

"*Dead*, sirs—Reassigned."

"Reassigned?" Pound strode up to Malmgren, gripped
his shoulders. "Reassigned? But how . . . ?"

Malmgren held a hand up to his neck, slid it across
his throat. "A blade to the jugular. He was still warm

when I found him." Malmgren looked down. "The White Eagle has fallen to death once again."

Pound looked at Nobile, raised a finger, pointed at him. "*You*," he said, "Umberto."

"Can you not bring him back?" Nobile asked. "Your connections . . . ? Have him Reassigned here?"

"It is not so easy . . . You did this, Umberto. You killed Amundsen. As before."

"Me? You judge me wrongly, Signor. I have been with the *Italia II* all morning." Nobile waved at his crew. "Ask my men."

"I—of course, Umberto. Of course." Pound bowed to Nobile, waved his right hand at him. "My apologies. Of course. You could not have done this." He turned to Malmgren. "The body—it is returned to Satan?"

Malmgren nodded. "I saw it sink into Hell myself."

"Then there is nothing we can do now, except continue. Umberto, you will command the ship—following my general orders, of course."

Nobile clicked his heels together, bowed slightly. "As you wish, Signor Pound."

"*Benissimo*. Let us leave now." Swirling his cape behind him, Pound led them onto the blimp. "Let us avenge Amundsen."

The peninsula thrust out into the northern sea like a crooked finger. Pink pack ice surrounded the peninsula, a flat bay along the peninsula's southern edge, extending perfectly flat and smooth to the far horizon. Hovering above the foothills ten miles to the south, the *Italia II* waited for the brief dawn to break. Campfires flickered in the lowlands and valleys of the foothills— the fires of the Dissidents. Halfway up the crook of the peninsula searchlights blazed, barrage balloons blackening the sky. Occasionally a mortar burst from the area of the searchlights, and another mortar would be returned back from the foothills.

Flying over the Great Range west of New Hell—they'd

become the Smokies, and then turned into the Alps to the north—the blimp had wound its way through shifting mountain passes, across the great desert controlled by Mao, and up the coast, along ranges that changed not into new mountains, but new nations. Malmgren had charted a new course daily, one map at a time, as Pound saw fit. The poet hadn't even let Nobile know where they were going—he had only said, "Fly the ship."

Pound stared through binoculars at the blazing lights to the northwest. He let them rest on the cord around his neck, turned to Nobile and Malmgren. "Good work, signors. We have reached our destination." He waved a hand at the searchlights. "Free Hell—home of the Democratic Resistance."

Nobile nodded. "Ah: I'd thought we were carrying cargo for them."

"Cargo?" Pound snorted. "Of a sort. What do you think our mission is?"

Nobile waved back at the hold. "Guns, ammunition, medical supplies, food . . . Are we not running supplies to the Resistance? You'd said in your broadcasts that they had taken back part of Hell from Che and the Dissidents." He smiled at Pound. "You never *did* say where."

"There," said Pound. "Purgatory, general. The Purgatory Peninsula." He unrolled a map of the area, tapped an X penciled in two-thirds of the way up the peninsula. "This entire coast is controlled by the Dissidents, but the Resistance has liberated the peninsula. The peninsula is all that keeps the Dissidents from sweeping north across the ice and into Purgatory—all that keeps them from seeking the justice they think they deserve."

Nobile nodded. "And we will go resupply them?"

Pound smiled. "Hah! Resupply them? Hardly." Pound reached behind him, and pulled out his Teller. "No, signors. We go to Free Hell not to save them, but to destroy them. We go . . . to wipe them out. And when we have destroyed them, and nothing stands in our way—" Pound looked forward, at the horizon beginning to glow dull red "—then *we* will escape—escape, si- gnors, to Purgatory!"

"*Escape* . . . ?" Nobile whispered.

"Escape," said Pound. "Are you with me?"

"Escape." Nobile smiled. "I had thought you . . . a slimy, conniving bastard, Pound. I misjudged you. How do we know that you won't betray us? How do we know that Satan won't stop us?"

Pound shrugged. "I have come this far. It is God who is all powerful, not Satan. Well?"

Nobile turned to the rest of the crew. "Finn, Giuseppe? Francis? Ettore? Vincenzo? What do you say? Is this madness? Or should we join Pound?"

"It is madness," said Malmgren. "But we should join the poet."

"Si," said Giuseppe. He turned to the other men. "We will fight with you, with the poet."

"I do not like this, Pound," Nobile said. "It stinks of treachery." He stared out at the mountains below, then smiled. "*You*—Roald knew. You had him killed because he would not go along with you?"

Pound smiled. "He was . . . reluctant."

"But won't he betray you on the Undertaker's table?"

"No—well, perhaps, but not for a while. The Under- taker is so, so *busy*. And he babbles so much: he hardly cares what the resurrected think." Pound grimaced, recalling his last Reassignment. He stared at Nobile. "Are you with me, general? Shall we make a go for it?"

"It still stinks, Pound." He looked at the other men, at Pound's Teller. "Still, I don't have any choice, do I? We'll do it, then, Pound. We'll wipe out this counter- revolutionary camp, and then make the run for Purgatory."

"*Benissimo*," said Pound. "*Benissimo*." He slipped a piece of paper to Giuseppe. "Broadcast a message on this channel to the Resistance: PAPIOLS, COME! LET'S TO MUSIC!" Ez turned to Nobile, held up his right

hand like a claw. "When the day breaks, and Paradise is
at our back, we will attack. The Dissidents will fire at
us, but we will be too high for their rockets to have any
effect. The Resistance will lower the barrage balloons
and let us into their encampment. When we are in—"
Pound smiled, closed his hand into a fist, and shook it.

"Si," said Nobile. "Stations, men. Malmgren, take
the ball turret. Vincenzo, Francis, Ettore, your stations. Signor Pound, I give you the honor of the bow
turret."

"*Grazie*," said Pound. He climbed forward.

Paradise rose behind the mountains east of the blimp,
lighting the plain of the frozen Sea of Purgatory into a
flaming mirror. The steel roofs of the Resistance camp
glowed in the dawn, the windows of the fort blazing
back the Holy Planet's glare. Nobile steered the *Italia
II* into a gentle wind from the west, and kept a level
altitude over the Dissidents' camps. Flak burst a hundred feet below them, the bursts of smoke silver puffs
against the white plain.

Giuseppe broadcast Pound's message, and the reply
came back from the Resistance: BERTRANS, TO THE
MUSIC.

"To the music," Pound whispered, and then, to Nobile. "Descend, general. Let's take them out."

The blimp roared down, a cloud of vengeance, its
engines screaming, a low, shrill screech rising from a
loose fold of rubber flapping in the descent. Someone
in the Resistance compound began winding the barrage
balloons down. The *Italia II* came over the edge of the
compound, high walls like a crater's rim. Nobile yanked
the wheel hard, to the right, swinging the blimp around
so that the nose swiveled on a point five-hundred yards
dead center over the compound.

"I'll keep her in a low circle, nose down, Pound!"
Nobile yelled to the poet. "Fire at will!"

Pound sighted down the barrels of the Minigun at
the fort below. Low buildings circled the parade ground

in the center, the searchlights mounted on the roofs. The barrage balloons were winding down on giant spools mounted in the esplanade running the length of the compound wall. Pound expected to see men coming out of the bunkers, men ready to bring the blimp down. His eyes flicked right to left, searching for a watchman, a lookout, anyone. A lone figure suddenly appeared at the center of the fort. Pound smiled, flicked the Minigun's trigger forward, and fired.

The bullets fell down in long, lazy loops, a narrow funnel of fire descending down to the figure, surrounding it, enveloping it. The blimp came down, lower, the Minigun's rounds tightening into a column of lead. The lone figure raised its arms at the blimp, spread its wings, and caught the bullets.

Dust swirled around the creature below, dust and fire and smoke and eviscerated bullets, sweeping the Minigun's force into it, pulling the bullets down, yanking the bullets, the charge, the powder, the cartridges, the very gun itself down into it. Pound pushed back from the gun, let go, pulled his cape before him as the GE Minigun was ripped from its supports and out of the blimp.

More, Ez, the voice said inside his head. *Give me more.*

Pound pulled his Teller forward, squeezed ten quick plasma bursts through the broken turret, waited for the gun to recharge, then fired ten more. The plasma charges fell down on the thing, its blue light flickering, enveloping the cloud around it, joining the dust, the smoke, the lead, the steel. The thing opened its great mouth, swallowed, and sucked the tornado into its maw. Pound heard his Teller cycle and fire, cycle and fire, until its batteries were exhausted. Behind him, Nobile fought for control, fought to take the blimp out of the spiral, to no avail.

Dust cleared. The thing at the center of the Resistance camp rose up, larger and larger, its wings spread-

ing to cover the sky. It reached up with a hand the size
of the blimp, and with a gentle finger, touched the
blimp's nose. The *Italia II* swirled around on the tip of
the finger, slowing and slowing like a top, until it rested
level in the sky.

"Lord Satan," someone behind Pound whispered.

EZRA, Lord Satan said, YOU HAVE DONE WELL.

Pound gulped. "I came to please you, Lord Satan."

YOU CAME TO DESTROY MY RESISTANCE, Lord
Satan said, BUT *I* AM THE RESISTANCE.

"I . . . I see that, Lord."

WHY? HAVE I NOT BEEN GOOD TO YOU?

"Very good," Pound said. "But . . ." *The Truth*, the
voice said inside him. *The Truth, Ez.* "I . . . It is not
enough. I wish to escape."

OH, said Satan. WELL. I AM HURT, BUT NOT
SURPRISED. ALL WISH TO ESCAPE MY DOMIN-
ION. EVEN *I* WISH TO ESCAPE MY DOMINION.
Satan lowered a finger, and drew a charred gash across
the peninsula, across the Resistance compound. THERE.
MY POWERS DIMINISH THERE. I AM TOO CLOSE
TO PURGATORY, DO YOU SEE? ESCAPE THEN.
CROSS THE LINE AND SEE.

"Props full reverse," Nobile whispered back to Ettore.

NOBILE KNOWS, Satan said. YES, PROPS FULL
REVERSE. RUN FOR IT. I GIVE YOU A CHANCE.

Satan touched the nose of the blimp again, and pushed
it. Pound glanced down, saw the *Italia II*'s shadow pass
over the black gash in the peninsula. Satan smiled,
pursed his lips together, and blew. The blimp slipped
backwards, her props screeching as they gasped for
purchase, and then Satan raised his wings.

"Props forward!" Nobile yelled. "Finn, Pound, get
out of the turrets. All hands—brace for impact!" Nobile
swung the wheel around again, turning the blimp's
stern behind them, their back to Satan.

Pound came up out of the nose turret, pushed by
Nobile, and took a jump seat against the port wall,

across from Francis at the elevator controls. Finn rose up from the belly turret, strapped himself in next to Pound.

Satan's gale hit the blimp from behind, tossed it forward on a wave of hot air, like a cork in a raging surf. Nobile gripped the wheel, twisting and turning with the buffets of Satan's wrath. Struts creaked and groaned from the spine of the blimp, the engines sputtered and gasped as the carburetors adjusted to new qualities of air. A chill spread over the blimp, frost forming on the walls of the nacelle. Pound pulled his cape around him, then smiled.

This is how it should be, he thought. *It will work.*

He stood up, spread the cape back, and went up to a wall of the nacelle. A dark cloud spread across the peninsula, and a horrid flapping whipped the air into hundreds of small tornadoes. Snow swept by the ports of the nacelle in streamers of broken white. Pound rubbed frost from a port, looked up at the blimp bag above. A thin sheen of red ice slowly built up on the flat-black rubber. He turned to Nobile.

"General?" Pound asked.

Nobile glanced over at Pound, nodded, looked away. "Now what, Pound? Do we still escape? Or incur Satan's wrath even more?"

"Escape, signor. Escape in the only way we know."

He nodded. "Die again?"

"Another spin of the wheel."

"Another torment?"

"Perhaps it will be better." Pound shrugged.

"Perhaps."

"I only meant to say general, that . . . that you showed great nerve." He jerked his head back, toward the sound of Satan flapping his wings. "I mean, thinking ahead of Satan."

"I'll probably pay for that, Pound." Nobile shrugged. "What now? What next?"

"There is a village ahead, near Purgatory. If you can make it?"

Nobile smiled at Pound. "If." he tightened his grip on the wheel. "Where?"

Pound took the chart that had been spread on the table, held it in front of Nobile. He pointed at the tip of the Purgatory Peninsula. " 'Middle finger,' " he said. "Qitiqliq. There is a small camp there—mostly whalers and such. It's something. If we live . . . ?"

"*Bene*," Nobile said. He looked at the map, then stared forward into the gloom.

Pound went back to the port, opened it, and leaned out. His black cape flying behind him in Satan's gale, he watched the red ice spin off the props and strike the underside of the blimp bag. The ice built up on the cracked wood blades, flew off in fist-sized chunks, and tore into the bag of the blimp. In the scream of the gale, he thought he heard the gentle hiss of the hydrogen leaking out of the bag. The Purgatory Peninsula seemed to rise to meet them, seemed to grab at the *Italia II* and yank it down to Hell.

Pound ducked back inside the command nacelle. "The ice is building up," he said.

"What?" Nobile yelled back.

"The ice. It's building up on the propellers, breaking off in little chunks, and shredding the blimp bag."

Nobile turned back, smiled. "No problem. Amundsen installed shields. He checked them himself, assured me they would work properly. We had that problem on the *Norge*."

Pound stuck a hand out the window, reached up, pulled a piece of tattered rubber inside, handed it to Nobile. "Amundsen's a son of a bitch."

"Fock," said Nobile.

Pound stepped forward, to Nobile's right, leaned against the console and looked at Nobile. "Odd, isn't it," he whispered, "how only Malmgren saw Amundsen die?" Pound pointed with his chin back at Malmgren, hunched in his jump seat. "And how Amundsen isn't here to see us crash?"

Nobile jerked his head toward Pound, bit his lip, then looked over at Ettore. "Ettore, take the wheel, please."

He strode up to Malmgren, Pound following, and grabbing the lapels of the navigator's jacket, yanked his head up. Malmgren reached for the catches of the safety belt holding him into the jump seat, but Nobile slapped his hands away.

"Finn! Did Roald die?"

Finn Malmgren looked up. "Die? Of course—that's why he's not here."

Nobile reached down into Malmgren's shirt, pulled the gold chain looped around his neck, the ebony tag at the end of the chain with Malmgren's vitals encoded in it—a ripcord. "Ah, Signor Important," Nobile asked, "what is so special about *you* that you need a ripcord? What information could you possibly possess that would make you want to suicide instantly?" Nobile looped the chain around his hand, twisted it lightly. "What *is* this little toy, and what happens if I pull it now?"

"Umberto," Malmgren croaked, "*No*, no . . ." Malmgren bit down on his tongue, but it moved around in his mouth, a viper aborning, bloody froth dripping out his lips. "I . . . I must speak." His voice changed its timbre. "You have asked for the truth. The ripcord is not a suicide device, not a gadget for spies and saboteurs, though that is what those who wear it would like you to believe it. It is a *torment*—my torment. The coward's curse, we who wear it call it. I am forced to tell you this. Lord Satan tests us, sends us into battle, gives us special missions. The ripcord is our way out, a clean death, a painless end. It wipes the slate clean, takes us back to what we were when we came into Hell."

"That is so bad?"

"No, no—yes, it is bad, for the one thing we remember is that we pulled the ripcord to escape dying, escape pain, escape suffering—escape *truth*, do you see?" Malmgren looked down. "I have pulled it seven times already. Each time I come closer to enduring, to going beyond my fear. If you pull it . . . The Devil does not make such fine distinctions. I will wear the cord again, forever and forever, until I die an honorable death."

Nobile twisted the chain in his hand. "Then. Then, answer me: Did Roald die?" He turned the chain tighter, until its links cut into Malmgren's pale throat.

"No . . ." he croaked. "No, I lied. *He* told me to lie."

"Kill him," Pound said. He reached for Nobile's hand.

"*He?* Who?" Nobile asked. "Roald?"

"*Pound*," Malmgren said.

Nobile turned, let the man drop. Pound reached forward, snatched the chain, and pulled. Malmgren's mouth opened, gasped, then his eyes dilated into black pools, and the body fell into itself and disappeared. The air popped around the space where Malmgren had been.

"*You*," Nobile said, staring at Pound.

Pound smiled. "Me," he said. "Well, who else? Who helped you build this blimp? Who had Amundsen and Malmgren assigned to you? Who thought up this mission?"

"You," Nobile whispered. "But why?"

"Think, Umberto. *Think*. Think why Amundsen died in the World."

"But . . ." He shook his head. "But we settled that."

"Oh?" Pound snorted. "Oh? Is anything *ever* settled in Hell? Ever?"

Nobile looked down. "Never," he said quietly. "*Amundsen* thought up this whole operation?"

"Amundsen? No, hardly—but close. Close."

"Satan," Nobile said.

"Ah, yes—our friend, Lord Satan." Pound stepped away, held his black cape out like wings. "Satan, Lord and Master." He flapped the cape back and forth, then wrapped it around him and sat back down. "Did you really think the Big Guy would actually let you *fly* to Purgatory?"

"*You* said that. You said he is not All Powerful." Nobile glanced aft, at the bulkheads of the blimp. "As you pointed out, Satan *did* let us build the *Italia II*."

"Yes, He did," Pound said. "Oh, he certainly did. And why did Satan let us build this blimp? Why did He let you get this far?" Nobile has to know, Pound thought.

"To torment me," Nobile said. "To punish me." He looked out the window, at the raging storm.

"Yes. *Yes.* And why else?"

Nobile stared at Pound, looked into his dark brown eyes. Pound smiled, tobacco stained teeth glinting out from black lips. Nobile turned away, shook his head. "*You*," he said. "To deliver you—to *this*?"

"*Bene*, Signore Nobile. *Bene.*" He fluttered his hand, making a mock bow.

"Fock," Nobile said. He straightened up, smoothed the lapels of his wool jacket. "Fock *you*. You will get where you will. And I, I will do then what I am to do: I will land this ship safely and protect my crew."

Nobile walked forward, took the wheel from Ettore. The clouds had parted briefly, and the tip of the peninsula stretched before them. "Okay," he said. "Then we go down there." He waved at the crew. "Landing stations—crash stations. Spread the word. I want everyone ready to jump if we have to. Dress warmly, too." He glared at Pound. "*You* just stay out of my way."

"As you wish, captain." Pound bowed at him, swept his cape across the deck, and sat down again.

The *Italia II* spun around in the gale, turned into the wind. Footsteps rang on the steel deck of the catwalk as Giuseppe, Ettore, and Vincenzo ran to the landing stations fore and aft. Francis remained at the elevator controls, with Pound and Nobile in the main nacelle. Pound reached into the chest pocket of his black jacket,

pulled out a tin case of cigarettes. "Captain?" he asked
Nobile.

"Fool!" Nobile said. He reached over, and with the
back of his hand, knocked the tin out of Pound's hand.

"Signore, those are *Sobrannies*," he said. "Do you
realize how hard they are to get?" He went down on
hands and knees, began picking up the cigarettes.

Nobile ignored Pound, gripped the oak wheel, fighting to keep the blimp into the wind. Francis struggled
next to him, turning the elevators, the two men trying
to fly the blimp down. She barely responded. Pound
gathered up his cigarettes, stuffed them in his vest, and
stood. He looked out at a frozen lagoon looming before
them, watched it recede below. Nobile turned the blimp
about, let the wind take the airship into the coast,
trying for another approach.

"Release ten-percent gas, all ballonets," he shouted
in the ship's intercom. The needles on the gas gauges
jerked, then began to fall down. They lost more altitude.

"You want to come down fast?" Pound asked.

"Shut up," Nobile said.

"I just had an idea," he said.

Nobile sighed. "All right. Let's hear it."

"Send all the men forward. Pump the water ballast
forward, too. The nose will drop." He held his hand out
straight, then pointed the fingers down. "See?"

"*Bene*," Nobile said.

Pound shrugged. "You learn a few things in poetics,"
he said.

"All hands forward," Nobile shouted. "Pump ballast
forward."

The *Italia II*'s nose dropped, the deck slanting at 45
degrees, pencils rolling off the console. A cigarette
rolled by Pound's foot. He stomped on it, reached
down, pulled the flattened cylinder up, stuck it in his
mouth. The ice rose up to the blimp, faster and faster.
Francis turned the elevator wheel level, but the blimp
stayed nose first, at forty-five degrees. Nobile locked

the rudder wheel, stepped over to Francis, and heaved with Francis to pull the ship out of the dive. Something screeched overhead, and Pound looked up. He heard a loud snap, then something whipping around above them. The elevator wheel spun back, tossing Nobile and Francis to the floor. The *Italia II* fell into a steep dive. The lagoon came at them.

"*Damnazione!*" Nobile shouted. He got up, yelled into the intercom. "All hands aft! Quick, quick." He looked at the intercom light; it didn't come on. He hit the switch, then pounded the console. "Francis! Run! Tell them to go aft!"

Francis nodded, climbed up into the catwalk above. They heard his footsteps thunder forward.

Nobile grabbed the main wheel, looked over his shoulder at Pound. "Ez! Prepare to crash!"

"Right," Pound said. He went back to the jump seat, strapped himself in, pulled the cape around him.

"Shit," Nobile said.

He fought with the helm, not daring to leave it, alone with Pound, all his men forward. Qitiqliq rose up to greet them, a little cluster of huts on a small mound between the great sea of ice and the Purgatory Peninsula. As they came down, Satan's gale seemed to stay above them, and they descended into calm, the light of Paradise gentle on the ice. The ice rose up, and Nobile gripped the helm as the blimp hit.

The nose of the blimp hit first. Like the nipple on a great baby bottle, it collapsed, pushing in. The forward section of the catwalk hit next, the edge of the keel cutting a long groove in the ice before the force crumpled the steel, pinning the men in the forward section between the base of the catwalk and the top of the spine, crushing them as the crash bent the steel. The command nacelle hit next, the B-25C fuselage ridiculous-looking upside down, the nose wheel bouncing on the ice, then wedging into an ice crack. The nacelle cracked at the top, ripping loose from the spine, separating from the blimp. The four engine nacelles broke apart, one propeller spinning into the ice, the others spinning up into the blimp bag, cutting it to shreds. The bag split open, and the ballonets inside burst, hydrogen spilling into the air.

Nobile slammed into the console, was thrown against the starboard bulkhead, then yanked from his feet and slammed shoulder-first into a seat post. A bone cracked in his back. He turned his head, looked up at Pound. The poet remained strapped in the jumpseat, head down between his knees, arms crossed over his head. Pound looked up, saw light pouring in as the remains of the blimp rose up and away, freed from the weight of the main nacelle. Ettore waved from part of the spine still attached to the stern.

The main nacelle slid across the ice, then came to a stop. Pound sat up, unstrapped himself, walked over to Nobile. He stood over the General, a limp cigarette in his lips, then kneeled down.

"You okay?" Pound asked.

"Fock no," Nobile said. "I think my back's broken."

"Yeah?" Pound reached down, pressed against Nobile's spine. A searing pain roared through Nobile; he winced, closed his eyes, cursed. "You're right, general," Pound said.

"Leave me," Nobile said. "Let me go back . . . back to Reassignments."

"To Fart Breath? No, you'll be fine," Pound said. "Let me move you."

"No!" he screamed. "Let me—"

"Ah." Pound reached underneath Nobile, rolled him over. Something cracked at the base of Nobile's neck. "How's that?"

"I . . ." Blood bubbled from his lips. "I . . . thank you, Pound. That's better." Nobile stared up at the caped poet. "Lord Satan, I have failed."

"No," Pound said. "You have done well, Umberto.

You have fulfilled your mission. You're a . . . *heck* of a pilot. Thank you for delivering me to Qitiqliq."

Nobile grimaced. "*Ebbene*, signor."

"An admirable job." Pound waved at the wrecked nacelle, shrugged. "A bit rough on the landings, but otherwise . . . fine. I'll go get help."

"Not . . . necessary, Pound." Nobile spat. "Ah. Ah. Back I go."

"Hold on, chum."

"No . . . no, I go."

Pound shrugged. "As you like." He stood, looked down at Nobile.

"See you, Pound," Nobile hissed.

"Not bloody likely," Pound said. He watched as Nobile heaved one, two, three last ragged breaths, and then went back to Reassignments. He reached down, closed Nobile's eyelids, and got up.

"Hell of a way to fly," he said. He took the unlit cigarette out of his mouth, smoothed it, stuck it back in. From his vast pocket the man in the black cape pulled out a book of matches, lit the cigarette, turned, and tossed the flaming match back at the remains of the *Italia II*. Pound pulled the cape over his shoulders, pulled the Teller forward, and began walking to Qitiqliq. A cloud of hydrogen burst aflame behind him, the flames licking at Ezra Pound's cape, and then receding. He sucked at the Sobrannie, and smiled.

GIVING HELL A SHOT

Bill Kerby

I ask you to forgive me.

I'm an actor. A damn good one, too. I wanted to be an actor since I was a little boy and fell in love with Montgomery Clift in *Red River*. Wasn't that an incredible performance? The sheer force of his commitment, of his persona blew my former hero, John Wayne, right off the screen. When I walked out of the theatre in Shaker Heights that day, my life direction was basically decided.

Although you don't realize it, you've seen me in movies, TV, plays; heard me doing voice-overs and books for the blind, I was even the voice of a caboose on a kid's radio show. Acting, as Brando once pointed out, is everywhere. Once I saw that I was not going to be a star right away, that it wasn't going to break bright and fast for me like it had for Monty in New York, I settled into a pretty good career playing featured parts, working my way up from the third guy on the right to speaking roles with a continuity of scenes. When I come to work, I come knowing my lines, who I'm supposed to be, and how to not bump into the furniture. If I ever break out, it will be from the experience of ten or twenty years of solid work. The way Harry Dean Stanton has. I'm told I have the younger version of that kind of face.

I look at what sneaks by for good acting these days and I just don't know. Some guy has a good moment and pretty soon they are talking Academy Award. So I keep working, keep studying the great old movies on the VCR—Olivier's *Henry V*, Bogart's *African Queen*, Harlow in *Red Dust*, O'Toole as Lawrence, Walter Huston as anything—and I dream. I am working with Pacino when he was still Pacino or Streep or Brando and we have a perfect script by Frank Pierson or Robert Towne or Nunnally Johnson, and Kazan or Wyler is directing and, awww shit, even then I know I'm going to have to wake up from this dream and I'll be back in my life, hammering on Mediocre's door to get out in the sunlight where I can be who I really am. Most people out here are just acting dreamers. I'm a dreaming Actor. There's a difference, believe me.

When I was cast in *Tootsie*, playing Bill Murray's best friend (apart from Dusty's character), it looked like things were going to finally change. But it cooled right back down when they screened the first cut at the Directors Guild and I was gonzo. Pollack and company had left my performance on the cutting room floor. I was pretty horrified, but I had to admit the movie was good. Very good. It's just that it would have been better with me in it.

Don't get me wrong; I'm not really complaining. Even though sometimes it seems like I don't matter, like my dreams and drive don't really count for anything, I truly love my life's work and I can make fifty, sixty thousand a year what with TV residuals from "Starsky and Hutch," "Police Story," etc. It's a good living, the crews are really great guys, you get to be in the sun a lot, and—who knows—maybe one day Red-ford or DeNiro will see what I'm doing back there and say, Marty, let's give Hell a shot in this scene.

See, my name is Warren Hell. I took it from my ninth-grade teacher who hung it on me for reasons that she thought were all too appropriate. My last name isn't Hell, of course, but it's close. I'm thirty something, 5'10" (almost), and 165 lbs. of decent bodd considering what I have been known to put into it. It's probably a reaction to the current fad of Squeaky Clean (as if that could hide the moral cancer), but I started to smoke, drink, and do light drugs again. Go figure.

I play karate two nights a week since long before the Bruce Lee craze hit. My master is a barrel-chested Eurasian named Shigamitsu Grover who thinks different-ent colored belts are bogus. The last time he competed, he buried all the so-called black belts anyway. Belts are for holding up pants. Shig and his classes are for karate, the real thing. There's only four of us in his Master session. And sometimes we teach. This is where I met the man who got in my life and just drove it away.

In Hollywood, no one has a real name and Zero wasn't his, but it was the one he used. He'd been a LURP, one of those long range reconnaissance patrol guys early in Viet Nam until he came home and turned into a screaming hippie. Zero says he grew his hair long in about a week, took lots of acid, and hooked up with the Black Panthers; remember them? He hung out with The Dead, got drunk in Montana with Brautigan, and was a no-show for the counter culture panel on the Cavett show. Zero came into my life at a time, I suppose, when I needed him most.

Even though I am bi (or maybe because of it, I don't know), in the seventies I had become a pussy-whipped oh so vulnerable, ever-understanding, waffling weenie; a clear-cut fallout casualty of the Women's Movement. Toward the end, the only hold I had on maleness was the karate class and even that had not gone unscathed. Shig Grover could immortally kick ass but he was un-

prepared for truth and justice in pantyhose. His wife
gave him all he wanted and some he didn't.

So the day Zero walked into the beginner's class was a
banner day for many of us. See, on top of everything
else, he is a funny, giving, and loyal human being. You
can't help but like the guy. On one arm he has tat-
tooed, "Death Before Dishonor," and on the other one,
"Oh, Wow"; I suppose I was the first to notice that
these two inscriptions could be talking to each other.

He had no more than a normal fascination with the
semi-success of my profession. All he really wanted to
know was if I had seen any movie stars taking dumps.
Unfortunately, I had and I totally shared with him the
theory that once this has happened, the thrill is gone, I
don't care who it is. It was our first laugh and right now
I get a cold chill when I remember it. As members of
Shig's classes are wont to do, we began hanging out;
dinners, screenings, mouth-puckering espressos at the
Farmers' Market in the mornings. We got cohesive
which is comforting for those of us not married with
kids and a real life. Occasionally. I would look at Zero,
laughing in the sun behind his Wayfarers, and I would
feel the old tug but—as I was in a relationship with a
fine woman named Suzanne who deserved better but
wasn't going to get it—I put those impulses to cryonic
sleep. It was okay; what I was getting in reality was
worth more than a high-dude quickie in fantasy. I was
beginning to feel like a man again.

And not a minute too soon, a voice inside me said;
did being "sensitive" mean I had to miss the Lakers on
TV if it was opposite "L.A. Law" and the VCR was
down? Why did I have to order seafood or salad and
Perrier if I wanted a porterhouse and a shot of JD?
Wasn't I allowed to flip the bird to a woman in a
Mercedes who cut in front of me? What if I thought
Richard Pryor was funny back when he was paranoid
and mean and a sexist and what if I didn't think Lily
Tomlin was all THAT great? If a woman did something

unconscionable and calculatingly treacherous invoking
the name of sisterhood, you couldn't call her That Word
but if a guy did something dumb, he practically begged
to be flogged down Wilshire Boulevard. TV commer-
cials with castrated, ignorantly well-meaning husbands
left me shuddering. Especially the one I did. Why
suddenly were most Corvettes driven by women and
most Saabs by men?

These (and the other Great Questions; like, where do
missing socks go?) were just a few of the things we
would muse on. I shared my history with Zero, the way
you do with new friends who have the patience of
hearing it for the first time. And in turn I learned about
him; tigersuited psychokiller in Indochina to barefoot
and babbling in People's Park in less than a year. Listening and laughing as his experiences heaped one on
top of the next until he was simply agog at the whole
rock and roll tapestry. Wherever he went, his movie
stars were taking dumps. Scholars wanted to be pop
stars, writers wanted to be in real estate, and guitarists
wanted to be dead. When he'd had enough, he went
home to New Orleans.

We got him after he'd graduated from some toney,
experimental mental program connected with Duke or
maybe it was Tulane. He just walked into our lives like
somebody named Bob Anderson who had a normal life
with normal things in it and had never even so much as
passed a special person like Zero in the streets.

The first time we tried floatation samadi tanks was an
unnerving experience for both of us. There in the separate dark silences, suspended in warm salt water, the
image of William Hurt in *Altered States* faded away into
an unbelievably complex nothingness which grew and
grew until it filled our whole minds, from the center of
the cylone out to its farthest edges. We both had combat flashbacks; his from the rainy ridges and hot jungles
of Southeast Asia and mine from the days of my youth
when everything I did was wrong and there was no

center or comfort or familiarity. Because one day, when
I was very young, my mother simply disappeared from
my life. I never learned what had happened to her. It
was something I was willing to live with if I didn't have
to think about it too much. Zero felt a little differently
about his flashback. He was eager to live with his,
chapter and verse, if he could add to it, changing little
details to modify the memory of the event, itself. "Combat is like shit ice cream," he said. "It's horrible, no
doubt about it, but it IS ice cream. We were barely out
of high school, gwonks that didn't even matter and suddenly, here they give us guns, man, and told us to be
war movie guys. It was great. It was something to BE,
you know?"

I did.

"When the incoming started," he continued, "it was
like a kind of hot midnight jazz that was so secret, you'd
never even heard about it. You knew this time was for
keeps and it was so exciting that some guys got hard
ons. Or is it hards on?"

"Do you want to go back, to do it again?" I asked
him.

"No. Just as long as I can remember it. Because it
was as real as I'm ever going to get, Warren."

It was a warm Hollywood night and we were riding
in my Bronco on the way to Musso & Franks to get a
couple of steaks when he first told me about The Games.
"You should come out with me this weekend, man."

"Where?"

"Different places. This week it's the desert east of
San Diego. Hotter'n forty hells."

"Sounds heavenly," I said laconically.

"It's the game that's great."

"What game?"

"You heard about the survival dorks playing war with
CO_2 guns? They had an article about it in *Esquire* or
someplace."

I had heard. Macho men sneaking around in camouflage makeup blasting away at each other with B.B. guns that shot red paint pellets. Rambo bullshit.

"Well," he continued, "ours isn't like that. We actually re-do a firefight. And we don't dick around. It's like terminal muscle chess, babe. You could find out for yourself what the deal is about combat. Such a deal!" He laughed.

Sitting at the counter at Musso's, I waved to friends, we ate, and I thought about what he had said. By this time, Zero and I were really good friends and I knew instinctively that he would never recommend something to me that would be either wrong or dangerous. As I wouldn't to him. This is what friends are for, I thought. It had gotten unusually hot that night, even considering that we were sitting across from the open mesquite grill. While I asked him about those weekends, my hypnotized eyes never left the spitting red coals of the fire.

"We meet in the nearest motel and map out the action," he said, spearing a shrimp out of my salad with a grin. "Then, we choose up sides—like when we were kids—and head out. The weapons vary; sometimes it's pellet guns, sometimes just hand-to-hand. We take no prisoners."

I assumed he meant figuratively as I pressed on, asking him why he thought I'd like a weekend of scrounging around in the deserts one jump ahead of the tarantulas and armed psychos trying to beat me senseless.

"Fun on the edge," he said. "Here, you know what's going to happen. You'll go to the Raincheck and get ploughed. You'll cruise Santa Monica Boulevard thinking about the 'good old days' as you head home alone to watch a cassette of *An Officer and a Gentleman* with Suzanne and you've seen it before and you've done it before and besides, this weekend, Shig's coming out with us."

"Shig?" I exclaimed. "How the hell did you get him to come?"

"I told him you'd be there," Zero laughed. "Plus which, I said two of my guys are aikido and they said he wasn't jack shit. You should have seen Shig smile."

"Guys with guns in the desert," I mused, "riding around with no shirts on, scratching their nuts, playing army. Sounds terrible to me."

"Au contrair, mon frair. It's bitchen. And if you sounded any more Alan Alda, this'd be his wife sitting here instead of me."

The ride to Palm Springs was nice. I had told Suzanne that I was going there to shoot a location commercial. She was going home to see her mother in Ojai anyway, so it worked out smoothly. I kept telling myself that was why I was with Zero and Shig on my way to some weekend warrior foolishness; it was going to be An Experience, I would use it for some character or other. We had a great time listening to an old Marvin Gaye tape and smoking those painless little cigars with the wooden tips. I am sure we looked like three happy, overgrown kids on our way to camp. "They'll appreciate the Bronco," he said. "We use vehicles sometimes; this will be hot and it will be ours."

"I don't want to tear it to shit, man."

"Then we won't. We'll tear them to shit instead." After a moment, he went on. "You know, I think it's pretty cool the way you both came this weekend."

"When my wife finds out where I been, she's gonna call some Beverly Hills divorce lawyer named Sid," Shig said.

"What are friends for?" I asked, grinning, "except to utterly beat up and ruin forever."

"Took the words right out of m'mouth," he said, doing W.C. Fields.

Out of Indio, it really began to get hot and as we turned south on 86, my fuckshitpiss air conditioning unit gave up the ghost. So we rolled down the windows and let the hot wind carry the smell of the sage though the car. "Aww, what's goin' on, tell me what's goin' on," we sang with Marvin at the top of our lungs. Here I was, out in the desert, between the Santa Rosa mountains on one side and the Salton Sea on the other, driving fast with buddies, headed god-knows-where and, you know, I felt just great.

Our side, if you can call us that, was completed by the addition of four more guys. Zero knew them all, of course, and they seemed nice. The big roly-poly one was a Korean War vet, older than he looked. He had hard blue eyes that didn't go with his mouth which rattled off every offensive joke you ever heard, but this time they were funny. Then, there were the twins; Rob and Bob something from San Diego. Identical twins are eerily fascinating, you always want to sneak looks to see what they're doing, how they're reacting. Is it the same, do they move in sync, are they mirrored, somehow? Graham filled out the group. He was impossibly tall, a thoughtful long-faced man in his forties from Orange County who taught political science at one of the colleges down there. Graham was a planner, an organizer. It was he who calmly informed the men in the motel room that, this week, they would be using live ammo. I thought it was a joke of course. Until he started handing out the .22 caliber pistols and rifles from two foam lined Haliburton suitcases. I looked around at the men who seemed to take this stunning bit of news calmly. Even Shig, which really began to frighten me.

"Hey, guys—" I started.

"Warren will be with me," said Zero. "He is not a target. Until he feels comfortable with it. Okay, buddy?" He was smiling at me, warmly. Something was wrong. The air smelled too rich, too pungent in the way that desert air can. It was too hot, the laughter was too easy and loud. And, for a second, I absolutely could not remember Suzanne's face. One of guys came out of the shower, naked. He had great divets out of him, shrapnel scars that walked up one side and out the other.

Somebody turned on the Magic Fingers, another snapped on the TV to "Wheel of Fortune."

"Don't buy a vowel, you asshole!" one of them yelled.

Somebody broke out the weed, we ate cold pizza and French dip roast beef sandwiches and I wondered casually if I was actually losing my mind. Was this it, was this what it was like, could I just tell the shrink what this room now felt like and she would understand and give me a safe conduct pass back to sanity?

I was afraid because I liked it, it was that simple. Somewhere in the last hour, I had gotten very comfortable. I was even playing with a little .22 Beretta and it felt real, real good in my hand. I decided just to go with the flow of this. These were American men, like me, and whenever whatever was going to happen was over, we would all go back to our lives and it would be just like before. I was up for a movie with Tom Cruise and I'd go to karate with Shig and Suzanne and I would have Zero over for barbecued chickies. That would be my future, one that I understood. Now, this was my present and if I didn't exactly understand it, I was determined to go with it.

"Warren and Shig and I will take the twins and Graham and Tubby. Okay?" Zero asked brightly. It was. So they began to make the Master Plan in which, apparently, they planned to combine one of the minor firefights from Bull Run with your average Mekong Delta ambush. It was all Greek to me, even if the sound of their voices was oddly calming.

We took two vehicles, my Bronco and Graham's Volvo wagon, and headed up some tiny road out of Ocotillo, toward the Vallecito mountains. It was beautiful. The blowing sand almost covered the ribbon road in some places and towering century plants that bloom only once in a hundred years wagged in the hot sun.

"Do they all bloom together or sort of one at a time?" I asked.

"By family. The kids bloom every other century. One

of nature's miracles," Tubby explained with a grin. Pretty soon we were all doing Marlin Perkins and Mr. Rogers and I chimed in my deadly imitation of Joe Campanella voice-over on the National Geographic Specials to much laughter. On the radio, the last AM station faded out. We were out in the toolies. Way, way out.

"What the fuck is that?" asked one of the twins.

"Where?" asked Graham.

"Three o'clock," said Zero, out his window. From horizon to horizon, a great undulating wall of something seemed to be moving toward us, eating sky from the bottom as it came. It was both far away and near; its size was incomprehensible.

"All right, honk for Graham to stop. Let's turn the ass end of the vehicles to it and roll the windows up," said Zero.

"Dust," said the twins. Together.

"Jesus," muttered Shig. "That's all we need."

I honked and Graham stopped his wagon. When I got out to go tell him the plan, the air was crackling with life. I had never felt anything quite like it. Graham rolled down his window. "Hi," he said.

"We got a storm coming in. Zero says to circle the wagons. You want to come over with us?"

"I saw it. I'll stay here." He had a tape of Gregorian chants on his car's stereo which seemed to blend perfectly with the quality of the atmosphere outside. The wind was picking up. "Take care," he said. I barely got back to the Bronco when it hit.

I have never been in anything like that in my life and I don't suppose I ever will be again. It was deafening; the howling wind must have reached in excess of seventy miles per hour, driving before it sand and dust and plants and small animals and anything in its path. It almost turned the Bronco over several times. Unidentifiable things were seen in that maelstrom bashing into the windows, webbing the safety glass, denting the hood and roof. I was frightened enough so that I never once thought of the damage and the subsequent cost of repair. A snake was flayed open on the windshield, writhing in agony. Something splattered blood over the back windows which was nearly wiped clean by the wind blown sand. Inside, it was dark as night and hot as noon while six men sat in jittery voiceless awe at the power roaring around us. Only Zero seemed calm. There was something about his face. And from outside came the unearthly howling of the storm which sounded nearly human in pitch and intensity. When a gust almost flipped us, we immediately threw ourselves on the floor to lower the center of gravity. Crouched down under my tilt steering wheel, I thought, what a bizarre ending this is, lost in a dust storm out of "Sands of the Kalahari." Even my death is going to be from a movie. Just as I was rolling the closing credits, the wind let up and the trailing edge of the storm drifted over us, headed west. Goodbye, it seemed to say, sorry about the Bronco.

When I looked up, I jumped with fright. Zero was looking at the horrifying face of an old man, his features pressed flat against the window glass. His mouth was working, his eyes were so red, they looked to be bleeding. He slid downward, out of view. No one spoke. I'm not sure anyone believed what they had just seen. No one out there could have lived through that hell.

He was Mexican or Indian or something. He'd gotten lost in the storm, he said as he gulped down Gatorade. One of the twins carefully sopped out his eyes with a boric solution. He was a mess.

"Where are you from?" asked Zero.

"San Miguel."

"Where is that?"

"There." He pointed. "Or maybe over there," he said and then pointed again in a different direction. He smiled helplessly. You couldn't help but feel empathy for the man.

"Where were you going?"

"To find someone to help us."

For a moment there was a silence in the car. Then, there was a soft tapping at the window and I rolled it down to see Graham's smiling face. "I see you've got company."

"Someone to help you do what?" asked Zero softly.

"Someone to save us. Before they kill us all. Before they wipe us away so that we will have never even been here."

We had ridden for what seemed like hours in all directions, on roads, trail, and in the desert itself. I know we'd been through what must have taken a tank of gas and still the Bronco said a half a tank. I was exhausted.

Now, high on a ridge, god knows how many miles from anywhere, we looked down into a desert valley to a small town of maybe ten or fifteen buildings at most. There were no cars moving, only a wrecked pickup on its side. There didn't seem to be more than one or two power lines running anyplace. It was nearly something out of history, out of a John Ford picture. When the wind blew our way, distant yelling and shots could be heard. Zero handed his binoculars to Tubby who looked down into the town. "Damn. Choppers, five, maybe six. They're Harleys and one old Indian."

"Yeah. Bikers."

"El Diablos," the old Mexican said. "Every week they come. We are almost gone. I was sent to find help."

"Hey, guys," I called out. "I've seen this movie. This is *Seven Samurai*. Look, there's even seven of us!" I was embarrassed to point this out, but the coincidence was overwhelming, at least to me. Toshiro Mifune gives one of the greatest performances ever seen on film in that movie. Brilliant!

"The Magnificent Seven," a twin said softly. "Sonofabitch if we aren't," said the other one.

Zero and I took a leak together. He wrote his name on a flat rock. I ran out, as I always do, on the second "R." "This is it, you know that, don't you?"

I said I did.

"Are you ready for it, buddy?"

I said I wasn't.

"This is your shot, Warren. This is where you get to matter, we all get to matter. This is us being the cavalry and the good guys and the white hats all rolled up into one. This is the payback," Zero said.

"The payback for what?"

"For everything." He turned away and walked back to the rest of the guys standing around the backs of the cars, getting into their uniforms, buckling on their gear. I stood there for a moment, alone high on a rocky ridge somewhere in south California or north Mexico—who knew?—and caught sight of a vapor trail from an airliner at thirty-five thousand feet, headed someplace that made sense, filled with people who knew what they were doing. Then, I shook my head sadly (I can almost see it in the dailies) and joined the other men.

By the time we had suited up, we looked pretty fierce. Tubby didn't seem so tubby anymore. And the twins had painted themselves up in dark streaked paint which hid their features beneath what seemed like a map projected on their faces. They still looked the same, it was strange. After he was outfitted, Zero prepped me. Thinking of Randolph Scott in Carlson's Raiders, I began getting into it. With line cord, he showed me how to tie down my legs and sleeves so they wouldn't flap in the breeze. He made sure nothing rattled, nothing jingled. He covered my face in Fullers Earth and then began to paint on it and as the sun went down behind the ridge, suddenly the light seemed to be a part of my face. "Hard to tell where one starts and the other one begins," he said. "How do you feel?"

"Scared. But excited."

"Yeah. We fell into something, here. You'll never

forget it. Take this, hondo." He handed me the Beretta I had been toying with back at the motel. It seemed like weeks ago, now. "You'll probably never use it, but what the hell." I took it, slipped it into a pocket. I could instantly feel the weight of it, down near my crotch. Me, who hates change in his pocket with a passion. It felt right.

In the twilight, we gathered in front of the Bronco. I would drive us and the old man would show us a road to get down. Now, all eyes were on Zero. He looked from me to Shig to the twins to Graham to the old man to Tubby and back to me again. I don't know why, but I think he was talking primarily to me. "All of you have been in combat before. Of one kind or another. This time, no sorrow or confusion, no panic. This time it goes slow enough to follow. This time, all the way to the end." There was something in his voice that raised hackles on the back of my neck and I thought his eyes were much darker than I remembered them.

We decided to hit the town at dawn. The old man had drawn us a surprisingly detailed map on the back of one of my old scripts (*Big Trouble in Little China*, I think it was) with one of Suzanne's million or so abandoned eyeliner pencils, so we were able to make a fairly detailed plan of attack. The old guy told us where the bikers slept; they had more or less divided up the town territorially between them. I would be with Zero. Shig would go with Tubby. The twins would be together of course and Graham was with the old man, now beaming as if he was sunbathing in the very light of Salvation.

There was a last-minute weapons check, then we got into the Bronco and headed down the far side of the ridge. Way below us, screaming and wild laughter were borne on the wind.

Sometime after midnight, we sent the old man back into town. "When we hit, you make sure all your people stay the fuck down. In a firefight, a target's a target; we can't be real selective, bustin' caps."

"I will hide the women and old men," he said as if he were twenty. "Then, we will come help you. To the end." With that, he left, disappearing into his darkness with a suddenness that was quite alarming.

We strung out to wait. It was odd how it could be so hot in the pitch black night and we all sweated so that little moonlit creeks ran down our faces across the camo paint, down the smalls of backs into shorts. Desert night crawlies ran over our legs and blind bugs flew into our faces. Wanting to slap them, to wipe the streams of sweat away, I cut a quick look over to the rest of the men who were stilled now to a point where they had simply become the moonstruck landscape. No one moved a muscle as they waited. I saw their faces as they looked towards the ramshackle little town and I wondered—I know these men, two of them very well— what in god's name could they be thinking? About food? Or sex or something that happened last Wednesday or their wives and kids?

Or were they, like me, thinking about Mr. Death?

Suddenly, Zero raised his arm. Quickly, I looked at my watch. Jesus! Five o'clock already? Slowly, with the aches and pains of the middle-aged men we'd all become, we got up in dead silence. On the far horizon— like a sign—the full moon drifted behind a cloud, and as the sun came up behind us, we began to walk toward the town. With each step, my heart seemed to be beating faster and faster until I thought everybody in the whole world would wake up and stare at me and ask, what the hell's wrong with you, Warren, that your heart is doing Mahler? I felt someone grip my arm, I looked over, and Zero smiled at me, bright teeth in the dark of the camouflage. I nearly laughed aloud but he shushed me. He cut his eyes down to my hand and I started as I saw that I was carrying the .22 Beretta. I absolutely did not recall taking it out. Zero just nodded, like he knew it all along. Some people know about acting, I remember thinking, about creating a character that brings light. This is what I know. Others know about darkness. Right there, right then, almost mid-stride, I looked over at Zero and realised that there is nothing anywhere without its opposite. And I felt a momentary surge of primal feeling that chilled me because I knew that I had tapped into something horrible and true.

Seven men walking, side by side, to their destiny; and just for a second as the red sunlight splayed around us, our long shadows made us look like Wild Bunch poster children.

It was Tubby who first saw the enormous El Diablo biker who'd staggered out to take an early-morning leak. He had one hand on his schlong and the other on a long leash which was attached to a cowering young Mexican girl. Her eyes jumped open when she saw us and a slow smile crept across her beaten features. With no warning she jerked away and ran from the biker who swore at her for disturbing such a pleasurable moment. That was when he saw us. "Who're you guys?" he called out tentatively. "Where're your hogs?"

"We're your future," said Zero, bringing up a shot gun. The mammoth biker's face fell as he tried to get his Mac 10 and he screamed for his gang with near operatic pitch just as he was blown, the top of his head gone, into the still-steaming puddle of his own urine.

All hell broke loose. I don't know what it must have looked like from the other side, but from where we were, it was horrifying but very beautiful. It was like Zero had said: things were in slow motion so that, for us, there was none of the confusion or panic that you hear pervades combat. This time, this morning, the nightmare was real and clear enough so that anyone could sing along.

And, don't you know, they did.

There were seven of us and maybe thirty of them.

Discounting me, that rationed out to five apiece if the citizens did nothing. I don't know why we figured that was going to be so easy but, as Shig wheeled around into the dawn and caught a biker with a chop to the bridge of his nose killing him instantly, I knew that it would be.

By this time, Zero and I had slipped in the dark doorway of one of the hovels. It took our eyes a moment to get used to the interior; when we had, I wished we hadn't. A wolf-like man, ropey thin and tall he was, had risen halfway to his feet and was in flight, wearing some kind of animal skin that sent a chill over me. Zero yelled as the man fired a flare gun at us. As he bounded out of the door, the room burst into a trembling white light from the phosphorus flare stuck in the wall next to me. It had missed me by only inches. Its light revealed what kind of skin the man had been wearing, for on the floor were perhaps four bodies, in bloody parts. One of the arms was split open where the skin had been peeled back. Whoever he was, he was wearing human skin.

"My god," I said, bracing myself on a rickety table, trying to focus on something else. There was nothing else.

"This is what it's like," Zero said, breathing heavy. "When you have the power, you can do what you want. Anything goes, then. You okay?"

"No."

"Welcome to the club," he said and moved through the door with his shotgun held high. I smelled smoke and I followed him.

Looking out an open window, I could see the twins in the next house. One of them had an axe he'd picked up outside and was whirling around, yelling at the top of his lungs, chopping into bikers who were trying desperately both to subdue him and to get out of his way. The other twin was shoving civilians out the far window as fast as he could. There was a resolute glow on his face that lasted right up until a burst of automatic gunfire hit him in the back. One of the young Mexicans tried to pull him through the window after them and when he couldn't, the boy vaulted back through the window to get this man who had come with the sun to save them. Then the boy was pinned to the wall with a spear of some kind. The remaining twin was knee deep in dead and wounded bikers who clawed up at him until they finally—arms tearing and flexing bloody hands—out of sheer number, pulled him down out of view.

Suddenly, I heard bellowing and was picked up from behind by someone with amazing strength. He held me aloft for a moment and threw me like a floppy stuffed animal through a flimsy room divider covered in old calendar pages. It knocked the breath out of me, which even in this madness, as it always had, engendered complete panic on my part. As the biker came at me, I lifted my hand holding the little pistol and, taking dead aim at his twisted face, I pulled the trigger. Nothing happened but a click. He laughed uproariously. "Your popgun ain't even loaded! You better hope that sucker got chocolate handles, Mern, because I'm gonna feed it to ya." He leaned down for me, a linoleum knife in his hand. "I like that face," he continued, "I think I'll give it to the Wolfman!"

Slowly—for now time seemed to slow down again for me—the sewer rat in stinky black leather came closer and closer, his eyes waltzing gently across my features as he imagined how they might look stretched across someone's else's face, I lifted the little Beretta again and pulled the trigger. This time, there flowered a tiny explosion, my hand jumped in a wave, and a twirling .22 lead slug walked across the red air full of horrific intentions and right into his open mouth. He bit down, slamming it shut just as the expanded slug came out the back of his neck. The linoleum knife dropped into my lap and he collapsed all two-hundred-fifty pounds onto me. For a few seconds, we lay there, like spent lovers, and I could feel the heat drain out of him. Looking down, I could see his little ears so vulnerable and cute. This frightened me; I thought bizarrely of his mother somewhere holding him as a baby before all this started and could suddenly see things the other way around. I pushed him off me with a spasm of revulsion. And then, I did what anyone who has just killed his first human being does. I ran.

Two beauties roared by on a Harley chopper. The guy in the side car had a twenty-foot bullwhip in one hand and some kind of sabre in the other. From one of the houses, someone had put on a radio real loud, adding to the surreal confusion with its early-morning news and wake-up music and Mexican laxative ads. As they swept by, the Diablo in the sidecar snapped his whip's circle in half, shooting out the black snake, slow as a dream, toward me—I didn't even want to pull away from it—and I watched it, entranced, as it wound around my upper arm with a stinging whisper. There was a moment where everything seemed stopped cold, then it exploded back to life and the whip almost jerked my arm out of the socket as they pulled me along behind the careening bike. I could have grabbed the whip with my other hand, but that meant I would have had to drop the little Beretta. No chance on that one. Besides, for some reason, my arm had stopped hurting and I didn't seem to be able to feel the dirt and rocks and cactus that I was being dragged over at 40 mph. Bouncing around helplessly, I caught a glimpse of the most beautiful dawn sky I had ever seen. The color was indescribable; the closest you could come was blood, but lighter.

The guy must have gotten tired of dragging me around, because he finally let go of the whip. The sounds of the radio were gone and someone, somewhere was singing what sounded like *Tosca*. Either that, or old Doors songs. I reeled in the whip—now I had two weapons— and sat up. I was a mess, evidently, because when my old buddy Shig got to me, his face went white until I made a sound.

"I thought you were dead," he said.

I tried to say something, but I couldn't. My mind was working, I could see everything, everything in the world, Christ, I could see things that weren't even there . . . but I could not talk. Around us the noise was deafening, coming in slow waves like everything else. Shig reached out and touched my face and then was gone. Dumbly, I watched Graham running past me, searching frantically for something in his pockets, headed toward a flaming building down the street from where the music seemed to be coming. "This is the end, beeeyoutiful friend," Jim Morrison's dusty voice sang. Suddenly, in the wind, I heard more than just that ancient, wonderful, deadly voice. I heard my destiny.

I got to my feet and began to stagger down the street after Graham. Tubby joined me, shocked at my appearance until I gestured that I was okay. What I saw next shocked but no longer surprised me: the twins, still alive and still the same. Last time I had seen them, they were covered in gore, headed South on the Long Train runnin', brought down by flailing Diablos. I tried to call out to them, but still I could not speak.

So there we were, headed up the street at sunrise for the house of music. "The killer awoke before dawn," Jim sang, "he put his boots on . . ." As I passed an open doorway, a twitching biker jumped out and leveled a sawed-off shotgun at us. I turned without breaking stride, held out my little Beretta and said, "Bang." A bullet slammed into his chest, nearly tearing it open. I wasn't fazed. This was death magic and the fact that Tubby had shot the prick at the precise instant I had pretended to didn't dim its power at all.

A few of the Diablos had made it to the rooftops thinking, take the high ground, but it was of little consequence to the lords of the low ground. We simply pointed, aimed, and fired. Like a dream, every slug

hit meat, every spraying squib was real, every body
fell, and every stunt was a six plus.

As we got closer to the house at the end of the
street, the music from inside became louder and
louder until it seemed as if it *was* the house. One of the
twins raked fire from his assault rifle across the side of
an adjoining building and, from the screams inside, hit
pay dirt. God, we never stopped walking. We did what
we had to do on the move—it did seem like slow
motion for us, regular for everyone else—and we all
arrived at the house together.

Inside, there was this incredibly bright light which
had a quality to it I had never seen before. It was warm
and golden and inviting and I did not want to go any
farther. I looked at that light and instinctively I knew
that it was something or came from somewhere that I
was afraid of. If this fear was shared by Graham or
Tubby or the twins or Shig, they didn't say anything.
But we were stopped in a semi-circle at the front of the
adobe house, held there by the force of the music and
the quality of the light. Isn't that it, though? Music and
light together, so strong it binds you to a moment in
time that might last forever, if only in your mind.

Slowly, without thinking at all, I saw my goddamn
feet—hey, what are you doing? What the fuck do you
think you're doing?!—moving in measured steps toward
the doorway. Helplessly, I saw the other guys looking
at me with concern that went from fear to awe. Yet I
could not stop walking to the door. As I got closer and
closer, the other senses in me, I can't even begin to
suggest what they were, opened up. I could feel things
in ways that I wouldn't have believed possible; seeing
everything and remembering everything at the same
time. Like that'd ever happened to you? That kind of
"everything." Other people you had been in other times,
other lives. It all came back on a huge, endless ruby
red wave and just took me away.

Through the open door, into the heart of that light, a

man stood in the middle of the room, head down for a
moment, hanging on a microphone stand; then, he
lifted his leonine head and sang. The face, the posture,
the agony and (yes, yes) the ecstasy, he just flat-out
became James Douglas Morrison, slack poet and loonie
rocker, film-making pre-vert and alcoholic selfdestructo—
destined for greatness, destined to disappoint, destined
for this hellish moment when he became the light of
darkness, the light he'd so often dreamed about as a
boy.

Of course, I knew it was Zero. Did they?

By now, all the rest of us had come inside, out of
Death's cruel storm, into the healing light that seemed
to make us younger, stronger, happier, more alive than
we had ever been or had any right to expect. This,
now, was ours alone. Hours ago, days ago, lifetimes
ago, we had been different people. That was then, this
was now.

"Father, I want to kill you," he sang, "mother . . . I
want to—" and the figure at the microphone swung
around in that horrifying, death-defying scream and
suddenly, he had an Uzi submachine gun in his hands
and began firing at the open windows which were now
filled with faces that stared into us, faces of the live and
faces of the dead, the face of the man I had killed and
the face of the wonderful old Mexican man, faces of the
young and the old and the men and the women and the
adults and the children and I knew with every fibre of
my being that we had to kill them all.

They had seen the unseeable, witnessed the unholy
miracle and now, it was time to pay up.

This time, it wasn't a dream at all. It went fast and
furious and horrible. Faces exploded, blowing skin and
hair and blood everywhere. Bodies were cut in half
with the fire; the tops went one way, the bottoms
another. There were screams and howls and maniacal
laughter and yelling and hysterical sobbing. And that
was just from me!

I saw the face of a Caesar, I saw Patton's face, the face of ancient warriors; I tell you, I saw gladiators and deal-makers, gunfighters and judges, I saw Presidents and bums, I saw the faded and the glorious, I saw the quick become the dead, I saw a man in armor who had a Gila monster coming out of his mouth, I saw them all and they were as real as anything in this or any other world.

In the end, beautiful friend, we killed every one of them.

In the past, I had marched against the war, gone to jail for the draft resisters, I had wanted to pull the switch on Lt. Calley and his massacring animals myself. Now, here, I knew that somehow I had become that man, those men; I had turned into all of them, the ones in rags in the bottom of that My Lai ditch and the ones with the guns in uniforms on top. And my horrible secret, the secret all seven of us in that bright and blazing room shared was: it's the same, hondo. There are no innocent bystanders because we're ALL innocent bystanders. And being in the ditch is the same as being out of the ditch.

Because all of Here is the ditch. What counts, it turns out in this simple, cruel joke that was playing itself out before our tired and desperate eyes, what counts is what comes afterward!

The last bullet in the last gun killed the last person in the last window. The trigger finger was mine.

I was home in my rose garden; drinking a diet Coke and listening to an old Jefferson Airplane record softly on the stereo's outdoor speaker when it happened.

It'd been real nice weather. In the seventies during the day, light and steady rain at night. Good for the roses, not bad for me, either. I hadn't seen Suzanne for some time. We'd had a blowout and we pretty much decided that life was hard enough without making it any harder. We were friends, we always would be. But these days, she said, I hardly ever talked, I couldn't seem to really concentrate on anything, my mind always seemed a million miles away. It was like I just didn't care anymore. I told her I did, I squeezed her hand and gave her the look I used on Bette Midler in that Janis Joplin rip-off (the bastards cut that scene, too) but Suzanne, who knew me too well, smiled sadly and told me goodbye. I was glad to see her go, still it hurt. She was pretty much the last friend I had.

I hardly went out anymore at all. I banked by mail, a kid from Jurgenson's delivered groceries, the mail brought dumb magazines that I secretly loved and residual checks (what were these? I'd ask, turning them over, looking them like they were artifacts). Now, it was just me and the silence and the roses.

And my dreams, of course.

That afternoon, when I saw Zero sitting out in my yard, I nearly dropped the diet Coke. Suddenly, I sensed something and looked over, and he was sitting in the old swing. How he got there, where he came from, I'll never know. But it was him, with that same neat grin and shyly forceful manner. I put down the hose (yes, I did think about squirting him) and went over. "What the hell are you doing here?"

"I'm here for you, Warren." I wasn't real sure I liked the sound of his voice. "You and me are gonzo, outta here; a hot, cheap historical novel with a big ending."

"Look, Zero, it took me a long time to get over that little desert expedition . . ."

"That's why I'm back," he said. "I need you."

Well, shit, I'm some kind of romantic movie-suckled fool for those three words; all I ever really wanted was to be needed. In their secret heart of hearts, who doesn't? I thought, whatever happened . . . happened. Besides, I like this guy. He's crazy— probably certifiable—he's self-centered, he's totally odd, he's erratic, and he's mine.

"Yeah," is what he said about that.

"Where are we going?" I asked him and he smiled, knowing full well he had me.

"War, hondo. We're going to war. Where I'm taking you is black as ten feet down, weirder than Dracula's jockey shorts. You heard about this place all your fucking life and never really believed it. Well, believe it."

I did. But my stomach didn't take a lot of comfort in it. Inside my body, my blood was suddenly like freon.

"You were a star in boot camp; out there in that 'little desert expedition.' Now, I need you. Now, you finally get your real shot. Know what I mean? From now on it's going to be you and me—with a few million others—up to our knees. Payin' it back!"

This time I didn't have to ask him paying back what. This time I knew. And this time with a clear heart and a light conscience, I knew I would go with him. Finally I knew Zero's real name.

I was Zero and with one firm and terrible stride, I stepped through his center and into the endless wild night-time of hell.

ROOK'S MOVE

C.J. Cherryh

Motors rumbled and echoed in the Armory garage, staccato orders rang off the girdered ceiling, and legionaries clustered in groups around their gear, waiting.

Hell was in turmoil, the Devil had ordered a game of musical chairs among the Seats of Power ringing New Hell, and nothing was working since Paradise had come up in Hell's murky red dawn—motors failed, tires blew, communications went down for reasons that might have to do with the freakish weather—boiling tumult in the skies, unsavory shapes appearing like shadows and vanishing— Or again, Hell needed no excuse: the Assyrians who had once attacked Rome's twin villas, the Seat of the Republic and that of the Empire, were on the move again, and the investigation which Administration had launched into Pentagram irregularities made for a logistics nightmare—Rome got a lot of its equipment by creative bookkeeping with the Pentagram's accounting system, and now was not a safe time to use those channels.

So they went with what they had, which, dammit to Tartarus, was not enough: they sent messages which

might or might not get through, to various of their
allies, calling in old debts—but as Hell would have it,
other Seats were threatened, allies had their hands full;
and they began to get a wider and wider picture of a
Hell upside down, everything breaking loose at once.

It was Rome against the Power that had recently
tried to supplant it. On the Legions depended the
welfare of the more distant establishment of Roman
folk—*in* this zone of Hell or dimensionally divided from
it, one was never sure—but there was a part of Hell's
more pleasant regions that afforded paradise to Rome's
more ordinary people—the Elysian fields, the Forest of
Lost Souls—and which also, rumor held, afforded
Tartarus for betrayers and traitors, and extended into
other places and times, holding certain criminals and
powers helpless to work harm.

That was the time the Legions were fighting to hold.
Paradise for the shopkeepers and the weavers, the
smallhold farmers and the retired soldiers and the kids
and the ordinary folk—not the paradise that rolled above
them and lit the sky, but the Roman one, the one that
they, who held the Seat at New Hell, could never reach
and never share. They could only lose it—and thereby
damn the Power that was Rome to leave the plane and
sink into one of the Nether Hells, in whatever conditions failure deserved.

So with such things at stake, the Legions did not
intend to fail.

They were veterans in Hell. Few things flapped them,
and among the legionaries there was the usual bitching,
the usual grumbling about things specific and general:
things broke and they swore, things stalled and they
swore, and the *number* of things that were breaking
and stalling only rated more swearing, shakes of experienced heads and an occasional judicious spit at the
ground, at the perfidious demons of luck.

It was bad, they knew it was, and knew that, with all
Hell uncertain, so was the Luck that returned them to

their own cohorts when they went the Trip in Hell—so old friends were a little quieter in this load-up, attention to equipment was that much more meticulous.

There was the chance that some of them were not coming back from this one; or that no one would: the Devil was not reputed for fairness.

But there was comfort in routine; and the Old Man walked among them, calling them by name and making bad jokes—shouting orders now and again to straighten out some tangle or expedite a situation.

The Old Man called Spurius Maecius by name, and clapped him on the shoulder in passing, and Maecius, who was nineteen—who had been nineteen since he died in 354 from the Founding, and who had fought campaigns enough in Hell that he had forgotten where and why, under Fabius, and Marius, gods knew. Now it was Julius Caesar—who knew his name, hailed him like an old friend, and walked on, passing here and there a word that would fly like rumor through the legions. That was Julius' style. Commanders came and they went, but it had been Julius longer than anyone—Julius who had started out Marius' co-commander in Hell and stayed on after Marius was lost. Maecius had seen it all—campaign after campaign, crisis after crisis; but he was never older than nineteen.

Maecius had gotten bad habits in Hell—acquired a taste for Irish whiskey, 15th century Italian women, and 20th century American cigarettes, all of which were hard come by in the 14th legion; but he managed—and carefully pocketed the cigarette he had pinched out and palmed when the Old Man came by.

The order was going out now: into the trucks and hit the road. He had figured that, if Julius was making his walk-through. So he gathered up his gear—that was 20th century American too, the Old Man got them the stuff; except Maecius still kept his sword for close work—*that* never jammed, and you couldn't say the same for any rifle in Hell.

On helmets, up kits, and into the trucks—that was
better too: it beat 50 mile marches. Except this was a
short one, *too* short, like a mile or so the other side of
the villa, the fucking Assyrians were kicking up again
and the rumor was the Allies were not going to make
this party. The Allies had stuff coming in on their own
turf, rumor was moving faster than any other kind of
information: communications were shot and no few of
them *were* hiking in—there were that many trucks out
of commission.

"Hell of a mess," Maecius said to his mate, a nine-
fingered kid from Volterrae. Maecenas, his name was.
Maecenas never talked much. But they shared a tent,
they cooked their rations together, and Maecenas had
carried him ten miles through Stygian swamp the time
the 14th had gotten chewed up by the Parthi. Which
was good enough for a friendship.

Maecenas spat and nodded, and clambered up into
the truck to give him a hand up.

Then a kind of a cold wind blew over Maecius—like a
draft out of the armory door; but it wasn't that. He just
stopped cold, holding onto Maecenas' hand and seeing
their hands locked like that, and thinking that somehow
they *were* locked together, and everything around them,
all the noise and everything—just faded out.

We're not coming back. he thought. *We won't do this
again. We won't come back from this one.*

He wasn't sure why he thought that, or what had
changed. He wasn't sure whether Maecenas had caught
it too—there was no change in Maecenas' expression,
nothing but the same bored indifference as he settled
down and arranged his gear—not a flap at all.

We're going to lose, Maecius thought, a certainty he
had never felt in all his time in Hell; and felt sick at his
stomach. But there was no profit in spreading panic
around. So he clamped his jaw down on it, took his
place by Maecenas and edged tighter as they crammed
another half dozen men in on the benches, gear and all.

The truck lumbered out, not the back way this time, that led around through the woods, but right up the north side of Park Avenue, past Decentral Park.

Decius Mus was already holding the line up there. There was more coming. So the Old Man had said. So he needed them—the 12th to hold the Armory, the rest of them on the field.

The Assyrians had some heavy stuff. If their luck was holding at all, it was subject to breakdowns too. If it wasn't—

They said they were going in again right over crazy Tiberius' lawn. That the Old Man had gritted his teeth and *asked* for the Praetorian Guard to turn out and lend the resources the Empire had—

A madman and a drunk. Tiberius and Marcus Antonius.

And the Praetorians, who had sold Rome itself for bonuses, and auctioned off the Imperium to the highest bidder.

That, more than anything, might be the source of that chill Maecius still felt. The knowledge that they had *that* to rely on.

That the Old Man had become that desperate.

It had an unreal feeling—going right down the tree-lined street in view of the skyscrapers.

Time was you couldn't bear arms in the City . . . in Rome. Time was, when an army got to the city limits, your officers stopped you there, you covered your shield and wrapped up your sword and bundled your spears and, damn, you *remembered* that, you remembered it drunk or sober—there was something sacred about that line, and something especially safe about the City where no weapons could come without the gods taking offense at it. But Romans had forgotten that—forgotten it when Italians fought with Romans over voting rights; forgotten it when emperors created the Guard to protect themselves from protest; forgotten it when the Guard ran roughshod over the bleeding City—

So here they were headed up Park Avenue, to stand beside the Guard.

The Old Man said so; and if it were any other officer said it, the 14th would not have gone. But Julius said, and they went; though for Maecius' own part, if he could have gotten a Praetorian under his sights he had rather shoot him than an Assyrian, hands down.

Maybe it was that, that made that queasy feeling.

Or maybe it was that—that might damn them.

We're going to lose this one, we're going to lose it, we're going to lose.

That was what the tires said on the concrete.

There was smoke over New Hell. It came from places all around the horizon.

Tiberius plucked another morsel from his plate and laid it on the table. Caligula reached out a paw and snatched it—Caligula, his own murderer and heir, sitting in regal splendor on the tabletop, grooming his fur between morsels and insolently refusing to prophesy.

That Caligula had returned in the shape of a baboon did not astonish him. Nothing in Hell astonished him. That Caligula had first appeared atop the statue of murdered Drusus was fraught with omen—Caligula had an affinity for murder, point; and Caligula had gone to nether hells, point; Caligula had come to perch on dead Drusus' bronze head, point; ergo Caligula had returned from the nether hells with an oracle regarding Drusus' whereabouts; and Tiberius, who could have ordered any of a thousand inventive punishments for his damned nephew Caligula,—Little Boots, who had smothered him with a pillow *and* permitted angry mobs to seize his body from the funeral procession, and drag it with hooks through the streets and fling it into the Tiber— like some convicted patricide, as if it were *he* who was responsible for Augustus' death—

Damned, damned, *damned* Augustus—

Damned, quadruply damned Caligula—

—Tiberius was patient. "Dear nephew," he said, "have another. *Tell* me where my brother is. You know. I know you do. Augustus murdered him, you know. They say Mother did, but I know the truth. I'm no fool. Don't you act like one. Stop this silliness. If you want to be a god, I'm sure I've no objection. I'll make you a temple. Anything you want. Virgins. I'm sure we can find a few. How's that? Bargain? All you have to do is tell me where he's hiding. I *love* him, nephew. I killed horses getting to his bedside—damned, damned horses—I *walked* all the way back to Rome with his body, a thousand miles I walked, nephew, you can't imagine—rain and mud and all, and his body stinking and shriveling in the salt—gods, *gods*, gods, it was awful; I'm sure you understand; I walked all that way to tell Augustus to go to hell and here we all are, bang. I mean, that's justice. And you can't trust anyone unless you're a god, because if you're not they can kill you, can't they? So don't you want to be a god? Tell me and I'll sign the papers. Just tell me where he's gone, there's a good lad. . . ."

The baboon picked up another bite with its curiously agile fingers, thoughtfully carried it to its mouth and regarded him like some canopic image, dark eyes glittering as it chewed.

"I really always loved you," Tiberius said; and brought his fist down. "*Dammit, why won't you talk to me?*"

It bared fangs at him, leapt off the table and scrambled up into the marble lap of a priapic faun.

The door opened. Tiberius whirled about in panic, stumbling as he gained his feet. The chair skidded and wood squealed on stone, and Tiberius grabbed after the plate and hurled it at the intruder.

The plate hit an upraised arm and fell clattering. And the vice-commander of the Guard stood there saying: "Treason, divine Tiberius. I have treason to report."

Tiberius gazed at him, distracted from his hope of prophecy to the certainty that there were plots, there were always plots: daily his enemies attempted to murder him, because there was no one to trust, no one to stand at his back the way his brother Drusus had once stood—

Plots had murdered Drusus, and murdered *him*. There were mobs outside, always mobs.

And the vice-commander said: "Marcus Antonius is trying to subvert the Guard, divinity. If he knew I had come to you he would kill me. I risk my life, divinity, for love of you."

Harmodias. Tiberius remembered his name. *Pretty* boy. *Nice* boy. *Love* of him, it was. "How nice," Tiberius said. "Tell me—what treason?" And to Caligula, who bounded down and grabbed a bit off the floor before the nervous sycophants, glowing spots in the air, could snatch up the debris: "Stop that, nephew!"

Antonius took a drink—the last of the whiskey and soda—he *swore* he was on the wagon again; but gods, a man needed it today—and grabbed up his pistol and the charts and headed for the door, hastily: you had to move fast to avoid the sycophants—never look like you were after what you were after; and never look guilty. "Move!" he yelled at one that cluttered his path, his best field command voice: *that* got them too, because sycophants never liked to be on the receiving end of trouble, and they smelled power and went for it. He actually *gained* a few on his way down the stairs, little points of light that darted and dodged around him as he headed into the yard where the Guard was forming up.

Get the Guard out there, Julius had said. *I don't care how—get them out on that line.*

Part of the Guard *was* on the line—those unlucky few cohorts that were on the line between Tiberius' villa and the Assyrians, but not facing the Assyrians—facing the two cohorts of the 10th that were on the aforementioned line facing *their* way.

Now Julius wanted the rest of the Guard out there

facing the Assyrians, and both items together were a tall order indeed.

But so far they were taking orders.

He had lied—a little. Said that he had Tiberius' sanction for the move. Which, privileges and bonuses coming from where they did for the last two thousand years of a corrupt service, meant, as he had put it: "Get your asses out there, or find yourself a cushy spot in a lower hell, friends, the emperor will get the name of the last man to volunteer."

"Get it moving!" he yelled down at the resplendent ranks under the balcony—gilt and glitter and solid gold armlets and spear-points reflecting a roiling red sky. The Guard kept to the old ways. So did everybody under Tiberius' roof; but some things got by. Like silk; and polyester; and a faddish taste for gold chain and Rolex watches.

Di immortales, he had *this* to lead—guard the flank, Julius had said, expecting from the Praetorians at least a healthy regard for their own lives.

They had learned—everyone learned, who served in Tiberius' villa by the sea, that no matter how incompetent the old emperor might be, no matter how crazed— malignant luck dropped the dead *back* here—where equally malignant fortune operated on Tiberius' behalf.

Meaning no one, no matter how desperate, had ever gotten the old bastard, no one had ever dislodged him from control, and the ones who had tried him—came to Tiberius' special attention. That was what ingenuity won you.

A glass of Scotch was not enough to still Antonius' stomach—

Not when he saw a veritable cloud of sycophants come through a closed door on the other side of the practice yard, and that door open, and Harmodias strut out into the yard to give an independent order, detaching a squad of men who gathered half a dozen others.

All of whom came in his direction.

Antonius drew his gun and fired, one, two, and three, and number one was Harmodias.

"Move it," he yelled, "keep going."

But the sycophants left him in a rush, which was a bad sign, and one the Praetorians knew.

They stood still.

He climbed the stairs again, with men starting after him from either side of the yard, up his stairs and up the one at the other side of the balcony.

Getting to the emperor and getting Tiberius to back him was the only hope in Hell at the moment; and Antonius gave up all pretext of dignity. He hit the balcony running, got the door open and bolted it behind him.

But he heard it blow behind him, heard the view-halloo of the Guard in hot pursuit, and he took the corner at a skid, toppled a marble and obscene nymph from her pedestal, and ran all out, downstairs again and down a long corridor.

The Luck had it, of course, that the door at the end was locked.

Law of things in Tiberius' palace.

Or damned efficient sycophants.

The whole house was in confusion—attack imminent, that was the word that had come to Augustus' villa—Julius was down gathering the 14th and the 15th to bring them up where Mouse was holding the line across from the Assyrian villa and Tiberius. The Assyrians were beginning their big push.

Brutus kept his head down, that was what. It was what any seventeen year old boy could do, who had thrown all Hell into chaos.

It *was* all his fault, the whole war and the chaos in Hell honestly, truly was his fault, and nothing his father Julius could say could take that away. He had run away with his half-brother Caesarion, Klea's son, gotten them both caught by the Assyrians, Julius had come after them and the shockwaves and revelations of treason in high places had run through the length and breadth of Hell—right to Administration.

Then Julius, having gotten him home, had told him who he was—what he had grown up to do, he, Marcus Junius Brutus, forever seventeen, because Julius' enemies had done that to him. Marcus Brutus the assassin, Julius' illegitimate son.

The one who loved Julius in death more than he had ever loved anyone and anything in life.

Stay here, Julius had said to him when he left to take command of the defense. And devils could skin him before he would budge this time or break Julius' orders.

Himself and Caesarion. Because Caesarion had gotten cut off from his own side—Tiberius' side; and gotten caught on Augustus' lawn in the fracas—*So lock me up,* Caesarion had yelled at Julius. Which was the way Caesarion managed things—not that Caesarion wanted to blow up and get himself in trouble. He just did— every time he got near Julius.

Don't try me, Julius had yelled back, with a fistful of Caesarion's tee-shirt—Brutus' tee-shirt, as it happened, since Caesarion had not exactly come with bag and baggage. *Do something right, son, just for once, do us all a favor and keep your mouth shut and your ass down—*

But Julius had let Caesarion stay in the house, and not put him in handcuffs and not locked him in the basement, which confused Caesarion considerably.

"Damn him," Caesarion muttered over a slow card game. And winced as a shell screamed over and hit with that peculiar dull thump.

"Viet Cong," Brutus said. "That happens, is all." And laid down a jack, trying to keep his hand from shaking. "That's over in the park."

"Nice neighborhood." Caesarion picked up his card.

There was the sound of engines very distant, getting

closer. Brutus looked at his hand and counted cards. English math. It was hard to concentrate.

"That's coming in the drive," Caesarion said, and threw down his hand and went to look out the window. Brutus was right behind him, leaning over his shoulder to watch the trucks round the corner by the villa's parking lot, and just keep going—their father in the jeep out there in front and the overloaded trucks with the legionaries; and finally a lot of men afoot.

No big guns. No artillery. Just the soldiers and the trucks and the gear they had aboard.

A terrible cold feeling grew in Brutus' stomach. "Guess he couldn't get the stuff he wanted," he said. And felt Caesarion's hand grip his shoulder till it hurt. There was a lump of ice in his throat to match the one in his gut.

"Shit, he'll pull it out," Caesarion said. "Always *does*, doesn't he?" Caesarion shook at him. "Listen, there was Hannibal. That was a mess. That was a real mess. You think our father came out with a scratch? No such luck."

"Shut up," Brutus said, and tore his arm loose and crossed the room—his bedroom, which was where they had to stay, which was better than Caesarion being in prison. He snapped his fingers and got his own, his private sycophant, a wan, frightened little thing, but it came. "What's going on?" he asked it. "What are they *doing* down there?"

Meetingsss, it whispered. *Yes, yesss. Augussstussss and Machiavelli, Kleopatra. And the woman King.*

Julius was not stopping. The sound of the trucks died away.

Trouble, trouble, trouble, the sycophant said.

"Where?" Brutus asked.

Caessssar, it said, and it vanished.

"Divinity," Antonius said, mumbled, from a bruised mouth, and tried to get an arm free—he had a terrible compulsion to talk with his hands; and facing Tiberius in the hands of his own soldiers was more than humiliating, it was terrifying.

More so, since the Luck had dropped Harmodias back inside ten minutes, fresh from the Undertaker and mad as hell, standing at Tiberius' elbow.

"That man—" Harmodias said, "shot me."

"To protect you from traitors," Antonius objected. "Divinity, Harmodias has subverted your orders, defied your commands, he works for his own interests—you *told* me to take the Guard out to your defense, divinity, and the Assyrians are on the move while this traitor, this unconscionable traitor, plots your death—"

The baboon screeched.

"To the basement," Tiberius screamed. "To the basement with him! Death to traitors."

"Majesty, the Assyrians are marching to take the villa—to overrun your walls and slaughter all of us—"

"To the basement!" Tiberius howled.

They were not gentle about it. They hauled him downstairs, backed him up against the wall, and Harmodias showed up through the door.

"Later," Harmodias said and patted Antonius on the shoulder, while he stood there with a Praetorian's fist in his hair, making him face the man. "You're *his*, friend. Remember Flaccus? Remember what the emperor did to him—just for the suspicion of what you did,—friend."

Then Harmodias hit him in the gut, once, and left him puking on the floor.

Augustus watched out the windows and winced as a shell thumped into the earth far beyond, in the trees.

While the might of Rome, such as they could spare from the other perimeters they guarded, went out to defend the holdings they felt most threatened.

Dante's computers told them nothing, nothing but short supply and the hazards of getting into the Pentagram computers—where a probe was still running, ferreting out irregularities.

Perhaps, Augustus thought, the *Assyrians* would make the mistake if they could prod them enough, and the *Assyrians* could find themselves on the receiving end of trouble.

But there was no guarantee of that: there was no justice in Hell, only Administration's whims, and a malevolent sense of humor that might reward fools and traitors and punish loyalty—simply because Hell was self-destructive.

One learned such lessons fast, when one administered a sector of Hell.

"Are the phones working?" he asked, turning a glance toward Niccolo Machiavelli—who, black-clad bird of ill omen, hovered at his back, dialing and re-dialing on the office phone while Kleopatra and Hatshepsut, the Egyptian contingent, fretted with the charts and maps that papered the large table, and argued over their own memory of the Assyrian grounds and front entry—in the case they should get that far, in the case luck should strike and they might have the chance to deliver an explosive present to Assurbanipal's very doorway.

"*Signore*," Machiavelli said, "this cursed thing—"

And vanished, elegant, slender hands in mid-gesture. Just—vanished, with a thunderclap that hurt the ears, fluttered the folds of Augustus' toga and showered papers off Augustus' overburdened desk and maps off the table.

Augustus stared in shock.

He had seen a great many things in Hell. But having one of the Household snatched out of midair—

The wind continued, sweeping maps with it, whipping at Klea's skirt, at Hatshepsut's hair. Pharaoh threw up her arms of a sudden, cried out:

"Typhon is unleashed!

"The leopard is discovered!

"The pharaoh of the lake has risen!

"Woe to the sons of the wolf!"
Bang!
A second clap of thunder, maps whirling away into oblivion where Hatshepsut had stood—
Reports of thunder from elsewhere in the house—
Bang! and *Crack!* Glass fell from the windows.
"My son!" Klea cried, and ran for the doors and out them, a clatter of high heels ringing away on the terrazzo.
Leaving a bewildered Augustus staring at bewildered legionary guards, amid the wreckage of the study, wondering if he would be the next to go.

The thunderclaps had stopped as quickly as they had begun, but the villa still seemed to reverberate. "What *was* it?" Brutus exclaimed—and suddenly there was a clatter coming down the hall, a frantic female voice raised in protest against the guards—"Gods, that's my mother," Caesarion said, headed for the door with protective mayhem in every line of him.
As the door opened and Kleopatra flew in. "Son!" she cried, and flung her arms about him, held onto him as if the world were coming unhinged, held his face between her hands and looked up at him. "Rome is losing its base," she said. "It's all coming undone, all the threads— Niccolo and Hatshepsut— All of us—the allies of Rome— Antonius is taken—Tiberius is onto us and I can't—I can't—Hell is taking us out—those of us foreign, who don't belong—"
Bang!
As suddenly she was gone, Caesarion stumbling in the gust of wind. Brutus grabbed him, grabbed him hard with both arms around his middle.
Bang!

Closer and closer, still aboard the trucks, with the lads afoot bringing up the rear—jolt and jostle, a ride that threw body into body in a bruising monotony. Maecius thought about the cigarettes in his pocket, finally pulled the half-smoked one out and lit it, cupping the match with his hand, took a drag and passed it to Maecenas.

It ended up going from hand to hand, all the way around again, and men who had never smoked took a drag to see what it was—generally made a face about it, and passed it on.

So he got back a stub and smoked it down.

Which the centurion would skin them for. But hell, there were some pleasures due them.

They said the Praetorians were going to take left flank.

There were a lot of Praetorian jokes going the rounds: like: How many Praetorians does it take to beat the Assyrians?

Answer: Depends on who's paying.

Bang!

Brutus fought for his balance and Caesarion's, with ground suddenly under their feet and both of them off-center in a murky hall, a place of cold and fire and incense.

They found a mutual brace and held that way, leaning together as Brutus found himself facing a brazen god with glowing eyes; and Caesarion said passionately: "Oh, *shit!*" and grabbed him by the arms and shook him. "Dammit, why'd you hang onto me?"

"I d-d-don't kn-kn—"

"We're in Tiberius' damn front hall, brother!"

"T-T-Ti-berius?" Brutus took another look at the fearsome statue. Drusus, not a god. Tiberius' brother, who, Augustus said, had died in a fall from a horse; whose death had tipped Tiberius over the edge and turned him sullen and withdrawn, and finally driven him mad.

Syphilis, had been Sargon's dour comment.

"Come *on*," Caesarion said; and started running, pulling him with him, and Brutus asked no questions.

But there was the sound of footsteps elsewhere, coming toward them in the direction they were going; and Caesarion came to a fast stop as a cluster of glowing lights broke in front of them and vanished with a hiss like serpents.

"Oh, damn, they've seen us!" Caesarion said; and an instant later a hue and cry broke out down the halls. Caesarion changed course, pulled him in among the pillars on the right; and there were shouts from that direction too.

"Where are we g-g-going?" Brutus yelled, and yelped, as Caesarion changed course a third time and crossed the open hall toward the statue and suddenly down a stairs and around again and then up and up and up a narrow twist of steps that even tennies found treacherous.

Through a door then, and into a bright place filled with machines, with levers and controls and things that belonged to another world.

"Wh-What—"

"Quiet," Caesarion hissed, and clamped his hand over his mouth and pulled him over against the wall. "This is the heart of the oracle," he whispered. "It's all a trick. The emperor uses this place to frighten people. Look!"

Brutus edged close as Caesarion first pressed his own eye against a hole in the wall, and then pulled him in line to take a look.

It was the atrium below, and there were soldiers going back and forth searching among the columns.

"We're in the s-s-statue," Brutus whispered.

"In the wall above it," Caesarion said, and leaned against the counter and caught his breath. "Damn," he said then, and wiped his face with a shaking hand. "The old goat gets his hands on us now we'll wish we were dead."

"Your m-mother—"

"I don't know where she is. I don't know what's happened."

"She said—said Antonius was c-c-caught. Antonius is *here*, he's g-g-got the Praetorians. . . ."

"Not anymore he doesn't," Caesarion breathed. "If the old goat's got him—he's in *bad* trouble—and the Praetorians are just apt to go at Julius, Julius has got his comeuppance this time, he's got it good—"

Brutus sorted through it three times in a dazed blink of an eye and grabbed Caesarion by the arm. "They've got to h-h-*help* him! If he f-f—*can't hold them off out there*—"

Caesarion fixed him with a hard and sidelong glance; and a curl of his lip. "*Rome* buys it. Too fucking *bad*, brother. See any tears? Only worry I've got—is the damn system dropped me back in *this* hellhole—with Tiberius, dammit. . . ."

"*Treason*," an old man's voice wailed, from somewhere below. "*Treason!*"

And from below, a voice deep and sonorous as a god's:

The way from Gaul is rain and mud.
The way to the throne is kinsmen's blood.

"What's th-th-that?"

"Tiberius talking to his dead brother," Caesarion said. "Sometimes he talks from here. Sometimes old Drusus talks back. I told you. It's an oracle."

"He runs it with m-m-machines? And he *b-believes* it?"

"I told you—he's nuts. Just hope he doesn't come up here. With luck, he'll go away and we can slip out the door."

"*Antonius has betrayed us*," the mad emperor wailed up at the statue—Brutus stole a fast look, at a stout man in a black toga, at a man frothing at the mouth and waving his arms at the dead. "*Antonius has betrayed us—he tried to steal my Praetorians, he tried to lead them after Julius! What should I do? What should I do with traitors?*"

Brutus drew in a shaken breath. "He's c-c-coming this w-w-way—"

"Damn!" Caesarion shoved him over and looked.

Brutus grabbed his shoulder. "Come *on*, we c-can still g-g-et *out*—" As something came up the steps and bounded in.

"AAEIEEEIIIIII!"

It yelled, they yelled, faced with a terrified baboon at tight quarters.

"*Treason!*" Tiberius' voice howled. "*Treason!*"

"Run!" Caesarion yelled, and they followed the baboon down the stairs and down and down.

Right into a cluster of Praetorians with leveled rifles.

A shell landed and the ground shook under the truck: Maecius bailed out and grabbed up his gear and ran for it. Six other men were in front of him and Maecenas and the others off the truck were behind him, with more rounds coming in.

"That's it, that's it," the centurion yelled, beckoning them to cover in the trees while the first to cover kept up a steady chatter of weapons-fire.

Close as they could get.

Maecius got belly to ground and got his rifle to bear, trying for a moment to catch his breath and get his nerves to stop fluttering. A man hit the dirt by him, slithered up to the little vantage they could get and lay still.

Assyrians had pushed over toward the woods. That was what they were into.

Meaning the Praetorians had failed.

Or never shown in the first place.

"Damn 'em," Maecenas said.

Damn them for sure.

They were in bad trouble, the convoy shot to hell and the Old Man's jeep lying on its side up ahead, where an Assyrian shell had blown it.

Fire was going out from that direction too. The Old

Man and Curtius were pinned down, but they had a
vantage of a kind, and they were using it.

"Why don't they run for it?" Maecius wondered.
"What in hell do we do?"

"No way we can get up there," Maecenas said. "*No*
damn way to cover more than they got."

"Got to take those Assyrian guns, is what," Maecius
said.

"*Who's* got to get 'em?" Maecenas asked, and looked
behind him. "*Mars fornicator,* lookit."

Maecius looked.

And got sick at his stomach.

The shells had got a direct hit on the truck behind,
taken the one after that.

And behind the whole field was littered with Roman
bodies only some of which were glowing and vanishing
as dead would in Hell.

"Undertaker's busy," Maecenas said.

Twenty, thirty of them had made it up to the cover of
the woods. Not even a full century left of the four
cohorts that were the 14th's advance units.

No way in hell they were going to make their rendezvous: there was action going to come out of the woods,
the 10th was going to be pushing hard, from the South,
and there was nothing on this side but a unit cut to
ribbons—

Gods knew whether or not they or the 10th had a
working radio.

"*Pretty* boy," Tiberius said, and patted Brutus on the
cheek. "What's a pretty boy like you want to kill me
for, hmmmn?"

Brutus backed up against Caesarion and the wall, the
frescoes on which were enough too make it clear enough
what kind of trouble they were in.

"Let him alone, damn you," Caesarion said, and tried
to get a kick in, but handcuffs took his balance, and
Brutus shoved with his shoulder, desperate, the two of

them ringed by Praetorians no saner than their emperor by the look of them.

Wit, boy, Niccolo would tell him.

"I—" he said, and knew he was going to stammer, *knew* that he had no way to make a madman listen. "M-My brother—and I—w-w-we ca-came—to t-t-*talk* to you, m-m-majesty,—"

"What's your name, boy? —What's his name?"

"Brutus," a Praetorian said. "Julius' other bastard. The assassin."

"Assassin!" One of Tiberius' eyes unfocused, the pupil very large. A line of spittle ran from the corner of his mouth. "Julius wants to kill me. Julius blew up my atrium. Killed my Egyptians. His mother—*his*—his mother—stole my Germans. It's a plot,—isn't it?"

"M-M-Majesty—Augustus s-says—"

"Augustus murdered my brother! *Murdered my brother!*"

"—s-says you were a g-g-great s-soldier,—m-m-majesty."

The single focussed eye turned toward him, as the emperor leaned close.

"Great soldier. I was a *genius,* I was the best damn soldier Rome *had,* I conquered the east—I kept the empire together while Gaius-damn him-Octavi*anus* Au*gus*tus plotted to murder my *brother*—"

"A g-gr-great s-s-soldier—a h-h-hero of the R-R-Republic—"

"There *was* no Republic, young fool! The Republic was dead!"

Brutus shook his head, clamped his jaw and tried not to throw up when Tiberius grabbed his shoulder and leaned close to him, spitting with every syllable.

"Dead and buried, boy. No more heroes. No damn heroes. Look what they did to *us,* to me and my brother, boy—"

"You can s-s-save it. My f-f-father n-n-needs you,

m-m-majesty. N-Needs the P-P-P—Guard. Out there.
Against the East. Ag-g-gain."

Tiberius drew back. Looked at him a second time.

And backed away.

"The East," the emperor said. "The enemy at the
gates."

And whirled and ran, his black toga flapping away
into the dark.

"Put them away," the captain said, and smiled at
them, a terrible, thin smile. "The emperor changes his
mind three and four times an hour. And he may *want*
his toys. Gods are fickle. Especially this one. We learn
to anticipate him. Don't we?"

Another shell. Maecius tucked low and wormed his
way under the pelting clods and ruin of trees, trying for
another vantage.

They could *not* get position on the bastards. An hour
of crawling on their bellies, running where they could,
trying to work around through the thicket, but that
damn great gun kept moving, a half-track howitzer, that
kept battering hell out of them, where the 10th had
come under fire—a duel between the couple of mortars
their own lads had gotten off the truck, the single field
piece the 10th had and the howitzer and the Assyrian
tank that kept repositioning and hammering away at
them at long and short range, a deadly combination to
cover—gods knew—an Assyrian push past their left
flank—where the Praetorians should have stood.

The radios gave back static. They were down to delivering messages and orders by runner, and they were
far out beyond reach of the runners now. Going on the
last orders they had from the Old Man, who was still
trying to hold onto the only vantage point they had to
work with, while the halftrack tried to get position,
covered by the tank.

They were down to a handful of equipment on both
sides—all the Devil left them.

And damn, there was not a whole patch of skin on Maecius' elbows or his knees, and not much more on his stomach.

He lay panting a moment until Maecenas came wriggling up to his small hummock, and then there was deceptive quiet, just the distant whump of the Assyrian howitzer.

He wiped an eye with the back of his arm and lay still a moment. Both of them did.

And blinked, because there were two horsemen in the gully below them.

Two kids in white. On white horses.

Everything came sharp and clear then, the taste of earth and sweat and the smell of oak-leaves and cordite. The distant hammer of the shells.

"You see that?" he asked Maecenas.

"What?" Maecenas said.

But the one rider beckoned then, and got off his horse and led; the other followed, up the leaf-strewn ridge.

"Where you going?" Maecenas asked. But Maecius was on his feet, no matter the shells, no matter the danger of snipers.

"After them," Maecius said. Because it was the Dioscuri.

Because he was old enough to know them—old enough, at nineteen and twenty five hundred years—that when the Twins led you, you followed—

And then maybe Maecenas could see them too, because Maecenas turned and looked, and stopped pulling at his arm.

As the sound of the tank carried to them on a gust of wind.

"Shit," Maecenas breathed.

Perhaps because Maecenas understood then what the gods were asking. The way they had asked all along Rome's long life.

This time the question came to them.

He found Maecenas' hand half-blind, gripped it and let it go. But Maecenas stayed with him on the course up the ridge and through the brush.

Down again, where a creek ran, as the sound of the tank's engines came nearer and nearer. As the monster loomed up on the ridge and started down it.

Used to do this with chariotry, was Maecius' thought —a lot of time to think, while you pulled a pin on a grenade and figured where to put it. *Let 'em come, climb up and send 'em the Trip.*

No coming back from this one.

"You holding?" Julius asked, and Curtius nodded, thin-lipped. The leg was bleeding again, soaking the cloth, but Curtius kept trying with the field-phone, getting sputter, mostly. Hell of a job for a general—forward spotter; but it was the only position of vantage they had been able to hang onto, the only one that enabled them to keep track of the firepoints and get orders back—by runner, the way another of the decimated 14th was ready to run the gauntlet back, because there was no word out of the 10th, just an intermittent blind firing, because they could not get word through on the damned phone.

He eased up again around the hulk of the jeep they had braced up with dirt and turned into a kind of fragile bunker, there on the hilltop, risked his head with a look out across the landscape, aware suddenly of two faint explosions from down off the ridge.

"They got help?" the courier wondered uneasily.

Then: "I've got them!" Curtius breathed, and rattled off coordinates, latest they had, into the miraculously working field-phone.

Julius sat down, hard, his back to the wreckage, his heart pounding with the realization *something* in their luck had broken loose; he turned and stuck his head up again, and of a sudden saw the distant plume of a shell from the 10th's guns—landing close, *damned* close to the Assyrian howitzer position.

He used the glasses, tried to get a clear view.

"*Imperator!*" the legionary breathed, beside him; and he swept the field-glasses left, suddenly seeing armored coming over the ridge.

"Shit!"

Then he saw the Praetorian insignia flying.

Saw the damnedest sight—a stout old man in a general's armor sitting in the lead jeep, hazed in light-scatter and the binocs' wobble.

"*Edepol! That's Tiberius!*"

Bang! Bang! Bang!

". . . all hope of . . ." Niccolo Machiavelli finished, and blinked, and looked around at Augustus' study. Klea was there, disheveled and distraught; and Hatshepsut, still reaching for her pistol.

Bang!

Dante Alighieri, in his bathrobe, bewildered.

"*Maledetto!*" Dante cried.

As the Emperor Augustus gripped Niccolo by the arms and shouted: "Where were you? What's happened?"

As Klea assailed both of them with: "Where's my son, dammit?" And: "Caesarion?" then, with a sudden turn to her left.

The boys *were* there, but the edge of Niccolo's eye saw something else. Saw something blinding bright, and what might be Legion uniforms—two dusty, sweaty men with the insignia of the 14th, or two young Greeks, or something—

"Everything's fine," said the one who looked like Caesarion. "Don't worry. The battle's done. We got Them. The Luck is with us."

And they walked out, but no one stopped them— Niccolo had it on his tongue to call out; but somehow it was like a dream, in which, stopping them, something dreadful might happen; or in which one might learn too

much or face something unmasked which one had no
wish to face.

He had seen some of the Powers of Hell—much too
closely. Perhaps, he thought, that was why he stood
still. And why he still delayed, until there came the
sound of horses from the broken window, and the emperor went to look.

Then they all did.

There was smoke all across the horizon. But the
shelling had stopped.

Of horsemen crossing the lawn—there was only the
sound—further and further away, and rising up to
Paradise.

Epilogue

The guards were back. Caesarion heard them in the
hall, from the little basement cell where they waited,
with only the light from the barred window, coming
from the hall. Beside him, Brutus. He reached out—
the guards at least had let them free within their cell—
and took Brutus by the shoulder, a tight, reassuring
grip.

And thought about the things that were ordinary in
Tiberius' house.

"Easy," he said, "probably just a guard change."

But he thought—thought as he had all these long
hours, that at some time it would not be, at some time
the emperor or one of his pets was going to get around
to them.

He would not play the hero, not himself. He had
learned a long time ago what that was worth in this sty.
You lived, and you waited, and you got even in small
doses, because no matter how often you died, Reassignments only sent you back, and you got it worse if you
were stupid. He saved his heroics for the outside world,

because he knew where the heart of Hell was, and if he got killed—he came here.

Like Antonius. Like all of the half-sane who lived here.

But gods knew what Brutus' fate was, or where Reassignments would send him if he took the Trip.

That was what tormented him. There was, for Brutus, the chance of a deeper hell.

Or this one.

And that was all that held Caesarion from killing his brother—sending him the Trip and getting him out of here.

The guards got to the door. A key rattled in the lock, and he got up; Brutus did, and Caesarion took him by the arm and pulled him close against him, a sudden jerk as he recognized the stocky, armored man who shadowed the doorway and walked in with the guards.

"*Roma est,*" the emperor said: *Rome Is.*

"My f-f-father?" Brutus asked. "Is my f-f-father—?"

The old lecher walked close. Caesarion pulled Brutus against the wall, got his shoulder between him and Tiberius.

And thought about where he could kick the old goat, and how slow he could die.

"You distrust me," Tiberius said.

"No," Caesarion said. "Of course not, divinity."

"We are," the emperor said, "a *great* soldier."

Bang!

Brutus was gone.

And the soldiers who had flinched and leveled their guns, and the emperor who had leapt back—stared.

Caesarion smiled and shrugged, and despaired, feeling that lack of presence at his back. "So, well, sorry, divinity. I know he'd like to have stayed."

And thought to himself: *Hope you're home again. Brother.*

SIGN ON

Chris Morris

Blaise Fuego here. You roger me, anybody? Come back . . . No? Well, I didn't think so. Not yet, anyhow. I just got here, see. So let's call this Day One, even though it's dark as the *Stark*'s hold in here. Can't see squat.

But I can feel the computer keyboard under my hands, and sometimes a scope comes up. So I'm just going to log what I get, like a good electronics specialist. That's what I was, see, on the *U.S.S. Stark*, until the Exocet(s) hit.

Remember that fine, you bet. Remember my whole Gulf tour, clear as a livelong day, dickin' around with Iranian and Iraqi overflights, and trying to project American power—only our guns weren't loaded. But then, you probably heard about that.

Bet you didn't hear how come those other two Exocets didn't go bang. It was me and Skip Rogene and Alf White, sittin' on 'em. Well, not exactly.

See, I was the fool who didn't leave his gun station when the first shell hit. I was blown right up into the air and I was kissin' my ass goodbye like you always think you're going to do when the worst happens. And then that sweet whiteboy ass of mine came

271

down. Right back down onto the *Stark*'s ripped-to-shit deck . . .

There was lots burning. A black-boy's-pecker to the left was our own ordnance magazine—you know, where the ammo was kept. If that Exocet had gone a little left . . .

But it didn't, and somebody was yellin' that at me, right as my feet hit the deck in the middle of all this black belching smoke and red and yellow-green fire. Hit the deck and didn't hurt none.

I was standing up in all that flame and I didn't get it, not until Alf came up and Skip was with him. But wasn't nobody else standin', though there were lots of pieces of guys lyin' around.

I heard Skip clear as day though he didn't open his mouth and *Whoosh*, there came the other two Exocets, just like he was tellin' me they would.

We jumped for 'em, me and Alf on the one, and Skip takin' the other by his lonesome. Snagged those suckers out of midair and laid 'em on the deck.

Then's when we sat on 'em. And we were some proud of our Navy butts, until we figured out nobody could see us.

Alf was the first to admit it, because he was callin' to one of the fire detail and the guy walked straight through him, before he stumbled on the Exocet. And I do mean stumbled.

So we looked at each other and we realized that we shouldn't be standing, not in the middle of that white-hot mess, not without protective clothing. I remember Skip realizing we were dead, ghosts, like. But nobody used their mouths to say anything—we didn't have real mouths, I guess. You just knew what the other guy was sayin', in your mind, like.

So in our minds Alf started hollerin' about how he never wanted to be no ghost, and Jesus loved him and was going to take him up to heaven and *Blooie!* Alf was gone in a blast of white light that made me think one of the two Exocets we'd kept from exploding had decided to go off after all.

So that left just Skip and me, and Skip, you know, he's one of those orange-haired blacks that's covered with freckles because there's lots of white mamas in his family tree, he started howlin' for his mama, and then I saw this big white lady in a robe and she came up and stood on the Exocet behind me and she holds out her arms to him.

This is still in the middle of that melting hot fire and the billowing smoke and all the fire-fighting that's goin' on right then, remember.

Skip, he yells "Mama!" like he had a mouth to holler with, and she hugs him up against her big white breasts and they's as gone as the guys fried when the first Exocet went off. It just got white where they were, and that was it.

I was all by my lonesome with all these dead guys who were black like somebody's left 'em on the barbecue too long, and the fire detail, and the smoke.

Now the smoke and the heat didn't bother me none, and neither did the fact that if I'd had a chance—had a go order, had fire orders, had a damned Order of Battle or even a little buckshot in my popgun, I probably coulda' saved the whole friggin' ship with my system's Elint capability. We had great tracking, sufficient rate of fire to take out the incomings, everything except power-up orders and a chance to defend ourselves.

That's my story about it, anyhow. Even though maybe some guys will tell you different. We weren't drinkin' that much, and we weren't that lazy, and we weren't that stupid—and none of us, not even Skip whose mama came to get him right off the friggin' deck, were all that anxious to die.

But die we did, there in the Gulf, and you can tell those Iraqis that I'd like my apology in the form of a transfer to Paradise.

The thing that's bitchin' me is where the other guys

went, because they sure didn't come here with me—wherever 'here' is. I'm the only guy I've run into, and where I am, it's like bein' the single operator in a submarine on hush running: can't see nothin' but my scopes, like I said, and the terminal I got here, which looks like an emergency com and control system. . . .

DAY TWO: I guess that's right, if last message was DAY ONE. I'm leaving off the comint garbage on these messages. If there's anybody around to give me demerits for 'failure to encode' or slug this stuff properly, I'll just say it was personal stuff, cause it is. And I don't know if you're receiving me out there, anybody. Still, beats counting radar sweeps. Bad as sheep for makin' you sleepy.

So I was sayin' (wasn't I?) that I got real freaked on the ol' *Stark*, bein' invisible and not real solid. I'd come up to guys and they'd walk right though me. Felt weird. Some little while into that (yeah, I cried and cursed and carried on some, but nobody noticed), my Exocet, the one I'd grabbed out of the air, got found, and the EO disposal guys came to move it.

That was what displaced me. I know it, but I don't know who told me. Something came down, like a skyhook, and grabbed me by the collar, and then I really thought I was dead. I shot up through the clouds and I was howlin', and then there was this whiteness, like Skip's mama's tits, and then I started to fall.

I fell a long time, and then there was this elevator that I noticed I was inside. So I wasn't falling, or I was in what guys laughingly call, 'Controlled Descent.' And I kept tryin' to tell somebody, anybody, that it wasn't my fault that the battery didn't fire. There just wasn't time to do your systems check and get it up and running and target the enemy and . . .

Anyway, when there was somebody to listen, it was this giant B-girl, fatter than a Calcutta hooker, who was tellin' me I was going to do just fine.

She asked my specialty, and I told her, and she said, "Down that corridor, to the right." She had these ugly, purple lips, and I think I walked that whole way to the door she'd told me to go through without askin' any more questions because I didn't want to look at those lips.

Once I got through that door, the black time started. Shit, I gotta go . . . There's somethin' on my scope.

DAY NINE: Well, I know more about this stuff, now. I've got the whole electronic command center for this war at my fingertips, except I don't exactly know who's fightin' us. Or even who 'us' is. But I know, this time, I'm not going to be caught without somethin' up my spout. Metaphorically speaking, as the War College types say.

So I was telling you about how it was when I first got here. After I came into my duty station, I kept trying to find a way out again. But there isn't one. I went all through that with this guy from up the chain of command.

He's a real guy, but I'm . . . well, it took me awhile to get used to this. I'm in this equipment to stay. Now, it bothered me last week, which is why I didn't write you none, but I'm gettin' used to it. Can't lose what you ain't got, right? I'm COMINT/ELINT/COMMAND &CONTROL AUTOTARGETING ARRAY—thats CECAR to you, buddy.

And I hope you're out there, somewhere. Because I'm stuck in this system, I been told, till judgment day. I asked how come I couldn't get out, where the real fighting was, at least, and this guy—at least I think it's a guy: somebody with rank's been inputting the hell out of this system I'm running. . . . Anyway, this guy says I got to stay here, and be the Intelligent Interface for this particular war toy, or else.

I'm working on finding out what the 'or else' is, since this isn't no damn way to spend the rest of eternity. I'll let you know—

* * *

DAY TWELVE: Whew, that was a close one, in the interval. Seems the rebels, or whatever they were, got close to a hit on a strategic island we're protecting, and we had to fire on 'em. Which meant I had to get my battery up and running. And you know what? Somethin's wrong with this system. It won't come on line fast enough, and even though I'm sure I ordered it loaded and ready to go on ninety seconds' notice, I couldn't get a bang when I needed one. So it's kinda messy in here.

Anyway, that's all over. Most of what I've got still works. And, oh yeah, I did find out what the 'or else' was. If I don't like this duty, I can go back 'topside,' as they call the land of the living, and be a 'haunt.'

That means I gotta try to get through to guys who've pulled berths like mine, before they make the same kind of mistake. (I ain't arguing, no more, about whether or not I made any mistakes. I'm here, so that says somethin'.) But I tried talking to the fire detail on the *Stark*, and they weren't real receptive.

I've got a rating here, and it's called Sycophant 1st Class, but I'm really just one more of what they call 'haunts.' Even outside this battery control center, there's those around who've got real bodies. And they can't see me no better than the live crewmen in the Med could, although I know they know I'm there, cause they give me orders and I can't tell 'em where to stick those orders.

Seems this is a demotion, of sorts. I been thinkin' about takin' up the CO on his offer and becoming a haunt, goin' back and trying to help the poor swabs in the Gulf, but I was always kinda superstitious.

I mean, they can call me a 'haunt' or they can call me a 'sycophant', but what they mean is, I'd be a ghost, back on Earth. And if there's one thing Blaise Fuego always hated, it was ghost stories.

So I think I'll stay here. A haunt in a machine's got

some kinda rank, whereas your basic sycophants are just gofers for the brass.

Anyway, I gotta go see how come I couldn't get my HELLFIRE battery to work any better than a PHA-LANX . . . It's gotta be a little switch somewhere, and I'm little enough, now, to find that switch.

If you need me for anything, just power up your system and type HELLFIRECOM. Unless we're in the middle of hosing down the west coast of Hell, of course. In that case, leave your call letters. I'll get back to you.